ROCKS
in my BED

ROCKS
in my BED

A Novel

Craig Nettleton

SANTA FE

Book design and type composition by Vicki Ahl

Sunstone books may be purchased for educational, business, or sales
promotional use. For information please write:
Special Markets Department, Sunstone Press,
P.O. Box 2321, Santa Fe, New Mexico 87504-2321.

Library of Congress Cataloging-in-Publication Data

Nettleton, Craig, 1949-
  Rocks in my bed : a novel / by Craig Nettleton.
    p. cm.
  ISBN 978-0-86534-597-3 (pbk. : alk. paper)
  1. New Mexico--Fiction. I. Title.

PS3614.E525R63 2007
813'.6--dc22
                              2007020804

WWW.SUNSTONEPRESS.COM
SUNSTONE PRESS / POST OFFICE BOX 2321 / SANTA FE, NM 87504-2321 /USA
(505) 988-4418 / ORDERS ONLY (800) 243-5644 / FAX (505) 988-1025

For my parents, Jack and Vera Nettleton
and
In memory of Luke, a brave cowboy

My heart is heavy as lead, because the blues have spread rocks in my bed.
Of all the people I see, why do they pick on poor me and put rocks in my bed?
All night long I weep. Tell me how can I sleep with rocks in my bed?

—Duke Ellington, 1941

Acknowledgements

This book is the product of several years of research and the much appreciated collaboration of friends who have contributed their time and knowledge. I am grateful to have had the opportunity to know Al Hutton, whose years of prospecting for the Lost Adams Diggings gave me the impetus to begin the search. I thank my friend, Michael Gray, for encouraging me to take the writing of this tale seriously. Will Franz was my knowledgeable and patient tutor on weaponry. Richard Gibbs shared stories of surveillance on college campuses. Mike Currica told me about growing up Basque in the malpais. Tom and Sandy Kieft not only gave me feedback on an early draft, but also gave me access to the library at New Mexico Tech. Pen LaFarge's critique was useful at a seminal stage of writing. Pat Ward was an enthusiastic companion in the field, as well as driving me to the haystack mountains on a road that wasn't really on the map. I thank the many shotgun riders who accompanied me to remote places in the Zunis, the Datils, and the malpais. I am grateful to the reference librarians who helped me find old books and pamphlets about the Lost Adams Diggings. My thanks to Jan Hayes and the many others who have read parts of the manuscript and given me feedback. Molly Backes's consultation gave life to a moribund manuscript. Dr. Tom Steele S.J. encouraged my progress and corrected my Spanish. The mistakes that remain are my own. I am grateful to the people of Lebanon who welcomed me and taught me about Arabic culture and language. My attempts to present the Arabic language in Roman script defy convention, so I ask your forgiveness. Thanks to Max Oelschlaeger and Howard Ignatius for the map. I am very grateful to Jim Smith of Sunstone Press for the opportunity and guidance to bring this work into publication.

My greatest thanks are to my family who has supported me during the years of creating this book. My parents, Jack and Vera Nettleton, have always believed that I could do anything I attempted and demonstrated that faith throughout this project. My sister, Barb, has been one of my greatest fans and has provided nurture all along the way. My brother-in-law, Howard Ignatius, has given me invaluable technical support. My daughter Claire's writing has always been an inspiration. My stepson, Tommy Damico, has been a trooper on treks and camping trips in the land of the legend. My wife, Sandy, has not only been supportive of my obsession, but she has also given me the love that I needed to sustain my efforts.

This is a work of fiction. All of the characters are products of my imagination.

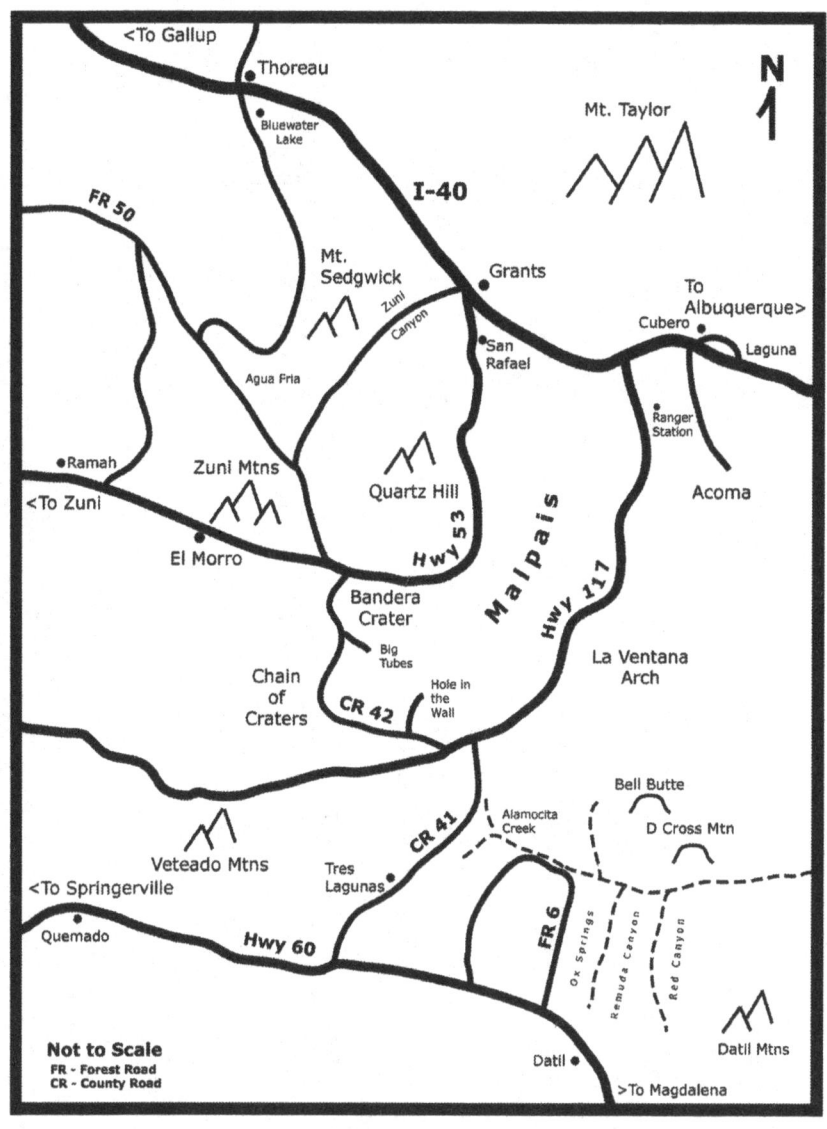

1

Buck Cavanaugh died as he had lived, surrounded by blood and controversy. Sometimes he had worn a badge, but no matter which side of the law he was on, nobody crossed him. Philip Habib wondered why a dead outlaw who had shot his last victims when he was over ninety years old needed to be investigated. Yesterday's phone call from his cousin George had pulled Philip out of his workshop in the Sandía Mountains to drive west across the volcanic badlands that had been Buck's domain.

George had asked, "Do you remember Buck Cavanaugh?"

"The one-man Wild West Show of the *malpais*, Western New Mexico's malevolent man of mystery. How could I forget? He must have died five or six years ago."

"Seven, actually. His granddaughter asked me to help her through probate with her father's estate. Buck's youngest son died a couple of months ago."

"Did she inherit some of Buck's estate?"

"All of it, her dad was the only one of his children that outlived Buck. She wants to understand some issues that will require investigation. So, I recommended you. Are you available?"

Philip tried to imagine what the old desperado's granddaughter would be like. Whatever questions had arisen in probate weren't likely to be answered from beyond the grave. The changing landscape drew his attention back to the road.

Red rock pillars loomed on both sides of I-40. The twin portals marked Philip's favorite part of the drive. The rolling dun-colored hills, punctuated by the green of piñon and juniper trees, were being replaced by the drama of blood-red sandstone. The long curve of the highway up the sandstone cliff gave way to the view of the sand dunes to the south. After the top of the rise, Laguna Pueblo spread out across the hill like a 1950s tinted postcard. Adobe houses clung to the hillside, red chiles drying on the tin roofs in the late August sunlight. The mission church of San José topped the prominence above the village, its cross reaching up to Mount Taylor. He smiled when a freight train appeared, lumbering along the tracks below the village, and bringing back memories of the Santa Fe streamliners of his childhood. Philip remembered his excitement whenever he saw the village on the Sunday drives west to his grandparents' ranch. He was looking forward to seeing his grandmother again, but George's call sounded as if this trip would be more business than pleasure.

Eighteen-wheelers, pickups, and cars filled the tribal casino and truck stop parking lots. Looking up the road toward Cubero, Philip reminisced about his Lebanese grandparents' trading post that stood on the corner of Route 66. The dimly lit store was packed with flour, lard, tobacco, blue jeans, and ranching supplies. Pawned jewelry, kachina dolls, and pottery filled a display counter, and the open bins of spices smelled like Middle Eastern markets. When he visited the trading post as a kid, Philip teased his rural cousins about the washboards and udder cream. George, from the lofty pinnacle of five years seniority, had reminded him that the store has been the beginning of all that the family had. The store was going to put George through law school and make him the governor of New Mexico someday.

George had been right on at least one count. Clerking at the trading post during the summers had helped him get a bachelor's degree and graduate from the law school at the University of New Mexico. The Cavanaugh investigation was part of George's law practice in Grants.

However, George's political ambitions didn't look likely to set Cíbola County on fire. He seemed content with a small town law practice and taking some of the state's movers and shakers on an elk hunt on the backside of Mount Taylor each fall. As his SUV climbed the hill, Philip looked over at the failing businesses along old Route 66, the mother road of diminishing returns. The only businesses that could thrive in Budville were the bars. Buck had probably spent some time in them, drinking down the line. He drove past the Acoma Pueblo village of McCartys and entered the *malpais*, the bad country. The black volcanic flow of lava extended for thirty miles to the south and fifteen miles to the west. The highway cut through the lava, and the lava filled the charcoal-colored canyon at the base of Mount Taylor. Tumbled jagged rock lay next to slabs of smooth dark stone. Spines of cacti and yucca protruded from the crevices. The Rio San José peeked through the low valleys and left ponds with ducks swimming inside cattail borders. Aside from these incursions, the bleak dark landscape looked like Hades spilling over onto the upper world. He could almost envision Buck, the old rounder astride his horse picking his way through the desolate lava.

Philip's image of Buck Cavanaugh was formed at the age of six when he first saw him. Like most red-blooded American boys of his era, his view of the world relied heavily on the Saturday morning television horse operas. Pointing Buck out to his father, he shouted, "There goes a bad guy."

Nobody looked more like a bad guy than Buck Cavanaugh. His long salt-and-pepper hair and beard gave him the look of a bygone era. He wore black from his boots to his cowboy hat. A .45 caliber Colt revolver sat in a black holster for all the world to see.

Philip's father agreed. "Sharp eyes, scout. He's a bounty hunter. Most people steer clear of him."

Buck lived on a ranch in the middle of the *malpais* south of Grants. Pueblo Indian people had conducted rituals on the lava flows for over a thousand years, leaving offerings in their beautiful polychrome pottery.

In a remote part of the lava beds, two men had unearthed some pots and prayer sticks in a shallow cave. When Buck found them, he demanded tribute. After all, they were trespassing on his grazing lease. The men laughed at the idea of grazing in the lava. The younger one made the mistake of pushing the elderly desperado. Buck ended the argument with a gun. After their relatives reported the two men missing, the state police helicopter found their bodies in the midst of the dark lands. They traced their gear back to Buck's ranch. He was arrested and found guilty, but justice came before the court decided his fate. He wasted away from cancer in the Grants jail while awaiting sentencing. The Wild West was dead.

The exit ramp off I-40 turned into Santa Fe Avenue, Grants' main street. Philip wondered why Buck's granddaughter needed his help. George was right; he was available. He tried to earn the bulk of his living as a woodworker, but he often grew tired of the popular Spanish Colonial style furniture that he sold under "Carving by Felipe." Occasionally, he would decorate a *trastero* in cowboy funk, or make *padre* benches in a German expressionist style. Nobody bought his most creative ventures, so he ended up living with a strange collection of furniture and not much money.

He turned off Santa Fe Avenue and down a side street toward George's office. It shared space with an insurance agent and a realtor. In the parking lot, Philip looked in the rear view mirror and straightened his bolo tie, a silver Hopi sun god his father had bought years ago on Second Mesa. He checked his dark brown hair, noting more gray around his temples, and curled the ends of his moustache into parentheses. Unfolding himself from the 4Runner, he pulled on a silk-blend tweed sport coat over his jeans and white button-down shirt. He dusted off his boots on the backs of his calves and strode across the parking lot.

Entering George's office, Philip swore he was having a flashback. There, staring out the window, was a figure dressed in black from riding boots to leather vest, wearing a belt adorned with silver *conchos* and a gambler's-style black cowboy hat. Silver medallions also trimmed the hat above the gray hair that reached the shoulders. The ghost of Cavanaughs past haunted him.

"Philip, meet Marlene Cavanaugh. Marlene, this is my cousin, Philip Habib."

The figure turned to reveal an attractive woman in her mid-fifties. Her gray hair was actually closer to platinum. Her face was smooth and her figure looked as if a professional trainer had shaped her. She gave him an appraising inspection. Her gaze lingered long enough that it seemed that she approved of Philip's lean muscular build.

She locked onto his eyes and said, "I knew I was back in New Mexico when we were looking for a P.I., and George said 'I have a cousin who ...'"

George started to defend himself, but Marlene stopped him with a look and turned back to Philip. "Well, *primo*, can you earn your keep or do you just stand there looking handsome?"

The family resemblance was there, not only in the piercing blue eyes, but also in the confrontational style. Philip shook her hand. "A pleasure to meet you, Ms. Cavanaugh. How may I be of service?"

"And *para servirle* to you too, *primo*. Didn't George tell you what we had here?"

George interrupted. "Just the bare bones. These days, portable and cellular phones compromise confidentiality to anyone with a scanner. I try to avoid discussing the details of private matters on the telephone. Philip, Ms. Cavanaugh has inherited her grandfather's journals, which shed a different light on the circumstances of the alleged murder."

"I think it was more than alleged, since the sheriff's deputy found Buck with the smoking gun. Later, during the trial, he admitted shooting them." Philip mentally kicked himself for saying the first thing that popped into his head.

Marlene looked as if she were tired of having to deal with fools. "Everybody agrees that Grandpa killed them. The more important question is why did he kill them? Read this."

Marlene thrust a yellowing composition book under Philip's nose. After reading for a moment, Philip frowned. "So the argument and killing had nothing to do with Indian pots. Are you sure this is your grandfather's writing?"

"As close as anyone can tell without an expert. He sure tampered with the evidence, didn't he?"

George shook his head. "As if that would matter when you're facing murder charges. Why would he make up that entire story about the Indian pots as a reason for the fight?"

"That's where you two come in. There's something behind all this. Grandpa was cantankerous, but he didn't kill on a whim. He had a reason for his killings. What else could those men have been doing out there in the *malpais*?"

Philip said, "Ms. Cavanaugh, I could understand if you might want to clear the name of an innocent man. You know, local history says that these were just the only killings that anybody arrested Buck for."

George added, "A number of the men that he found as a bounty hunter came in draped over their saddles. And those two weren't the only people who disappeared in the *malpais* that Buck was suspected of having dispatched."

Marlene walked up to Philip and stared at him hard. "Times sure did change during his lifetime didn't they? I could give a rat's ass about Buck's reputation, and neither did he. No, the issue here is greed, not honor. Buck never took a paycheck after he quit the Pinkertons, and he stopped bounty hunting decades ago. That ranch out there sure never made anything, but he always had a jingle in his pocket. Daddy never knew where the money came from. It sure as hell dried up after Grandpa died. I want you to find out where Buck got his money, and I want it for myself."

Philip imagined her stomping her foot. "This is a pretty cold trail. The cops say that if you haven't solved a murder within twenty-four hours, your chances are pretty slim. This one is over seven years old."

"We're not trying to solve a murder; we're trying to understand it. When the *Malpais* Monument was established, they paid my family some money for the ranch. George tells me your fee is three hundred dollars per day plus expenses. I'm willing to invest a couple thousand dollars of Daddy's money, plus expenses. I want you to find out what happened and where Buck's lucre came from. Are you really interested or do you want to go back to woodworking?"

"Ms. Cavanaugh, I am intrigued. However, I want you to understand the difficulty of what you're asking. Most of the people who knew your grandfather are dead. You also need to understand how slowly the wheels of the bureaucracy grind in New Mexico. I'll need to read the journals just to get started. But you're right; this sounds a lot more interesting than carving headboards. I'd be willing to dedicate a week of my time to your case."

Marlene gave him a thousand-watt smile. "Let's at least get it out of the chutes. I understand that you've spent enough time here to have doors open for you. Hopefully, you're not so much of a local that you're contaminated by the prejudice against my family that I've found in Grants. I'm staying at the Cíbola Inn east of town. I'll expect a couple of progress reports before the week's over."

Moving closer to him, she shook his hand and looked into his eyes intensely. Then she turned and walked out the door.

Philip felt as if he had just emerged from some kind of power vortex. He asked George, "Aren't we supposed to have a contract or something?"

George smiled and handed him a file folder. "I took the liberty of drawing up a boilerplate and having her sign it. You didn't do all that well at the Spanish Market in Santa Fe this year."

Philip glanced at the contract. "Since you've taken care of everything else, I hope you've arranged for lunch at your mom's."

"As a matter of fact, she's waiting for us right now."

A black Lexus with tinted windows pulled out of the parking lot. Philip watched Marlene accelerate up the street. "That appears to be one high maintenance woman."

George nodded. "Several husbands thought so. At least they paid her a lot of money for a divorce. I've got an appointment back here after lunch, so let's take separate cars."

Philip drove north. He was looking forward to finding out more about Buck, but his primary duty seemed insurmountable. How was he going to find the source of the money with as little information as he had? Marlene had just swept him along in her quest. Domineering women made him feel anxious. He was looking forward to some comfort food.

George's parents lived on the outskirts of town, with a view of Mount Taylor. The ranch style house was filled with the aroma of garlic and cinnamon.

"*Ahlan w' sahlan*. Welcome Philip," Aunt Mary called out.

"*Ahlan w' sahlan fiik*. It smells like *kibbi*."

She came in the living room wiping her hands on her apron, "Of course, I know you like the family recipe for Lebanese meatloaf, and the pine nuts are from Mount Taylor. There's rice with spinach and *tabbouli* too."

He hugged her and kissed both of her cheeks. "Have you seen *Sitti* recently?"

"Your grandmother was here just this morning. We did some grocery shopping together. You have to stay with her if you're going to spend some time around here. Now sit down. Everything is ready."

Aunt Mary was the older sister of Philip's father. Philip and George not only shared Levantine ancestry, but both older Habibs had married Hispanic New Mexicans. Philip's mother was from Northern New Mexico, and claimed direct descent from Spain (with an Irish shepherd grandfather thrown in). George's grandfather Martinez was from Los Lunas. The result was that the cousins shared their dark good looks, the slightly aquiline nose, and the full moustaches. Philip was a few inches taller, and he had a scattering of red hairs in his moustache and flecks of gold in his eyes, the result of the intermingling of Celt, *Castellano*, and Crusader ancestry. George had always been thicker in build, but middle age was making him thicker yet.

They sat down and passed the food around. "The *kibbi* is delicious. Did you gather the *piñon* nuts yourself?" Philip loved the similarity of climate in Lebanon and New Mexico that led to the use of pine nuts in the cuisine of both locales.

"I spread my clean sheets under the trees to gather them and washed them carefully." She passed the pita bread. "Speaking of dirty, what was that thing you entered in the Spanish Market?"

Philip was waiting for this after George's earlier comment. "It was a *retablo* depicting Santa Teresa. She wrote about her dreams and meditations, and I carved them. It sold the first day."

"To perverts in Santa Fe. Philip, why do you embarrass your family? Everyone in the parish was talking about the scandalous carvings of Philip Habib. People were sending digital pictures of them from phone to phone, hissing their disapproval."

Philip imagined that some of them might be having a different reaction in private. He thought about a discussion of the lives of the saints, and Santa Teresa's mystical union with Christ. He remembered the stone carvings in Kujaraho, India, from an art history class. In intimate detail, they celebrated the unification of the masculine and feminine aspects of the deity.

Instead of making another unsuccessful attempt to defend himself against his family's religious conservatism, he said, "This *tabbouli* is wonderful. Did you grow the parsley? It tastes so fresh. And how's my cousin Cissy doing? I'm going to drop by to talk with Don this afternoon."

George nodded. "That's a good place to start."

"The kids are keeping Cissy busy. Lessons and practices; she's like a chauffeur. What are you going to talk to Don about?"

"The investigation that George called me about. What do you remember about Buck Cavanaugh?"

His aunt shook her head. "I remember staying out of his way."

"Okay. So, George, what do you really know about Marlene Cavanaugh?"

"You mean, aside from *Destry Rides Again* being her father's favorite movie? Not a whole lot. She says she was named Marlene because of Dietrich's character. Her dad, Mack, nicknamed her 'Frenchy' too, just like in the movie."

Phillip was never sure when his cousin's obscure movie references were true, or if George made them up on the spot just to amuse himself. "Sounds like quite a guy."

"Buck was not the most nurturing father on record. From what I hear, he eventually took interest in his boys when they were big enough to help with a roundup. Apparently, he was able to persuade their doubting mothers that the cowboy life was a wholesome summer experience for young men."

Philip smiled. "It worked for our parents."

Aunt Mary nodded. "You bet it did. You boys had your grandparents as examples. But those Cavanaugh boys were a sight to behold on a summer Saturday night. Their father would bring them into town and give them a few dollars. Then he'd go off on a toot at the VFW or somewhere. You couldn't walk down Main Street without being accosted by those hooligans."

George nodded. "Marlene's father, Mack, was the only one that lived longer than his father. None of them escaped from being under Buck's shadow. Where Buck could command respect, his sons were merely bullies."

"Bully doesn't go far enough to describe those punks."

"They intimidated the defenseless and bowed to anyone in a position of authority. That evidently made Mack a good master sergeant.

Marlene was born in California where they lived for most of Mack's military career. He put in his twenty and retired with a good record. Marlene's mother divorced Mack as soon as Marlene turned eighteen. His ex-wife took half of his pension and had nothing more to do with him."

Philip said, "Sounds like this sort of thing runs in that family."

"And you boys would be better off having nothing to do with that family."

"You're right, Mom, but it would be nice to get paid for my work occasionally. After retirement, Mack knocked around the oil fields in California and eventually ended up back in New Mexico in the Four Corners area. Mack made quite a reputation in the border towns around the Big Res. He drank like an Irishman."

"Irishman nothing. He drank like a fish."

George rolled his eyes. "After he got himself plowed in bars with fellow roughnecks, he fought for honor in dusty parking lots. God forbid you should ever cross him on the morning after."

"He must not have known about *menudo*, the breakfast of champions. What about Marlene?"

George smiled longingly. "You couldn't have missed how fit she looks. I hear that she used her skill at tennis, golf, and horseback riding to gain entrance to California's post-war gentry. She attended the University of California at Santa Barbara and married well. Marlene has parlayed knowledge of Southwestern Indian crafts and contacts in California into a moderately successful wholesale operation. She lives in Orange County and makes forays into Indian country periodically. She's combining this inquiry with buying rugs in Crownpoint, jewelry at Zuni, and pottery at Acoma. I don't think she's happy unless she can either make money on a deal or write it off on taxes.

Aunt Mary disagreed. "I've seen her a few times over the years, and I don't think she's happy unless she's got some man fawning over her."

"Yes, mom. She's been married several times and came out of

each divorce with substantially more money than she had going into the marriage."

Philip observed, "Sounds like success, Southern California style."

"Take Buck's genetics, and temper it with the skim milk of human kindness from her mother. Give it the female variant, and you end up with Marlene. She's a shark, but not a man-eater."

"Did you get a retainer?"

George laughed. "I did, but you're on your own."

"What a family: killers, carousers, and cutthroat businesswomen."

Aunt Mary started picking up the dishes. "Why do you two always go looking for trouble? You've been like this when you get together ever since you were boys out on the ranch. Philip, wasn't your arrest after September Eleventh enough excitement for you?"

Philip hated thinking about the incident that his aunt had brought up. After the terrorist attacks on the World Trade Center and the Pentagon, the whole country was horrified by the fact that *Al Qaida* had been able to attack America at home. Intelligence gathering agencies were caught with their pants down, so they began a roundup of Arab males aged eighteen to fifty. By the third day after the attack, a dark American-made sedan drove up his driveway. After IDs were shown around, the FBI agents asked if they could talk with him about his connections to the Middle East. Immediately, a confrontation arose. He remembered the conversation.

"Your name has been linked with Palestinian terrorist organizations. You spent a lot of time with Al Fatah, the militant arm of the Palestine Liberation Organization."

"Look. I worked with those groups under orders during my Marine Corps duty. I reported back to military intelligence in Beirut. I haven't had contact with any of them for more than twenty years."

"Your assignment was to infiltrate Palestinian student organizations to gather intelligence, but it's funny how talk gets started about double agents."

"I don't know what had happened to any of my armchair radicals since they've grown up. How can I be a double agent if I haven't had any contact with them since I was discharged back in the seventies?"

"Not having contact would be real good. A couple of them have moved over to *Hamas* and might be involved with blowing things up."

"When I knew them, they were students who published left-wing newspapers and printed inflammatory leaflets. The most dangerous thing they did was to inflict second-hand smoke on the bourgeoisie in the cafes of the *Hamra* district."

The agents continued to hammer him, asking him if he knew Sheikh What's His Name or *Abu Shu Ismu*. As the questioning became more heated, they asked to look around. Philip had nothing to hide, but he was tired of their Gestapo tactics. So he refused, and they said that they would get a warrant. Philip protested that the Fourth Amendment requires probable cause for a search. He asked what crime they suspected. The agents looked at one another and gave him a list of possibilities: treason, conspiracy, or just obstructing justice. They handcuffed him, and led him to the sedan.

They had allowed him a phone call to his lawyer, which was more than hundreds of other Arab detainees were given. George arranged for a high-profile defense attorney and fellow elk hunter to represent Philip. His parents rallied support in the Lebanese community. At the bail hearing the next day, the federal judge noted that he usually didn't see so many prominent members of the educational, legal, and commercial establishment in attendance at these proceedings. He looked at the charges of interfering with a federal agent, read the arrest report, and shook his head. The prosecutor emphasized that America was under attack, and that Philip refused to cooperate in the war against terror. The defense attorney pointed out Philip's family's long connection to New Mexico. He called attention to Philip's honorable discharge after antiterrorist duty for his country. Because the prosecution had produced no current evidence linking Philip to terrorists, he also asked for Philip to be released on his own recognizance. The judge not only agreed, but he also admonished the prosecution.

"At the next hearing, you better bring me evidence of a real crime. These tactics are like the internment of the Japanese during World War II. The United States government needs to ask for help from experienced Middle Eastern operatives, not arrest them."

The prosecution dropped the charges, but Philip felt that he had been victimized by the very system he had defended for four years. Thousands of Arab men were detained, and the Special Registration program interviewed and fingerprinted more than one hundred thousand men from Muslim countries. Not a single conviction for terrorism resulted from these heavy-handed tactics.

Philip changed the subject again and asked about his other cousin, Mary's younger son. "So what do you hear from Sy?"

Aunt Mary shrugged. "It's back to Simòn, again. Now he's in Costa Rica working for a consortium of fruit importers. He's heading up a project to teach the *campesinos* to wash their hands so Americans will buy their blackberries."

After chatting about his cousins and their families, Philip brought Mary up to date on his sisters as well as his nieces and nephews. After they said their goodbyes, he wondered if the exquisite food was worth the chiding that he always received from her. He called his cousin Priscilla's husband, Don Abeyta, at the Cíbola County sheriff's office.

Don was in, doing the mountains of paperwork that came with the job. He looked relieved to have an excuse to take a break. As they drank the acid wash that passed for coffee, Don chuckled. "It's a good thing Sister Mary Katherine passed away before you carved that Santa Teresa thing, or you would have had a slap across the knuckle with her ruler."

Philip sighed. "No one who took such obvious pleasure in spanking her adolescent charges would have had any room for criticism. Besides, she was the one who taught me about the patron saint of the church here in town."

"I was in Santa Fe delivering a prisoner. Someone else was covering your booth, but I saw the offending thing."

How many times was he going to hear about the infamous carving? "The thing was a diptych illustrating her dream about her baptism and her visions as a bride of Christ."

"And you were the dip that ticked them off." Don laughed at his own joke. "That sure looked more like your experiences than Santa Teresa's. Who was the model?"

Philip's memories of Teresita had a bittersweet taste. She always referred to their first night in the hot tub as "our baptism." It was less than six months since she had left him and the wounds were just beginning to heal.

"Artistic license, a product of my imagination. What do you remember about the Buck Cavanaugh trial?"

Don tipped back his chair. "That takes me back. I was a rookie then, just out of the service. I drove him back and forth from the jail to the courtroom a few times. He was real sick, looking kind of gray, and he lost a lot of weight. He coughed up blood, like a TB patient. They offered to treat his lung cancer, but Buck asked, 'Why bother?' He didn't last long after they found him guilty."

"Did you talk to him at all? Did he say anything that made you to think that there was more going on than he was saying in the courtroom?"

Don looked lost in thought. "It was a long time ago, and I didn't have the antenna for that kind of thing like I do now. He'd talk about how things used to be when he first moved here, when it was still the frontier. People took care of their own problems then. He said that, in the old days, there wouldn't have even been a trial for shooting somebody trespassing on a man's grazing lease."

"Any scuttlebutt in the department that might be enlightening?"

Don studied Philip's face. "What are you looking into? You're kicking up the dust of ancient history."

Philip remained silent and grimaced as he sipped the wretched coffee.

"Okay, you've got a client. My superior detective ability spotted Marlene Cavanaugh at the Cíbola Inn coffee shop when I was at the Lion's Club meeting yesterday. I won't press you any further, but Buck was before my time. Let's call Old Man Matthews."

After Don arranged the meeting with Tim Matthews, the retired sheriff of Cíbola County, Philip rose and thanked him. Don walked Philip to the door and reminded him, "You know, our little Melissa has a birthday party coming up."

Philip smiled and shook his hand. "I wouldn't dream of missing her birthday. I'll see you there."

2

Tim Matthews lived on the way to the old Cavanaugh ranch, south of San Rafael. As Philip passed through the village he saw a few monuments of a former time, large *haciendas* for extended families. There were more doublewide trailers now. Kids wanted a place of their own. With a minimum down payment, they could buy the house of their dreams on a lot on Central Avenue in Albuquerque. They'd have it set up on the family's land by the next week. Philip was reassured to find that former Sheriff Matthews lived in a modest ranch-style house that dated back to the first boom in Grants in the fifties. The former sheriff greeted him at the door. As Philip entered the living room, he noted that the decor dated back to the nineteen fifties as well. Over the blond furniture, there were a few pictures on the wall of Tim Matthews shaking hands with dignitaries, but there were many more photos of family.

Old Man Matthews had been the Sheriff of Cíbola County before there was a Cíbola County. Before the western end of Valencia County seceded, Tim Matthews had been the under-sheriff in charge of the Grants substation. He answered to the sheriff in Los Lunas and complained about being neglected in the boondocks. When Cíbola County was established in 1981, he won the sheriff's election hands down and kept the job until he retired. Some said he should have retired some years before he did, but Tim Matthews kept showing up at picnics and the meetings of fraternal organizations. He always wore his silver-belly Stetson hat, and pressed the flesh so that every registered voter knew him personally. He had liked being sheriff a lot more than he liked being retired.

Philip almost didn't recognize him at first; he had never seen him without his hat. He had always suspected that Sheriff Matthews was bald, and that was now confirmed.

"Sheriff Matthews, thank you for agreeing to see me."

"I'm glad to do it. I knew your grandfather well, and I remember you from the summers you stayed with your grandparents. Besides, I got nothing better to do, don't most days. Every so often, we get in a real social mood and go visit the doctor. We talk about not sleeping and waiting days to take a crap. Now there's an exciting conversation for you. Come on out to the back porch, Millie's got some iced tea set out."

"Maybe this will be more interesting. I'd like to pick your brain about Buck Cavanaugh."

A smile crept across Matthews' face as they sat in the old metal tulip chairs on the porch. "Buck Cavanaugh. Now there was a genuine reprobate for you. Millie, this is Philip Habib. Buck wasn't his given name, came to him from cowboying, buckaroo, you know. Seamus was his Christian name, but nobody used it. It didn't fit him."

"I've never even heard his given name before."

"There wasn't enough money in working cattle to keep Buck's interest for long. He used his time on the range well though, practicing shooting. He turned out to be one of the best shots I've ever seen. The thing that scared you about Buck wasn't just how good he was with a gun. It was how willing he was to use it. He was born a few years too late, thought it was still the Wild West."

Millie said, "Most people around here live the cowboy life, but Buck acted like it was still frontier days."

Sheriff Matthews nodded. "He got in on the end of that era. He hired out to the outfit that paid him the highest, always wearing black, always packing that Colt Peacemaker. He tried working for the

Pinkertons, said he loved it. He was down in Silver City for that mess at the Santa Rita mine. Breaking strikes meant that he got to scare large groups of people, not just individuals. He said that working mobs was just like working cattle, pick off the leader and they would stampede to get away from you. But he couldn't follow the rules enough to stay with the Pinks. He would've never lasted in a real law enforcement agency. Bounty hunting was the right job for him."

Philip gestured to the northeast. "You've got a great view of Mount Taylor and the *malpais* from this porch. In Buck's day, bounty hunting must have meant being a good tracker in some pretty wild country."

Sheriff Matthews agreed. "Buck didn't miss much. That made him a good tracker. He brought in some criminals that the rest of us had given up any hope of finding."

Philip noted the respect that Matthews had for Buck. "I hear he spent more time on the wrong side of the law."

"Well Buck wasn't a dyed in the wool criminal. He just had his own views, which rarely took the law into account. He was smart enough that he didn't flaunt his law breaking, couldn't abide the idea of being locked up."

Millie interrupted. "I think being locked up is what killed him. It just ate him up."

Her husband agreed. "He couldn't tolerate being indoors for that length of time. He even asked for a cell with a view of the *malpais*."

Millie refilled the tea glasses. Philip took a sip and remarked, "I've been hearing that Buck always had money, but that he never worked steady after the Pinkertons."

Millie smiled. "He sure did dress nice."

Philip wiped his brow. "I can't imagine that a ranch in the *malpais* would be much of a moneymaker. Where do you think he got his money?"

Sheriff Matthews shrugged. "That ranch would surprise you. There's a lot of grass and quite a few springs back there, if you know how to get to them without breaking a leg or getting snake bit out in the lava. Buck also did work as a guide for deer hunters and people looking for Indian pots in the lava fields. Besides, he did a lot of bounty hunting when he was younger. Some of those fellows carried a substantial reward. Back then, it was a manhunt across mountains, plains, and the desert. Buck got out when it came to be nothing but skip tracing."

Philips finger's traced a design in the condensation on his glass. "I'd like to see the ranch, but isn't it part of the monument now?"

Matthews nodded. "Sure is. Give me a few phone calls and I can get us out to the ranch."

"Do you really think he earned all his money from ranching and guiding deer hunters and Indian pot hunters?"

"You're probably right. I always thought Buck had something else going, but I couldn't find evidence of any wrongdoing. I'd drop by, just to be neighborly. I'd happen to have the State Police dog with me, but it never alerted to drugs or explosives. I never saw any signs of smuggling *mojados* up from the border either."

Matthews raised a furry eyebrow. "I thought I was the only one suspicious of Buck. Why are you looking into this now, Philip?"

"I'm doing a series of cowboy carvings and I wanted some local color."

Tim Matthews took a long look at Philip and walked into the house. He wasn't buying Philip's story, but he called in a marker. A ranger agreed to meet them at the road to the Cavanaugh ranch. Philip joined him inside.

"I had to promise this intern ranger, who's working on her doctorate, that I would talk to her about the place. Ain't many people around anymore who spent time out there. Besides, I got nothing better to do."

As he put on his lace up Ropers, he griped. "Too old to walk in a proper pair of boots, had to have these built up so I don't waddle like a duck."

He kissed Millie at the door. "Goodbye, dear. Don't wait up, I'm off chasing ghosts."

Sheriff Matthews looked more like his pictures as he donned his Stetson and hoisted himself into Philip's 4Runner. "Air conditioning, CD player. You ever spent any time on a horse?"

Philip reminded Matthews that he had served on a posse on horseback with him during one fall weekend when he was in high school. Some deer hunters had wandered away from their camp on Mount Taylor, and a horseback search and rescue had been mounted. Philip and George had borrowed horses from their grandparents and joined the party. After a hard day's work, the search party found the hunters. By that point, Philip had decided that pleasure riding was a better experience than spending all day in a saddle. He was dog-tired and saddle-sore after ten hours clinging to a horse's back in rough country. He put Patsy Cline on the CD player, which seemed to placate Matthews.

As they drove toward the Cavanaugh ranch, Philip looked more closely at the *malpais*. It wasn't as continuous as he remembered. Near San Rafael, there were sections of the roughest rock imaginable, small hills rose where pressure had pushed the lava upward. There were also deep sinkholes where the lava had collapsed. Everything that grew there had thorns. But there were also rivers of grass that ran along and through the lava. Wildflowers splashed purples, yellows, and reds across the meadows. *Piñon* and juniper grew densely on the north sides of hills and sparsely elsewhere. It was a complex ecosystem, with microclimates determining what vegetation grew where.

Philip asked, "What's your favorite story about Buck?"

"I can do you one better. Let me tell you about where Buck's favorite stories came from. He enlisted in the Army shortly after Pearl Harbor and was assigned to the Pacific Theater. They figured out that he was one hell of a sharpshooter. They put him in one of the units that did reconnaissance on the Japanese controlled islands. He loved to be the advance scout and make the first contact with the enemy. One on one with Jap snipers was his all-time favorite game. He made a lot of kills and came back with a chest full of medals. Buck was a warrior to his bones, and armed combat was as good as it got. He really missed it when he came home. He tried to throw himself back into bounty hunting again, but his opponents were disappointing. He said that those Japs really knew how to fight."

The road climbed as they approached the Cavanaugh ranch. Ponderosa pines began to replace the scrub forest of the lower elevations. The lava looked older, veiled by the New Mexico dust.

"Buck couldn't live closer to people than this," Matthews explained as they waited at the gate for the ranger. "After a few days in town, he'd get a burr under his blanket and get into some kind of trouble. Every so often he'd attract some woman who fancied she could change him. Buck was too self-centered to think that romance meant anything other than sex. The women would get fed up and split the blankets, but there was always another one on the horizon. Like they say, 'ladies love outlaws.'"

Pillow talk, that was his problem. Philip remembered the number of women he'd told his deepest secrets to and felt embarrassed. He was too Mediterranean to be the strong, silent type. Maybe he could be a sensitive brute, sort of a cross between Alan Alda and Clint Eastwood. When they first met, Teresita had been attracted to the fact that he was a man who could talk about his feelings. Later, she accused him of wallowing in his depression, massaging his anger, and being generally neurotic.

His reverie was interrupted by the arrival of a Park Service Jeep. His resolve to be a loner like Buck disappeared as soon as the ranger opened the door of her Jeep. He had expected a historian to be a bookish mousy sort of woman. The blonde with the French braid did wear horn-rimmed sunglasses, but Philip barely noticed them as he tried not to stare at her long shapely legs as she swung out of the Jeep. As she walked over, Philip had to admit that he didn't know that uniforms could be tailored so well. Her face had exquisite bone structure, with a patrician nose and high cheekbones.

She extended her hand to the men and introduced herself. "Sarah Johnson, I hope I didn't keep you waiting. Let me unlock the gate so we can talk at the ranch. There's some shade there."

Tim Matthews held the gate as the vehicles passed through. He locked it and rejoined Philip. They drove down the dirt road between and over the dark flows of lava. The hills and valleys came in successively larger series. Cottonwoods appeared as they topped a ridge and dropped into a hidden valley. The house was nestled in the shade of the big trees. Barns, sheds, and corrals spread out as the valley opened to the south. A fenced meadow ran between the volcanic hills. They pulled into the dusty parking area.

Sarah pointed out the hand pump. "The water's not bad. There's a windmill and storage tank, but we don't keep it filled since nobody's using the place. What brings you two out here? There's not a lot of interest in the Cavanaugh place."

"Philip claims he's doing background research for a Western art series. I'm just a sentimental old fool who don't tolerate being put out to pasture," Matthews replied with a twinkle in his eye.

Sarah smiled at Sheriff Matthews. "You were the sheriff for many years. I bet you spent some time here in an official capacity."

"There were complaints about Buck. Any crime in the malpais was laid at his feet before we tried it on anyone else. But I came out here more often as a neighbor than a sheriff. Weren't many people between Buck's place and ours in them days. Besides, we were both fossils from a bygone time. When I started patrolling the county, Route Sixty-six was an improved gravel road. Highway Fifty-three out here wasn't much more than wagon tracks. It took all day to get to Zuni, and that was on a good day."

"Times have changed."

"That reminds me. You ever hear the one about the Texan who's bragging in a bar in Grants? He says, 'These postage-stamp sized pieces of ground y'all got around here ain't ranches. Hell, back home it takes me all day to drive my pickup from one end of my ranch to the other.' The old man from San Rafael looks up from his beer and says, 'You know, I used to have a truck just like that.'"

Philip was as interested in the archivist's reaction as he was in Matthews' joke. "Ms. Johnson, what can you tell us about the Cavanaugh ranch? How many head of cattle do you think Buck ran out of here?"

"It's Sarah, and I'd guess between seventy and eighty depending on how many calves dropped each spring. Is that about right, Sheriff Matthews?"

Matthews looked at the pasture and nodded.

"The grass is good because the land's too rugged for it to get overgrazed. Remember that big horn sheep used to forage out here until they got killed off. But a lot of the springs are seasonal, and he only had two other windmills besides the one here."

Philip shook his head. "That sounds like subsistence ranching. Buck cut a pretty wide swath around Grants. My dad told me that when Buck got pretty well juiced up, you could count on him buying a round for the house down at the Grubstake Bar. Do you think he made that much money selling a few steers every year?"

Sarah smiled. "No. That's why, when I heard that the former Sheriff of Cíbola County and a private investigator wanted to look at the Cavanaugh place, I wanted to be here. My doctoral dissertation in American Studies at UNM is on outlaws and rustlers of the twentieth century."

"I only studied them enough to catch 'em," responded Sheriff Matthews.

"Buck is one of my favorite subjects. Few people with such notoriety in the early days of New Mexico statehood committed their final criminal act so recently. Sheriff Matthews, where do you think Buck got his money?"

"Like I was telling Philip, I tried to pin all kinds of nefarious schemes on Buck. I never found any evidence. If he's a pet of yours, what do you think?"

Sarah opened the gate to the front yard. "I've been trying to link him up with the known robberies and payroll heists in the area, and there are a couple of possibilities. He certainly knew some of the players.

Philip looked back up the road. "Living out here, he could be gone long enough to pull a job and get back without anybody knowing."

"You're right. But the thing that bothers me about the big score hypothesis is that Buck didn't go through the boom and bust cycles that most criminals do. He didn't do anything particularly conspicuous, but he always had more money than most small time ranchers. I don't know. He was far more intelligent than the average hoodlum, so maybe he learned to live on a budget. I don't really have an answer, but it's nice to talk to people who are asking the same question. Let's go inside."

The cottonwoods created a filtered light, and the leaves rustled in the breeze. Lilacs defined the front yard. Hollyhocks and cosmos grew along the portal adding pink, purple, and indigo to the dappled palette. The cabin consisted of a large square built from logs chinked with concrete with a frame addition to the east. It was all roofed over in tin. Sarah led them down the flagstone path to the front door. The door was made from hand-hewn lumber, and the hinges, nails, and latches looked hand-forged as well. Sarah unlocked the deadbolt and ushered them in. There was the stale dusty smell of abandonment.

As a woodworker, Philip considered himself somewhat of a connoisseur of handmade houses. He was impressed. There were enough windows to provide good light. The floor plan was simple but elegant. The living area was to the right, the dining to the left with the kitchen behind it. The walled off area in the southeast corner was probably a bedroom. Philip instinctively moved to the kitchen cabinets. They were made of wide pine planks, again with hand-forged hinges, nails, and knobs. Philip asked Sheriff Matthews, "Did Buck do his own carpentry?"

"Buck was a really good carpenter. He built this whole place himself."

"So he was the blacksmith too?"

"Boy, didn't I just say he built the whole place himself? He did it all. Not to say that he didn't get help when he had to set these logs or heave beams that would have been too heavy for one person. He was skilled in every craft. In fact, anything that Buck put his mind to, he did better than most people."

Philip continued his inspection. "This whole cabin is well made. The flagstone floors have been set with precision, and this tile work is gorgeous." He rubbed his hand over the cobalt and russet figures. "This is an unusual pattern. He must have picked this up in Mexico."

Sarah beckoned them over. "Check out this cook stove. You don't see too many of these. It's half gas and half wood, not the usual meaning of dual fuel these days. There's also a reservoir over here on the wood side to heat water."

She walked over to the living room. "And look at this stove. It has isinglass windows so that you can see the fire. These porcelain cameos on the front are unique, but my favorite part is the base. Look at those castings of the god Borealis blowing cold air at us. And it's dual purpose too. You can slide away the top on this swivel, and there's a cook surface there."

Tim Matthews smiled at the memory. "Buck used to brew a pot of coffee on this stove when he had it going in the winter. He never used the gas stove unless he had to. He said he could gather all the wood he needed."

Sarah nodded. "He was either ahead of his time or lost in the technology of the Great Depression, depending how you look at it. Take a close look at those elk antler chandeliers. That's a thirty-two volt electrical system. A lot of remote ranches had these before the Rural Electrification Act. Buck had a really nice set up. She pointed out the window. "See that shed over there next to the smaller windmill? That windmill turns a generator that charges a bank of batteries in the shed. There are also a couple of transformers that he must have custom built that step the thirty-two volt current down to twelve and six volts. That way he could run a radio or anything else that was battery-operated. He had a gas generator out in the garage, but I bet he only used it to run power tools. Self-sufficiency, *malpais* style."

Philip glanced over at the wall where Mexican tinwork lamps hung in a row. "Those oil lamps suggest that the system wasn't always on line."

Tim Matthews laughed. "You're right. Later on, Buck had to tinker with it a lot. But he refused to hook into the power line out at the road. He always said, 'No dependency, no vulnerability.'"

Sarah agreed. "He had water pretty well taken care of, too. The bigger windmill filled that storage tank on the hill. The well's never gone dry that I've heard. He had enough water to irrigate a big truck garden out back as well as the trees. And from the size of that root cellar built into the lava, I bet he put up a lot of his produce. He probably canned fruit too, although that old orchard looks pretty well played out now."

She led the way into the frame part of the house. Philip was even more impressed by the woodwork; the addition was togged out in Carpenter Gothic. Beautiful moldings surrounded the doors and windows. As he admired the Queen-Anne-style porch, he asked, "Wasn't all this millwork expensive in its day?"

Matthews replied, "Because of all the lumbering in New Mexico back then, there was a mill in Albuquerque. So you didn't have to pay shipping, but it was still pricey. Not only did he have this fancy woodwork, but Buck also had one of the first flush toilets in these parts out here in this addition."

Philip looked into the bathroom. "Check out that big claw-footed tub."

"Buck had a coal-fired hot water heater that he stoked up when he wanted to take a bath. He picked up the coal by the truck load in Gallup."

Sarah's gaze swept across the distant ranchlands. "He didn't pay for all this from the proceeds of this ranch. I doubt that he made enough as a bounty hunter to keep up the lifestyle he enjoyed."

The old sheriff fanned himself with his hat. "I don't know. He brought in some hefty bounties in the early days, but the bounty money dried up later."

"I'll bet the IRS would have been interested in Buck's profit and loss statements."

Philip was intrigued by the ranger intern's chosen field, as well as being intrigued by the ranger. He turned to Sarah. "Outlaws of the twentieth century. How did a nice girl like you . . ."

Sarah laughed. "That sounds like a line, but I'll take you up on it. I've got to get up to El Morro for an interpretive talk. Can you gentlemen get together later back in town to discuss Buck?"

Time Matthews grinned, but then he protested. "I don't drive after dark, so I'll take a rain check on tonight. When you two need some first-hand memories, give me a call. This sure beats bingo at the Senior Center."

Philip suggested dinner at the Grubstake in honor of Buck and arranged to meet Sarah there. His red face was not just a result of the glaring sun. He followed her out to the highway and waved as she locked the gate behind them.

Tim Matthews looked amused. "The only female government employee out here when I was first elected sheriff was the county extension agent. Didn't have willowy blondes studying rustlers back then. By God, her legs are long enough to reach to heaven. Enjoy your youth, boy, it don't last long."

Philip felt far from young, but he didn't feel as old as he had earlier. Maybe her invitation was just professional interest on her part, or perhaps it was prompted by the prospect of another evening alone in Grants. Whatever Sarah's motivations were, he suspected that Buck would not be the only subject of his inquiries that evening.

3

Philip pulled into the parking lot in front of George's office. The building's red brick facing with green panels and aluminum windows reminded Philip that Grants didn't change with the times. His cousin seemed content with the small suite with its fluorescent lights and early business-as-usual furnishings. George was talking with a client in his private office when Philip entered the building.

Phillip knocked. "Sorry to interrupt, but could I look at those journals?

"No problem. There's also some information that I found while I was picking up records."

Philip went into the coffee room. He put an enameled pot of water on the hot plate, added Turkish coffee and sugar, and opened the file folder. George had given him Buck's arrest report and case summary. The arresting officer's report included some details about the victims. As he poured the thick sweet brew into an espresso cup, he wondered if their next of kin could still be reached. He decided to call the number listed for the widow of the older man.

A woman answered. After establishing that he was talking to Irene Talbot, he identified himself.

"Mrs. Talbot, I apologize for bringing up painful issues, but I'm doing an investigation of Buck Cavanaugh. Could I talk to you about your husband's murder?

There was a silence of several seconds. Her voice quavered. "I'm sorry, of course I'll try to help. Sometimes the grief hits you when you're not prepared, and it feels almost like you're being swept under by a wave. What can I tell you about the man who butchered my husband?"

"Again, I apologize. I've uncovered some information that suggests that the fatal argument may not have been over Indian artifacts. Do you know any other reason why your husband and Mr. Randolph might have been in the *malpais*?"

"I always thought that the pottery part was odd. You see, Bert and Travis were amateur treasure hunters. They would have picked up Indian pottery if they found it, but they were stuck on gold. They read these magazines about buried treasure and lost mines. They usually carried this expensive metal detector and a gold pan with them when they were out prospecting."

"Do you know what kind of treasure they were after in the lava?"

"Bert told me that they were on the trail of a lost gold mine. They had found some bogus treasure map that they were going to follow. I never paid much attention to their little hobby as long as I knew their general location. It never occurred to me that his harmless obsession would get Bert killed."

"Do you know anything more about the mine, Mrs. Talbot?"

"They said something about the Indians killing off the miners. But Indians killing off the miners was kind of a theme in a lot of their tales. That's really all I know."

"Do you think that Mrs. Randolph would know more?"

"We're not in touch anymore. Even if I knew where she was, I wouldn't tell you. She was devastated when Travis was killed. They had two kids less than three years old. She went back home to her family, somewhere in the piney woods of Texas. She blamed Bert for getting Travis involved in treasure hunting, so she didn't have much to say to me. We did go to the trial together."

By then Philip could hear the tears in the tone of her voice. "I have to say that I loved watching Buck Cavanaugh dying before our very eyes in that courtroom. His painful death made me feel like his sentence was being delivered by God Almighty, not just some judge."

"Thank you ma'am, and I'm sorry to bring all this back for you."

"Most of the time, I can handle it. I've got the kids and the grandkids. You just took me by surprise."

Sometimes the intrusiveness of investigating made Philip feel ashamed. The killings were a tragedy, but the treasure-hunting angle sounded promising. He warmed the coffee, poured another cup, and picked up one of Buck's journals.

Buck's writing was difficult to follow. His penmanship was poor, his style was telegraphic, and his use of abbreviations was idiosyncratic. Philip could decipher most of them, place names and ranching terms. But he was confused, why Buck would incriminate himself in writing? It was puzzling and fascinating, like listening to Richard Nixon's tapes during the Watergate hearings. Didn't these men fear discovery? Was their narcissism so great that they felt themselves to be invulnerable? He was fascinated by the bravado of the coarse first-person narrative in the composition books.

Buck earned a little money from cattle, and a bit more from acting as a guide to parties seeking deer or adventure in the lava beds. There wasn't any direct mention of money from other sources, but he hadn't expected to find that since he knew Marlene had read the journals before turning them over to him. Expenditures far exceeded income, and Philip didn't think Buck was using his MasterCard to finesse his cash flow. But what kept Philip's attention was the self-portrait that emerged from the musty books. Buck Cavanaugh feared no man and respected no woman. He lived large. Although he held title to a number of acres and leased several sections from the Bureau of Land Management, his perception of his realm covered far more territory. His dark influence spread as surely as the black rock covered the land. He was Lucifer, Lord of the Lava.

Buck considered anyone venturing into the *malpais* to be invading his domain. The journals contained several incidents of Buck chasing deer hunters and Indian pottery hunters off the lava. They also implied that at least one of the parties might not have left. Philip's earlier suspicion that Buck was responsible for more deaths than he had been charged with was accurate. How many skeletons were really in Buck's closets? He was beginning to know Buck better, but he liked him less with every page.

Philip called his grandmother and asked, "*Sitti*, can I stay with you while I'm in the area?"

"You're always welcome. George told me you'd be here. I just wish you wouldn't stay away so long."

Before she could nag him further Philip begged off. "I've got an important meeting over supper, so don't wait up for me. I love you, and I'll see you soon."

He looked in on George, trying to shake off the vague sense of guilt his grandmother often seemed to elicit. George's private office had the standard legal appointments. There was the wall of law books and the dark stained furniture with leather chairs. George's trophy wall had a double meaning, since his pictures of himself with dignitaries often included trophy elk.

Philip asked, "Did you get a chance to look at the journals?"

"Just enough to know that I needed my decoder ring. What did you find?"

"There are a lot of mundane ranching records, but he enjoyed writing about fights in the *malpais*. He had several. There's nothing out of the ordinary about money, but I did find out something interesting about his victims?"

"About them or about the money?"

"Both. I talked to Widow Talbot who said that her husband was an amateur treasure hunter. You know, lost mines and buried gold, that sort of thing."

"*Bismillah*, a clue!"

"It gives us a possible avenue to pursue, anyway. I'm off to the

Grubstake for dinner with the intern from the Monument."

"I know that it's a tough job, having to interview beautiful women. Don't stay out too late; you know that *Sitti* will wait up for you."

Philip focused his thoughts on the enjoyable business at hand and drove over to meet Sarah at the Grubstake. The restaurant and lounge were showing their age. Like much of Grants, it had been born in the boom of the fifties, and slid downhill until the oil embargo in the seventies sparked a renewed interest in uranium. Then it really hit the skids after the Three Mile Island incident, and the mines closed down. Philip was pleased to see Sarah emerging from her VW in the parking lot. She was wearing a floral print sundress that accentuated her model's figure as well as her tan. Her hair was loose, but uncombed, still wavy from the braid. As she leaned forward to give him a hug, he inhaled the heady aroma of patchouli. She not only looked ravishing, but she smelled delicious as well.

"I didn't feel comfortable waiting alone in there. I felt about as local as a fish in a tree." She half apologized. Philip offered his arm and they walked across the lot.

Sarah looked up at him and inquired, "Habib; that's Arab, isn't it?"

Philip found his face freezing into a mask. "Lebanese actually, and born and raised in Albuquerque. I was a good Catholic boy, as the Lebanese side has been for the past couple of thousand years and the Hispanic side has been for the last thousand. I even graduated from St. Pius High School."

Since the terrorist attack on September 11th, being asked if you were an Arab no longer felt like an innocent inquiry about ethnicity. Philip had been horrified by the carnage created by the terrorists and outraged at the assault on America. Because of his experience in the Middle East, he watched events unfold anxiously. As the days progressed, he watched the anger on television engulf anything Arab. The relative ignorance of most Americans regarding Middle Eastern politics made the learning curve too steep for most people. Backlash blossomed. A few mosques were set on fire, and an Arizona Sikh convenience store clerk was murdered because he looked like Osama Bin Laden. He hoped that Sarah's question was motivated by interest rather than paranoia.

Sarah looked at him quizzically as they entered the building. Philip noted that the caliber of lounge lizards had declined as much as the maintenance of the exterior. The men at the bar looked lost, desperately drinking their way through the evening. Three bikers and a skinhead were playing pool, but the rest of the crowd were solitary drunks. Although the people on the bar stools came from different ethnic groups, they looked like they shared a feeling of hopelessness. Like the tailings mounds surrounding the town, they were the human reminders of a boomtown gone bust.

The restaurant half of the Grubstake was a slight improvement; the rustic hippie carpentry was holding up better than the Naugahyde in the lounge. A few locals were scattered across the room. Philip waved to a couple he knew, who were grazing their way through the salad bar.

"I guess Buck could still reign in the Grubstake. 'In the land of the blind, the one-eyed man is king.'"

Sarah nodded as she slid into the booth. "This is the funkiest décor I've seen in Grants. Tell me, does being an Arab-American give you a special perspective on the war on terrorism?"

Philip remembered his night in jail and smiled ruefully. "In more ways than you could know."

"What do you mean?"

"I love my country and served it proudly in the Marine Corps. Like most of us, I took the September Eleventh catastrophe personally. I was enraged, but then the fear crept in. I lived in Beirut while it was in a state of siege. I hope that America never has to experience that level of fear. Anyone who watches the Middle East knows that violent hatred of Americans was on the rise. But I was shocked because, not only was the attack so abominable, but it was also so sophisticated. The *Wahabis* and other fundamentalist Muslims I knew didn't exactly embrace technology."

The waitress brought water and took their order for beer.

"Tell me more."

Philip continued, "I'm very glad that the allied strike against the *Taliban* and *Al Qaida* prevented the development of a full scale Messianic *Mahdi* movement in Afghanistan. Anti-American sentiment could have coalesced with Muslim fundamentalism to create a level of hysteria that could have threatened the entire Western world. This war in Iraq sure wasn't the way to win the hearts of the Arab and Muslim populace. Americans are familiar with the word *jihad* now, but they don't know that the primary meaning is not a holy war. One of the pillars of *Islam* is the greater *jihad*, the war within oneself to know and obey *Allah*."

"A couple of years ago, several of the Muslim professors at the University gave a colloquium on Islam and the Arab world. I knew that there were Sunnis and Shiites, but I didn't realize how many divergent groups Islam contained. A Saudi professor lectured on the influence of the *Wahabis*."

"Saudi Arabia is their stronghold."

"He said that the *Wahabis* gained power on the Arabian Peninsula as a conservative religious protest against the Ottoman Empire. They have dominated Saudi politics ever since. My favorite talk was about the *Sufis* from Afghanistan, Iraq, and Iran. I loved the wonderful stories from *Nasr u Din*."

"His name means victory of faith, but I think his real victory was his ability to teach through humor. The stories are used to lead the reader towards self-discovery. Unfortunately, it's harder to look inside oneself than it is to find outside enemies. America is missing its moment for introspection which could lead to long-term geopolitical solutions."

"Campus political scientists would say that America has rarely had a global perspective, and we're certainly unlikely to see it with this administration."

"So now anything Arab is suspect. I know that other groups have suffered much worse levels of racial profiling, but it's the first time I've experienced it myself. Almost every time I've flown in the last few years, I've been pulled aside for a search. Anyway, back to the Grubstake, the menu writer was more inspired than the cook, so I'd stick to meat and potatoes."

Sarah looked at him pensively, but she took his cue that it was time for a topic shift. "You don't live here, and from what I hear you never have. Yet people call you by name and you know the menu. What's your connection to Grants?"

"Neurotic," Philip replied. "My father was born here. My grandmother lives east of town, up against Mount Taylor, by Cubero. We came out for every holiday and birthday in the extended family. I spent most of my summers on my grandparents' ranch growing up."

"Just because it's family, it's neurotic?"

"In my family it is; we're enmeshed. My Lebanese ancestry is warm and generous, but is also critical and knows no boundaries. My Spanish ancestors have their own issues about being dominated by Anglo society. Both sides are religious to an obsession, and family focused to a compulsion. Any thoughts or actions not approved by the Pope are suspicious. But I love them all."

The waitress returned, and Sarah followed Philip's recommendation and ordered chicken baked with herbs and new potatoes. Philip ordered a beef filet *ranchero* style. They headed for the salad bar.

Sarah seemed thoughtful. "My family was close growing up, but we're scattered far and wide now. How many people in Cibola County are relatives of yours?"

Philip hesitated. "Counting second cousins? Now it's probably less than twenty; a lot of them have moved into Albuquerque. There are also some people around here who are closer to us than cousins, but aren't actually blood relatives."

"Close, but not kin?"

"No, but families who were so closely entwined with mine that intimacy counted for more than genetics."

Sarah smirked and leaned forward. "A private eye who uses the word intimacy. Are you on a speaking relationship with the term?"

"Not at the moment, but I have fond memories of the experience."

They returned to their booth, and Philip continued. "Since we're in the Grubstake, that reminds me of a story. There was this old prospector sitting over in the lounge one day. The boys were teasing him about being a loner. The bartender asked why he hadn't ever been married. He winked and suggested that the old geezer must have been waiting for the perfect woman. The prospector replied that he had never waited for good fortune; he always had searched for the things he wanted. When he was a young man, he had looked hard for the perfect woman. 'Never found her, huh?' the bartender grunted. The prospector replied, 'I found her all right, but she was looking for the perfect man.'"

Sarah smiled. "And there we have the human condition."

The waitress presented Sarah with her chicken, fragrant with fresh herbs, and gave Philip his steak and *papitas* smothered with homemade *pico de gallo* and cheese. Philip found himself staring at Sarah. She got a high score on the perfect woman scale; she was intelligent and beautiful. Her blue-green eyes were accentuated by the floral print of her dress. Her nose was too strong by Hollywood standards, but Philip's Arab influenced aesthetics found her exquisite. Her high cheek-bones gave her face a beauty that was accentuated by her coy smile.

"Did Buck ever find his perfect woman?"

Philip swallowed a bite of the surprisingly tasty steak and replied, "Several times, but he either lost her or chased her out after a while. A few of them lasted long enough to give him children, but stability was not his strong suit. The journals show a conflict between wanting companionship and needing solitude. I guess that's not an unusual trait in a cowboy."

"Tell me about it. I grew up in Southern Utah, and I think that cowboys have more conflicts than the average guy. There's something about the high lonesome that makes a man wish he had someone to share it with. But I got tired of waiting for men to get back from something 'a man's got to do.'"

"So were you raised on a ranch?"

"It was a small one, but really pretty. We had a few acres of irrigated bottomland with a stream through it. The rest of the section was grazing country, but it had a couple of awesome red-rock canyons. We leased a couple of adjoining sections too.

"Did both of your parents ranch full time?"

Sarah eyes widened. "You've got to be kidding. No ranch family can make it without side jobs these days. My mom taught history at the middle school in town. And my dad had a small mobile welding business, mostly serving local ranchers. So he had the monster truck, you know."

"Now you're talking. Tell me about it."

"It's obviously a guy thing. Actually he had several. They were all one-ton four-by-four crewcabs with a winch in the front and dualies in the back. They all had a custom steel-plate bed with the welding machine taking up most of the space. The whole family would pile into that rig, and off we'd go, exploring slickrock and mountains. My mom was a western history buff and would guide us back in time as well as in space."

"Is that how you got interested in outlaws?"

"Yeah, I grew up hearing about Robber's Roost and the Hole in the Wall Gang. I went to the University of Nevada - Las Vegas for my undergraduate work, haunting libraries, reading yellowing newspapers, feasting on the exploits of the knaves and the brave. I started hating that town; Las Vegas was too gaudy and too big."

"I can see that happening to a country girl."

"Ever since I've been in graduate school at UNM, I've been working too hard. My eyes were blurring from looking things up on microfiche, and I missed seeing the stars at night. When you're doing this kind of research, you have to get out of the stacks every so often or you lose the feel of the territory. That's why I jumped at the opportunity for a summer internship out here."

Philip smiled. "I'm glad you did. I really appreciate your help."

She savored a piece of chicken. "Do you know that they actually marinated this chicken in olive oil and lemon juice and the herbs taste fresh? It's quite good, and the tarragon potatoes are wonderful."

Philip whispered, "There are rumors of a Greek chef. I had an interesting conversation with the widow of one of Buck's victims."

"Really. What did she say?"

"That her husband and his friend were amateur treasure hunters. They were supposed to be looking for a lost mine, some kind of treasure trove."

"If they were after a lost treasure, the most likely source happened decades before Buck got to Cibola County. There was a train robbery in Grants before the turn of the last century. The robbers got away with the loot. They were hunted and I think most of them were killed in the Zuni Mountains, but the money wasn't on them. Most people think they stashed it in the *malpais*. Rewards were offered, but most of the people hunting for it had no intention of turning it in to get a much smaller amount. Nobody ever announced finding it, but who knows?"

"Didn't every square foot of this area have a Geiger counter held over it during the uranium prospecting days? Why didn't somebody find it then?"

"Good point. The *malpais* hasn't given up any uranium finds yet, and I don't think many prospectors actually set out across it on foot. Most of the surveying was by air. Even if you walked over every inch of the lava, there are nooks and crannies that nobody's ever poked into. It's too rough. We're not even sure that all of the tubes have been completely explored."

Philip cocked his head. "Tubes?"

"And I thought you grew up out here. When the lava flows cooled, a crust of rock formed on top. Sometimes the molten lava flowed on and left huge horizontal tubes in the midst of the flows, like tunnels in the lava. There are a couple of areas near Bandera crater that have trails built to them."

"How big are these tubes?"

"They're awesome! The Big Tubes are between forty and a hundred feet across. The ones near Bandera Crater range from a quarter of a mile to a mile long. They're part of a system that's almost seventeen miles long. It's a completely different experience from a limestone cave. There's no sense of a living, growing entity. You feel that you've found the hidden entrance to the kingdom of darkness. The Big Tubes are relatively level, but their rough floors made them tough to walk in. Some of them split and weave back together. I'll take you back there some day."

Philip was pleased that Sarah wanted to see him again. "When I was growing up, the only people who went in the *malpais* were hunting deer, rattlesnakes, or Indian pots. It sounds like I've missed out on an experience. You make it sound like it would be possible to hide just about anything in the lava."

"There are other stories about lost treasure in the *malpais*, but the A and P Railroad loot looks to be the most likely culprit. After all, they caught up with the gang just west of the lava fields, up a canyon in the Zunis. That's only a few miles from Buck's place, right in his backyard. A lot of people looked for the money right after the robbery, but none of them spent the amount of time out in the lava that Buck did."

"How much money are we talking about?"

Sarah shook her head. "I don't remember. What form it was in would make a big difference in what it was worth later. I'll look that up and give you more particulars about the robbery."

As they sipped their coffee after the meal, Philip found himself more intrigued by the intelligent, down-to-earth woman opposite him. He decided that he would accept her invitation to hike to the Big Tubes.

He was taken by the combination of beauty, brains, and assertiveness that Sarah Johnson displayed. He was somewhat intimidated, but completely captivated.

"How did you become a detective?"

"I was drafted."

"Really, conscripted into being a P.I.?"

"Actually, I was feeling lost after my freshman year of college. I'd had some heavy losses so I joined the Marines. When they discovered that I spoke Arabic, a rare matching of talent and location occurred. I was stationed in Amman, Jordan, for embassy duty. That's where they assigned me to that classic oxymoron, military intelligence."

A wry smile crossed Sarah's face.

"They spruced up my Arabic, helped me connect with my cousins in Jounieh, Lebanon, and sent me to the American University of Beirut. It was after Beirut self-destructed in the civil war between the right-wing Christian Phalangists and the left-wing Palestinian and Lebanese Muslims. Later, the Syrians took control of Lebanon."

"It looked like the Lebanese people were happy to seem them leave. It's too bad it took an assassination to make it happen,"

"They sure weren't happy when the Syrians came, but it was better than civil war. My job was to infiltrate radical Palestinian political groups at the university and report back. I found myself liking the people I was spying on more than the people I was spying for. The student radicals were cosmopolitan and compassionate, and some of my jarhead superiors were narrow-minded control freaks. So, I quit after I graduated from A.U.B., when my enlistment ran out. But, then I had a religious conversion."

Sarah leaned forward and grinned. "I don't think becoming a gum shoe is what most religious people mean when they talk about finding a vocation."

"It wasn't that religion. In Beirut, being a double agent meant that I eventually managed to alienate almost everyone I knew. After my discharge, I was disenchanted with cities, politics, and life in general. So, I went back into the Sangre de Cristo Mountains and rejoined my cousins in Cordova to work on my woodcarving. The satisfaction of bringing beauty out of the wood gave me a sense of purpose again. Being back with my mother's family in a mountain village helped me reconnect with people. Sometimes, we visited a friend in Tesuque, just north of Santa Fe. There was this wonderful old wood carver there, with the nickname of Archie, who made these whimsical animals out of cottonwood roots."

"Remind me to ask for the short version of things if I need information in a hurry. So was wood-carving your new religion, and does it give you such strong arms?" Sarah reached across the table and caressed his arm while she looked into his eyes.

Philip felt a pleasant flush come over him as he took her hand. "I was getting there. Old Archie made quite a few friends along Canyon Road with his drunken magic tricks, including some Sikhs who had a restaurant downtown. I started hanging out at the restaurant. I was looking for exotica, I guess, missing the Middle East. Then, all of a sudden, I found myself wearing funny clothes."

"You know, it's still hard for me to see Española as a major religious center."

The waitress brought the bill. "The Northern New Mexico brand of Sikhism is a unique subculture. But it's part of a greater Sikh tradition that values military service. So I was drafted. They had started a security agency that, like most businesses that the Sikhs develop, is prospering now. At that time, my résumé made me a player again. But I didn't last with the Sikhs' doctrine any better than I had with the Marines. When they wanted to arrange a marriage for me, I knew that it was time to leave."

Sarah appeared shocked. "How medieval."

"I realized after that adventure that I needed to be my own boss. So now I'm a part-time woodworker, part-time independent investigator."

As Philip put money on the table, Sarah said, "Well, I think we each have some investigating to do. You need to scour those journals, which

I hope you will persuade Ms. Cavanaugh to donate to the Monument after this is over. I need to look up those Atlantic and Pacific robbery references. I look forward to a productive collaboration." She looked into Philip's eyes and took his arm as they left the restaurant.

As they walked past the lounge, an *a cappella* version of an Arabic song assaulted their ears, "*Yaa habibi.*" Philip saw Ross McIntyre stumbling towards them, making up in volume what he lacked in skill in mastering the quartertone scale. His beard was unkempt, his hair hadn't seen a barber or a comb recently, and his clothes were rumpled. His pale blue eyes were almost lost under heavy lids, but he greeted Philip as if he were a long-lost brother. "*Kifak, yaa khayee.*"

Philip replied, "*Mabsut. W inta?*"

Philip was bathed in alcoholic fumes as Ross aspirated his response. "*Al hamdillah.* Praise God."

The skinhead at the pool tabled muttered, "Sand nigger lovers." His biker friends thought this was hysterical.

Philip put an arm around his friend to steady him and introduced Sarah.

"What are you doing back in these parts, my friend?" Ross asked.

"I'm doing some research on the *malpais.* Sarah's an intern at the monument."

Ross's eyes rolled back momentarily, he stiffened, then his face darkened and he took on the countenance of an Old Testament prophet. His voice began a crescendo, "Molten rock will cover the land. It's just a tick on the old geologic clock since the last eruption. It could happen again, any time now, rivers of fire."

Sarah pulled back in alarm. Ross clambered onto a chair, raised his hands above his head, and shouted, "Vesuvius reaching out for Pompeii, Mount Peleé incinerating Sainte Pierre. We'll burn for our sin of bringing radiation to the surface world. The earth will cleanse herself of the vermin. The Rio San José will boil, and the pitiful pretense of existence that is Grants will be consumed in flames."

A drunk at the bar raised his head and said, "Praise the Lord." The bikers were laughing so hard that their missing teeth were showing. The skinhead gave them all a look of pure evil. The bartender came around the bar with a hostile look on his face.

"What are you drinking there, *amigo*, whiskey and holy water?" Philip was torn between the pain in his friend's eyes and his embarrassment in front of Sarah. He helped Ross down and asked, "Why don't you walk us out to the parking lot?"

A waxing moon sat on the eastern horizon, but the harsh lighting of the parking lot emphasized the darkness of Ross's eye sockets. "You look like you've had enough for one night, Ross. Why don't you let me drive you home?"

Ross grabbed Philip's arms with both hands and stared at him. "Not you too, Philip. The sobriety storm troopers are everywhere. Christian temperance, my ass!"

He pulled Philip close and whispered, "You're not twelfth stepping me, are you?"

Philip pushed Ross and his fumes back. "No, Ross. I remember that the first miracle was turning water into wine at the wedding feast at Cana. But, it's going to be a miracle if you get home without Grants' finest throwing you in the drunk tank after that scene in there."

Ross looked down. "I guess you're right."

Sarah was holding her arms tight and shivering. Ross hung his head. "I'm sorry if I offended you, ma'am."

Philip raised his hands, palms up in supplication. "Sarah, could you follow us in your Beetle? Ross, give me your keys to your truck."

As they headed north into what little residential area Grants had, a police cruiser pulled along side of the pickup. The officer nodded to Philip and continued past.

"You were right, amigo. I would have lost my license this time for sure. Thanks."

They were silent as they pulled up to the frame stucco house, a

1950s Pueblo-style bungalow, in one of the neighborhoods that hadn't changed much since Grants' first boom. Ross mumbled apologies as he lurched up the walk.

As Philip climbed into the Bug, Sarah asked, "Is Ross typical of your friends?"

Philip apologized as she drove back to the Grubstake parking lot and his car. He told Sarah that he and Ross had known one another since he was a teenager, but he hadn't seen Ross in years. He tried to explain Ross' behavior. "Underneath it all, he's a good man, a brilliant geologist. He was a local boy made good, from an upright Mormon family, who won a scholarship to Brigham Young University. After he graduated, he volunteered to serve in Vietnam. He came back to the community after his tour of duty wearing decorations for bravery. He found work with one of the uranium companies, and married a local girl. They took Mormon self-sufficiency to an extreme, combining it with the back to the land mentality of the times."

Sarah stared straight ahead as she drove. "You don't have to tell me about Mormons. Remember, I'm from Utah."

Philip went on. "I was a teenager when I got to know them through a food cooperative. They built a cabin way up in the Zunis with a wind generator and a propane refrigerator. They had a beautiful baby girl and a huge truck garden. Then Ross had to go to an overnight natural gas exploration conference in Albuquerque. When he came back, he found his wife and daughter dead in the master bed. The propane refrigerator had fouled and was spewing out carbon monoxide."

Sarah touched Philip's leg. "Oh my God."

"It gets worse. Ross not only blamed himself, but he also went a little crazy. After the funeral, he set fire to the cabin and drank himself unconscious while it burned to the ground."

Sarah face had softened. Philip tried to plead Ross' case. "He's never been able to stay sober for more than a few months ever since. Mormons are very protective of their own, but they don't tolerate drunks.

Eventually patience is proven to be finite. After one too many outrageous drunken blasphemies, he lost the support of his family and the church."

Sarah glanced at him. "The same kind of thing happened to a girlfriend of mine from high school. They sent her to a church sponsored treatment center, but her family didn't tolerate relapses either."

"After he had burned his bridges around here, Ross hired on with an oil company in Saudi Arabia and did well for a few years there. That's where he picked up the Arabic."

"Were you there at the same time?"

"Yes. While I was in Beirut, we met up in Jordan and toured the rose-red ruins of Petra. We even got caught up in an all-night Bedouin coffee-drinking, rifle-shooting, dancing revel. If it weren't for the moon, we wouldn't have made it back."

Sarah pointed up to the sunroof. "We've got a nice one tonight too."

Philip looked up. "You're right. I want to tell you again how sorry I am that the evening ended this way. Let me finish Ross' story; I'm almost done. American oil enclaves in Islamic countries are a unique microcosm. Alcohol is prohibited in those countries, but a blind eye is turned toward consumption that stays within the compound. This leads to the same pattern of abstinence and binges that Ross had already adopted, so he fit in for a while. But his ghosts followed him, and his drunken ravings were full of the apocalyptic bullshit he cranked out tonight."

Sarah said, "He's so bleak that he makes Sartre sound like Norman Vincent Peale."

"The small American compounds couldn't handle his haunted madness. He bounced around the Gulf States, getting excellent recommendations for his work, but remaining an emotional cripple and a social outcast. So he came back to Grants where the past looms over everyone."

Sarah shivered. "Poor, Ross. What a tragedy. I hope that he can turn it around. You make Grants sound like it's the only boomtown and bust scenario in the West. There are a few played out mining towns in Utah too."

"It's the only one I've known up close and personal. I've been to most of the classic ghost towns in New Mexico, like Elizabethtown, White Oaks, and Mogollón. But it's different when you're living it, instead of reading about it. It's like having a manic-depressive around. 'It was the best of times; it was the worst of times.'"

"You don't look all that stable, yourself, handsome." She gave Philip a peck on the cheek. "Call me tomorrow."

As he drove east on old U.S. 66, past the boarded-up storefronts, Philip recalled his description of Grants as a manic-depressive. When he thought of Sarah, his own mood felt like it might be lifting. He was tired of moping around, feeling betrayed. He looked forward to tomorrow and hoped there wouldn't be any of the weirdness they'd experienced tonight. He put Joan Osborne on the CD player as he continued on old Route 66 across the McCarty's lava flow towards his grandmother's ranch. He wondered if Joan's family had given her as much of a hard time about her *Saint Theresa* as his family seemed intent upon giving him.

The two-lane highway dipped under I-40 and wound around the ranches of outlying Acoma families. The moonlight emphasized the bleak darkness of the lava beds. He turned off old 66 past San Fidel and headed north toward the dark escarpment that surrounded Mount Taylor. He bounced along the washboard surface of the gravel road on the gentle climb toward his grandmother's ranch. She had surprised the family by staying on at the ranch after his grandfather died. He thought she would have moved into Grants or Albuquerque to be near her family. She had said that, as long as she could take care of herself, she would do so in her own home. She did have some help. The ranch foreman, a Basque shepherd, ran a few cows, goats, and sheep of his own and maintained the place. His wife helped *Sitti* around the house. But they were getting on in years too, and Philip wondered how long these relics would be able to keep up the place.

When he let himself into his grandmother's adobe *hacienda*, he was chagrined to compare the spotless beauty of the old ranch house to the chaos of his own lifestyle. There wasn't a mote of dust on the exquisite antiques in the living room. The brick floors gleamed. He heard movement and smelled honey and nuts and called out, "*Marhaba, Sitti.* I'm surprised that you're still up. Did you make *baklawa?*"

His grandmother's voice rang out from the kitchen, "*Marhabtayn. Ma"loum,* I have to feed you your favorites so you won't stay away so long." His grandmother bustled out and gave him a big hug. He felt guilty for thinking that this round bundle of energy was headed towards the old folks' home.

They went into the big farm kitchen and Philip asked, "So, did you bake it in that beautiful nickel plated cook stove of yours?"

Sitti shook her finger at him. "You know I just keep that for when the power goes out."

"I know you keep it because you couldn't stand to part with it."

"It is so much prettier than modern stoves." She sighed. "But I did get rid of the ice box, even though it was such beautiful oak."

Philip chuckled. "You just put it out in the tack shed. Now, George uses it for a TV stand in his den."

"I'm so glad you boys show some appreciation for craftsmanship from the past."

Philip could feel it coming; these compliments were usually followed by a reproach.

"I've always been proud of your woodwork. You know how much I enjoy your *padre* benches on the *portal*. But that carving at the Spanish Market! Why did you have to choose the patron saint of our church to show naked and sexy? The whole parish was in a hubbub."

Philip shrugged. "Michelangelo's David created quite a stir in his day."

"That was just naked, not naked and sexy."

He was feeling quite defensive by now, but he realized that talking about Michelangelo's David as a homosexual demigod wouldn't get him anywhere. "But I took the work from the writings of Santa Teresa herself."

"That's what I told them at church. I knew this issue wasn't over between you and Santa Teresa de Avila. Do you remember the scene with that Irish priest when you were a teenager?"

Philip realized that, for all her criticisms, his grandmother had stood up in defense of him throughout his life. He remembered the argument his grandmother mentioned. In his youth, Philip had been fascinated with the mystic saints, Teresa and John of the Cross. Grants' Irish priest had been horrified by Philip's readings of some of Saint Teresa's more arcane experiences at a Catholic Youth Organization meeting. Reacting impulsively, Philip had accused the priest of being more interested in the proceeds from their car washes and bingo nights than in their religious life. Philip was then banned from the Grants CYO, the first of many groups that were happy to see him leave, taking his iconoclastic views with him.

He remembered his grandmother admonishing the priest. He recalled the way she described the encounter.

She had said to the priest, "No foreigner, whose Celtic ancestors were painting themselves blue while my ancestors were spreading the gospel, is going to interfere with my relationship with God or the saints."

The priest replied, "Your grandson's interpretation of Santa Teresa's dreams and visions didn't sound as though they were inspired by God."

"This congregation chose Santa Teresa because of her mysticism. Look around you at the *moradas* in the Spanish villages, and the *kivas* in the pueblos where secret rituals were performed regularly. Local shepherds and cowboys, looking in the starlit sky, felt the mysteries every night."

"Philip seemed more interested in the mysteries of sex."

"Santa Teresa touches women deeply by describing her union with

Christ as a sexual metaphor, an accessible experience of bliss. I trust that your lack of understanding comes from your celibacy. Hopefully, you haven't been assigned to Grants as part of your sexual rehabilitation from the retreat houses in the Jémez Mountains. Father, if you want to be our shepherd, you need to truly understand your flock. Don't just impose your genteel conventional morality upon us."

Philip was sure that *Sitti* had served some harsh penance as the result of that little statement of faith. His grandmother had stood by him then and now. He thanked her, apologized for being a burden, and gave her a hug. They ate the delicious pastry, talked about the family, and said goodnight.

4

The light streaming through the lace curtains on the windows gave a glow to the old oak table and the sideboard behind it. *Sitti* had set out a breakfast of fresh bread, homemade goat cheese, and her raspberry jam. He assembled the ingredients and took a bite.

"*Laziz*. I don't get enough homemade food, *yslamu dayki*. What do you remember about Buck Cavanaugh?"

She replied brusquely, "I don't want to remember that scoundrel. He came into the store a few times, but I tried to avoid him. Your grandfather waited on Buck. Ask Hank, they rode together in the *malpais* many years ago."

It was clear that the subject was closed. After he finished eating, Philip headed over toward the foreman's house across the compound from his grandmother's house. Enrique Echeverría, better known as Hank to his friends, was leaning against the top rail of the corral. The old ranch hand approached Philip with his bow-legged gait.

"¡*Hola, amigo!* Any decent horseflesh left on this string, Hank?"

Hank smiled. "*Buenos días. Dios mío*, it's good to see you, Felipe. There are a couple of good ones, and a bunch of old broken-down ones like me." He pointed back to the corral. "Let's take a look at them. Going for a ride?"

"Not today, but I hope I can while I'm here. George called me in for an investigation of Buck Cavanaugh. Grandmother says you knew him."

Hank's expression hardened. "I spent time around him, but I couldn't say that I really knew him. He played it pretty close to the vest. There are a lot of stories about him, though. Everybody has at least one."

Philip put a boot on the corral fence and looked over the horses. "*Abuelita* said that you used to work with him."

"Out in the *malpais* of course, a long time ago. I worked for another Basque who had a huge flock of sheep out in one of those grassy areas in the middle of the lava. It was like a big island in the rock. Buck used to come by, and sometimes he helped us move the sheep down to the pens where they trucked them up to the railroad in Grants."

A big dappled gray walked up to the fence and nuzzled Hank's hand. "Back in the fifties, we moved them all the way down to Magdalena when the other stockyard offered the *jefe* a better deal. Buck was in on that one. He worked the roundups for the last of the big cattle drives across the Plains of San Agustín to Magdalena too. I think that they tore up the railroad tracks around nineteen seventy or seventy-one."

"So, was he pretty good on a horse?"

Hank pushed back his hat. "Since Buck trained him, I guess he gets the credit either way, but that horse of his was amazing."

"What do you mean?"

"He was real well schooled. I never heard Buck say anything to him to change gaits, so he must have responded just to leg aids. And that horse could really side pass; Buck made opening and shutting gates while mounted look easy. He was a good cutting horse too. He could spin on a dime, and he seemed to sense where the sheep or cow was headed next. He was as sure footed as an Indian pony, but bigger and black as coal. He looked half Arab, with that dished out face and big nostrils."

"Did he run with his tail up in the wind?"

"*Claro*, you should have seen him. That horse and Buck could go places in the *malpais* that would have cut up the feet of any normal horse. The horse was named *Diablo*, and it was like they had made a pact with the devil."

Philip sang, "'Tryin' to catch the devil's herd across the endless sky.'"

"It was like that." Hank shooed the gray back from the fence. "Buck always wore black, and with that black tack and saddle on Diablo, they would just disappear out in the lava. Then they would show up some place that I couldn't have ridden to on any horse I've ever known."

"Quite the cowboy. I hear that Buck was pretty skilled with a gun too."

Hank pointed to a spot on the mesa, "See that juniper. Once I saw him shoot a jackrabbit about that far away from his horse at a gallop. He said, 'Left eye.' I rode over to it. It was further away than anybody else could have hit it with a handgun, much less on a moving horse. The bullet hole was in its left eye."

Philip was impressed. "What was it like to work with him?"

Hank kept staring into the distance. His brow was furrowed and his hands gripped the top rail tightly. "Like I was saying, he was great at moving a herd. You had to respect him; he could work any position. But he made me nervous when he was riding drag, just knowing that Buck was behind me with a loaded gun. He was spooky in camp, too. He kept to himself most of the time. But if somebody had a bottle, he'd join in. He'd get drunk and tell stories that would make your hair stand on end. The tales of revenge made you vow never to cross him."

"What kind of stories?"

"Buck had been a bounty hunter for years. You could tell that he really enjoyed a manhunt. When he was working for the uranium companies, Buck loved to humiliate the claim jumpers. He would tie his captives to trees or fence posts with barbed wire overnight."

"It sounds like a crucifixion."

Hank nodded. "*Mas o menos.* In the morning, he took those wretched men to the sheriff. I wonder if some of those guys ever made it to the safety of a jail."

"What makes you say that?"

Hank looked down at his boot on the corral rail. "It felt like there was something missing from Buck. The rest of us were like animals to him, like the sheep were to us. He was a lone wolf, always keeping an eye out for the weak ones."

"Scary guy." Philip recalled Buck's writing in the journals.

Hank glanced over at the main house. "I was relieved that I wouldn't have to work with him any more when I started working for your grandparents. Why are you and George looking into him after all these years?"

"We're trying to figure out where his extra money came from."

"I'll bet old Fred Russell would remember more about him. He said that he used to run into Buck when he was prospecting in the Zunis, along the edge of the *malpais*."

Philip smiled. "Really. Is he still around? I thought that he was old when I first met him as a kid."

"*De veras, el es un viejo.* He's kind of a fixture around these parts, Gallup too. He's in his eighties, and he's lived it hard. Now he's got a one-man coal mine."

"I know that a lot of the old prospectors ran a one-man gold or silver outfit. But I've never heard of a one-man coal mine."

"Fred was looking for gold and silver originally, then uranium later, but I guess it's come down to coal. He found a seam in the checkerboard area in the red rocks north of Thoreau.

"How does he mine the coal?"

"He attacks it with a pick and shovel, loads it in that two-ton fifty-four Chevy, and drives into Gallup where he sells it. Then he buys groceries and goes back out to the mine. He doesn't spend much time around people these days. He never has, I guess. He lives in one of those shiny old travel trailers."

Philip shook his head. "Subsistence mining. How do you know so much about what he's doing?"

They walked across the yard. "There aren't that many of us old timers left. I ran into him at the hardware store a while back. He was buying shotgun shells and thirty-aught-six cartridges. He said that he had a bear problem."

"Can you direct me to him?"

"No, but the coal yards in Gallup would know where the mine was to make sure he wasn't on Indian land."

"*Muchas gracias, amigo.* I'll get back to you about the trail ride. *Adios.*"

Philip went back to his grandmother's house. He called the monument headquarters and asked for Sarah. Waiting increased his anxiety. When she came to the phone, he asked her out for lunch. She said that she had a working lunch, but she could take him to the Big Tubes after work if he was still interested. Philip happily agreed; he was relieved. The debacle with Ross hadn't soured her on him completely. She said that she would meet him at the turn off to County Road 42, near Bandera Crater, at five o'clock.

Michael Martin Murphy's songs of outlaws went in the CD player as he drove out to old Highway 66. He headed west, then south on NM 117 to the Malpais Monument Visitor Center. He looked at the exhibits, the geology as well as human incursions into the lava. He bought a map and picked up brochures and a single-page handout on the Big Tubes. After returning to the 4Runner, he unfolded his Malpais Monument map, placed it on the passenger seat, and drove to the Sandstone Bluffs Overlook. Philip got out of the four by four and walked to the edge of the weirdly eroded red and white layers of sandstone. To his left, there was a promontory whose top layer was strewn with grotesque freestanding pillars of rock, hoodoos. On the right, there was a canyon carved by the torrential rains of the summer monsoons. Directly in front of him stretched the *malpais*. He could see across the width of it. Miles of black lava stretched up to the village of San Rafael and the foothills of the Zunis. Much further south, he could see the Chain of Craters, the volcanic cones on the southwestern boundary of the monument.

Bandera Crater, on the north end of the chain, was where he was to meet Sarah that afternoon. To both the north and south, there was lava as far as he could see. Fueled by Hank's description, he imagined Buck and Diablo riding across the foreboding landscape, disappearing into the blackness and reappearing in the distance. Had anyone taken Buck's place as the Prince of Darkness? Jet black ridges alternated with the sand-filled lowlands, ribbons of green and tan. These little valleys supported *piñon* and juniper trees and a variety of grasses, shrubs, and wild flowers. However, some areas remained devoid of vegetation. There were big tilted slabs of the ropy-textured lava the brochure called *pahoehoe*, and vast fields of the jagged *aa-aa*. Hawaiian words were used to describe the types of lava.

Philip decided to drive further to the Acoma-Zuni trailhead to walk on the lava. As he drove south, he saw a group of Acoma Indians moving cattle in the grassy plain between the sandstone and the lava. Philip saw that the grass was thick, the cattle were fat, and the horses' coats were glossy. It appeared that water collected in the areas next to the rock and supported areas of vegetation that were far more dense than the high desert climate usually allowed. This marginal land apparently provided a good return for those who were hardy enough to use it. He waved at the drovers and thought about Hank and Buck driving a herd of sheep south towards Magdalena.

At the trailhead, the information plaque told of ancient trail makers who dropped rocks in crevices to make bridges across the lava. Both Acoma and Zuni Pueblos had tales of rivers of fire, so their ancestors must have seen eruptions more than a thousand years ago. Trade and communication between these two ancient pueblos of western New Mexico went back hundreds of years. West of Bandera Crater, there had been another pueblo that sat high on the sandstone cliffs at *El Morro*, just the way that Sky City at Acoma stands perched above the plains today.

Philip hiked down the trail through a sandy mix of meadow and scrub forest. He reached the lava and noted the rock cairns that marked the trail through the rough rock. He followed them into the lava far enough to feel surrounded by the volcanic blackness. It looked like a moonscape. The only plants were desert succulents that stored water in their leaves, stems and roots. The spines of the narrow leaf yucca were so sharp they were known as Spanish bayonets. The flowers of the claret cup cacti glowed wine red, the *tunas* of the prickly pear were ripening, and the waist-high spiny *chollas* stood guard to punish any deviation from the trail. He felt as if he were on another planet, a land with its violent early history closer at hand. It was no accident that Buck lived in this frightening environment. He had surrounded himself with lava, the way a spider lurks in its web.

How could you find your way back without the cairns to guide you? A misstep could put you on unsteady slabs that led to holes that dropped deep beneath the surface. He saw what Sarah meant about being able to hide anything out here.

Humbled by his encounter with the *malpais*, he drove back north to I-40. Guiding the 4Runner west, he looked more carefully at how the Rio San Jose ran through the collapsed lava. The ponds were green, surrounded by reeds and duckweed. Mallards swam contentedly. The river as well as the desert encroached on the black rock over time. He exited into Grants and let himself into George's office.

George had said that he would be in court, so Philip made himself coffee and got back into the journals. He read about conquests of men, women, and the lava. A pattern of spending emerged after trips to El Paso and Juárez. In addition to obtaining cheap booze and running typical south-of-the-border errands, Buck came home noticeably more comfortable financially. It also looked as though he may have gone further into the interior of Mexico. What did Mexico have to do with Buck's money? Tim Matthews said that he had checked any smuggling possibilities.

Philip called Sheriff Matthews to arrange another interview before he met Sarah. Then he called Gallup and found out the location of Fred Russell's camp. He had time to find Fred before meeting the sheriff. He drove west to the Thoreau exit and took the Crownpoint road, aware that he was almost due north of Buck's ranch. On this side of the Zunis, the terrain was quite different with sandstone mesas and sandy draws. North of the freeway, the colors tended toward the reds of Haystack Mountain and Church Rock.

He turned east on a poorly maintained dirt road. After several wrong turns, Philip saw the glint of a shiny metal trailer in the distance. When he came up to it, he honked his horn. An answering honk floated down the canyon from the end of a primitive road to the works. Fred's 1950's two-ton Chevy flatbed with stake sides sat in front of red cliffs with a black line across their base.

Fred was holding a pick and sweating. He was black with coal dust and smelled a little ripe. He greeted Philip and said, "You look familiar. Ain't you from around here?"

Philip acknowledged that they had first met at his grandparent's trading post more than 25 years ago, when Fred was prospecting around Mount Taylor. Fred had always remained around the periphery of mineral exploitation.

Fred gripped the pick tighter. "Why did you come looking for me, anyways?"

Philip invoked Hank's friendship, and he could see Fred drop his guard. "Fred, can you take a break? I need to talk to you about Buck Cavanaugh."

Fred put down the pick and moved into the shade. "Always got time to talk about Buck. Last of the old ones."

Philip took a couple of steps back from the odiferous old miner. "What do you mean by that?"

"Buck acted like it was still frontier days. He took what he wanted and to hell with the rest. Nobody these days acts like the government can't control 'em. Them Catron County boys may talk about secession, but they still pay their taxes." The old man spat out his tobacco.

Philip moved upwind and deeper into the shade. "How did you meet him?"

"I was prospecting on the east side of the Zunis, back in the Depression days."

Philip was puzzled. "Did you think he was prospecting too?"

Fred took off his hat. "He knew a lot about gold and silver. I ran into him several times around the edges of the Zunis, places that were better for finding color than cattle. Sometimes he was leading a mule packed with panniers, but he always covered his load. So I don't know for sure what he was packing. But I got the feeling he was doing some prospecting himself."

"I heard a story yesterday that he might have found some gold."

Fred took a swig of water out of a canteen. "If he did, he never told anybody. But you'd never get anything out of Buck he didn't want to tell you. Hell, all us prospectors are that way until we file a claim. We're a paranoid bunch."

Philip fanned himself with his hat. "Did Buck make you feel more paranoid?"

"If you weren't a little paranoid around Buck, you weren't paying attention. Don't get me wrong. Buck always greeted me like he was glad to see me. I just heard too many stories about what he did to other people. I was always polite and accommodating with Buck."

"What kind of stories did you hear?"

Fred looked away, scratched like an old hound, and dipped some more snuff. "No sir. I've had enough nightmares about Buck Cavanaugh that I'm not interested in dredging that claim again."

Philip tried a less threatening topic. "I hear he was a pretty good horseman."

Fred nodded and mopped his brow. "I grew up running cattle on the Canadian, I've been a mule skinner, and I broke ponies for ranches. But, in all my days around horses, I never saw anything like Buck. Over the years, he went through a few of those black stallions. *Diablo*, he called every one of 'em. Each one had a better configuration, and more spirit than the last. Having Buck ride up on you out of nowhere kind of reminded me of that old story about the headless horseman coming out of the night."

Philip remembered the time he and his friends had rented horses in Giza, Egypt. They rode around the Sphinx and south into the desert on the mares the Arabs loved. They trotted back to the Great Pyramid of Cheops at the same time that some of their classmates from the American University of Beirut appeared with their tour guide. The superiority he had felt as a horseman gave him some insight into Buck's pact with *Diablo*.

Fred invited him back to the trailer, and they had coffee amidst the blond paneling and heat. Fred took another pinch of Copenhagen. Their talk about the old days was punctuated by the old miner spitting into a coffee can. He told Philip about the many times he had come close to striking it rich only to have it snatched away by some twist of fate. Philip felt the same way about women.

As he drove off, he thought about how disturbed Fred had been by the thought of Buck's cruelty. He was also intrigued by Buck's knowledge of prospecting. Fred had a claim in the Zunis just waiting for gold and silver to hit a price when it would be commercially viable. Philip wondered if Buck had found something that turned out to be a bit more lucrative. He also wondered how many more geriatric eccentrics he would be talking to in this case.

Philip drove past the chain fast-food restaurants at the I-40 interchange to the Blake's Lotaburger further into Grants. His old high school drive-in was more comfortable for him than the new ones. He ordered a Lotaburger with green *chile* and cheese and a side of seasoned fries. As he bit into the burger, he realized he was almost as stuck in the past as the old codgers he was interviewing.

He headed to Tim Matthews' house on the outskirts of San Rafael.

Matthews looked pleased to see him. "What are you finding out about my favorite outlaw?"

"I found out that some of the prisoners he delivered in the fifties weren't always in the best shape for arraignment." Philip cursed himself for his impulsivity. Why couldn't he think first so he wouldn't offend people?

Matthews' face clouded. "That was decades before the Miranda decision. I didn't always like what Buck had done to those claim jumpers. But the fact is they were criminals in his custody. I had no say unless those boys pressed charges and they were way too scared to complain. They were better off in jail than they'd been with Buck."

Matthews gestured for Philip to sit down in the living room.

"It sounds like he handled them the way you said he talked about strike-breaking, like they were animals."

Matthews shrugged. "Maybe. His prisoners probably felt that way. When he was with me, I felt like I was his pal. But the way he talked about other people made you wonder how he talked about you when you weren't with him. He sure enjoyed dominating people more than he did animals."

Philip tried to get their conversation closer to his investigation. "I've been reading in Buck's journals that he made regular pilgrimages to Mexico."

"Sometimes, when people were swapping stories at a bar, he'd brag about those trips. He had this route that he followed, first to Truth or Consequences. I thought that was the damnedest thing when Hot Springs changed its name to Truth or Consequences."

"That was a strange one. I remember seeing the hot spring pools on the TV show."

"As an officer of the law, I had to admire the motto. Anyway, he'd 'take the waters' and hole up in some motel for a couple of days and soak in the mineral baths. Then he'd go down to Juárez. If he didn't have a woman with him at the time, he'd whore around for a couple of days.

Then he'd disappear for a couple of weeks. I got the feeling that he went deeper into Mexico most visits."

"What made you think he went further into Mexico?"

Matthew appeared amused by the memory. "Sometimes when he got real juiced, he'd go on about Guadalajara, Cuernavaca, and San Miguel de Allende."

Philip was excited. "Cuernavaca is known for its silver mines, and San Miguel de Allende is in the middle of a mining district. Even though these days San Miguel mostly imports tourists and exports arts and crafts, almost every village around it mines something."

"What's that got to do with Buck?"

"I talked to the widow of the older man that Buck killed. She said that her husband was a treasure hunter, obsessed by gold. Fred Russell said that Buck seemed to be knowledgeable in prospecting."

Matthews scowled. "There's a big difference between prospecting and doing the scut work and manual labor it takes to run a mine."

"I haven't figured out what he was doing down there. And you never found any evidence of drugs or smuggling aliens?"

"And I really looked. I saw the same pattern of spending you did. I confronted him on it once. He said that he'd done well at the horse track at Sunland Park. I checked that out with the Doña Ana County Sheriff's Department down in Las Cruces. They said that their snitches confirmed that Buck was a major player at the races."

"Do you think that's where his money came from?"

Sheriff Matthews smiled ruefully. "I doubt that it was the only source. He had enough horse sense that he probably could have made a fair amount of money at the track. Doña Ana said that he placed some hefty bets. But he couldn't have done that with what he made around here."

Suddenly Matthews stared into Philip's eyes with his famous "I know you're guilty" look. "I've checked around and I know that Marlene Cavanaugh's in town. So stop giving me this cowboy culture bit. I won't ask you to break your client's confidentiality, but don't bullshit me."

Philip felt chagrined. "I'm sorry. I should have known that you wouldn't buy such a lousy cover story. Sarah Johnson thinks his money might have come from a bank job or payroll heist. What do you think of that idea?"

"I don't know of any big robbery in the Four Corners region that I didn't try to pin on Buck. We never found a shred of evidence against him."

"Sarah talked about a train robbery."

Matthews clapped his hand on his forehead. "My God, you mean the old A and P. I thought that one had been wrapped up in mothballs years ago."

"She said that it was still unsolved."

Matthews got up and saw Philip to the door. "So are a lot of things in life, boy."

5

Further south on Highway 53, the ridges of black rock rose above the sandy valleys and plains less frequently. Drought-tolerant grasses and cacti enveloped the rock along with scrub oak and four-wing saltbush. Gray-green stands of chamisa bloomed in waves of yellow, and purple asters contrasted with the pale desert colors. In the distance, dense stands of *piñon* and juniper covered the hills. A mixture of excitement and anxiety distracted him as he thought about meeting Sarah. At the point where Highway 53 began to head west and gain elevation, tall ponderosa pine replaced the *piñon* and juniper. It looked like the transition took place at a lower altitude than usual.

He slowed as he passed the road to Buck's ranch. He felt Buck's presence, but all the stories he had been hearing had created a figure larger than life. He remembered the trial pictures in *The Uranium Reporter* showing an old man, but his mind's eye could only summon the image frozen in his six-year-old brain, the bad man. Buck had been at the top of his game then, a bounty hunter. He could almost see Buck and *Diablo* ambling up the ranch road. There was irony in Buck's journal entries about being a bounty hunter, the fox guarding the hen house. He was paid well by the uranium companies and saluted by the cops for doing the things he enjoyed most, stalking and domination.

As the SUV climbed, Philip saw the peak of Bandera's cone looming in the distance and a flow of *aa-aa* lava creating a rough black scar at its base. As the road scaled the side of the volcanic cone, the red and black cinders covered the hillside. Philip remembered a boyhood trip to the Bandera Volcano and the Candelaria Ice Caves. His single excursion into the *malpais* as a child occurred when Philip's family took a Sunday drive to the only tourist trap in the Zuni Mountains. The current billboards still evoked the Route 66 era of roadside curiosities.

The Ice Caves were a short walk into the *malpais* and consisted of what he now knew to be a lava tube filled with a sheet of ice. The existence of all this ice surrounded by lava had piqued young Philip's curiosity. In the midst of the summer's heat, the descent down the rickety wooden stairs to the ice was an oasis of refreshing refrigeration. The anomaly of the ice in the middle of the sun-baked black rock stimulated countless questions from the boy.

Philip had asked, "Where did the water for the ice come from? Why didn't it melt when the snow melted? How far back do the caves go? Why can't we go further into the caves?"

His father's patience had been exhausted, but now he could satisfy his youthful longing to explore the depths. A quarter mile after the turn off to the Ice Caves, Philip turned south on County Road 42. He crossed the cattle guard and parked in a grove of trees. He was looking forward to this expedition not only for the adventure of exploring the tubes but to see Sarah again. He pictured her tall slim body, her sculptured face, and her blond hair streaked by the sun. He especially liked her hands, the long slender fingers that had caressed his arm last night. He hadn't reacted to a woman like this in years, and he vacillated between hope and fear. It wasn't just her looks; he was intrigued by her incisive intelligence. Unlike Teresita who often kept her own counsel, Sarah certainly wasn't afraid to say what was on her mind. He smiled when her Park Service Jeep pulled down the incline and parked next to him. He greeted her with a hug and felt the warmth of her response as she lightly kissed his cheek.

Sarah said, "I wonder how Ross is doing today?"

"Better than he would be if we hadn't driven him home. Thanks for your patience last night."

"Poor man. We should take your vehicle since this isn't exactly the official Park Service tour."

Philip bowed. "I'd be happy to drive. Where have you been this afternoon?"

"*El Morro*, again. With the two monuments so close together, I spend some time there as well. I usually just give interpretive talks over there, since the history of the inscriptions is pretty well established. I like the freshness of the *malpais* project better."

"I haven't been to see Inscription Rock in many years. The part I remember best from visiting it as a boy was the Beale expedition."

As he opened the door for her, she asked mockingly, "Does everything relate back to the Middle East for you?"

"No. I thought that Oñate's *Paso por aquí* was impressive too."

"Beale's camels didn't work out. Even though they did well with the geography, no one could handle them."

"That's because they only had one Arab. Camels' personalities are completely different from horses. You have to be sensitive to their moods; they hold grudges. Once they get mad at you, you have to give them your clothes to destroy before they'll forgive you."

Sarah cocked her head. "I had a boyfriend like that once. Is this camel business a commercial for understanding Mediterranean males?"

"No, I just thought a historian might want to know the facts. But we're burning daylight, let's go."

They got into the SUV and drove over the ridge into the *malpais*. Philip couldn't understand why their conversations sometimes made him uncomfortable. Were they jockeying for position? Was this sexual politics Wild West style?

He decided to change the subject. "So tell me about the Big Tubes."

"You'll see them for yourself soon enough. These features are part of a tube system that is over sixteen miles long. There are two intact tubes and two canyons where the tubes have collapsed. We have to hike across the *malpais* for about a half-mile to get to them. We'll probably have just enough time to go into one of the tubes. The trails are marked by rock cairns that can be hard to spot at dusk."

"This is quite a road for a national monument. If this mud is left over from the summer rains a few weeks ago, I'd hate to drive it then."

"If you think this is bad, you should see the road to the Braided Cave. At least you know you're on a road here. I'll bet conditions were even more primitive in Buck's heyday. In a couple of miles, you'll come to a sign, *Cerro Rendija*. Turn left there."

The challenge of negotiating the mud limited Philip's conversational ability. He saw the rounded hill in the distance and turned down the side road. He was relieved to see that this section was gravel that had been graded recently. Shortly afterward, a wall of lava loomed on the left. It was taller than the ponderosa pines, and towered black, rugged, and ominous. A short distance later, a sign pointed to the Big Tubes. The parking lot consisted of an information board and a sign-in sheet.

"Where are the RV hookups?"

"The Park Service has plans for a portapotty. Some people avail themselves of primitive camping here. Do you have a flashlight?"

Philip looked in his emergency kit in the back of the 4Runner. "I have one and the batteries look strong."

"I brought a couple of spares, a first aid kit, and some water. Have you got some gloves and extra water? Good, let's hit the trail."

Sarah hitched up her fanny pack, Philip hefted his daypack, and they signed the visitor log. As they passed by the first lava cairns marking the trail, Philip realized that there were aspen trees growing at least a thousand feet lower than they normally did. Their pale bark made a stark contrast against the black rock.

It wasn't much of a trail. Rock cairns pointed the way, but the footing was difficult on the rugged rock. Philip was glad that he was wearing heavy-duty hiking boots. The crunching sound of the loose rock was reminiscent of the cinders from the archaic coal furnaces of his early memories. The ponderosa were more sporadic, and aspen broke through the lava in lonely groves. Although Philip was aware that they were generally traveling east, he couldn't locate discreet landmarks. He felt disoriented. They would climb up a low ridge and scramble down a shallow valley. The lava was smoother here and rougher there, but after a few minutes, it all looked the same. How had Buck found his way through this kind of terrain? Philip had brought his GPS device, but he didn't want to look like he didn't trust Sarah's sense of reckoning. After crossing the most desolate, boot-destroying piece of ground he had ever had the misfortune of walking upon, Philip saw a sign.

Sarah noticed his interest. "Don't pay any attention to that. It's misleading."

"Your tax dollars at work. Where do we go from here?"

Sarah led the way up an incline to a huge hole in the ground. The lava dropped off precipitously to a floor about one hundred feet below. There was a land bridge across the structure on the northern end and a tunnel to the southeast.

"This is the Big Skylight. It's a little tricky getting down into it and the floor is a constant scramble, so we'll just go across the top to the skylight and look down."

Leading the way, Sarah pointed out the hole in the surface of the lava that opened into the Big Skylight Cave. "Notice the moss growing down below. It's the about the only green thing that grows in the tubes, and then only in a few places where holes let in light."

Philip was overwhelmed by the immensity of the tube. Sarah had said that they were big, but he was not prepared for cathedral proportions. Because his brain could not quite comprehend the processes created by molten rock, he automatically compared the tube to sandstone canyons scoured by water. Images of red-hot rivers of rock cooling around the edges to form tubes, benches, and layers that peeled backward towards the floor belonged to a primordial time. Yet here he was staring at the remnants of a flow just a few thousand years old.

Sarah led the way to the Four Windows Cave, a short journey northeast over the lava field. The terrain was smoother, there was more soil, and vegetation filled the pockets in the lava.

"A couple of the old geezers I talked to today said that Buck could ride his horse across the lava. It sure looks possible here, but I can't imagine it in that aa-aa near the Big Skylight."

"You would have to choose your path carefully and it would take quite a horse."

"Both Hank, my grandmother's foreman, and Fred Russell, the old prospector, said that Buck's horses were among the finest that they'd ever seen. They were well-schooled too, so he was a damned good trainer as well."

"It sounds like Sheriff Matthews was right. Buck was good at anything he put his mind to. I heard some Buck stories today, too. A couple of the older women who work at the Park Service said that Buck was quite the ladies' man. They said that once a woman was in his sights, he could charm the birds out of a tree. One of them said that a friend had confided to her that Buck was an exciting lover, but he was a little too rough for her taste." A faint blush came over Sarah's face.

Philip smiled. "Maybe that's part of the reason that he couldn't keep them long. You have to try a little tenderness."

Although he enjoyed the direction that the conversation was going, Philip thought it was a little too early in their relationship to pursue it. As they hiked from cairn to cairn, he saw a small lizard disappear down a hole in a frozen basalt bubble. A long-eared squirrel scampered up a ponderosa, and a couple of birds flitted from bush to bush.

"Not a whole lot in the way of wildlife," he noted.

"Actually, we've seen a fair amount. Wait a couple of hours. It's still hot enough that most of the residents hide out during the day. There are lots of rodents in the cracks in the rocks. Rattlesnakes hunt more by thermal location than by sight, so they'll be around later when it's cooler. We might see deer or coyote on the drive out. Maybe an owl, or are they really witches? I haven't heard you say much about your Hispanic side."

Philip held his head high. "I'm proud of my Spanish blood. We sing *Las Mañanitas* on birthdays, and my uncles still go to the *morada* on Good Friday. I don't know much about this *buho* or *brujo* thing with owls; we call them *tecolotes*. But, if I spend any more time out here, I could believe in just about anything."

He pointed to the canyon to the north. "Hey, is that where we descend into hell, like the last scene in *Don Giovanni?*"

Sarah looked at him intently. "A detective who knows opera." She shaded her eyes with her hand. "That's it, the Four Windows Cave, our descent into the netherworld. It's easier to get into on the other side. Watch out for the pin-cushion cacti as you go down, they're in a lot of the crevices."

As they walked to the other side of the pit, Philip explained, "When I stayed with Archie in Tesuque, we'd get standing-room-only tickets for the Santa Fe Opera. After all, it was just up on the hill above the village. When I saw *Don Giovanni*, a thunderstorm broke out during that last scene. The old opera theater was mostly open air, so you could see the lightning through the stage. Mozart would have been proud of that production. While the lightning lit up the Jémez Mountains, the thunder overpowered the orchestra. The first raindrops hit as Don Giovanni disappeared into the bowels of the earth. Speaking of which, these tubes do bear a resemblance."

Sarah cautioned him, "They're a lot sharper. Your gloves will help you feel more comfortable about using your hands, which might save your neck. NASA studied these tubes because of the similarity to the ones on the moon. They thought that underground shelter would protect against cosmic rays. However, they decided that space suits wouldn't survive the hazardous conditions. This one's a stroll compared to some of the others, but even here you have to pay constant attention to safety."

Philip responded, "'Eternal vigilance is the price of freedom.' Thomas Jefferson."

"Do you channel *Bartlett's Quotations* or what?" Sarah led the scramble down into the tube.

Philip was mulling over her comment, but the climb down demanded his concentration. He had to use his hands because the rocks underfoot were wobbly. They walked along the east wall and looked over at the bright green moss growing on the slopes of the blocks that had tumbled from the roof. The skylights made beams of light that looked like spotlights on the moss. Philip learned quickly that he could either walk or look at the roof. Trying to do both led to stumbling on the loose rock. They passed the mossy break down and dropped down to a relatively level floor. As the light from the windows dimmed, they turned on their flashlights and made their way down the tube. As they walked around the bend and left all light behind, the floor became smooth.

"This feels like walking in an underground parking garage," Philip exclaimed.

"The floor is *pahoehoe*. See the rough-edged ripples on these little mushroom-like things? The roof is strong enough that nothing has fallen down. They call this hallway the Cauliflower Passage. That little crevice on the left is supposed to go back to the entrance, but I'm too claustrophobic to try it. The walking gets tougher up ahead in the One-Foot-in-the-Gutter Gallery."

After they turned the corner, the floor became uneven again. The name of the gallery proved to be accurate. They climbed over blocks, scrambled on loose rock and crisscrossed the tube to find better footing.

As he clambered over some break down, Philip asked, "So, how long ago did these blocks fall?"

Sarah laughed. "They fall all the time, but most of them fell in the first few years after the tube's birth."

Eventually, they came to a balcony where the lower level ended a short distance further. Philip could feel air moving through the upper tunnel.

"Have you been further on the top level? It must have an opening for the air to be flowing through."

"There's another entrance, but remember I'm not good in small spaces. These big tubes are fine, but the narrow passages aren't for me. Let's take a break. Sit down beside me on this block and turn out your flashlight."

Philip was very aware of Sarah's body next to his. Wherever the wind was blowing from, the opening wasn't close enough to contribute any light. Philip had never been in darkness so complete before. Tourist caves leave the lights on. He remembered a story that his mother told him about visiting Carlsbad Caverns when she was a girl. They turned out all of the lights in the Big Room. Then, the rangers lit torches and sang "Rock of Ages" as they approached that formation.

After a minute, there was no improvement in Philip's ability to see, no adjustment. The debate between the Hindus who declared that eyes should shut during meditation and the Buddhists who meditated with eyes open was meaningless here. After a couple of minutes, his eyes started playing tricks, and dim colored glows appeared before him. They moved with him when he moved his head, so he knew it wasn't light in the cave. Eventually he became restless and turned on his light in the lantern mode, which gave a glow to the area around them.

"I was trying to wait for you, but I almost couldn't do it." Sarah breathed a sigh of relief.

Philip couldn't resist. "It's always better when it's simultaneous."

He winked, but he wasn't sure if Sarah could see it. He put his arm around her shoulder and she laid her head on his shoulder and snuggled into him.

Sarah sighed. "This feels wonderful, but it's getting dark outside. I want to show you one more feature."

They disentangled and made their way back up the tube, picking their way through the rubble. When they got back to the Cauliflower Passage, Philip shone his light down the side passage that Sarah had pointed out earlier. He voted with Sarah. It was narrower than he felt comfortable negotiating. They saw the light of the windows and the entrance. It seemed odd to turn off the flashlights and see with available light again. The Kelly green of the moss seemed especially intense after a world of black and white. As they climbed out, Philip was sweaty, and he could feel the strain on his muscles. The Tubes were no walk in the park.

Sarah was more confident back on the surface. She looked at the sun. "We've got time for a collapse structure. Let me show you one that isn't on your flyer, Seven Bridges."

She led the way back toward the Big Skylight, however she skirted the entrance, passing further east as she continued south. The footing became even stranger. The lava was smooth, but consisted of gently convex plates about a yard across. It was like walking across a pile of manhole covers. The ponderosa were growing more thickly. As Philip started to become concerned about their course, he saw a cairn. There were only a couple more before a large space opened up ahead of them. They emerged from the trees and walked along the north side of a canyon that twisted through the lava.

"Caterpillar Collapse is like this, but it's not as big and doesn't have the bridges that Seven Bridges has. They're both tubes that collapsed," Sarah explained.

They held hands as they walked across the first bridge. The canyon extended beyond, with more stone bridges visible. Philip was amazed by the thin smooth conduit of lava that spanned the canyon. It was thinner than the sandstone arches he had seen. Not only that, but there were tall ponderosas growing on the bridges. As the wind whistled through the pines, he knew he wouldn't want to be on these bridges during a windstorm.

He turned to Sarah as they watched the colors in the western sky.

He wanted to kiss her and feel her body pressing against him, but the timing didn't feel right.

She interrupted his fantasy by saying, "It's getting dark, and we've got to get out of here."

They walked back, following the cairns. Philip now really had the sense of having visited another world. His previous walk across the lava had led him to feel that he was in an alien landscape, but the exploration of the tubes confirmed it. The isolation of the place heightened that feeling. He had visited Carlsbad Caverns and experienced the marvels of a limestone cave, but those caves were filled with people. Aside from having his own personal ranger, there was little sign of the presence of the Park Service here. No one else had been at any of the features.

Dusk was falling and the cairns were hard to spot. He saw movement out of the corner of his eye, a man in black? It was just a long-eared squirrel with a black bushy tail scurrying up a Ponderosa.

He breathed a sigh of relief when they returned to the parking lot. Philip looked at the sign-in book again. There had been one other party earlier today, and less than a dozen more over the course of a week.

"I can't believe there aren't more visitors. These are incredible geological phenomena."

Sarah shook her head. "We were just starting to market the place, but the budget-cutters in Washington are rolling back the funding for the Park Service. There are plans to improve the road and establish a better trailhead, but there are also rumors that the Monument is on a hit list of poorly visited parks. Enjoy it while it lasts, one way or the other, it will change."

"I can't believe there isn't more local knowledge of this place. I've been around this area most of my life, and I've never heard of these lava tubes until you mentioned them at dinner last night."

They put their packs in the back and climbed into the SUV. Sarah tossed one of the water bottles to Philip and took a long drink from her own.

"They scare most people. I've asked people to come out to see them, but I get polite refusals most of the time. Some of the fear comes from the lack of development. People are much more willing to tour caves that have smooth paths and an electric light system. But, I think the main deterrent is the *malpais* itself. There is something about this place that scares off a lot of people. I don't think it's just the isolation, or the rough rock. You were joking about the descent into hell, but I think that's it. It is too much like the archetype. To a lot of people, this place is symbolic of evil."

"And the perfect place for Buck's evil empire. It's a good place to hide things or hide out yourself, lost treasure and lost souls."

6

Derek Gruber slowed as he crossed the cattle guard onto County Road 42 and saw the Park Service Jeep. What was the ranger doing here at this hour? His experience of federal employees told him to be wary of anyone who didn't clock out at five. If they weren't after a paycheck and pension, they were likely to be Boy Scouts of one persuasion or another. County Road 42 was the long way home from his job as a security guard at the uranium mines at Ambrosia Lake. He made sure to go through the west side of the monument at least once a week to keep his eye on the Feds.

He was glad that he had decided to observe today. There was something going on between the woman ranger and the dark-haired man standing next to the Toyota. They looked at him and took a step back from one another. They were in the shade, so he had some difficulty seeing details, but he could sense the tension between them. As he drew closer, he recognized them, the couple from the Grubstake. They knew the crazy drunk who sang love songs in Arabic. The stylized cedar-tree window decal on the 4Runner jogged his memory, Lebanon. The man was must be an Arab; did the Lebanese symbol mean he was Hezbollah? He quickly jotted down the license-plate number on the notepad on his dash.

As he drove past, all of his anger about the September 11 terrorist attacks boiled up again. Fundamentalist Muslim radicals had infiltrated the United States with impunity, hatched a diabolical plot, and carried it out while federal authorities sat on their asses. Since returning from Dubai, he had warned everyone he knew about the impending Armageddon that was brewing in the Middle East. They had ignored him, preferring their own comfortable existence to the work of forming militias to defend America. After 9/11, G.W. Bush finally focused on the importance of homeland security, but all that really meant was the consolidation of federal agencies into an even bigger bureaucracy. At least G.W. had done better than his dad had done in Iraq, toppling the tyrant. Now he looked like a fool with no weapons of mass destruction and a growing civil war. By pushing the Taliban out of Afghanistan and establishing a new government, Bush had made a credible show of force against international terrorism. Now his Operation Iraqi Freedom was distracting us from the real work of stopping terrorism. Why hadn't they found Osama Bin Laden and his *Al Qaida* lieutenants?

The heavy-duty four by four truck climbed slowly uphill and entered the *malpais*. The intrusive memories were taking his concentration away from steering around the rocks. The desert camouflage Dodge Power Wagon bounced around the bend. Once he was out of sight, he slowed and pulled off the road. As he reached for his pack, he remembered his excitement at the prospect of fighting in the first Gulf War. What a fiasco! Rather than focusing on battle readiness, they got lectures about cultural sensitivity. He remembered the deference shown by American brass toward the Kuwaiti and Saudi military. Instead of being given the respect due them as liberators, American GI's were sequestered away from the populace as though they were an embarrassment. Now the American fighting forces were being kept away from the Iraqi populace as a safety precaution against suicide bombers. The Sunni insurgents had actually invited *Al Qaida* to join them.

Derek left the truck behind and ran up the hill. Why was there an Arab out here now? Even the way he stood with his hands together behind his back was so typical. If there had been another man with him rather than a woman, they probably would have been linking pinkies the way that the Arab soldiers did. It looked like they didn't feel lonely in the bunkers at night.

Climbing up the hill quickly, he was careful not to make sounds that could be heard by the couple below. The training regimen that he had learned in Special Forces kept him in shape for this kind of threat. He had been studying tactical strategies and realized that the first Gulf War had been a plot by the Arab fundamentalists to get the U.S. to reveal their weapons technology. Because of Operation Desert Storm, Osama Bin Laden had realized that the forces of Allah couldn't win a conventional war. So he brought the terror to America's doorstep. After all, if Saddam Hussein had really been a threat to international security the first time, why was he allowed to remain as the ruler of Iraq? George Bush the Elder must have been bought off by the oil sheikhs. Both Bushes and Vice President Cheney were connected to oil companies, after all. It was interesting that the highest priority by the American forces in Iraq this time turned out to be securing the oil fields.

Why hadn't Saudi Arabia been the target of investigation rather than Iraq anyway? The majority of the 9/11 hijackers had been Saudis. But rather than sending the CIA to investigate, the Bushes sent former Secretary of State James Baker to negotiate oil contracts. Gruber saw that oil money flows downhill to the bottom feeders. He had provided personal security for oil executives while he worked for a private security company in the United Arab Emirates. They were narcissistic parasites.

Derek went over the top of the ridge to the north and crouched behind a juniper. He pulled out his field glasses and made sure he wouldn't be reflecting light down to the couple below. They were each in their vehicles now and pulled out as he watched. Both vehicles turned right and headed east on Highway 53. What were they doing here? Could this be the beginning? Lebanon had become one of the entry points to the West for Islamic militants since the puppet government that had been controlled by the Syrians had come to power. Even though the new government was independent, the Iranians still moved arms to Hezbollah through Syria. And now that Hamas was part of the government in Palestine, terrorists crossed back and forth across all three areas. There were enough Lebanese in America to provide good cover for an operative. Derek mulled over the possibilities as he moved down to the grove of trees below. The Jeep hadn't gone beyond parking area, but he would try to track the 4Runner. He pulled out his digital camera and took shots of the tire pattern of the 4Runner. The aggressive off-road tread would be easy to spot in the mud holes.

He jogged double time back to his old four by four. He felt his excitement growing. All these weeks of watchful waiting, and now it was unfolding in front of him. After he left the corruption of the Gulf States, he had decided to keep a watch for *Al Qaida* in America's uranium country. A radioactive dirty bomb was probably the next horror. He remembered the drunk and the Arab greeting each other in Arabic. Was that song some kind of code? He'd seen the drunk slugging them down at the Grubstake for the past several weeks. Maybe the drinking was just a cover. Had he been waiting for the Lebanese all along? Derek tossed his pack on the passenger seat and locked the hubs into four-wheel drive. He started the engine and drove south. The energy that came from a new mission was flowing through him. His counter-terrorism and surveillance instruction at Fort Bragg would be put to use here on the home front, where it was needed most.

Derek turned off CR 42, down the road to *Cerro Rendija* and followed the 4Runner's tracks to the Big Tube parking lot. There were footprints heading from the parking lot to the trailhead and return prints coming back. What were they doing in the lava fields? Derek's mind searched for options. Could it be the Tubes themselves? Were they planning to use them for storage of ordnance? If they looked far enough down the system, they might find his own weapons and supply cache. Derek had carefully researched sites for several caches that he had established. The *malpais* seemed an obvious choice for one because of its isolation, the rugged inaccessibility, and the irony of using the fed's own preserve as part of their downfall.

He turned the truck around and returned to County Road 42 to continue south. It wouldn't be long before the top-heavy federal bureaucracy would topple from its own weight. He knew many people who would be happy to assist in the process. They would restore America to the kind of democracy that the true patriots of the American Revolution had envisioned. Homeland security couldn't be forged by the same bureaucrats who had failed us before. Federal intelligence agencies hadn't even communicated with each other, much less coordinated their planning. He knew that the founding fathers had been right; only a well-armed militia could protect America. America was in the same situation now as the Minutemen were in during the Revolution. A hostile force was invading our country with the aim of forcing us into submission. By mobilizing citizen soldiers, we could have observers everywhere. Vigilant civilians had found the *Al Qaida* cell in upstate New York, as well as the truck driver who wanted to blow up the Brooklyn Bridge. Suspicious activities could be dealt with immediately within the militia network, instead of sending memos that would never be read. The Internet would move information instantaneously to the community of patriots. We beat the British through guerilla warfare, and we can do the same with these rag-heads.

He wished that he could steer his way through local politics as well as he made his way through these mud puddles. Derek moved to Catron County in order to join the movement to secede from the Union. Instead of the freedom fighters that he'd expected to find, he discovered that the secessionists were mostly a bunch of poor ranchers who just wanted to graze cattle on federal land for cheap. He sought forward-thinking men of action who would dare to secede from the United States, modern day versions of Jefferson Davis and Robert E. Lee. This wasn't just a Sagebrush Rebellion; the militia movement was growing in every state. The Posse Comitas was trying to return the building block of democracy to the county level of government. Catron County had the historic imperative to begin the restoration of the true intentions of the founding fathers.

However, Catron County wasn't interested in international conspiracies. They could see how federal regulations regarding the Mexican Spotted Owl had closed the sawmill, how the Gila Wilderness was being turned into a playground for city people, and even how the Very Large Array radio telescope was bringing internationalism to their doorstep. But they remained provincial and focused on local issues. Terrorism was just a problem for the big cities. There were a few who had a wider perspective. A couple of them had been involved in the Committee of the States in California several years ago. They understood that the corrupt federal government only served the rich, but they weren't interested in working with a greenhorn who had just moved here.

Derek was used to being persecuted for his views. As he drove down the rugged extent of County 42 past the Chain of Craters, he reflected on the number of times he had stormed out of meetings with expletives hanging in the air. He had been teased in high school, called a skinhead, a Nazi. They didn't understand true patriotism. Just because he was of German descent didn't mean that he was a Nazi. In fact, his grandfather had opposed the National Socialist Party's rise to power, a position that was more safely maintained in America than in the Fatherland. His grandfather was proud that he had become an American citizen. On the other hand, Derek remembered cleaning out the attic at the farm after his grandmother's death and finding the framed picture of the Kaiser. Hans Gruber had respect for rule by law; he had been a policeman and was proud of it. Derek's father had been just as rigid, but he lost respect for the government over the years. He had fought for the American way against the godless Communists in the Korean Conflict. Gerald insisted that Derek join the boy scouts to learn to respect God and country. He had been very demanding as Derek earned his merit badges and progressed through the scouting program. It was hard to live up to his father's standards, but his dad had drilled him through the rifleman badges and made sure that he was an expert marksman. Gerald Gruber had never been as proud as the night that Derek obtained the rank of Eagle Scout.

As time went on, Gerald Gruber complained that the government was allowing this country to "go to hell in a hand basket." He decried the erosion of values and rampant liberalism that were destroying the American way of life that he had fought for. Gerald turned to the right-wing beliefs of William Potter Gale as a beacon in the dark times of racial strife. He admired the call of the Posse Comitas for armed insurrection against big government that was giving our taxes to people who were too lazy to work.

Derek left the cinder cones behind as the road turned southeast. The trees thinned out as he drove toward the Hole In The Wall. He had been shocked that his views weren't accepted when he joined the Army. Some of the things he held sacred, such as the Second Amendment, were also important to his buddies. However, his G.I. chums were uneasy with his belief in the importance of the military to protect America from the international conspiracy of bankers, who were now controlled by the oil *sheikhs*. Between his beliefs and the racial tensions in the Army, he had been in a lot of fights during the first few weeks of his enlistment. In due course he learned that it wasn't worth getting caught up in other people's ignorance, especially if he wanted to advance in the ranks.

The Power Wagon passed through the sparse prairie grasses to the intersection with State Road 117. Derek got out of the truck and turned the hubs to take the Power Wagon out of four-wheel drive. The vast emptiness of the North Plains stretched to the horizon. He got back in the truck and turned left on the pavement.

In order to cope with the Army, Derek became a loner. He indulged his love of weapons and ordnance and used every opportunity to learn more about them. He was in better shape than anyone else and read tactical manuals for pleasure. Before the end of his first tour, he went before the promotion board and qualified for noncommissioned officers school. He knew that his squad thought he was too tough on them during training exercises, but he had learned from his father to do it until you did it right. They were prepared when they went into battle during Desert Storm, and he'd been able to bring them through it alive. They distinguished themselves and certainly didn't complain when they were given their medals. His commanding officer was so impressed with his leadership that he recommended that Derek apply for Special Forces. There, he found soldiers with the same level of dedication that he felt and faced challenges that taught him to execute covert missions and survive.

After a few miles, he turned right on to County Road 41. The gravel road stretched on into the distance. Soon, the monotony led him back into his reverie. Every so often he had found like-minded pals. A couple of his Army buddies were involved in the Identity Church movement. When he came back stateside, he visited them in Elohim City. He listened to them go on about the martyrs in Waco and Timothy McVeigh. They didn't realize that the world had changed. They still believed that blacks and Jews were the root of America's problems. They were locked into the wrong Semites; the Islamic fundamentalists were the real enemy now. The world economy was no longer controlled by Jewish bankers; it was controlled by oil.

After his frustration at Elohim City and the Catron County debacle, he had decided to go underground. He would focus his efforts on the Internet. There were plenty of web sites where truly important information was posted. There were also chat rooms where like-minded people supported the cause of freedom. He didn't need to associate with people whose political education was so lacking. He stayed in touch with fellow patriots via the Internet and limited his face-to-face contact. Encrypted email kept their plans safe from government spying.

Although women were attracted to his chiseled good looks and muscular build, his relationships didn't last long. Very few women understood the immediacy of the danger to our country, and most of them thought that he was obsessed by it. Derek had been surprised that his acquaintance with the Aryan Brotherhood bikers led to an introduction to a woman who understood his views. He was looking forward to visiting Gloria at the women's prison and telling her about his suspicions.

His experiences in the Gulf taught him that energy resources were crucial for world domination. Derek knew that *Al Qaida* was seeking nuclear material for a dirty bomb. Although the former Soviet Union was the most likely source, the Cíbola County uranium mines were also a possibility, so he decided to defend them. Therefore, Derek Gruber took a job as a security guard in the Ambrosia Lake mining district and bided his time. He would run the Arab's license plate and check his databases. He would also ask the few people that he trusted in Grants about the Arab and the drunk. His Aryan Brother friends would have noticed the blonde for sure, and they might know something about the Lebanese. Strangers attracted attention in Cibola County. What was a beautiful blonde doing with that swarthy foreigner anyway?

7

Philip turned onto the road to the Ice Caves. He didn't want to tailgate Sarah all the way back to Grants. Their parting had felt strange. She had pushed him away when the Power Wagon appeared. He understood that she had to maintain professionalism while in uniform, but it felt like ice water had been thrown on the growing warmth of their relationship. The guy driving the Dodge had slowed and stared at them. It looked as if he had taken down Philip's license plate number. Was he someone Sarah knew?

He drove through the ponderosas to the Ice Caves parking lot to no avail; it was closed for the day. The buildings looked like they had been caught in a time warp from the heyday of tourist courts. Small cabins surrounded a log building that housed the office and museum. He wondered what happened to the two-headed snake he remembered from his boyhood visit.

Driving downhill on 53, Philip was perplexed by Sarah. She seemed interested, but she could turn cold faster than weather in the mountains. He wondered if something in her past had left bigger scars than she was letting on. She talked about men having conflicts, but it felt as if her knowledge of that concept was first hand. He remembered the graduate student in psychology who had taught the behaviorism lab at the American University of Beirut. He had demonstrated the concept of approach-avoidance conflict by shocking male rats whenever they approached females in heat. When the male rats were far away, they were drawn to the females. But, when they approached the area where they had been punished, they became fearful and withdrew. Did Sarah have a trauma in her past that gave her such mixed emotions about men?

He was on his way to report in to his client. Marlene Cavanaugh had suggested that he give his findings to her over a late dinner at the Cíbola Inn. After his talk with George about the Cavanaugh clan, he was intrigued by Marlene. What impact had growing up with Buck's son as a father left on her, and what was Buck like as a grandfather?

He drove the length and breadth of the *malpais* to his grandmother's ranch. She was under the portal listening to the sounds of the stock settling down for the night. He pulled a rocking chair up next to her. They talked about Fred Russell and Tim Matthews. His grandmother seemed wistful for the days of the trading post. He realized that she felt isolated at the ranch. She had been at the hub of activity "down the line," as the strip of land between the Laguna and Acoma reservations was called. The trading post had been on the west side of Cubero, away from the bars that provided most of the gossip in the area. Saints and sinners alike traded with the Habibs. His grandparents functioned as much like a bank as a store for the people of the area. Credit was extended to ranchers and farmers until they brought in their harvest. People told their tales to his grandmother who always took the time to listen. He remembered her smile as she gave pieces of sesame-honey candy to the children. The kindness of the Habibs was repaid with loyalty from their customers, who could have driven to Albuquerque for better prices. They preferred the homey atmosphere of the little store. He could appreciate the appeal of their hospitality as he tried to limit himself to one small spinach pie offered by his grandmother. Refusals of food were almost impossible with *Sitti*.

"N*"aimen*," his grandmother called as he emerged from showering and changing clothes. "*Yaa Allah "ainem a le'ek*," Philip replied and smiled. He enjoyed having grown up in a culture that had a ritual greeting and blessing for every time someone noticed that you bathed or had your hair cut. "We see you. May God have his eye upon you." From what he saw in some of his friends' families, people barely said hello and goodbye to one another.

Marlene Cavanaugh gave him a warm greeting in the lounge of the Cibola Inn. She was in black again, but this time it was a form-fitting little black dress that emphasized the curves of her body. He suspected that some of that perfection might have been the result of cosmetic surgery. Whatever the cause, the effect was stunning. Her blue eyes were highlighted by the matching turquoise necklace, earrings, and bracelet. She hugged him, and he was drawn to the sharp musky perfume she wore. She was overdressed for Grants, but Philip had to admire the result.

"That looks like Zuni needlepoint jewelry. Did you do some buying out there?" he inquired.

"I thought I'd mix business with pleasure. Don't you enjoy doing that, Philip?"

Philip bowed slightly. "It's a pleasure to see you, Marlene."

"That's better. Let's go into the dining room and order our dinner. I hope you have something to report."

They began with *margaritas* and *guacamole*. The menu hadn't yet been converted to the Nouvelle Southwestern Cuisine that was sweeping the tourist routes. Philip ordered *carne adovada* and Marlene asked for the trout and a glass of Chardonnay.

"Well, it's clear your grandfather was into something. Not only do the journals confirm it, but the people who knew him saw the pattern too."

"What pattern? Tell me what you've found out."

Philip told her about his conversations with Tim Matthews and Sarah Johnson. He thought he detected a female radar alert when he was talking about Sarah. He reported Fred Russell's speculations and asked if Marlene knew anything about Buck and mining.

"I can't imagine Buck doing anything that was tedious, repetitive, and required back-breaking labor, so that leaves out hard-rock mining. He was more interested in locating gold that was easier to find. I visited him once in the nineteen eighties. It was during the time when F. Lee Bailey sued the Air Force into allowing the descendents of Doc Noss to explore Victorio Peak."

"I remember that. The media had a field day, but they didn't find any gold."

"Buck knew every nuance of Noss's story. He was convinced that the searchers would come up with bars of conquistador gold. He'd heard the story many times while drinking with Noss in saloons from Truth or Consequences to Old Mesilla."

She finished her *margarita*. "That was tasty. Buck got a kick out of the fact that Noss wasn't a doctor of podiatry as he claimed. He might have been as much of a scoundrel as my grandfather, but he didn't cover himself as well as Buck did. Didn't he get shot by a partner?"

Philip nodded. "The partner claimed self defense. There's no honor among thieves. Didn't Noss make most of his money selling shares of the mine?"

"Another reason Buck admired him."

"The story was that Noss had taken some bars of bullion out before he blew up the opening. Did Buck ever see the gold?"

The waitress brought their meals. Marlene inspected the fish and apparently decided it was edible. "He didn't say. I couldn't really tell if Buck was more interested in the recovery of the gold or Noss being so ballsy in selling the story. When the expedition didn't find any gold in Victorio Peak, Buck claimed that the Air Force had stolen it. What's all this got to do with Buck anyway?"

Philip shrugged. "It's somewhat indirect. Ms. Johnson thinks Buck might have found the loot from a robbery that was stashed in the *malpais*. The thieves robbed a train in Grants and were eventually caught in the Zunis, but the money was never found. It's a long shot, but there are some parallels to the Noss story."

Marlene's manicured fingers drummed on the tabletop. "So you really haven't got any hard leads. I'm surrounded by incompetence. Waitress, I did order my wine so that I could drink it with dinner. I would like it now."

Philip quickly tried to show some progress in the investigation. "I've uncovered a pattern of trips to Mexico that are related to his having money when he came back. But it doesn't make sense to be smuggling anything into Mexico."

Marlene paused in her assault of the trout. "Except maybe gold. Buck told me that Noss had been worried about the laws against U.S. citizens possessing more than an ounce of gold and freezing the price at thirty-four dollars an ounce. He said that Noss converted the bars of gold to cash in Mexico. Buck said that there were black markets all over Mexico. He even told me where you could get the best prices, depending on the people you knew. They repealed those federal gold laws in the seventies, I think."

"So it sounds like he had a working knowledge of the Mexican gold markets. Could he speak Spanish?"

Marlene smiled at Philip. "It was crude. He learned it from the cowboys and shepherds that he rode with. But the power of Buck's personality carried a lot of weight in nonverbal communication. I bet he could've made himself understood."

Philip gulped water after a particularly spicy piece of pork. "He sounds like quite a guy. What was he like as a grandfather?"

"I didn't see him that often when I was young. But when I did, he was very indulgent. I know everybody talks about what a scary guy he was, but he was good to me. He was different with us. He was more relaxed at home than he was with other people."

Philip could feel the red chile marinade on the pork heightening his senses. He asked for more water and a beer. "I was impressed by the wonderful craftsmanship at Buck's cabin. It looked like he was quite a farmer as well."

Marlene's face softened and she seemed lost in reminiscence. "You know, I think I had some of the freshest vegetables in my life there. Buck was really proud of his sweet corn. He'd get a pot of water boiling before he'd pick the corn. Then he'd shuck them as he walked and got them in the pot in a flash. He said that you lost sugar every minute after you picked it. He was good at preserving food too. I loved that root cellar; it was full of treasures. Buck learned how to can food from one of his wives, and he developed quite a canning operation. His pickled peaches had a strong taste of cinnamon and bristled with cloves. He turned his cucumbers into great pickles too. I loved to see the garlic and dill in the jars. Don't you love the image of Buck entering bread-and-butter pickles at the county fair?"

Philip tried to imagine it. "I can't see Buck in a ruffled apron."

"When I was a kid, it felt like he was the king of that ranch, lord to all those animals. I was growing up in base housing, rows of identical fourplexes. When I visited Buck, I was riding horses through the old West. I was thrilled and he knew it. I helped him feed and groom the animals. He had a way of commanding the respect of his stock. As a little girl I loved those horses, cows, sheep, and goats. I loved the man who encouraged me to be a cowgirl, too."

Marlene dabbed her mouth with her napkin. "As an adult, I've heard horror stories about him, but to me he was a real live cowboy hero. He regaled me with stories of the range and cattle drives. I really loved to hear about his days with the Pinkertons and as a bounty hunter bringing criminals to justice. He was the heart of the West to me, and I identified with him. Every time we moved, the first thing that I told the new kids was that my grandpa was a cowboy."

"It sure doesn't sound like the stories I've been hearing. On the other hand, both Tim Matthews and Fred Russell said that he always treated them like they were his long lost friends. He certainly had a way with women, so he must have had some charm."

She laughed and winked. "When it served him, he did. A lot of what he did was calculated. Once he put his mind to it, he could turn any situation to his advantage. He was an excellent listener when he was on the prowl. I realized later that he had done that with me when I was a girl. He could rephrase what people, especially women, told him so that they felt like he was looking right into their souls."

Her expression brightened again. "And his image! He never wore that black stuff when he was home on the ranch, just jeans, t-shirts, and flannel shirts like anybody else. But in public he was the man in black, marked by mystery. He loved to drive his shiny black nineteen forty-six Chevy pickup to town. You know, he had functional late-model four-by-four trucks that he used for ranch work. But that long, curvaceous, chromed relic was his cruise mobile."

"Those were some of the prettiest trucks ever made."

"I remember one time when he must have been riding a wave of fortune. When I was in junior high, he invited my family to have dinner at a fancy hotel in Los Angeles."

She looked around the restaurant. "Nothing like this cheesy highway motel. It was in Beverly Hills. He greeted us in the lobby wearing these two-toned wingtip shoes, nicely draped taupe gabardine slacks, a chocolate brown silk shirt, and a well-tailored natural linen sport coat. He had trimmed his beard short, wore a Borsalino at a jaunty angle on his head, and sported a huge diamond pinkie ring. I mean he looked sharp. The hotel staff treated him really well too, like he was a player. I remember that we had a fabulous feast."

"Before we ate, Buck called for our attention. He held a fat Cuban cigar, looked over each member of his family, and smiled. 'I had a very good year, children. And the ponies at Santa Anita have been even better to me. Order whatever you want, and let's enjoy it while we can.'"

Marlene's eyes locked onto Philip's. "I want to know where that money came from. After I'd grown up, he got drunk in front of me a few times, and I saw some really ugly things come out. He was a complicated man, and my feelings about him are complicated. But I'd feel a lot better about him if he left me wealthy."

"I think we're doing pretty well for the short time I've been working on this. The gold hypothesis is looking better all the time. I wonder where he found it. We need to find out more about this old train robbery."

Her eyes narrowed. "So you'll be seeing that intern again. You better check some other sources about gold stories too."

Philip was sure he felt the green monster this time. From the way Marlene had been leaning toward him when she was telling him about Buck, he was very aware of her. The change from the confrontational style of their first encounter to her wide-eyed little girl stories felt like a conscious decision. She was trying to pull him into her web of influence, and it was working.

He replied, "I have a friend who is a geologist and a local boy. He'll know anything about gold around Grants."

Marlene looked pleased as she charged the meal to her room. "He sounds like a great resource." She got up from the table. "Why don't you walk me to my room?"

Marlene took Philip's arm as they left the restaurant. She brushed against him as they walked down the hall, making Philip aware of how long he had been celibate. As they stopped in front of Marlene's door, she turned into him and stared into his eyes.

"Why don't you come in for a nightcap?"

Philip felt conflicted. He knew that it would complicate his work if he became involved with Marlene. He also felt some need to resolve where things were going with Sarah, but Marlene's predatory approach was exciting. He hadn't felt desirable in months, and now two women were showing an interest. His body was responding to her physical charms and the closeness of her contact. He had to find out what that perfume was. In spite of his struggle, reason prevailed.

He said gently, "Marlene, I don't think it would be a good idea."

Marlene moved closer and caressed his cheek. "Am I too old for you? Don't you know what Benjamin Franklin said about older women as lovers? We're so grateful." She snuggled against him.

Philip had a hard time catching his breath; he was aroused. "My dear, seeing you in that dress makes chronological age unimportant. I'd love to, but let's wait until I'm not on your payroll."

Marlene pushed Philip back and jerked open the door. Anger distorted her face. "And I thought you were my private dick! You might not have me around after this is over."

Then she struck a pose and said, "If you change your mind, just whistle. You do know how to whistle, don't you? Just put your lips together and blow."

She wheeled around and slammed the door in his face. Luckily, hanging out with George, the movie fanatic, had exposed Philip to that scene in *To Have or Have Not*. Marlene had imitated Lauren Bacall's parting shot to Humphrey Bogart after a similar encounter. It was their first movie together, and the sexual tension between them was palpable. Maybe this woman's life was one classic film after another. She must have been Jane Wyman in the dining room, and maybe she was channeling Barbara Stanwyck in George's office. He shook his head as he walked out to the parking lot.

Talking to Ross McIntyre would remind him of his duties to her as a client. Philip drove up to the residential section of Grants. He was surprised to find his friend's dented Ford F-100 pickup in the driveway of his house. Ross greeted him enthusiastically.

"*Amigo*, I've been thinking since last night. You were right about my driving drunk. Even though it's just a few blocks away, I'm not driving back from the Grubstake drunk anymore. I'll either drink a few beers there and finish up with whiskey at home, or I'll walk over there."

"Well, I'm glad to see you taking better care of yourself. I worry when I see you that far out of it."

"One step at a time. I'm not promising sobriety, just no more drunk driving. In fact, let me make you a drink. I've got some *ouzo* that's just like that *araq* you used to drink in Beirut. Come on in."

Philip sat down on the threadbare couch. "Just one, Ross. I need a favor. I want to know all the gold, lost treasure, or hidden robbery loot stories there are in Cíbola County."

"Shiver me timbers, it's lost treasure you're seeking. Do you want me to start with Acoma gambling stories about the origin of the *malpais* or Spanish treasure? Don't you love the smell of the anise in this stuff?"

Philip raised his glass. "*Kassak.* Anything that might have been found within the last few decades."

Ross sat in an easy chair that was leaking its innards. "In the last few decades? I haven't heard of any finds, but I was out of the country for a long time. So do you want them ranked in the order of probability or what? Starting with the oldest, there's the Spanish padre's treasure by Cubero. I'm surprised that you don't know that one since it's supposed to be somewhere near your grandmother's back yard."

"I'm after anything in the lava beds or the Zunis."

Ross took a long drink. "Why all this interest in the *malpais?*"

"I'm trying to find out where Buck Cavanaugh got his extra funds."

"Cibola County's favorite gunslinger. Well, there's that old train robbery."

"The A and P, I know about that one. Anything else?"

The ice in their glasses was turning the clear liquor into a milky brew. Ross poured himself another. "Only the most famous lost-mine story in New Mexico. Have you ever heard of the Lost Adams Diggings?"

"The name rings a bell, but I can't place it."

Ross chuckled. "That's kind of the issue. If anybody knew where it was, it wouldn't be a lost mine. Adams came out to western New Mexico from Arizona during the Civil War. His party of miners was supposed to have found the richest placer strike in the Southwest. Then, the Apaches wiped out almost all of them. No one has been able to find it again. Adams spent his whole life trying to get back to the canyon."

"Where was it supposed to be? I thought that the Apaches were further south."

"Four days from Fort Wingate. Fort Wingate was located in San Rafael in those days. So the Diggings should be somewhere near the edge of the lava. Adams said that there was lava near by, and that there were two sugar-loaf mountains within sight. The Apaches ranged pretty far, they were probably up near the *malpais*."

"Was there any evidence of this gold, or was it just the imaginings of an old man?"

"Actually, one of the other survivors told the same story independently of Adams. There were also supposed to be witnesses who said when Adams was picked up by the cavalry, he had a nugget the size of a turkey egg. Hundreds of people have looked for it during the century after Adams returned to search and started telling the tale."

"If people have been looking for over a hundred years, why does anyone still search?"

Ross shrugged. "People keep looking for the Lost Dutchman too. I heard the story from the early Mormon settlers who knew some of those old prospectors. Some of the elders believed that the treasure was part of the bounty of the Promised Land. They mounted search parties periodically; I guess the latter day miracle craze was upon them. Anyway, I never heard of anybody finding anything like Adams described. There are a bunch of books and articles about it. It's in every lost mine book."

"Thanks. I'll check the library."

"I heard your name being mentioned at the Grubstake tonight."

"For being your true blue friend and getting you home safe?"

"No, weird people too. Do you remember the skinhead and the bikers who were there last night?"

"Vaguely. I couldn't pick them out of lineup of skinheads and bikers."

"They were back again tonight. There were a bunch of other bikers there too. You probably haven't had a chance to observe the latest sociological phenomenon in Grants. People who are visiting their friends and relatives in the two new prisons we've acquired are struck by the abundance of cheap housing and business properties. We've therefore acquired a couple of motorcycle repair and rebuilding shops. I don't think they're chop shops. Anyway, there are these outlaw bikers who hang out at the Grubstake now. These are the hard drinking, cigarette smoking, tattooed grease monkey faction, rather than the paranoid meth-lab rapist contingent."

"They sound like great drinking companions."

Ross ignored his sarcasm. "Some of these bikers were involved with the Aryan Brotherhood while they were in the lock up. Their political views make Rush Limbaugh sound like Jesse Jackson. Anyway, this blond skinhead-looking guy was asking the bikers about you. One of the locals was telling him about you having family in town and being a private eye, when the skinhead noticed that I was listening. Then they started talking softly amongst themselves, but they'd glance over at me every so often."

Ross wasn't talking about rich urban bikers riding shiny new Harleys on weekends; this was the flotsam and jetsam of humanity. Philip asked, "How about the skinhead? Have you ever seen him before?"

"He's hung out with these guys before. I think he's a security guard at one of the closed mines. He looks like a prototype Hitler youth, classic Aryan features, looks good in a uniform. This is a rough crowd who's interested in you, *amigo*. What are you up to?"

Philip's brow furrowed. "Nothing that would have anything to do with Neo-Nazis. Anyway, the Lost Adams' Diggings sounds interesting."

"Damn right. It's part of what made me a geologist. I grew up on a carrot farm in Bluewater when everybody and their brother were trying to find uranium. Several of the elders of our church had ranches on what turned out to be the Ambrosia Lake uranium district. They became millionaires, and tithed on their gross earnings, making the bishops really happy. The Lost Adams Diggings had the same kind of appeal. Because it was a historic enigma, it was more exciting to me. After I heard the old men's stories, I read J. Frank Dobie and followed Howard Bryan's column about the west in the Albuquerque papers. We Latter Day Saints have a strong sense of history, and being 'chosen people,' we always felt entitled to the riches of the kingdom. I poked around a little trying to find that zigzag canyon myself. But, I don't see any connection between the A and P or the Lost Adams and the brown-shirt faction."

"Neither do I, but it looks like I've got some reading to do. *Shukran.*"

"*Afwan.* Thanks for the help last night."

Philip was happy that Ross was able to be more responsible with his alcohol consumption. Although he understood what had turned a curious, hopeful boy into this burned-out cynic, he hoped that Ross could eventually make another life for himself. How could he find redemption? It would probably take another woman, another chance for a family. Philip wondered if it was too late for both of them.

8

The morning dawned crisp and bright. Philip's grandmother had left early to baby-sit for his cousin Priscilla's kids. Philip took his coffee over to the corral where Hank was feeding the horses.

"*Buenos Días, Enrique.* Are any of these ponies surefooted enough to be able to get through some rough mountain country?"

Hank came over and shook his hand. "You sound like you're getting more serious about this trail ride. I use a couple of these old *caballos* to gather sheep. You know that these hills out back are full of volcanic rock and cactus, and they come back without getting nicked up. One of them is pretty good at cutting too, but I doubt you're going on a round up. Take a look at the big gray over there. Where are you headed anyway?"

"That's the other piece. How's the horse trailer holding up? I'd like to go up into the Zunis."

Hank nodded and started off across the yard. "*Vamonos.* Let's take a look. I just put a new floor in it last year. You can see that the paint's scratched and faded, but the lights and the electric brakes work all right."

Philip stepped into the trailer and bounced a little on the floorboards. "*Bien hecho,* Hank."

"*Gracias.* I doubt that Japanese rig of yours can pull the weight when it's loaded with two horses. What are you doing up in the Zunis?"

"Prospecting."

Hank laughed. "You sure you don't want a burro and a pick and shovel?"

Philip shook his head. "No, this is about Buck. I've got a hunch that he found some gold. I just want to get back in the country around where the *malpais* and the Zunis meet.

"Buck prospecting? *No lo creo*. What makes you believe that he'd be carrying a gold pan?"

"I'm trying to find out where he got his extra money. Some people think it might have been gold, and Fred Russell ran into him while he was prospecting. Ross McIntyre's been telling me about the Lost Adams Diggings. Have you heard of them?"

"I've heard some stories in the bars from geezers looking for a grubstake, but I don't pay attention to those old fools. If they'd put their energy into some real work instead of traipsing off after dreams, they wouldn't have been broke in the first place. *Qué bobos*. I'm sorry, but you've got to go back to Fred again. He knows all about the diggings and wasted a big part of his life looking for them."

"I wish I'd known about all this yesterday. *No importa;* I enjoyed talking with him. I might ask a friend to join me tomorrow on the ride, so I'll need two horses.

Hank winked. "A friend, I see. I hope she can ride."

Philip's ears felt warm. "She grew up on a ranch, so I'm sure she knows how to ride. If you don't think my Toyota will haul the load, can I trade you for your V8 Ford tomorrow?"

"Fine by me. When do you think you'll leave?"

"In the morning, but not too early. Thanks for the use of the F-two-fifty." He waved goodbye as he started back to the main house. "*Mañana por la mañana, amigo*."

Feeling some anxiety about where he stood with Sarah, Philip phoned to ask her to join him on a trail ride tomorrow. He was relieved when she enthusiastically accepted. In addition, she asked him to pick her up to have dinner at the Atomic Café. Whistling a hopeful tune, he drove into town and went to the Mother Whiteside Library.

He remembered that Ross had mentioned J. Frank Dobie's books. He used the reference computer to track down the author. The titles bewildered him; Dobie was a prolific writer. He went over to the librarian, a tired-looking Hispanic woman dressed in a broomstick skirt, tailored chambray blouse, and tapestry vest.

He inquired, "I'm looking at J. Frank Dobie's citation list, but I don't know which one I'm after. Could you help me?"

The librarian replied, "Sure. What are you looking for?"

"A reference to the Lost Adams Diggings."

She laughed. "The gold bug bit another one. That would be *Apache Gold and Yaqui Silver*. Going prospecting?"

"No, it's more the mystery of it. I like unsolved mysteries."

She led him to the book. "A man of mystery. Would you like some other works regarding the Diggings? I can pull a couple more while you start with Dobie."

Philip found himself pulled into the story of a fortuitous encounter between Adams, the wagon driver with a herd of horses, and a group of prospectors in the Pima villages near Tucson. A "gotch-eared" former Apache captive laughed at the prospectors' attempts at panning gold. He said that he knew of a canyon where nuggets were scattered like acorns. He led the party northeast across mountains, rivers, plains, and lava beds through an opening in a rock wall to a zigzag canyon where they found the richest placer strike in New Mexico. Their joy was short. A band of Apaches led by Chief Nana descended upon them. Nana told them that they would allow them to work the valley as long as they did not go up to their sacred site above the falls. A short time later a prospector brought Adam's the fabled gold nugget the size of a turkey's egg. He found it above the falls. The violation of their agreement with the Apaches made Adams nervous. The next day Adams and a friend rode out to look for their overdue relief party that had gone to Fort Wingate for supplies. They found them slaughtered and the supplies scattered. They cautiously returned to the canyon and approached an overlook where they saw that everyone in camp had been killed. The Apaches were celebrating their grisly victory. They crept away, only to be lost for days across western New Mexico and eastern Arizona. Soldiers found them near the site of Fort Apache. Adams' companion was treated by the army surgeon, but died shortly afterwards. Adams spent his entire life trying to find the site of the gold again. His memory was notoriously poor and he became lost over and over. Several bands of explorers turned on him for appearing to lead them on wild goose chases.

Philip's reverie was interrupted by the librarian's return with a few other books about the Diggings. Dobie pulled him back in and he continued to skim through the book. He glanced at the others and wrote down the titles of the ones that looked most promising.

Approaching the librarian, he said, "This book is wonderful. Do you know where I could buy a copy?"

"Yes, they finally ran another edition. Dobie is a great storyteller, isn't he? The copies around here are getting pretty dog-eared. You might be able to find it at the bookstore in Gallup. But it's more likely that you'll have to order it online. These two recent books about the Diggings seem to be good reviews of the legend, but they place it in completely different places. Dobie's version of the tale is the best written, but who knows which has the most accurate information."

"It sounds like you've pulled these books a few times before."

She smiled. "About once a month, more during good weather. Today's prospectors are sunshine soldiers. Since you know how to use the computer and I haven't seen you before, I'd guess you're from out of town. Did the Diggings bring you to Grants?"

"Hardly, my grandmother lives near Cubero. I spent a lot of time out here when I was a kid." He rose and offered his hand. "My name is Philip Habib."

She gently shook his hand. "Lorraine Sánchez. Your grandparents had the trading post. Where do you live now?"

"La Madera, in the northeast foothills of the Sandias. If you know about the trading post, you must have been here awhile yourself."

Lorraine grinned. "Trailer trash from Milan. My parents came here during the second boom in the seventies. I was born in Peñasco and spent my childhood in the *Sangre de Cristo* mountains, but I graduated from Grants High School."

Philip gave her an appraising look. "Trailer trash doesn't dress like you do. You've spent some time away from Cíbola County."

"We didn't stay in the trailer long. Contract mining made my dad a wealthy man by blue-collar standards. My parents encouraged me to get an education to get out of this dying town."

"Why did you come back?"

A sad expression crossed her face and she lowered her eyes. "My dad developed lung cancer from radon exposure while working in the uranium mines. My mom needed help. A master's degree in library science puts me in a good position here, and I can help my family."

She looked up quickly. "You know, Mother Whiteside, the namesake of this library, used to have a boarding house on the edge of the Zunis and the *malpais*. I bet she knew some stories about the Diggings, but she died back in the fifties. If you're serious about researching the Adams Diggings, you should look into the Gallup library too. They've got a much larger collection, especially in western history, cowboy culture, and all that. And their newspaper archives go back into the time period you might want to research. If you want more primary sources, Special Collections at the Albuquerque Public Library would have some of those old pamphlets that Dobie mentioned."

Philip stood up. "Thanks for the help and the advice. It's a pleasure to meet someone who combines a modern education with the traditional values of helping the family. I hope your father's illness isn't too painful."

She grimaced and her shoulders tightened. "It's too late for that. We try to keep him comfortable, but the pain wakes him up in the night. All his miner friends who smoked as well as breathing radon are already dead. The mines have given him a pittance. How can you pay someone back for their life? I'm sorry; I didn't mean to go on like this. Good luck with your explorations."

Philip was having a difficult time concentrating on his research. Lorraine's story had triggered painful memories. He was all too familiar with that kind of dying. His girlfriend's death from leukemia during his freshman year at the University of New Mexico had left him crazy with grief. That was when he dropped out and enlisted in the Marines. Forcing himself to stop brooding over the past, he gently inquired about the location of the Gallup library and the bookstore and left with a sad heart.

Intrusive memories haunted him along I-40 and north of Thoreau. The beauty of the red sandstone mesas and blue sky began to soothe him as he drove down the dirt track to Fred's claim. The roughness of the road required his concentration, bringing him back to the present. He continued past the trailer up to the coal mine. Fred was working there, hitting a hand drill with a small sledgehammer.

Philip called to him. "Fred, I'm impressed. Not only are you one of the hardest working people I've met, but you're also the oldest hard-working person I've met."

Fred grinned as he straightened up. "They go together, Philip. You do better at any age if you exercise regular. I used to walk with my burros. I enjoyed that a lot more than I enjoy this, but this pays better."

"If I take you out to lunch in Gallup, would you be willing to take a break?"

Fred pushed back his hat. "You're on. I can't remember the last time someone took me out to lunch, much less from out here. Do you want to talk some more about Buck? Take me back to the trailer and let me change clothes."

Philip waited in the shade of a tall juniper and looked at the red cliff with the black stripe across the bottom. A red-tailed hawk screamed trying to flush out its prey. A mild breeze flowed up the canyon. He looked over at the trailer. He realized that Fred was spending his eighties just the way he wanted to. He could think of a lot worse ways to do it. Fred emerged wearing black Wranglers, a charcoal, pink, and white striped cowboy shirt, and a handsome straw hat.

"You look like my uncle's nineteen fifty-seven DeSoto. But, of course, that was pretty good looking. Let's mount up."

Philip engaged Fred in small talk so that he could negotiate the decrepit road. Once he got to the pavement, Philip asked, "Do you think that there could be any connection between Buck and the Lost Adams Diggings?"

Fred looked stunned and grabbed the safety handle above the door. "Whew! You set me back a minute there, boy. But why else would he have been prospecting the same places I was? What got you thinking about the Lost Adams?"

"I've been reading his journals. Some of them are almost indecipherable, but it looks like he went to Mexico every year and came back richer. Tim Matthews says that it wasn't drugs or *mojados*. Besides, it looks like he was smuggling something into Mexico, not out. His granddaughter says that he knew about the black market for gold there. I think he was smuggling gold."

Fred slapped his thigh. "That scoundrel! I guess if anybody could have found the gold, Buck would have a good shot at it. He went places nobody else went, and he had a keen eye. I didn't take his prospecting very seriously, I guess. Now that I think about, I suppose that bounty hunting is sort of similar, being able to find something that nobody else can. Why do you think it might have been the Lost Adams?"

"Do you know any other lost mine stories around here?"

"Actually I do, but you're right. It's the most famous one. 'The Adams Diggings is a shadowy naught. And they lie in the valley of fanciful thought.' Nat Straw carved that on an aspen long ago. And after many years of searching, I agree with him."

"What if Buck actually found it? Fred, tell me what you know about the Lost Adams."

"How much do you know already?"

"I skimmed J. Frank Dobie."

Fred exploded. "Dobie! That smooth-talking storytelling Texan. I read his book years ago. He did have some good things in it; he got the basic story straight. I did like the way he talked about the great old prospectors, like Nat Straw, Ben Lilly, Bear Moore, and Mike Cooney. But some of that stuff was pure hogwash. I mean, the guy who got the Yaquis to bring him the head of the Apache Kid. Bullshit! The Apache Kid is buried in the San Mateos, northwest of Apache Peak. There's a monument up there. As far as I know, his head is still attached to his body. Anyway, you've got a working knowledge of the legend, right?"

Philip piloted the 4Runner west onto I-40. "I think that I got the gist of it."

"Okay. One of the stories that Dobie wrote about was told by a rancher, A.M. Tenney, who lived near Springerville, Arizona. Tenney's ranch was close enough to the route of the Adams' party coming out of the White Mountains that several searchers stopped in on him. Captain Shaw, Adams' faithful partner in several expeditions, hired Tenney to take him east to find the landmarks for the Diggings. They also went up into the White Mountains to try to find a tree that Adams said pointed the way, but they never found it. Then Shaw went up to the Fort Wingate near Gallup and found the same store keeper there who had been at the Fort Wingate at San Rafael. He remembered a party of men who came across the lava to buy supplies, mining tools, and hardware to make sluice boxes. They paid in coarse gold and left immediately."

"So he verified Adam's story."

"It would seem so. A few years later, who walks onto Tenney's ranch but the leader of the supply party, John Brewer. Adams had assumed that Brewer was dead, and Brewer had assumed that he was sole survivor of the massacre. Brewer had been farming in Colorado, but eventually he had to come back to look for the Diggings. He told Tenney the story of his escape. He was wounded in the initial attack on the party. But he was able to crawl off under a dense juniper until nightfall when he snuck back to the edge of the canyon. From the screams he had heard and the glow of the burning cabin, he was sure that everyone had been killed. He knew the Apaches would be watching the wagon road to Fort Wingate. So he realized that his only chance would be to head east to the Mexican villages on the Rio Grande.

"That sounds like a long walk." The sign for the Continental Divide flashed past.

"People weren't soft like they are now. After two days of wandering through the desert, he fell into a pool of water in an arroyo. He was found there, half delirious, by Pueblo Indians who brought him to their home. He was able to talk Mexican with them and asked to see the *alcalde*. When he was well enough to walk to the main village, he met with the Pueblo leaders. He asked for their help to go back to the canyon to check for survivors and bury the dead. They refused. The Pueblo people knew all too well what the wrath of the Apache was like. They said that he could ask for help at the fort, but he would have to cross territory that was claimed by bands of both Apaches and Navajos."

That was an option that he'd already rejected."

"Rightly so. They showed him the path to the Rio Grande and gave him a couple of gourds of water for his journey. For two days, he walked east to the Rio Grande. From one of the Mexican villages, he worked his way north to Santa Fe. Then he found a job freighting on the Santa Fe Trail and made his way back to Missouri. Later, he came back west to Colorado, took a Ute wife, and farmed and raised cattle. Until the lost mine pulled him back here."

"You're still sharp as a tack, old codger. You really do know your stuff. So it's another source for the legend, and it gives us some more markers. The only Pueblos east of the *malpais* are Acoma and Laguna."

"So there's a line from Springerville to Acoma and Laguna. The more landmarks from the legend you know, the better chance you have of finding the Diggings. Check out the size of that truck stop."

"I heard that it has its own zip code. There are some books I'd like to buy in Gallup."

Fred sputtered. "Books! When I started on this, we didn't depend on books. We started walking the country. Every prospector knew the story. Do you think we would have ignored the little door, or gone through a zigzag canyon without thinking of it? And I can tell you from my own experience that there are a lot of twin haystack mountains in New Mexico. Just look at the map. The names of the searchers are all over it: Cooney Canyon, Shaw Mountain, Patterson Canyon, Lilly Mountain, and McKenna Park. We didn't go to the bookstore; we went to the old timers. We heard some of the stories first hand, but more of them took on a life of their own. They were retold around campfires all over the Southwest."

"It sounds like the best way to hear them, but there aren't a lot of you old sourdoughs left."

Fred looked troubled. "No, we're a dying breed. I can see that I'm going to have to teach you how to do this right, and I thought you were an investigator. We've got some serious talking ahead of us. Now I know the perfect place to have lunch."

9

Fred told Philip to exit in the middle of Gallup. He needed to get his bearings by going by the historic El Rancho Hotel, home away from home to the stars of John Ford's westerns. He directed Philip west down old 66 and then told him to turn right and cross the Santa Fe railroad tracks.

"It might be the wrong side of the tracks, but this place has the best barbecue in Western New Mexico and Eastern Arizona. The owner is somebody you should meet if you want the real story behind the Diggings."

They pulled into a gravel parking lot and parked under the cottonwoods. The restaurant had the look of a roadhouse, and Philip wondered if they played music at night. The air had the smell of hardwood fires and sweet tang of barbeque sauce. After they entered, Fred led the way to a large elderly man wearing bib overalls. He had an interesting mix of African and Indian features: a hooked nose, big lips, prominent cheekbones, and wavy gray hair combed straight back.

Fred introduced them. "Clarence, this is Philip Habib. Philip, this is Clarence Williams."

"Any relation to Cootie?"

Clarence laughed. "No, but I'm a jazz fan too. I'll put some Kansas City swing on the stereo."

Fred had a gleam in his eye when he said, "We're here for some of your brisket, but we'd like some of your time too. Can you join us after we order?"

"Sure. Find yourself a seat and my granddaughter, Corrina, will take your order."

With the strains of Count Basie behind him, Clarence walked over to their table. He asked, "Habib, are you one of those traders down in Zuni?"

"No, my grandparents were traders in Cubero."

As he gave them their iced teas, recognition dawned across Clarence's broad face. "The trading post down the line. Your people have been here almost as long as mine."

"What brought your people to Gallup, Clarence?"

The big man sat down at the table with them. "Well, you could say that some of my people have been here for several centuries, since Apachería was not far from here. But, I assume you meant my African ancestors. My great-grandfather came to New Mexico as part of the Ninth Cavalry."

Fred interrupted, "Philip, that's why I wanted you to talk to Clarence. He's the Buffalo Soldier-Apache connection."

Clarence's face clouded. "Fred, you didn't. You're not trying to sell some greenhorn a treasure map, are you?"

"See, he knows exactly what I'm talking about."

"Fred, of course I know. Ever since I told you about Sno-ta-hay, it's the only thing you want to talk to me about. We used to have civilized conversations."

The grizzled old prospector defended himself. "Philip came to me asking about the Adams Diggings, not the other way around. So I told him that you had a piece of the story that didn't usually get told."

Resigning himself, Clarence said, "Well, since you're eating at my restaurant, I'll tell the story. But I have to tell it my way. My great-grandfather, Ezekiel Williams, was born a slave. His father had been captured as a teenager in West Africa where our family had been herdsmen. So Zeke's father was eventually placed in charge of the horses and cattle on a plantation in Virginia. Zeke grew up around animals, and he developed some skills that would serve him well."

Clarence was interrupted by the arrival of savory platters of barbequed beef, beans, coleslaw, and cornbread. As Philip and Fred attacked their food, he continued.

"When the Civil War broke out, Zeke was eighteen years old and couldn't be stopped. He stole a horse and headed north to join the Union Army. Zeke's horse sense and his skill as a farrier put him in the Cavalry. He had the zeal of a man fighting for his freedom, so he distinguished himself in battle. But, when the war was over, the offer of forty acres and a mule didn't appeal much to him. Like Hank Williams used to say, he'd spent too many years looking at the wrong end of a mule."

Fred nodded. "Been there, done that."

"He joined the all Negro Ninth Cavalry for the Indian Wars. After spending some years on the plains, Zeke learned some more horsemanship tricks from the Kiowas and Comanches, like using your legs to guide your horse to free up your hands for fighting. Their teaching went deeper; they showed him how to be one with his horse, to become the wild stallion."

Clarence paused and then shouted, "Corrina, could you please bring these gentlemen some more iced tea?"

The skinny teenager hurried over with the pitcher and filled their glasses. She walked back to the kitchen and stared at the ceiling-mounted television.

Clarence shook his head. "I put that TV in so the cooks wouldn't get bored. But that girl is addicted. She'll do anything that you ask her to do, but when you're not looking, she's staring at the tube. Anyway, back to Zeke. The Ninth and Tenth Cavalry, as well as black infantrymen, were sent to New Mexico in the eighteen seventies to put down the Apache uprisings. They fought across most of the southern half of the state, picking up the Apache's trail in the Guadalupes, just across the

Texas border and following them west across the San Andrés. Most of the raiding at that time was done by Victorio, who was the chief of the Warm Springs Apache. Do y'all know the area where they used to camp, the Ojo Caliente west of the Rio Grande, between the San Mateos and the Black Range?"

Fred had a mouthful of slaw and just nodded.

Philip answered, "Since that's mineral country, I'd expect Fred to know it. But I haven't been that far back, just to the ghost towns."

"Those ghost towns were just beginning to boom then. Silver mining had started in Winston and Chloride, and settlers were moving into the land that had been Apache territory for centuries. The Apaches tried moving west, but gold strikes at Piños Altos and Mimbres meant more miners there, too. Victorio was pushed into a corner, so the Apaches embarked on a reign of terror, killing every white person they met. They struck such fear into the settlers that they caused a mass exodus, getting just what they had hoped for. When they were near the Rio Grande, they would band together with the Mescalero Apache. On the western end of their range, they joined their cousins, the Chiricahua, raiding anywhere along the border."

Clarence stared at the brownish-red barbeque sauce dribbling down the miner's gray stubble. He handed him another napkin. "How long has it been since you've eaten with human company, old timer?"

Fred shrugged, and Clarence continued. "The U.S. Army eventually put thousands of soldiers, black and white, in the field against a few hundred Apache. Since the Mexicans had fewer resources, Victorio would retreat to the mountains of northern Mexico when it got too hot in the U.S. On one of those excursions into Mexico, Colonel Hatch was supposed to have 'misinterpreted' a communiqué to authorize the U.S. Army pursuit of Victorio across the border. So Zeke and the cavalry invaded Mexico. They helped push the Apaches into an encounter with the Mexican Army at Tres Castillos that left Victorio and most of his band dead."

Clarence looked at their plates. "Are y'all ready for some more sauce? Corrina, bring a cup of sauce to Fred and Philip, will you?"

The girl kept her eye on the TV while she poured the sauce into a cup. Then she walked over, all knees and elbows, and set the sauce on the table. Philip thanked her.

Fred asked, "Clarence, could you speed this up?"

"Hold your horses, Fred. I told you that I was going to tell this my way. Have you got a date that can't wait? Chief Nana's role before Victorio's death had been as much spiritual adviser as war chief. His special power was that he could always find ammunition, a power that kept the Apaches in the game against the army. *Kas-Tziden,* as he was known to the people, was in his seventies and half-crippled when Victorio was killed at the Tres Castillos massacre. But the ancient warrior took up the mantle and took revenge with the few warriors who were left from the Warm Springs band. He was joined by Lozen, Victorio's sister, whose power was determining the whereabouts and number of enemy soldiers. Working his way back to the San Carlos reservation, Nana had a clandestine meeting with Noch-ay-del-Klinne, the shaman that the whites called the Dreamer. Guided by the Dreamer's ceremony, he saw the ghosts of Mangas Coloradas, Cochise, and Victorio ascend into heaven."

Philip said, "I've never heard anybody talk about the Apaches as spiritual people before. In the movies, they're always portrayed as blood-thirsty savages."

"The movies are shameful. The Apaches became blood-thirsty in their revenge, but they weren't savages. They had a highly developed moral code, and spiritual practices dominated their lives. Anyway, strengthened by his vision, Nana gathered an additional small band of Mescaleros to his Warm Spring warriors. Then he began his infamous last raid. In two months they covered three thousand miles, killed more than thirty enemies and wounded many more, as well as stealing hundreds of horses and cattle. It was a reign of terror that is still studied by military strategists. The Army pursued them relentlessly. The Ninth Cavalry was involved in that pursuit and engaged Nana's raiders in Carrizo Canyon. They lost a quarter of their force. Zeke said that it was the most frightening battle of his career. Then, Nana slipped back into the mountains of Mexico for prayer and meditation."

Philip was impressed. "Quite an accomplishment for a senior citizen."

Clarence scowled, but his eyes twinkled. "You watch your mouth, boy. Your turn is coming. Years later, after Gerónimo finally surrendered, the Ninth was reassigned to Kansas, but the Indian wars were over. The combination of boredom and bigotry from the white officers of the corps finally got to Zeke. He left the Army when his term of enlistment expired. You know, he told my dad a story about a black soldier who had been joking about hunting turkeys when they were on a wood-gathering detail down in the Black Range. The white officer warned him not to shoot anything but an Apache. When the soldier actually shot a turkey, the white officer was so incensed about his disobedience that he chained the turkey to the soldier's back and made him wear it until it rotted off."

Philip flinched. "Sounds like 'The Rime of the Ancient Mariner,' Southwestern racist style, doesn't it?"

Fred and Clarence looked at one another, then back to Philip. "Sorry, it's poem about a sailor who shot an albatross and had to wear it. Those birds must have smelled pretty ripe by the time they rotted off."

Fred glared at Philip. "Nice story for the lunch table and you two complain about my manners."

Clarence said, "Let me finish this up. On the other hand, the Apache had always treated him with respect. He deeply admired their horsemanship, their love of the wild mountains, and their perseverance. So he went back to New Mexico to find the Apaches."

Philip smiled sardonically. "So, he liked the people he was fighting against better than the people he was fighting for? That sounds familiar. Go on, Clarence."

"Zeke wasn't the only Buffalo Soldier who joined the Indians either. I've got a copy of an old photo around here somewhere of some White Mountain Apaches and a 'renegade Negro.' The Apaches usually adopted captive children from other races, but they were willing to include adults too."

"Nana had been the spiritual voice of the Warm Springs Apache. When he gave up the fight and was sent to Florida, the soul had been torn from the Warm Springs band. The few who remained free dispersed into the mountains. Zeke joined up with a small group that settled in the northern part of the Gila country. They returned to a semi-nomadic life. Eventually, futurists like Zeke introduced cattle herding as opposed to cattle theft."

Clarence stretched and an enormous expanse of overalls filled their view. "Now, back to the gold."

Fred muttered under his breath. "It's about time."

Clarence gave him a dirty look. "Adams had always been clear that it wasn't just any band of Apaches that had attacked them in the canyon, it was Nana and his warriors. Nana also told him the name of the region during their first meeting, Sno-ta-hay. Zeke eventually married a shirttail relation of Nana, who became my great-grandmother. When my grandfather was a boy, she told him about a fight between Nana and some miners who were some of the first to seek their fortune in central New Mexico. Nana had given permission to the miners to pan for gold in the canyon if they did not disturb the sacred sites near their camp, and promised they would only stay a few days. The miners broke their promise and violated the holy ground. They also sent a group back for more supplies and built a cabin. It looked like they were settling in. Nana ordered them to be killed for their sacrilege and lies. When my grandfather told that story, he used it as an example of how most whites could not be trusted."

Looking at Philip and Fred, he said, "Except present company, of course. Just remember to pay your bill." Philip put his wallet on the table.

Clarence smiled. "My grandfather felt that white people had no respect for what was important to other people, because they were so blinded by their own greed. The Apache had a special hatred for prospectors and miners, because they intruded into the realm of the Mountain Gods. Gold was known as the tears of the sun, the source of all life. Ussen, the Creator, had given the Apaches every thing they needed; wanting anything more was pure greed. In fact, while seeking ammunition, Nana once raided a Mexican mule train that turned out to be carrying silver ingots. He made the raiding party bury the silver to return it to the earth. My grandmother said that Nana considered whites to be like children whose impulsivity made them unable to see the consequences of their actions."

Philip had to interrupt. "Please forgive my own impulsivity, but did anyone in your family know where Sno-ta-hay was?"

"Did is the word. My great-grandmother did and possibly my grandparents. My father remembers that they told him that they were near it when he was a kid and they were hunting deer near the Zunis, or maybe it was that time at Mangas Mountain, or the other time in the Datils. He was too young, and the hunting trips kind of ran together. Anyway, it's somewhere south and east of Zuni, and north and west of Magdalena. But nobody in my family really knows where it is now. I guess us mixed bloods weren't to be trusted with knowledge of sacred sites whose riches might outweigh our conscience."

Clarence looked pained, so Philip quickly said, "J. Frank Dobie mentioned Adams attempting to get a reaction from Nana when he saw him years later. He also wrote that Nana told a storekeeper from Socorro about Sno-ta-hay. So there's definitely a connection between Nana and the diggings. Aren't there any more hints from your family?"

"Nothing specific."

Fred couldn't contain himself any longer. "Clarence's account proves that the Adams story is true. His great-grandmother's tale is independent of the legend.'"

"It would seem so, but it doesn't exactly point us to a location. Since your great-grandfather was in the cavalry, did he know anyone who was stationed at Fort Wingate?"

Clarence broke into a smile. "Sure, he knew a lot of people at Fort Wingate. But, you've got the time and place wrong if you're thinking about Adams and the fort. The fort at San Rafael was abandoned after the Navajo Long Walk to Bosque Redondo. When they were allowed to return, the fort was moved to where it is now, east of Gallup in the Navajo homelands. The Buffalo Soldiers were stationed at the second Fort Wingate years after Adams' placer strike."

Philip employed his family's time-honored way of dealing with frustration; he changed the subject, "Thanks for telling us your story. And where did you learn to cook such good barbeque sauce? I don't think this is an Apache recipe."

Clarence's smile broadened. "Kansas City, of course. But every so often I pay homage to Apache trail food by serving a brisket of mule meat."

His chair shook from his laughter as he watched Philip and Fred turning green. "Just kidding. How about sweet potato pie and coffee?"

After lunch they found Gallup's bookstore, and Philip bought a couple of the books that Lorraine had shown him. As they walked out to the 4x4, Fred asked if Philip would be willing to make a slight detour for another piece of the story. He knew someone in Ramah who also had first-hand knowledge about the Diggings. Afterwards, Philip could drive him over the Zunis and back to Thoreau.

Philip asked, "Does this person have a coffee shop with the best cheesecake in Western New Mexico?

Fred's jaw locked as he hissed, "You think I'm just trying to cadge another meal off of you. You don't understand how much time I've spent looking for the Diggings. But, if you don't want to utilize my expertise and get to people who looked for the Diggings before you were even born, you can just drive me home."

Philip quickly apologized and told Fred how much he appreciated his help. Philip called to get Lars Gustafson's number and handed the cell phone to Fred who confirmed that his friend was home. They drove south, climbing in elevation as the road headed towards Zuni pueblo. When they intersected Highway 53, they turned east to Ramah. The village of Ramah was founded by Mormons who established a farming and ranching community, as well as a center for proselytizing to the Navajo and the Zunis. They turned down an elm-shaded lane and drove up to a prairie style bungalow. A tall man wearing a plaid shirt and khakis was rocking on the front porch. He stood and greeted Fred, who introduced Philip.

"Fred, what can I do for you?"

"Well, Swede, Philip has been looking for information about the Adam's Diggings, so I thought you might talk to him about your dad."

"You know Fred; you're about the only person who still calls me Swede. I think that one of the reasons I went into teaching is that people would call me Mr. Gustafson instead of Swede. Philip, my dad was called Big Swede and I was Little Swede, which became somewhat amusing after I topped six-three. Call me Lars. Fred's right though. Being Swedish is part of what led to our settling here in Ramah. Please have a seat; the rest of my crew is off shopping in Gallup."

Philip was confused. "I didn't think Ramah was a Scandinavian community."

Lars chuckled. "In spirit only. No, Ramah is pure Mormon. It was named after a town in Judea where the prophet Samuel sheltered David from the wrath of Saul. It was a metaphor for the persecution of the Latter Day Saints. Anyway, my grandparents came to the Zunis with the logging boom of the twenties. My grandfather was a carpenter with the narrow-gauge railroad, building bridges and trestles. My grandmother tried to turn a tent in *Agua Fría* into a home without much success. She was one of the few women in the camp, and she was disgusted by the behavior of the loggers. Have you ever been to *Agua Fría*, Philip?"

"Yes, it's in a beautiful green valley, but I remember it being pretty isolated."

Fred added, "Back then, the railroad was the best way in and out."

"Grandmother was looking for spiritual comfort when my grandfather met some of the Latter Day Saints from Ramah. He talked to her about their teachings and she asked to know more. A man came by their tent the next day, stating that he was an elder of the church. He spoke to her in Swedish, and she immediately felt comfortable with him and the Mormon religion. She asked my grandfather to take her to Ramah the next Sunday. When they arrived, she asked to talk to the Swedish-speaking elder again. The men became agitated and talked together excitedly. They told her that there wasn't anyone in the Mormon community who spoke Swedish. My grandmother took it to be a sign and converted to the Church of the Latter Day Saints that very day. So when the railroad went belly up in the Depression, my grandparents moved into Ramah. And our family's been here ever since."

Fred jumped into the conversation again. "Tell Philip Ole's stories about the Diggings."

Lars shook his head. "Just a minute, Fred. You've been living alone too long. You've lost whatever social graces you might have had. Would you gentlemen care for lemonade?"

In the midst of the heat of the early afternoon, the shade on the porch was welcome relief. Sweet peas climbed up the railings, and planters of petunias continued the pink and purple color scheme. Honeysuckle blossoms along the fence perfumed the dusty air. The vegetables in the large garden looked plump and ripe.

When Lars returned with the cool drinks, he resumed his story. "The Depression was going to be my segue into my dad's search for the Diggings. The Mormons fared better than most during the depression. The church asks each family to have two years food supply in reserve. The town had constructed an irrigation dam and was able to mete out the water during the drought years. But, what really dried up was cash.

Farmers and ranchers had been earning cash from selling crops to the loggers. When the loggers went away, so did the concept of cash crops. So my father, Ole, who was a teenager at the time . . ."

He was interrupted by the roar of an old truck full of adolescents. Two boys stood in bed of the pickup with coiled ropes. They waved to Lars as they flew by and made a circuit of the village. A calico cat jumped onto the porch and into Lars' lap. The sound of the truck faded down the highway.

"Speaking of teenagers. Summer break is almost over and they're getting restless. Did you see Puss run away from them? Those two in the back are team ropers and good ones. Any dog or cat is fair game for them. When their testosterone levels hit a peak, they'll tie the rope to the bumper and jerk out mailboxes and sign posts. Did you notice that there aren't street signs in Ramah? We got tired of replacing them. I only have a few more years left of trying to teach them. Why bother with history, if you can't learn from the consequences of your own actions."

"Anyway, my dad and my grand-dad joined the hordes of depression miners in New Mexico. When you couldn't buy a job, panning for gold became an attractive proposition. All the old placer mines had prospectors panning the streams and dry panning the washes. There was even a township of Depression gold miners north of White Oaks. Anyway, everybody was looking for color, so it's not surprising that the Lost Adams became a hot topic. Fred, you and my dad talked about it a lot right here on this porch."

Fred agreed heartily. "And good talks they were."

Lars continued, "There was a family that lived near Ramah back then that had cousins near Old Horse Springs, between Datil and Reserve. They claimed that Adams himself had stopped by their ranch during his wanderings and told them about the mine. He inspired one boy enough to search for the Diggings several years later. He and his friends stopped by Ramah on his search one summer sometime during World War I. They hunted across a triangle from Gallup to Zuni Salt

Lake to the Point of Malpais. They claimed to have found every marker, the two haystack mountains, the range that looked like a woman on her back, and the zigzag canyon. The only thing they couldn't find was the gold mine."

Philip said, "It sounds like looking for the Diggings could become an obsession."

"You're right. My dad was definitely obsessed with the Diggings. He tried to follow up all the local lore as well as the clues that were published in those old pamphlets. He became convinced that the Diggings were somewhere on the edge of the Zuni Mountains and the *malpais*. There were a lot of homesteaders on the edge of the *malpais* those days that were trying to prove up their claim. My dad asked each and every one of them whether they had seen a glimmer of color. Most of them let him explore on their homesteads. He made a lot of friends and gathered a lot of stories, but he never found the Diggings. One rancher told him that there was an Indian who worked for him who said that there was gold in the *malpais*. To prove it, they went to a spot on the edge of the lava where the rancher had to wait. In less than an hour, the Indian brought back a gold nugget."

Philip replied, "It sounds like your dad spent a lot of time looking for gold. Ross McIntyre said that the Saints had mounted search parties for the diggings."

Lars looked pensive. "Yeah, Ross and I were on a couple of those as kids. My dad always organized the posse. It was such a shame about Ross's wife and daughter. It's not surprising that he took it so hard. We miss him around here. How's he doing these days?"

"Okay, I guess. He said that he's stopped driving drunk."

"One step at a time. Greet him for me when you see him again, will you please? What else did Ross tell you about the Diggings?"

"To read J. Frank Dobie. I'll be sure to give him your greetings."

Lars looked incredulous. "Ross knows more about the Adams Diggings than J. Frank Dobie ever did. And he sure spent a lot more time on the ground looking for them than Dobie. Dobie just collected stories; I don't think he actually did any prospecting."

Fred said, "That's what I was telling you before lunch."

Philip felt embarrassed. He was confused about why Ross had been so guarded with him, but he responded amicably, "Maybe I had to pass Adams' Diggings one-o-one before I could get into the advanced course. Did your dad have any specific places he would go back to?"

"He covered most of the western edge of the *malpais* pretty well. He kept talking about the Byerts' pamphlet. I think where he went depended on how much time he had. He spent a lot of time in the area between Paxton Springs and Quartz Hill, where the mountains meet the lava, but that's close by. Fred, didn't the two of you look around here and points north?

Fred grinned. "We sure had ourselves a time. Before you were born, your dad had this old Model A truck. We fixed a lot of flat tires on that rig looking for signs of the Diggings. He knew a lot about the legend; I really respected his knowledge."

Lars went on. "It truly was his obsession. When he had more time and the weather was good, he'd head down by what's now County Road Forty-two. He mostly looked west of the volcanic cones, but he'd look in the *kipukas*, those lava-free 'islands' as well. A few times, he brought back a little bit of gold in a vial, but there was never enough to make the effort worthwhile. He taught me how to look for signs of gold and pan for it. Unfortunately, my knowledge of gold has only served me well in my lectures about Coronado and El Dorado while I'm teaching history at Pine Hill."

As they drove back to Highway 53, Fred suggested, "Why don't we go back to Thoreau on a short cut and cover some of the country that Ole and I searched?"

"Why does the sound of a short cut make me nervous?"

Fred was defensive again. "If you don't want to do some first-hand prospecting with one of the most experienced Adams Diggings hunters alive, just go back to the freeway."

Philip again tried to smooth the old man's feathers. He unfolded the Cibola Forest map of the Zuni Mountain District and asked Fred to show him the route. He saw that Fred was right; his "short cut" would save them almost an hour's highway driving. He wondered how much extra time the rugged mountain roads would take.

They drove east and turned left on Forest Road 178. A short distance down the dusty road, Fred pointed to an overhanging cliff.

"What do you see up there?"

There were a few stone rooms built in the south-facing cave. "It's a cliff dwelling."

"Sure is, there are lots of them in these remote canyons. Wait a minute. Look, there's a fence around it and a bronze plaque. Those weren't here the last time I passed through."

Philip pulled over and read the plaque, "'Pueblo Three, inhabited between twelve and thirteen hundred.' That would put it right around the time of the abandonment of Chaco Canyon."

"The legend says that the Adams party passed a pumpkin patch that must have cultivated by Indians. That has most people thinking that they passed close to Zuni or Acoma, but there are little places like this all over."

As they continued on Forest Road 178, Fred drew Philip's attention to the weirdly eroded red and white sandstone bluffs along the road. "Don't they look like the kind of rock that Adams said the little door was in? Ole and I explored these and the rest of the sandstone east of here. There were a couple of boulders that might have been possibilities, but we didn't find anything real promising."

"Well, they're sure pretty anyway. This is a lot better road then I was expecting, Fred."

Fred scratched his head. "It's a lot better road than what used to be here. There's a sign up here for Timberlake Ranches. Maybe those folks improved the road."

As they rounded the sandstone bluff, they drove past a community of attractive vacation and retirement homes. Fred looked like he had entered a time warp.

"I never thought I would see the day when there would be a subdivision in the Zunis. Look at those green boxes; they've even got cable TV. It used to be that when you called something a ranch, you ran livestock on it."

Fred still had the deer in the headlights look as they passed graded and graveled side streets. After they entered a broad valley, a sign for a Y in the road appeared. The main road went west.

"Slow down, Philip. That's not right. The road didn't go this far west. Pull over; it looks like there's a wooden sign on the ground."

Philip got out and picked up the sign. Sure enough, the north arrow was Forest Road 178 to McGaffey. The road became a dirt track with a bar ditch, that was barely wide enough for one vehicle at a time. Philip shifted into four-wheel drive. They climbed and twisted through piñon and juniper covered hills. It took concentration to avoid the ruts. Oak groves appeared sporadically. After climbing for some time, they came over a ridge into a wide grassy valley surrounded by low peaks covered with ponderosa.

Philip admired the view. "Well, Fred. This is some of the prettiest ranching country I've seen. Are these the kind of ranches you had in mind?"

Fred nodded. "You're right. The grass sure looks green after the summer rains, don't it? I knew some ranchers back here in the old days, but only a few of the kids stayed on. I guess the other ones wanted little green boxes for cable TV."

"Civilization has found its way here, too. Not only are we on a good gravel road again, but that also looks like a four-way stop coming up. We turn right here on Forest Road Fifty, don't we?"

Fred grumbled. "Maybe you should just read the map. Seems like everything's changed from the way I remember it."

Philip turned right and drove along more lush pasture. The road climbed toward the continental divide. Aspen groves appeared in the side canyons, and the cattle and horses looked fat and happy in the meadows. Sarah kept invading his mind. A trail ride through this kind of country would be romantic; maybe *Sitti* could be persuaded to pack a special lunch.

As they neared the crest of the road, Fred said, "This looks like the country around Mount Sedgwick, where I found that vein of quartz with the gold and silver in it. A lot of times, gold is found in quartz. That's why we look for placer findings below veins of quartz. There's science of where to pan, mature mountains with black sand in the washes. Most of the Adams story goes against what I've learned over the years, but like they say, 'Gold is where you find it.'"

Philip replied, "I got the impression that you were going to take me to a place that fit the legend."

"Coming right up, Cottonwood Canyon. The road looks like it's turning back into dirt up ahead. Keep your eyes open for a road on the left as we wind down this canyon. Your map calls it Forest Road Four-Eighty-Three."

There wasn't a road marker for the turn off, but there were signs for the distance to *Ojo Redondo* Campground and back to McGaffey. Fred insisted. "This is it. We head north to Cottonwood Canyon here."

Philip watched the road disappear down the side of a steep *arroyo*. He put the truck into low range, dropped over the edge, drove along the bottom, and then crawled out in first gear.

Philip looked back at the *arroyo* as he shifted back into high range, and then scanned the sky. "We've got to watch these clouds carefully. They're scattered now, but if there's a cloudburst up the mountain, we won't get across this *arroyo* until the water subsides."

The road was just a two track along a green meadow that was bisected by a wide *arroyo* filled with grass and dotted with pools of water.

White-faced cattle grazed contentedly. They rounded a bend and Fred pointed excitedly.

"Look there."

Philip stopped the 4Runner. "Fred, I know that you want me to say that those are the twin haystack mountains, and they do look like them. If they are the markers, why couldn't we see them earlier? Adams said that you could see the haystack mountains from a distance. What other signs do you have up your sleeve?"

"Little door country and a zigzag canyon."

"Sounds great. Will we need a gold pan? Let's go."

They came upon an open gate, but the fence had "No Trespassing" and "No Hunting" signs. Philip was hesitant to continue. Fred pointed out that they were on a dedicated Forest Service road on their way to a canyon on Forest Service land. He maintained that private landowners have to provide access in such a situation as long as you stay on the road.

"If I'd stopped prospecting every time somebody didn't like me crossing their property, I'd never gotten anywhere. You've got to balance the rights of all parties involved. Now our main issue is to follow the Code of the West, 'Leave 'em like you found 'em.' We're going to leave the gate open and drive through, but we aren't going to trespass because we won't leave the road. The main things that ranchers are concerned about are rustling and having the fat run off their cattle. We're going to leave the cows alone and just go to that zigzag canyon."

They continued down the two-track until a voluptuously curving red sandstone monolith rose up on the left and went on as far as they could see. On the right, the buff colored sandstone cliffs converged in a canyon filled with aspens.

Fred was growing increasingly excited. "That's it, Cottonwood Canyon."

Philip was puzzled. "Why is it called Cottonwood Canyon when it's filled with aspen?"

Fred laughed. "There are cottonwoods on the lower end where it comes out near Thoreau. You probably haven't got far enough into the legend to know some of the markers that Adams mentioned on their escape from the Apaches. He said that they spent the night in an aspen grove and then walked across slickrock to hide their tracks. Those two features are right in front of us."

They took the right fork towards the canyon. They went through another gate. After Fred shut the gate, he told Philip that he could relax because they were back on public land. The road became increasingly filled with large rocks as they continued. When it dropped into what looked more like a streambed than a road, Philip stopped the truck.

"This is the end of the road for this vehicle. I'm going to back up to that wide spot to park and we'll continue on foot."

Fred smiled. "In fact, this is the only time that I've been here when I wasn't on foot. But I'm wearing my dancing boots instead of my mule packers, so we'll have to take it easy."

Philip took a couple of bottles of water out of his cooler and handed one to Fred.

After he took a couple of swallows, Fred said, "I always carried my water in a canteen with a horse blanket cover, which kept it from getting hot as long as you kept it wet. But I've got to say that it tastes better ice cold. Let's vamoose."

The sound of the wind rustling through the aspens accompanied the cool breeze that ran down the canyon. The filtered light gave the impression of movement and energy. They came to a spot where the rocky streambed opened up in front of them. Philip inspected the rock and sand carefully.

"All I see is sandstone and sand. I can't make out any of the black sand you were talking about."

Fred laughed again. "That's because there ain't any. This canyon has a lot of the markers, but there's no sign of gold. When I first found it, I thought that there might have been some igneous material that washed down from the high country. After all, Adams said that the canyon wasn't in a mineralized area. One spring, I spent several days here panning, but there isn't any color."

Philip had known that there wouldn't be a pot of gold at the end of this rainbow, so he wasn't disappointed. As he looked around, he gained a new sense of Fred. Prospecting put him in a lot of beautiful places.

"I'll bet this canyon is real pretty with the spring runoff flowing through it."

Fred smiled beatifically. "One of the prettiest spots I've camped in. You know Philip, I've never struck it rich, but I've got more treasure in my memories of the back country than most people ever accumulate."

They drove back toward Forest Road 50. As Philip put the 4Runner back in low range and crawled through the deep *arroyo*, he said, "I'm glad to be on the other side of that one. The clouds are bumping together now, and this would have a torrent in it if it rained."

They turned left and followed Forest Road 50 to the fork where Forest Road 480 took them towards Post Office Flats.

Fred observed, "There used to be quite a community down the road a few miles at *Agua Fría*. You remember that Lars was talking about his family living there. These days it's hard days to imagine how the Zunis boomed in the twenties. There was another camp just northwest of here at Sawyer. Since the trees have mostly grown back, you don't realize what it was like to watch these hills get clear-cut. The ponderosa were a lot bigger before the loggers came. This area was swarming with loggers and railroad men. Very few brought their families. It was a town of brawling bachelors. This country used to be wild, but the people who supposedly tamed it turned out to be wilder yet."

When they came to Bluewater Canyon, Philip said, "This gets a few points as a zigzag canyon too."

Fred agreed. "I panned it too, including the area that's under Bluewater Lake now. There's no gold here either even though it's closer to Mount Sedgwick."

"My dad took me to the area below the dam to fish when I was a teenager. I guess it's better for trout than gold."

As they drove alongside Bluewater Lake, Philip turned to Fred. "Thanks for the tour and putting me in touch with your friends. I think I'll take a look at the area around Quartz Hill tomorrow, where the mountains meet the *malpais*."

10

Philip smiled when Sarah opened the door of her apartment. She was wearing khaki shorts that emphasized her long legs and a red camp shirt with a petroglyph pattern.

"Welcome to my humble abode. It's furnished in the 'student as gypsy' style." Posters were on the wall, a Mexican rug covered the carpet, and a modular bookcase stood next to a desk covered with papers and a laptop computer.

Sarah pulled him close and greeted him with a passionate kiss; her body melted into his. As he held her, Philip felt the supple motion of her back. Her sinuous rhythmic movement excited him.

Sarah pushed away. "I would love to continue this, but I'm really starved. Let's head over to the Atomic before I'm unable to tell whether I'm swooning from passion or hunger."

Only Grants would have a Chinese restaurant that sounded radioactive. While they drove, Philip told Sarah that he had once asked the owners where they had come from. They replied "Gallup." Apparently their family had been involved in building the railroad and had stayed on in New Mexico. As they got out of the SUV, Philip's attention was drawn to a noisy group of bikers in the park across the street who were staring at them. Maybe they were just raising a little hell, but he remembered Ross's warning from the night before.

The café's red and gold Chinese decorations looked shopworn, and the bright colors couldn't disguise the fact that the restaurant was basically a diner. They found a table, ordered, and asked for chopsticks.

As they drank tea and ate pork dumplings, Philip reported on his day's research and described his obstreperous old tour guide.

Sarah was amused. "Fred sounds delightful, but isn't he awfully old to be working that coal mine?"

"Fred wouldn't have it any other way. He's been prospecting and mining for over fifty years. He's still strong in a wiry kind of way, and he swings a pick as well as anyone. Besides, you should have seen him light up when I asked about the Adams Diggings. There's plenty of life left in him."

"Well, he certainly knows some interesting characters. It sounds like he's not the only true believer."

Sarah was interrupted by the arrival of the eggplant with garlic sauce and the beef and snow peas with oyster sauce. "This smells great! Let's share them."

She scooped rice onto her plate, and they passed the serving bowls. "I did some interesting research myself. Sherry Robinson's book about this area is a wealth of information. Before the Santa Fe took over, the tracks through Grants were part of the Atlantic and Pacific Railroad. On October eighth, eighteen fifty-seven, the eastbound train was met by gunfire. The train crew took off, but the fireman was convinced to stay by a bullet through his cap. The robbers ordered him to unhook the rest of the train and take the express car to the stockyards east of town. The rest of the gang was waiting there. They blew the doors off the express car and then cracked the safe. They took one hundred thousand dollars of currency and gold."

"So, there was gold!"

"About half of it. This eggplant has quite a bite, but it's scrumptious. They handed the fireman a bottle of whiskey for his trouble and headed into the malpais. It looks as though they buried the gold somewhere in the malpais, took the cash, and headed west across the Zunis. A posse was formed that included a renowned Navajo scout from Fort Wingate who tracked the thieves to a hideout near Fence Lake. In the shootout that followed, some of the gang and the sheriff were killed. 'Kid' Johnson and Bronco Bill were captured, but apparently the others escaped. The gold was never recovered."

Philip furrowed his brow. "Fifty thousand dollars of gold at about eighteen dollars an ounce would be worth almost twenty times that now. That's a million dollars!"

Sarah gulped ice water, and then smiled. "It gets better. Robinson tells a couple of stories about a man named Twadell who came looking for the gold in the thirties. Apparently in eighteen ninety-seven, Twadell had been on the lam for something he had done in Mexico and holed up in a cabin in a *kipuka* in the *malpais*. Could I have more of the eggplant, please?"

As they dished up second helpings, Sarah called the waitress to ask for more water.

"The stories diverge. One version has him returning to the cabin after spending some time away from it only to find the place occupied by three men. He overheard them discussing money and making plans to go to Mexico. So, he stayed hidden when two of them left to get supplies. Then, he had a shootout with the remaining robber and killed him. Or as the other version has it, he and a pal rode up to the cabin and the three desperados spilled out with six-guns blazing. Twadell was the only survivor of the gunfight."

Putting down the break-apart chopsticks, she examined her finger. "I think I've got a sliver. Anyway, he entered the cabin to find fifty thousand dollars of gold on the table. He was afraid to get caught with the loot, so he buried it under the cabin floor. This next part bothers me. Something distracts him from a fortune for thirty years. Then, he comes back during the Depression to find the burned-out remains of the cabin, but no gold. Somebody beat him to it. Got any likely candidates?"

"You're right. Who was more likely than Buck to have found an isolated cabin in the lava? I was convinced that the Adams Diggings was going to be the answer, but this sounds like a very real possibility. What bothers me about this one are Buck's annual trips to Mexico. You brought up the boom and bust cycle of most robbers the first time we talked. What do you think now?"

As she pushed rice into the garlic sauce, Sarah said, "Consumer credit counseling? I don't know. Why would he go to Mexico periodically when he had all the gold at once? Fear of being caught with the whole bundle? Waiting for a better exchange rate? The same thing would be true if he found the richest gold strike in New Mexico, why spread it out over time? Why not just file the claim and work it legit?"

Philip shook his head. "I don't know. Both prospects look good, but neither of them quite matches up with Buck's behavior. Don't you just love a mystery?"

"Sorry. I wouldn't be studying history if I didn't want to know how it turns out. What do we do now?"

Philip reached for Sarah's hand. "Hit the trail. Let's go on that horseback trip tomorrow and get a better feel for the territory. Maybe if we sleep on it, something will come to us."

She squeezed his hand. "There's nothing like a trail ride to provide some time for thought."

"I was pumped up about the Adam's Diggings, but the A and P sounds good too. To paraphrase Lao Tzu, 'He who feels punctured must first have been inflated.' If the solution were easy, Sheriff Matthews would have figured it out years ago. So it looks like we've got some more work ahead of us."

Philip settled the bill, and Sarah took his arm. As they got into the 4Runner, Philip looked again at the group of bikers next to the gazebo in the park across the street. One of them jumped on his starter and peeled off. As they drove down Santa Fe Avenue, the Harley pulled up along side of them. The rider had well-defined muscles, chiseled features, and very short blond hair. He was wearing black leather pants and a matching vest without a shirt. Neo-tribal tattoos circled his arms. He rode an old pan head Harley with the gas tank and rear fender painted like black lace underwear. His black leather saddlebags were covered with metal studs. Philip wondered if this was the guy Ross had told him about from the Grubstake. The rider was grinning sadistically; then he started shouting. Sarah looked uncomfortable as Philip rolled down his window.

Derek Gruber yelled, "*Yaa, an dinak. Ibn charmuta.*"

Philip shouted back as he slowed down, "*Laysh bitul hayda? Shu bedak?*"

Derek laughed, "*Rasak.*"

⁄⁄ ⁄⁄ ⁄⁄

Derek kicked the car door hard, and flipped them off as he roared away. He wanted Habib to know that he was on to him. His digital directory showed that Philip Habib was a gumshoe from Albuquerque. His biker friends said that he was probably related to some Lebanese people here in Grants. What better cover to infiltrate America's nuclear reservoir. Maybe the story of Saddam Hussein attempting to buy yellow cake uranium in Niger had been fabricated, but some terrorist group was going to take the dirty bomb idea and run. The Lebanese government allowed terrorists to operate freely within their borders. Half a million people had gathered in Martyrs' Square in Beirut during *Hezbollah's* pro-Syrian demonstration. He wondered if Habib was connected to one of the Palestinian terrorist groups: *Hezbollah* or *Hamas*. *Al Qaida* seemed more likely since they had already demonstrated their willingness to take us on at home. Besides, they had recruited resident Arabs in other places in America.

He reveled in the surprised look on Habib's face when he swore at him in Arabic. His Special Forces language training continued to be useful. He also enjoyed the look of fear on the blonde's face; after all she was a collaborator.

Philip made a note of the motorcycle's license plate number, but he was concerned about Sarah. At first she had just looked frightened, and now she looked mad as hell, too.

"What the hell was that about?"

Philip responded, "I was about to ask you the same thing. He looks like the guy that Ross overheard asking the bikers about me last night. And, I'm pretty sure that he was the guy in the Power Wagon from County Road Forty-two yesterday. Do you know this guy, rejected suitor, that sort of thing?"

Sarah's eyes blazed. "Never laid eyes on him before tonight. Although you might be right about him being the guy in the Power Wagon. Besides, I prefer my men with hair that's more than a quarter inch long. What was that yelling about?"

Philip grimaced. "Pretty standard Arabic road-rage stuff. He cursed my religion and called me the son of a whore. I asked him why he was saying this and what he wanted. He said, 'Your head.' I'm going to drive toward Lobo Canyon and away from your apartment."

Sarah hugged herself. "So if you're taking evasive action, what do you think is happening here?"

Rage was bubbling up in Philip. "I have no idea. This makes no sense whatever. I see no connection between what we've been doing and this guy's taunts. But whatever his game is, he certainly wants us to play it with him."

After they drove a short ways up the mountain, Philip found a bumpy little-used side road. He bounced down the track for several yards, turned the 4Runner around, and killed his lights. He flipped off the dome light and got his 9 mm. out of the glove compartment. He asked Sarah to get out of the car and away from it. A glowing ring of clouds surrounded the moon. They listened to the quiet of the foothills, no engines groaning against the incline, just crickets. An uncomfortable silence developed between them. The heat of the day had dissipated and the mountain air was cool as it flowed down the canyon.

Sarah said, "Now I know what those fugitives felt like with Buck on their trail."

Above the pings of the cooling engine, Philip heard the deep-throated growl of the Harley. He urged Sarah behind a clump of fragrant *chamisa* and watched, holding the 9mm. Sig-Sauer with a two-handed grip in front of him. Sarah was shivering with fear as she crouched behind the ghostly pale branches. A Harley with a rider wearing a leather flight helmet and old-fashioned goggles slowed slightly, and continued up the mountain. Their anxiety slowly dissipated as the chopper's headlight followed the switchbacks. After a few quiet minutes, Sarah asked if they could leave. They got back in the car and drove back into town.

Philip took the turns too fast down Lobo Canyon Road. "That son of a bitch. Maybe I over reacted. I don't know what a uranium mine security guard who hangs out with the Aryan Brotherhood wants with us, the Lost Adams Diggings, or the *malpais*. I just don't get it."

"I don't think it's an over reaction when he really was following us. How do you think that asshole knew to swear in Arabic?"

"Well, I've got a Cedar of Lebanon decal on the SUV, and Ross said that the bikers told him that my relatives are Arabs. What's confusing is how he knows Arabic at all. He doesn't look Arab, and it's not exactly the usual high school language offering."

Sarah shivered, "You're right, I don't get it either. Do all of your dates have bizarre and scary events like the last couple have had? These threats and guns are giving me the creeps. Is it safe to take me home now?"

ⵌ ⵌ ⵌ

From the cover of a juniper, Derek Gruber used his night vision goggles to watch Philip park the 4Runner around the block from Sarah's apartment. They walked cautiously down the street. Did Habib really think that a woman who looked like that and drove a VW beetle would escape the notice of his testosterone driven friends? He felt assured that having Gloria's brother drive past them on the road had given them a false sense of security. Getting them to run gave Derek deep pleasure. His buddy had called him from up the canyon to say that he had seen a flash of reflection in the moonlight down a side road. So Habib was taking the harassment seriously. What did he have to hide? He would check him out with his online spooks bulletin board. Derek was convinced that Habib was suspicious enough that his intelligence buddies would know the Arab.

Gruber smiled as he watched Habib get Sarah's keys and enter the apartment with his 9 mm. drawn. Why did he pull a gun after a little road rage incident? This didn't look just an innocent visit home to see the family. As a P.I., Habib probably had a license to carry. After all he had obtained a concealed carry permit himself as soon as the New Mexico legislature had permitted it. Entering the blonde's apartment like there might be hostiles inside suggested that Habib didn't see himself as an innocent victim. What was his real mission?

⁄⁄ ⁄⁄ ⁄⁄

After Philip gave the apartment a quick sweep, he beckoned for Sarah to come inside.

"I don't think he's got a line on you yet. I'm sorry that I've involved you in whatever I've involved you in. I'm baffled."

"We've got to talk. The end of this evening has been just a tad too weird for me. I'm still very anxious about that whole scene. I think anyone would have been upset, but there's a reason why that really affected me. I grew up around guns; they were a necessary tool on the ranch. In fact, I got pretty good at picking off coyotes that were worrying the herd. But guns took on a new meaning for me a few years ago."

She started pacing. "Right after graduation, I married my high school sweetheart. As a honeymoon, I joined him on the road that summer while he started a professional rodeo career as a calf roper. He had won the calf-roping championship at the high school national rodeo final and was doing pretty well for a beginner on the Professional Rodeo Cowboys of America circuit. That fall we moved to Las Vegas so that I could start school at UNLV. Matt was away a lot, but he was starting to earn some money. By the following season, he was earning serious points to get to the PRCA finals in Las Vegas. But the cowboys he was hanging with were party animals. I tried to overlook the buckle bunnies that fawned over them. He spent most of his time on the road; so he started doing white crosses to stay awake while he drove to the next rodeo. Next, he was snorting crystal meth at these all night red neck rendezvous. By the time he got back to Las Vegas, he was not only using coke, but he was also into debt with some pretty seedy wise-guy types. Finally, the coke brought these thugs into our house. I got to watch them beat Matt. They held a gun on me and talked about what they were going to do to me later. We survived intact, but the next day I was out of there. I don't like being around violence."

Philip got up and held her to him. "Violence is a rare occurrence in my life. I still have no idea why this guy is confronting us. I'm sorry that this is bringing back unpleasant memories."

Sarah smiled ruefully. "I'll have those memories no matter what. I just don't want to add to the collection."

As he drove away, Philip was disheartened because the evening had turned out so poorly. He felt dejected and rejected. "We need to talk," anxiety overcame him every time he heard that phrase from a woman. The biker's interference in his love life, as well as his aggressive taunts infuriated him. He was determined to find him and straighten this out. He called Ross on his cell phone and left a message asking him to find out who this guy was from the bikers at the Grubstake. He'd call Don Abeyta in the morning to report the incident and to ask him to run the plate.

Philip picked up a six pack of *Negra Modelo* and a twelve pack of *Tecate*. He was in a melancholy mood as he drove out of town. The sky was clouding up and the temperature was falling. He put Susan Tedeschi on the CD player. Her blues in a minor key matched his mood. Knowing that he wasn't the only one who felt so low gave him some solace.

When he entered his grandmother's house, she came into the living room and said, "I bet you just had a fortune cookie. How about some dessert?" She took his arm and escorted him into the kitchen.

"Could you make *qtayif*?"

"Yes. But only because I already made the crepes, knowing that you would ask. It will take me a few minutes to make the filling, and they'll have to bake for fifteen minutes. Do you want some coffee?"

Philip opened a Negra Modelo. "I'll have one of these instead."

His grandmother cocked an eye. "You're home a little earlier than I expected."

"Me, too. This motorcycle hoodlum harassed us, and after that Sarah wanted to make an early night of it. She was scared, and I'm angry."

Sitti's eyes widened and she put her hand up to her mouth. "*Bismillah!* In the name of God, I don't know how trouble finds you so often. I won't even ask how it happened. Is she still going on the trail ride with you tomorrow?"

"Yes. I think she's still interested, but she may be having second thoughts about dating someone who attracts the attention of outlaw bikers. Even though she's studying outlaws, I think she prefers them one generation removed. She's beautiful and intelligent, and I'm getting a little fixated on her."

"I suppose she's a tall skinny blonde."

"*Sitti*, don't get started. I don't need a Lebanese girl to cook for me, I've got you." He gave his grandmother a hug.

She laughed and led the way into the kitchen. "You won't have me forever. At this rate, you'd better learn to cook these recipes yourself."

Sitti showed Philip how to make the sweet cheese filling. They spooned it into the crepes, rolled them, poured rose-water syrup over it all, and put them in the oven. He remembered all the picnics and dinners when *Sitti* or Aunt Mary would just happen to invite a single girl who they thought was an appropriate match. Their match-making efforts were nothing compared with Aunt Rose in Albuquerque. She was the wife of Philip's father's younger brother, Peter. The daughter of a Lebanese trading family from Bernalillo, Rose was the queen of networking. She and Peter ran a successful short-haul trucking firm in Albuquerque. There was an informal "Chamber of Commerce" among Lebanese people in New Mexico. Rose went through a period when she would call his father to command Philip to a brunch after mass at the little Byzantine Catholic Church in the near Northeast Heights. Girls from every Lebanese business family were paraded through these brunches. Philip's father couldn't keep a straight face when Rose finally tried to rope in the Maloofs. He asked, "Maybe you could get me some tickets? Any of the professional teams they own would do." Rose finally gave up when Philip reached an age at which he was no longer a prime candidate.

Philip told his grandmother that he appreciated her concern about his welfare. However, he made it clear that romance was an area in which he would make his own mistakes. When his grandmother opened the oven and aroma of roses emerged, Philip remembered the *dicho* in Spanish. *No hay ninguna rosa sin espinas;* there are no roses without thorns. The *qtayif* was delicious.

Philip bent down and kissed his grandmother on the forehead and went to his room. He loved the old adobe farmhouse with its sensuous curves in the walls and windowsills. Philip had slept in this room since he was a child, and he felt very comfortable in it. He built a fire in the small adobe corner fireplace to take the chill off the room and to warm his heart. Collapsing onto the Taos bed, he pulled off his boots. The old carved oak WPA desk that his grandfather had bought at auction was about to enter the digital age. Philip powered up his laptop and portable printer. He loaded the topographic maps of New Mexico disk and printed the quadrangles of the Zuni Mountains and the Malpais. He made close ups around Quartz Hill and the Chain of Craters. After untangling the phone cord, he plugged his laptop into the phone jack and logged on to the Internet. His search turned up a couple of short summaries of the Adams Diggings that didn't add much to his knowledge. However, he was intrigued by the discussions on the treasure hunters' bulletin board. A lot of people proposed that they knew where the Diggings were and cited references to back up their claim. But he couldn't find any news of a discovery. His eyes were growing weary from looking at the screen, so he decided to go back to the web another day.

He got undressed and crawled under the covers. He propped up the pillows and lay down to skim through the books he had found in Gallup. As he grew drowsy, he put down the books and turned out the light. He watched the firelight dance on the walls as he drifted off.

11

While Philip was drinking his first cup of coffee, he called Don Abeyta at the Sheriff's office. He greeted Don and reported the assault by the biker. Don agreed to run the motorcycle's plates and call him back. By the time Philip had eaten most of *Sitti's* hearty ranch breakfast, Don called.

"His name is Derek Gruber. He doesn't have a criminal record or outstanding warrants, so I checked some data bases. He served as a sergeant in the Army during the First Gulf War. Then he joined the Special Forces, and probably worked covert operations in the Middle East."

"That would explain how he knows Arabic."

"Now he works as a security guard for one of the uranium companies. One of our guys has talked to Gruber at one of the closed mines while he was out on patrol. He reported that Gruber talks like a Second Amendment militia type. This deputy also respects his knowledge of firearms; Gruber carries this impressive Kimber Combat Gold forty-five."

Philip's assessment of Gruber's threat potential went up several notches. "*Hijole*, Special Forces! And that's quite a pistol. Don't tactical weapons teams use them?"

"You're right. The LAPD SWAT team carries them."

"What else do your guys know about him?"

"One of our clerks has a cousin who works at the women's prison. She says that Gruber has a girlfriend there, a tough-case Irish redhead. The way that they're both built; they'd look good on a wanted poster, twenty-first century versions of Bonnie and Clyde."

"What's she in for?"

"I don't know, but I hear that she cuts a pretty wide swath at the prison. We see Gruber hanging with the bikers at the Grubstake sometimes. I think the redhead is the sister of one of them. I hear that Gruber's a pretty good pool player. He likes to talk to our guys and the Grants cops, pretending that we're all on the same team, wannabe stuff."

"So he hasn't caused any problems?"

Don paused. "I didn't say that. He's been involved in couple of parking lot scuffles where nobody pressed charges. Do you remember that hate graffiti was spray painted on the Lebanese businesses out here after nine-eleven? We thought that the Aryan Brotherhood was behind that. Gruber looked good as one of the perpetrators. But we never found any evidence, nothing that could have given us grounds for a search warrant."

Philip groaned. "So he's a Special Forces trained, racist gun-nut with criminal tendencies. I feel much better."

"He's not somebody I'd like to have pop up on my personal radar screen. I'm sorry that we won't be able to do much for you, Philip. We can pull him over for questioning if we see him, but he didn't even cause any property damage. We wouldn't be able to get anything done if we tracked down every redneck that swore at somebody. I'll let you know if I hear anymore on this end. Keep a look out and call me if he hassles you again."

The day was overcast with dark clouds hanging from the top of Mount Taylor. Philip thought about the small crater at the top of the mountain. The Acomas and Lagunas said that it was the source of the clouds, and the *sipapu* from which the *kachina* spirits emerged. Clouds were building up over the Zuni Mountains as well. He wondered what was building up between him and Gruber.

As he watched Hank feed the horses, Philip was distracted by the pleasant sensation of his full stomach. From years of cooking for ranch hands, his grandmother had developed a wonderful skillet scramble. Good food did take away some of the anxiety.

Hank called out, "*Buenos días. ¿Cómo estás?*"

Philip laughed and patted his belly. "*Panza llena, corazón contento.* If I stay much longer I'm going to be putting on weight. I sure do love *abuelita's* cooking. So, which horses do you think are your best trail riders?"

"How well does your lady friend ride?"

"I don't really know. She grew up on a ranch in southern Utah, so I suspect that she's pretty good on horseback."

Stepping into the corral, Hank offered an alfalfa pellet to the big dappled gray. "I think this old *caballo* would be good for you. He stands over fifteen hands high. He's a semi-retired ranch gelding, but he's still willing. He responds well to leg cues, and we call him Sam."

As he rubbed the gray's neck, Philip heard the horse chomping his treat. The gelding nodded his head up and down, asking for more. Hank walked to the other side of the corral and offered the bay mare an alfalfa pellet. The gelding followed.

"This half-Arab *yegua* is the one for the lady. She's a nice little bay, but she's got a few years on her, too. She belonged to a girl who showed her in dressage, so she's real sure footed. She does especially well if you can rein her English."

"I trust your judgment, Hank. How about if we let Sarah try this mare in the corral before we load them?"

A meadowlark trilled its song as Sarah's yellow classic Beetle appeared in front of plume of dust. The bug pulled up to the corral, and she climbed out. She was wearing Roper boots, Rocky Mountain jeans, a pink Western shirt with snap buttons, and a jean jacket. Her hair was in a ponytail pulled through a UNM Lobos cap. She greeted Philip with a warm embrace and caressed the brim of his hat.

"A four X beaver silver-belly with an old-fashioned deep-creased high crown and a horsehair band and stampede string. Nice. I like it when the good guys wear white hats."

She stepped back to take an appraising look at him. "Mule packer boots, Levis, leather vest, and a mustard-colored barn coat. Aren't you overdressed for prospecting?"

Philip winked. "I'm dressed for success with my lady friend on a trail ride."

"You're succeeding all right." Sarah kissed his cheek.

Philip beamed as they walked over to the corral. He introduced her to Hank, and Hank introduced them to their mounts. Philip approved as he watched Sarah approach the mare from the diagonal.

"What's her name?"

"We call her *Mi hija*," Hank answered, blending the words together.

"*Mija.*" Sarah repeated dropping the middle syllable as Hank had. "A term of endearment." She stroked the mare's chest and shoulder. Leaning into the *Mija's* face, Sarah breathed into her nostrils. The bay relaxed as Sarah proceeded to rub her neck.

"I'd like to brush her." The mare looked contented under Sarah's brushing, her ears and eyelids drooping. "Have you picked her hooves yet?"

"Not yet." Hank handed her a hoof pick forged from half of an old horseshoe.

Sarah moved her hand down the horse's shoulder to her leg. When she reached her ankle, the mare gave Sarah her foot. As Sarah bent over wielding the pick, Philip thought that there was something special about cowgirls. Not only did they have a way with animals, but all that riding also gave them a shape that couldn't be surpassed. Those Rockies sure did show off Sarah's.

Hank walked over to the tack shed. "This mare used to do dressage. Do you ride English?"

Sarah shrugged. "I used to, years ago. How would she do with a western saddle and English reining?"

Hank grinned. "We can do better than that. I've got an Australian saddle that I use on her. It's kind of compromise between a western and an English saddle. They were developed for herding sheep in rough country, you know. How about that?"

Sarah smiled back at Hank. "Perfect. Can we give it a try now so you could help me adjust it?"

Philip enjoyed brushing the gelding's charcoal gray mane and tail. He liked the contrasts. Sam looked pretty good for his age. Philip watched with interest as Sarah swung up on the bay. She sat well in the saddle and had gentle hands. The mare responded well. When Philip saw that Sarah was able to get the mare to back up and side pass, he knew that they would be fine together. He put splints on Sam and loaded him in the trailer. Sarah took off *Mija's* tack, put on a halter, wrapped the mare's legs, and loaded her.

The saddles and tack were piled in the bed of the pickup. As Hank tossed in a bag of alfalfa pellets, he said, "There's hay and water on the trailer. If you take these saddlebags to Fatima, Philip, she'll fill them full of lunch for you two."

After thanking Hank, they walked up to the house. Philip's grandmother was effusive in her greeting to Sarah. Philip was glad that he had talked to her. *Sitti* transformed herself into the Queen of Tupperware and Blue Ice and outfitted them well. They assured her that they would be careful and climbed into Hank's truck.

As they headed west, Philip asked Sarah, "So, there's a canyon in the Zunis you think we should go to?"

Sarah looked pensive. "Yes, for several reasons. Lars said that Ole spent a lot of time around there, and Fred told you that he ran into Buck at the edge of the Zunis and the *malpais*. I've already been in a zigzag canyon over there. Earlier this summer I went mountain biking with some friends around Quartz Hill. I've been thinking about it since last night. I don't think it's quite right, but I think we should go anyway and get the feel of it. Drive south on the road to San Rafael, take a quick right past the trailer park, and head up Zuni Canyon Road."

As the pavement turned into a well-maintained gravel road, Philip looked up at the tall sandstone walls. The canyon had been cut by a meandering stream, and the road curved back and forth following it. "It's going to get more zigzag than this?"

Sarah laughed. "Sort of. The lava will make it feel tighter. When you see the lava field ahead, look for the road to the left. It feels very different to me today, with the clouds hanging so low."

They passed the place where the lumberjacks used to roll logs off the cliff down to the railroad. Philip asked, "Are you all right after last night? My cousin's husband told me that the biker's name is Derek Gruber, and he sounds like trouble."

"I don't need anybody else to tell me that he's trouble. I had a hard time getting to sleep. I don't know; maybe he was just showing off for his outlaw buddies. If you didn't find out anything more about why he harassed us, I guess it won't do any good to worry. Let's try to get away from whatever his problem is and enjoy our trail ride."

At the lava field, Philip turned left and slowed to a crawl as they went over the cattle guard. "And we're going to take a side road off this bustling thoroughfare?"

Sarah held on to the handle above the door as they slogged through a puddle. She looked back to make sure that the horses had maintained their footing. "See that two-track up there that parallels the lava. We're going to go a few hundred yards down that and unload the horses."

Philip stopped the truck a short distance down the two-track. "Look off to the north. What do you see?"

Sarah nodded. "You're right. There are two haystack mountains down a long valley."

Philip handed her the digital camera. As she adjusted the zoom, Sarah said, "But those mountains are to the north and the mouth of this canyon faces east. They don't fit the story of the journey."

"Don't be so sure. Adams was notoriously bad with directions. If they went north of the Zunis, it's only twenty miles off the path we were thinking about. And those canyons between here and those haystacks have some red sandstone in them, so they could be the site of the Little Door. As you said, we can at least get the feel of a place like Adams described."

Philip pulled into a large meadow and turned the rig around so that they were facing out. "That fog in the canyon looks strange lying above the lava. Let's see if we can get the horses to drink before we go."

After unloading the horses, they took off their leg wraps, and gave them a drink from a canvas bucket. Then they put on blankets, saddles, and bridles. Philip secured the saddlebags, and they mounted. They rode over the ridge and entered a canyon filled with tongues of jagged *aa-aa* lava flows. Fog limited their visibility, and the low hanging clouds emphasized the rock walls' containment of the valley. The sandstone cliffs narrowed, barely allowing a rugged road to creep along the south side of the lava. The canyon walls continued their twisting pattern as the black rock flowed through them. Aspen grew at the edge of the lava, forming pockets of green along the black rock. Around the corner splatter cones appeared, tall black grotesque monuments among the ponderosa. The road continued through the pines and opened up on a wide valley, dotted with sagebrush. Lava divided the green meadow and continued until the road began a steeper climb.

Sarah rode closer to Philip. "This is a beautiful trail ride. I love the smell of the sage and the contrast of the fog and the lava." She leaned towards him, placed her hand on his shoulder and kissed his neck. Philip smiled and leaned toward her to kiss her on the mouth.

They left the fog behind, but deep ruts appeared in the road and narrowed the path. Sarah kept a good seat and shifted her weight forward to help the mare deal with the rough country. The big gray just muscled his way up the slopes. As the horses climbed, they saw a deep pit on the right. The road really deteriorated past the old mine. They stopped at the top of the hill where there was a fork in the road.

Sarah said, "That was a fun climb. The mines around here contained fluorspar, a hardening agent for steel. There was a big demand for it during the Second World War. There are test pits on the other side of the hill too. We're on top of Quartz Hill now. Didn't Fred say that gold was associated with quartz?"

Philip nodded. "Yes, and that he filed a claim on Mount Sedgwick which is maybe eight miles from here. He found traces of gold in a quartz vein over there.

Sarah reined the mare right next to the gray. Philip gave her a water bottle and she drank deeply. As she passed the bottle back to him, Philip pulled her close and kissed her deeply. When the horses shifted their weight, they broke apart.

Philip licked his lips. "*Laziz*. You taste delicious. Look to the left, there's lots of quartz in the pass over there. If you've already seen the east side and didn't discover the Diggings, let's go straight. We should be able to get to the other lava flow that's west of here."

As the horses picked their way down, sunlight tried to break through the clouds. The temperature was mild and the countryside interesting. Ponderosa pines provided shade, but when they hit the lava, aspen appeared again. The primitive road mostly skirted the black basalt, but occasionally it went over a ridge in the lava. They also traversed across hillsides that looked as though they could have been the lower elevations of cinder cones.

Philip turned in his saddle. "Not much in the way of little doors, deep narrow canyons, or waterfalls around here. Let's find a relatively flat grassy place where the horses can graze while we have lunch."

They unsaddled the horses and put them in hobbles and halters. Philip spread an old olive army blanket in front of the saddles. They reclined against the saddles, admitting that they both could feel the fact that they hadn't ridden in a while.

Sarah praised the Aussie saddle. "Now I understand what Hank meant, it really works well in this country. Have you ever tried one?"

Philip shook his head. "Never. The only times I've ridden English were in the Middle East and North Africa. I'm not used to the close contact, and my knees had a hard time of it."

"That's why the Aussie is such a good compromise. You wear the leg irons lower than on an English saddle. The saddle is deeper, and I love the feel of it. The English reining also gives you so much more communication with the horse. And, I'm as hungry as one. What have we got for lunch?"

Philip spread out the meal and offered Sarah a Tecate. "Do you know Middle Eastern cooking?"

"I can tell that the square one is *hummus,* and those are grape leaves, and that's pita."

"Good so far. We call the grape leaves, *waraq "ainab.* The round one is *baba ghanoush,* it means toothless grandfather, an eggplant dip. This delicious salad with parsley and mint is *tabbouli;* it's best scooped into baby Romaine leaves. And, of course, there are imported olives and cheese."

Sarah dipped pita into the *baba ghanoush* and gave a soft moan of pleasure. "Does your grandmother always serve lunch like this?"

"Only when her grandson, whom she doesn't see as much as she'd like, comes to visit. She knows how much I enjoy her cooking, and she shamelessly exploits it. How do you like the *baba ghanoush?*"

"It's fabulous. There's a little hint of a smoky flavor."

"The smoky flavor comes from grilling the eggplant; it's the traditional way. Try one of these *waraq "ainab.*"

Sarah closed her eyes as Philip offered her a stuffed grape leave. Philip stared as Sarah gave into pure sensuality as she ate. Watching the way her lips surrounded the grape leaf, he felt the stirrings of arousal. She opened her eyes and said, "I can't be the only one with olive oil on my lips."

Philip closed his eyes as Sarah fed him the other half. He couldn't remember when he was so focused on taste and texture. When he opened his eyes, Sarah's face was close to his. He pulled her to him and kissed her passionately. He could feel the olive oil on her tongue and tasted the hint of lemon. They turned their attention away from the meal and fed the flames of their desire. The cravings revealed in the kiss were heightened by intimate explorations by feverish hands. Philip pulled her even tighter against him. They kissed until they were breathless and their lips felt bruised. As his tongue gently circled her ear, her jaw dropped and she took a sharp intake of breath. He felt her hands caressing the muscles of his back. She worked her hands into his inner thighs, and it was his turn to gasp.

Philip pushed himself back, grabbed Sarah's blouse by the mother of pearl snaps, and said, "I love being a bodice ripper."

He tore open her blouse and kissed her small but perfectly formed breasts. Her nipples had the color, shape, and texture of raspberries. His tongue lingered over them. He mouthed the succulent suppleness of her breasts and licked her cleavage. His lips grazed her flat stomach, and then he kissed her navel delicately. After fumbling with the buttons of his chambray shirt, her mouth caressed the strong muscles of his chest and abdomen. Then she unfastened his belt and unbuttoned his jeans. Her hand found him, and he moaned.

They struggled out of their boots and jeans. Their eyes lingered over each other's body as they settled onto the blanket. Sarah wrapped her leg over Philip. She put her arms around his neck and pulled herself up to his mouth. Her tongue explored his as she rubbed herself against him until they were both writhing with desire. Sarah mounted Philip, and they both gasped as he entered her. She lifted her exquisite form towards the sky until the sun made her golden hair glow like a halo. He cupped her breasts as she rocked her hips as though she were riding at a slow gallop. Suddenly, she ground her pelvis into him wildly and locked her jaw. Just as Sarah cried out, Philip exploded into the electrifying, narcotic free-fall of total release.

Sarah reclined against the saddle languidly, an odalisque, like a painting hanging on a frontier barroom wall.

Philip laid his head on her lap. "That was wonderful. You are exquisite. I'm sorry that so many things have interfered with our romance. Are you all right?"

Sarah brushed his hair back from his forehead. "I'm more than all right. I feel fantastic; you are a very attentive lover. I felt a little vulnerable, making love outdoors. But it was so sensual that I lost myself in the moment. Thank you for asking. This has been the strangest courtship that I've ever experienced."

"I feel the same way. Whenever we talked I felt closer to you, but something bizarre has interfered every time."

"In spite of it all, you sure do know how to get a cowgirl in the mood."

They ate lunch leisurely. Philip poured olive oil and sprinkled pine nuts over the *hummus*. Sarah dipped pita into the paste and said, as she dribbled olive oil down her chin, "Mmm, this sure doesn't taste like store bought."

Philip licked the olive oil off her chin and in the recess formed by her clavicle. She cradled his head and kissed his forehead tenderly. They spooned up the *tabbouli* with the Romaine leaves. Sarah asked, "Do I detect a hint of cinnamon in the salad?"

"It's used in a lot of Lebanese dishes. Americans aren't used to it in salads or with meat, but it's a mainstay in Arabic cooking. I used to love walking through the *suqs*, the open air markets. The spice markets were a sensual delight, inhaling the aromas of all the spices in a kaleidoscope of color."

They finished the meal with a lingering kiss. Reluctantly they dressed. Then they packed up the lunch and walked over to the horses. They snapped on lead ropes and unbuckled the hobbles. As they walked back to their gear, Sarah held up the hobbles and winked at Philip. "I can't imagine what got me feeling this way, but right now I'm thinking about other possible uses for these."

Philip actually felt himself blushing. The Wild West sexual politics had reached a new level in their relationship. They rode south until the road forked. Sarah suggested that they take the east fork away from Paxton Springs. She explained, "Hundreds of the rowdiest lumbermen, cowboys, miners, and prospectors along the continental divide passed through Paxton Springs. Mother Whiteside ran a boarding house there when it was a railhead. I can't imagine that the wealthiest mine in New Mexico could be within a mile of that bunch. We'll go by the fluorspar mines and come down into Bonita Canyon."

"Sounds good. I've been thinking about the A and P robbery you told me about. Did the posse catch up with the robbers near here?"

"No, it was closer to Fence Lake. They probably rode through here, but their take was never recovered. That Twadell story is the only one that I know that gives a location for the loot. The A and P robbery happened twenty years before the railroad came into the Zunis."

"I still have a hard time imagining a railhead and a booming boarding house for loggers a mile from here. The trees have grown tall again, and we haven't seen a soul all day."

The horses climbed up a hillside that looked a lot like Quartz Hill. When they got to the top, there was a deep pit that was fenced by barbed wire. They dismounted and peered over the side, but they couldn't see the bottom.

Philip shook his head. "If they could find fluorspar this deep beneath the surface, why hasn't anyone found Adams' gold sitting right there in a stream bed?"

"I don't think we know much about mining. Let's look around. There's supposed to be another one with an intact wooden headstall nearby."

They explored a maze of dirt roads that connected mines until they found the one with the headstall, a lonely monument against the sky. Then they rode east until they found a series of progressively larger roads that ran into Forest Road 447. After riding north on FR 447 for a couple of miles, they spotted the lava flow.

As the horses ambled down the two-track, Sarah asked, "Isn't your friend Ross a geologist? Between the two of us, we don't know squat about finding minerals. Didn't Lars say that Ross was an expert on the Diggings? Let's invite him to dinner."

Philip called Ross on his cell phone as they drove down Zuni Canyon. They returned to the ranch, put up the horses, and returned the gear to the tack shed. Philip grabbed a quick shower. Sarah drove off to her apartment and cleaned up in record time. Philip admired the T-shirt-styled turquoise dress that showed off her figure and brought out both the blue and the green sparkles in her eyes. He greeted her with a low wolf whistle. After picking up Ross, they went to strip mall on the north end of town. *El Comedor del Norte* was filled with mouth-watering smells. They found a table, ordered Mexican beer, and started in on the fresh *salsa* and chips. Ross said, "Both the red and green *chile* are good here, and they've got chicken with *molé*, too."

The *pollo con molé* appealed to both men; Sarah went for the *chile relleno* with green *chile*. She wrinkled up her nose. "Chocolate and peanuts belong in Snickers, not with *chile* powder. Let's get some of the *espinaca con queso* appetizer too."

After they ordered, Philip looked straight at Ross and asked, "*Sadeeki*, why didn't you tell me that you were such an expert on the Adams Diggings? I felt pretty foolish in front of Fred and Lars."

Ross hung his head. "I feel pretty foolish now. I certainly didn't mean to cause you any embarrassment. I didn't realize how gung ho you were. I'm sorry, but the Diggings bring back memories of my naiveté, my hopes for a golden future that wasn't meant to be. 'Seek and ye shall find.' I told you that it was part of what got me interested in being a geologist."

Sarah tried to diffuse the tension between the two men. "How did the Adams Diggings get you into geology?"

"Lars's dad, Ole, better known as Big Swede, got me started looking for them when I was a teenager. After a few times out, it started feeling like a wild goose chase. Big Swede knew a lot about the legend, but he only knew a little about placer deposits."

The hot spinach and cheese dip arrived. Sarah dipped a chip in it and popped it into her mouth. "I love this dip. If you boys don't dig in, I'm going to eat it all."

Philip reached for the blue corn chips and dipped into the spinach cheese mixture. "By the way, Lars said to say hello. He said that he missed seeing you."

"I miss the folks in Ramah too, but the memories are too powerful there."

Changing the subject, Philip said, "Fred told me that there was a science to panning for gold."

Ross chuckled. "I'd call what Fred does more of an art than a science. What did he tell you?"

"To look for what he called mature mountains, that gold was associated with quartz, and to find black sand in order to know where to pan."

Ross replied, "That's fine as far as it goes. Mature mountain ranges have about the right level of erosion for placer finds, not too new and rugged, but not so old that the valleys have filled in. By black sand, he probably meant magnetite, which is a heavy ore of iron oxide. Most placer mining takes advantage of gold being heavier than most minerals. Since magnetite is almost as heavy, they're often found together in streambeds. And he's right about quartz being associated with gold, it's often found in veins in a quartz matrix. That abandoned mine near your place in La Madera, the North Star, was mostly fluorspar, but it had a little gold embedded in quartz too."

Sarah smiled. "I've got a feeling that you're going to tell us that it's a little more complicated than that."

Ross looked at Sarah with a new awareness. "Bright and beautiful.

It's a lot more complicated than that. When I got frustrated with Ole's searches, I started reading about gold mining and geology as it related to gold. I was convinced that those old prospectors had missed the Diggings because they weren't looking for the right things. Remember that Adams said it wasn't in a mineralized area. So with the egotism born of youth and the energy to match, I decided that I would obtain the knowledge that was the key to finding the Diggings. I went through the books in the libraries in Grants pretty fast. Then I drove to Socorro and haunted the School of Mines. There are a lot of minerals associated with gold. Sometimes it's found in oxidized sulfide veins in monzonite, or it might be associated with telluride. Then there are the places where it's derived from contact pyrometasomatic auriferous pyrite."

Philip was befuddled. "Pyromania, that's what I'll get, trying to follow this conversation."

Ross crunched down on a chip laden with *espinaca con queso.* "Listen. You don't need to know all this stuff, but I didn't want you to limit yourselves to what Fred told you. Suffice it to say that gold is usually found in igneous rock, but it can also exist in intrusions into sedimentary and metamorphic rock. Placer findings like the Adams Diggings are the result of the erosion of the original material. Adams talked about nuggets, so you're probably looking for free gold rather than an ore."

Sarah looked at Ross intently and asked, "Did you research the legend as well as you did the geology?"

Ross nodded. "As I told Philip, J. Frank Dobie is the place to start."

"Fred Russell wasn't all that impressed by the veracity of some of Dobie's facts."

Ross shook his head. "Consider the source; Fred is barely literate. He wouldn't be my first choice as a book reviewer, but he's right nonetheless. When I went to the original sources, I found that Dobie had edited them considerably. For example, the Byerts' pamphlet was one of the earliest accounts, published in nineteen nineteen. When I was looking, it was hard to put your hands on a copy of it. Byerts told the story of a woman who used to work for him and was homesteading just east of the malpais. A sick old man rode up to her ranch and asked if he could stay until he was well enough to ride again. His horses and outfit were the finest that money could buy. She gave him some aspirin for his rheumatoid arthritis and rubbed liniment into his hands and feet. On the fourth day, he was well enough to leave. It took three of them to hoist his saddlebags onto his packhorse. The old man tried to pay her, but she refused. She said that no sick person would ever be turned away from her door, and that she didn't know any rancher who would charge someone to lay over for a few days. He started to ride off, but turned around to tell her something he had never told anyone before. He said that he had been working a gold mine in the *malpais* for the past fourteen years. Because of her kindness, he told her where the gold could be found, that the *malpais* had to be entered from the south. Then he gave her point to point directions, but she never pursued it and had forgotten the details by the time she met Byerts."

The waitress arrived with their meals. As she set them down, she said, "Be careful, the plates are hot."

Philip was confused. "I thought that the Byerts pamphlet was supposed to be a first-hand account from Adams."

Ross agreed. "You're right. That's the meat of it, but there are corroborative stories as well. Anyway, Byerts is clear throughout the book that the *malpais* must be entered from the south. He also talked about the famous pumpkin patch, the first sign of Indian agriculture since the Pima Villages. The first pueblo to the northeast of the Pima Villages is Zuni. There are signs of habitation from the modern Pueblo all the way down to the Zuni Salt Lake. Philip, how do you like this molé?"

With his mouth full, Philip said, 'Far better than most. It's not too sweet."

"There's also an account by Ben Kemp that places Adams at some warm springs, which could be the Ojo Caliente between the Salt Lake and Zuni. At least, Adams visited one of the other likely contenders, the Gila Hot Springs, with Kemp's sister. Adams said it wasn't the right one; the water flowed in the wrong direction. So according to those lights, that puts the canyon somewhere in the Zuni Mountains or the *malpais*. Smack dab in the middle of your primary search area. Other sources emphasize that Gotchear, the half-breed guide, used the Spanish word *piloncillo* to refer to the "haystack" mountains that Adams described. It's commonly used for cones of raw sugar. Have you ever seen them in Mexican markets?"

Philip nodded. "They look like volcanoes. Do you think that takes us to the Chain of Craters?"

"That was my thought at the time."

Sarah leaned forward. "Let's go there tomorrow. Philip, did I see a stock trailer at your grandmother's barn? It sure looked like there might be another horse in that string that would work for Ross."

Philip smiled. "Ross, I would sure appreciate your help on this search. Could you join us tomorrow?"

Ross glanced at them both and looked a little sheepish. "Are you sure I wouldn't be a fifth wheel?"

Sarah caught his hand and stared into Ross' eyes. "Only a third wheel. The fifth wheel is for the trailer. Please come with us. It was apparent to us today that we didn't have the knowledge or experience to really search for the diggings. We need your help."

"Can I bring my gold panning gear?"

Philip laughed. "I hope we get that far, but I'd like to see you pan for gold just to know how it's done."

"I'm a little rusty, but I could give you an introduction. We'll need to bring some water."

"I'll bring a five gallon jug. We'll need to make a late start. I've got to give Marlene a progress report over brunch." Philip raised his drink. "To Eldorado."

Ross and Sarah chimed in, "To Eldorado."

After they dropped Ross off, Sarah invited Philip into her apartment. She put on a Latin-sounding David Grisman CD, took him into the bedroom, and lit a candle. "I didn't want you to get the impression that I was just swept away by the pelvic stimulation of that Aussie saddle this afternoon. Come here."

She pressed against him, and they kissed until they were panting with passion. They undressed each other. Philip had noticed earlier that Sarah wasn't wearing a bra, now he was happy to see that the thong she wore hardly qualified as underwear. Sarah leaned over the bed, and he kissed the smooth curve of her derrière. Sarah fell onto the quilt, smiling lasciviously as she beckoned for him to join her. Philip fondled her while he licked her skin and gave her soft love bites. Her hand caressed him. Philip's tongue explored her until she groaned and raked her nails across his back. She enfolded him, and they found a needy, ragged rhythm. Sarah's eyes locked on his, and he could feel her labored breathing. Her eyes shut and the muscles of her face tightened as she moaned with pleasure. Philip thought that watching a woman have an orgasm was the sexiest thing imaginable. Then he couldn't think of anything except his own experience of ecstasy.

12

When Philip knocked on Marlene's door, he was surprised to see her in a satin nightgown and robe. She looked like Rita Hayworth's classic pin-up. She led him into the suite, and smiled over her shoulder as she let the robe fall to reveal her sculpted posterior.

"I thought that our meeting might include some information that we wouldn't want to broadcast over the entire dining room. So I ordered in. I hope Eggs Benedict are all right."

Philip had been impressed by Marlene's figure before, but the satin gown left nothing to the imagination. A diagonal of lace moved across one exquisite breast, giving a glimpse of an erect nipple, the other prominently displayed by the satin. She moved close to him and caressed his cheek, capturing him with her azure eyes. She held his face with both hands and then kissed him deeply. Her hands moved across his back until they found his muscular buttocks and pulled him tight against her lascivious body. She nuzzled his earlobe as she moved her pelvis rhythmically against him.

She grinned and said, "Oh my, I can tell that you're glad to see me."

Philip was confused. He was in a state of high arousal, and there was that perfume again. Marlene's blatant seduction was having the planned effect. As she began to unbutton his jeans, he gently pushed her away.

Philip held her at arm's length. "This still isn't a good idea, Marlene."

"It's obvious that part of you likes the idea," she retorted.

"Very much, but it will complicate our relationship. The last time I let this happen; I didn't get paid and had a complaint filed against me. I'm a professional, and you hired me to do a job. I have a report to give you and a bill. Where does that fit into the morning's activities?"

"Afterwards. Don't get prissy on me; I know you want me. Do you want me to write you the check first, so you won't feel like a gigolo?"

Philip nodded. "Yes, I would like a check. I would also like to give you an oral report. These notes just cover the basic information, but you're not getting the point."

She smiled coquettishly and placed her hand on his crotch. "I'd like to get the point and do an oral report on it, but you stopped me."

Philip stepped back. "Okay, it's clear that I find you attractive. And under other circumstances, I'd like to do something about it, but . . ."

Anger twisted her features. "It's that ranger. You've hooked up with that little Girl Scout, haven't you?"

"My personal life is personal, and our relationship is professional."

Marlene shrugged her robe on. She snarled at him, "Don't give me that crap. If you were into ethics, you'd be teaching philosophy instead of hiring out as a peeper. Get out of here. I don't want to look at your lying face."

"Well, if you want to discuss the report or the bill, you can call George and arrange an appointment there. Any future contact between us will take place at George's office with George in attendance."

Marlene flung open the door. "Get the hell out of here, you pompous little prick."

As he drove back to the ranch, Philip called George on his cell phone. "I think I've ruffled some feathers."

"More. Who's this time?"

"Our client's." Philip told him the story.

"That's the kind of problem to have. You know to an old married man that sounds . . . Of course, I would have done the same thing. What's happening with this story that *Sitti* is telling everyone about you and the bad boy biker? You know, for a guy who got pretty far into the peace and love thing as a teenager, you seem to have a real talent for pissing people off."

Philip was annoyed; sometimes George's taunts went too far. "I just need you to cover me with Marlene. I'm doing the right thing here, and I just know I'm going to pay for it."

"No good deed goes unpunished."

"And 'hell hath no fury like a woman scorned.' You got me into this, and I need your help."

"All right, already. Haven't I always bailed you out of whatever trouble you're in? What happened with the biker?"

"You're right, you have. I'm sorry; being screamed at twice in two days has me on edge. Sarah and I had just left the Atomic Café when this tattooed creep pulls alongside and starts swearing at me in Arabic. When I tried to talk to him, he kicked my door and thundered off."

"I don't like the sound of this one."

"It gets worse. Don tells me he's a racist gun-toting Special Forces Gulf War veteran.

"Watch your back. *Maa" salaami.*"

When Philip returned to the ranch, he made a quick snack of pita with *labne,* a yogurt spread and *zatar,* a mix of Jordanian spices and sesame seeds. After soothing his spirits with comfort food, he took his coffee out to the corral. He greeted Hank and asked him about Ross's mount.

"I've got a sixteen-hand sorrel that came from a dude ranch. He's big, but anybody can ride him. He loves a good trail ride. Are you sure you want that rummy along? What if he gets hurt?" Philip scowled.

"Okay, Okay, mind my own business. It's just that your grandparents have been real good to me, and I don't want no drunk suing *Abuelita*. *Sabes?* You know that I've never had a better life than I have here. And I promised your grandfather that I would watch over *Abuelita* and the ranch. *Ten cuidado con el borracho!*"

"*Claro*. I'll watch him."

"Now, give me a hand getting this fifth wheel in the bed of the Ford, will you? I can't lift it by myself any more. That stock trailer can handle the horses all right, but it's not in as good a shape as the horse trailer. The lights all work, and it's street legal, but the brakes aren't that good. Take it easy with it."

Philip tried to reassure him. "I'll treat it with kid gloves."

"I know that road out there, Philip. The southern end of County Road Forty-two gets real rough in spots. Getting around those deep puddles is a little trickier with a trailer this size."

"The F-two-fifty was great yesterday."

Hank was emphatic. "That was in the high country. You just put it in four wheel drive as soon as you get on County Road Forty-two, Okay?"

"Okay."

Sarah and Ross drove up. They were talking excitedly as they emerged from her Bug.

Philip greeted them and gave Sarah a squeeze. "What's up?"

Ross grinned. "Our Internet detective downloaded some information about the Adams Diggings. It's good stuff."

"It's straight up history, but there isn't a lot of documentation." Sarah added as she kissed Philip, "Hi Hank. How's *Mija* today?"

"She's great. You took good care of her yesterday. So you're all going to the Chain of Craters?"

Ross extended his hand. "Yes, Enrique. It's good to see you again, Ross McIntyre."

Hank shook Ross's hand. "And this is your mount, Ross. By looking at his short tail and knowing my lack of imagination, can you guess his name?

Ross laughed. "Bob, of course."

"You just stay on his back. He's got heart; he'll take you anywhere you want to go."

Sarah asked Hank, "Could you tell us a little bit more about working with Buck in the malpais?"

Hank looked down at his boots. "Like I was telling Philip, I was glad to get away from Buck. He only joined us occasionally, just on the roundups and shearings. Sometimes he just happened by. He was an outsider, and most of us in the outfit were Basque. Most people would try to fit in, but not Buck. He kept apart from us unless there was a bottle. Now, don't get me wrong. As likely as not, Buck supplied the bottle. His drinking stories made me uncomfortable; they were full of violence. And he was always showing off his talent with a gun. He'd humiliate anyone who'd bite in a shooting contest. He'd just ask them to pick a target that they knew they could hit. Then he would keep moving the target out ten to twenty yards further until they missed. Then he would ask them to choose a target past that. He hit it every time. He won a lot of bottles of booze that way."

Ross inquired, "Wasn't there some controversy about how Buck shot those pot hunters?"

"At Buck's trial, the coroner reported that one of those pot hunters had been shot once in the chest and once in the back. The district attorney goes on about how Buck had shot a man in the back. Buck jumps up and says, "I couldn't help it. After I shot him in the chest, the son of a bitch wouldn't stop spinning."

Philip grimaced. "What a guy. So what was his secret to getting around in that volcanic hell hole?"

"It was more skill than secrets. He knew all the trails, but he really trained that horse how to pick his way through the lava. He also used rawhide over-boots to protect *Diablo's* legs when they were in rough country."

Sarah asked, "You know we're interested in his possible connection to the Adams Diggings. Did he ever talk about gold mining?"

Hank thought for a while. "Not directly, he wouldn't have. But I remember a bunch of us sitting around the chuck wagon talking about what we'd do if we struck it rich. You know, a typical workingman's fantasy. Buck said that he wouldn't change much. He'd just buy a new truck, drink better booze, go into town more often, take vacations, bet more at the races, and attract a better class of woman. He said that you couldn't buy a better life than being a lone cowboy. But no, he didn't talk to us about prospecting."

Ross asked, "You all worked in the *kipukas*, the grassy places in the middle of the lava. Did Buck show any interest in a particular canyon?"

"You just don't understand Buck. He was always aware of his surroundings. We'd set up camp, and the rest of us would be dying to get out of the saddle. Not Buck. He and *Diablo* would go check the perimeter. More often than not, he'd shoot a coyote or two as twilight was deepening. Pissing in the corners, establishing his territory. He always rode down the side canyons, claiming to sweep them for lost sheep. In answer to your question, I didn't see him focus on any one. I would have been surprised. If Buck had a real interest in something, he wouldn't show it. He would've come back later when no one was around. Look, Buck was capable of anything, but he didn't like to share. If he had wanted us to know anything, he would have told us directly. Otherwise no one would know. He was a loner, and he jealously guarded his privacy."

"Thanks for the information, and thanks for your help rounding up these mounts and setting up the rig. We might take a look at the Hole in the Wall this afternoon too. Doesn't that open to the south?"

"Yes it does. We spent a lot of time there with the sheep. I'd be real surprised if you found something there. There are also some grassy places on the west side of the malpais, near the Little Hole in the Wall, that face south. I wouldn't try to come up to them from the south on Forty-two with that trailer. Another day, take your SUV and drive south from Fifty-three. You're going to be near the ranch of a Basque family I know.

I ran into one of the kids at the Basco Fiasco at Elko last summer. He's ranching in the eastern part of New Mexico. They were good people; too bad they left. Philip, you keep in touch with that cell phone of yours."

They walked across the yard and picked up a lunch from Philip's grandmother. She was very gracious as always. She gave Sarah a little hug and warmly welcomed Ross back to her home. "*Ahlan w sahlan.*"

Ross replied, "*Ahlan w sahlan fiik.*"

Sitti smiled. "*Takee arabi, l'hamdillah.* It's been a long time since we've seen you here, Mr. McIntyre. Philip told me that you've learned a little Arabic in your travels. You were a good friend to Philip when he was a teenager. Don't be a stranger now."

She poured them each a cup of sweet mint tea and handed out cardamom flavored cookies. They chatted for a few minutes. Then, with Hank's help, they loaded the horses and gear.

As they climbed into the truck, Sarah scooted into the center of the seat. She announced, "The real cowboy sits in the middle because you don't have to drive and you don't have to mess with the gates."

"So what's this article that you printed off the Internet?" asked Philip as they drove south.

Sarah replied, "It's pretty well written. It's long enough to give details and short enough to be read. Of course, any website named www. theoutlaws.com is going to get my attention, and this was written by a female western history buff to boot."

"It was good to see the legend in print again. All my notes burned up in the fire." Ross turned away from them and stared out the window.

Sarah filled the silence by saying, "I especially liked the part about Adams repeating 'The Apaches made me forget.'"

Ross spoke softly. "He might have been right. From what I saw coming out of Nam, it looked like exposure to atrocities was a big part of what caused Post Traumatic Stress Disorder. Remember, first Adams found the bodies of his slain companions, and then he went back to the canyon to see his other friends being beheaded and their heads paraded around on lances. That's up there on the atrocity scale. Then they were pursued and barely escaped with their lives. That was followed by days of dehydration, malnutrition, and disorientation. If that wouldn't set you up for a PTSD, I don't know what it would take."

Sarah said, "I agree completely, but what about his knowledge of the trip to the canyon? That was at least a couple of weeks before the massacre. The PTSD shouldn't have affected that."

"That's another disorder. That's the one they keep warning me about at the Veteran's Hospital when I go in to dry out. Everybody talks about what a lush Adams was. They said he would stay drunk for six months at a time and then drink heavy for the rest of the year. Byerts talked about his sterling character, but nobody else was nominating him for any office other than town drunk. I think he developed an alcohol-related dementia. The V.A. psychologists tell me that alcoholic dementia affects visual spatial memory, which is not good news for geologists."

"That's scary stuff, Ross." Sarah placed her hand on Ross's arm.

"I still test out all right, but they just say that they're getting a baseline. One of the people that Adams stayed with when he was searching for the lost mine said that Adams couldn't find his way out of a one hundred sixty acre section without following the fence line. But I think that the real problem finding the diggings was that he couldn't compare new information about his current location to his old memories. It's a processing problem, a torn neural network. At least that's what they say will happen to me when I go in for detox. That should scare me, but I've got too many memories that I'd like to forget."

Philip knew that they shouldn't encourage Ross to talk about his losses. "You know, Dobie said that Adams also had typhoid fever when he was living in California after the Apache episode. It was supposed to have affected his memory, too. His wife and kids helped him remember what he had told them. What about Captain Shaw, Adams' partner who bankrolled him in the early searches? Everybody agrees that he was a good judge of character; and he trusted Adams."

"I don't know, maybe his dementia wasn't as bad in the beginning. Besides, Shaw kept the search going long after Adams died. Maybe it was actually better without Adams' interference."

Sarah intervened. "You know guys; psychohistory is conjecture, at best. Ross, I think you're probably right that there was something going on with Adams. Whether it was emotional or intellectual, I think he was a taco short of a combination plate. He must have had enough gold to convince people that the story was true, but nobody's been able to find it following his directions for almost a century and a half."

Ross disagreed. "Except maybe Buck. I don't know how much he knew about the legend, but I'm sure he at least heard the story in the saloons from Reserve to Magdalena. He might have even found a placer strike that wasn't in a zigzag canyon. I've been thinking about your question about the multiple trips to Mexico. It might line up with the Byerts story I told you last night, too. Maybe both men worked the diggings episodically, because you could only find gold episodically. The Adams group or somebody else might have worked the canyon more or less down to bedrock. Now the only gold that can be found is what washes down every year in the runoff and the summer rains. You would have to have water to pan. That would only be available during the summer monsoons, and he would have wait until the latter part of the rains. So, a couple of weeks panning would be the year's harvest."

Philip was excited. "That matches the timing of Buck's pilgrimages to Mexico. He usually went in the fall. And it sounds like the level of mining that he could tolerate. A couple weeks of panning every year seems more likely than ongoing hard-rock mining. It fits with Hank's story about lifestyle enhancement as well. Why wouldn't he look for the mother lode?"

"It might have already eroded away. The only remaining gold would be in the alluvial gravels."

They pulled off the pavement at the Point of Malpais, and Philip got out and turned the hubs. He shifted into four-wheel drive. Following

Hank's instructions, he pulled out his cell phone, but there was no signal. They headed northwest, up the rugged road.

Philip shared what Don had to say about Derek Gruber. Sarah's facial expression froze, and she stared straight ahead. Ross confirmed that Don's description fit with what little he knew about Gruber.

Ross turned to face Philip. "Maybe he just hates you on principle. As an Arab, you're a convenient target. People who hate like that need enemies in order to justify their paranoid beliefs. *Willkommen* to the Fourth *Reich*."

"Should I paint a bulls-eye on my chest? In the twenty-first century, I guess being anti-Semitic includes Arabs, too."

The countryside was a rolling grassy plain dotted with junipers and occasional lava outcroppings. After a few miles they came to the turn-off for the Hole in the Wall. They agreed to go to the Chain of Craters first and then come back to the *kipuka*. The road worsened, and Philip learned that Hank was right about the trailer and the mud holes. He followed the alternative tracks around them and didn't lose traction often, but he jostled the horses a lot more than he would have liked to. He was glad to see Cerro Brillante getting larger. He handed Sarah and Ross the maps he had generated two nights before.

Philip said, "I'd like to park this as soon as possible. It looks like there's a primitive road that goes behind Cerro Colorado and heads north up the Chain. Why don't we go over there and unload?"

Sarah replied, "Sounds good to me."

Ross looked discouraged. "From looking at these maps, it doesn't look very promising for zigzag canyons west of here."

Philip agreed. "No, but these craters sure look like *piloncillos*."

Ross turned to Sarah. "Let's get out, Sugar."

Sarah groaned. "Bad pun, but a beautiful day for a trail ride. We can't prospect west of here anyway. Cerro Alto, the tall one to the west, is actually on the Ramah Navajo Reservation. Federal law prohibits prospecting or mining on tribal lands except with permission by the tribe. But for Pete's sake, we're not forming a mining conglomerate to negotiate a joint powers agreement. We're just following up leads on a story.

Philip opened the trailer gate. "Let's saddle up and ride."

They unloaded, watered, tacked, and saddled the horses. Philip made sure that each of them was carrying enough water in the saddlebags. Shortly after they started up the road, they crossed an arroyo. Ross halted his horse and leaned over Bob's neck to examine the streambed.

"It's pretty much what you'd expect: sand, eroded basalt, remnants of pumice, mixed with broken-down lava from the 'bombs,' the projectiles that make up a lot of these cones. Not real promising for gold. Although from the color of some of this, there's probably a fairly high iron content."

Philip urged Sam upward with increased leg pressure. "We're not interested in iron. Now, wouldn't that sound exciting, The Lost Iron Mine of the Malpais, that's almost as good as the Lost Fluorspar Mines of the Zuni Mountains."

"Stop bickering boys," Sarah admonished them. "This is real pretty country for a trail ride. I've never ridden through a range of volcanoes before. I like the look of them. Ross, what did Byerts say about locating the Diggings?"

"He said that you had to go several miles west of the Point of Malpais. Somewhere in that vicinity was the 'Pumpkin Patch,' which could've died out in a drought without leaving a trace. Then go north to the little door and zigzag canyon. How far west and how far north seem to be the issues."

Philip said, "I don't think it's quite that simple. According to the maps, there aren't any zigzag canyons, much less little doors for miles."

"I know maps are a guy thing, and now this GPS stuff is so high tech. But all that equipment will just tell you where you already are and how that relates to what was drawn on this map, maybe thirty years ago. It's not going to help you find something new."

"You're right." Philip retorted, "'The map is not the territory,' Gregory Bateson. But the Apaches won't be able to make us forget; on the GPS, it's digitized."

"You've got to find it first. Besides, there's nothing wrong with establishing that it couldn't be here, so you can start looking someplace else. Let's enjoy this beautiful rolling country." Sarah moved *Mija* into a slow trot.

Philip enjoyed watching the horse and rider moving smoothly, rhythms complementing one another. On the other hand, Ross looked like he wasn't quite finding his seat on Bob's trot. Bob was looking back anxiously at his rider.

"Ross, let up and just move him at a fast walk. He's got such a nice long stride, and that way you won't have to do that bone-jarring thing I was watching. We don't have to hurry; Sarah just wants to ride. Watch, she'll break into a collected little gallop across the flats. Don't they look good together?"

After a gallop to the next ridge, Sarah turned *Mija* back toward them. She slowed her to a walk as she neared the other horses. She was beaming.

Ross greeted her. "You look happy, Sarah."

"I sure am. Great horse, wonderful trail, and fabulous companionship." She drew her horse next to Sam and gave Philip a long kiss.

Philip smiled broadly, "I thought we'd go up to Cerro Piedrita and maybe have lunch." He looked at Sarah with a lopsided grin. "Don't get your hopes up. I think we've just got sandwiches today."

Sarah led the way along the hills. Suddenly the sound of *Mija's* hoof beats changed pitch. "It sounds hollow underneath."

Ross shouted, "Sarah, stop. Bring *Mija* back slowly. You're over an air pocket, maybe a mini-tube. There's no way to know how thick the lava is."

Sarah backed her horse out of the area. They all breathed easier.

"Hank told me that the ranchers out here lost some cattle when one of these pockets broke through." Philip rode over to Sarah and kissed her. "I'm glad you're such a light weight."

The blue sky held a few wispy horsetail clouds. The sun beat down hard. They felt the warmth of the animals beneath them and took frequent pulls from their water bottles. When they reached Cerro Piedrita, they found a good-sized *piñon*, and set up a picnic lunch in its shade. They gave the horses a drink from the canvas bucket.

The sandwiches were delicious, and the Tecates were drained rapidly. Sarah announced, "You know, I've been thinking about the Apaches and Adams. The story about Nana sounds strange to me."

Philip asked, "Why?"

"Well, you've got to understand the historical context of miners and Apaches. Miners were the first encroachment of whites into Apachería. In the eighteen thirties Juan José, the chief of the Mimbres Apaches, and his people were invited for a feast at the Mexican copper mining town of Santa Rita. As Juan Jose and his band wolfed down the food, American bounty hunters fired cannon full of grape shot and killed most of them. Mangas Coloradas escaped and returned to the remaining Mimbres bands. He told the story of the massacre and whipped the warriors into a frenzied raid that led to the deaths of a couple dozen miners and numerous others."

Ross looked at her quizzically. "How do you know so much about the Apaches, Sarah? I read about them while I minored in history at BYU. There's a lot of interest in military history among the Saints. We're a breeding ground for the military. I focused on the role of the cavalry in the West. I know that story, something about the state of Chihuahua offering money for scalps, the slaughter of the innocents."

Sarah saw the thousand-yard-stare begin in Ross' eyes and quickly replied, "I took a seminar called "The Last Indian Wars and the End of the Frontier" and I did my term paper on the Apaches. I think they were probably the best guerilla warriors that ever lived, at least in terms of what a small disciplined band can do to an invading army. Back to the point, they hated miners. Miners desecrated the home of the Mountain Gods, the Ga'an. They dug huge holes into the earth and muddied the clear streams. In the eighteen fifties, miners found color at Piños Altos, right in the middle of the Mimbres land. Mangas Coloradas came to them under a flag of truce. He offered to take them to an area in the Sierra Madres that was far richer. The miners invited him into their camp, and captured him. They tied Mangas to a post and whipped him one hundred lashes."

"Probably the wrong guy to torture," noted Philip.

"Then, they made the mistake of letting him go. After recuperating in the hot springs at Ojo Caliente, Mangas Coloradas unleashed a blood bath. Later, in eighteen sixty near Fort Bowie, Cochise was also arrested after he came in under a flag of truce. He escaped, but his brother and nephews were hanged. Mangas and Cochise joined forces a couple of years later at the Battle of Apache Pass."

"That was the only time the Apaches employed a frontal assault. They built up breastworks on the ridges overlooking the pass. They did pretty well until the California Column of the U.S. Cavalry that was heading east to join the Civil War brought in mountain howitzers. The bombardments killed and wounded a lot of Apaches."

Sarah asked, "So why isn't there anything about the Civil War in the legend? The Confederates beat the Union forces near Fort Craig right in the middle of Apache country."

Philip broke in. "And in walks Adams. I can see why you think Nana's gracious acceptance of the miners was a little out of character for Apaches at the time."

Sarah continued, "The only thing that I can figure is that Nana was in his spiritual mode. Nana and Lozen, the mystic warrior who was Victorio's sister, were the spiritual core of the Warm Springs band. Maybe he threw a pinch of *hoddentin* at them, twirled the bull roarer around his head, and prayed for them to be content with what they could gather."

"That didn't last long."

Sarah concurred. "That's right, as soon as they broke their word, he attacked. His devotion to Ussen, the one god, required retribution from the greedy liars who defaced Ussen's creation. We need to look at the bigger picture. Victorio, Nana's nephew, was an anathema to white encroachment in the eighteen-sixties and seventies. Victorio, Nana, Cochise and Geronimo were the reasons why Adams waited to return to try to find the zigzag canyon. Because Nana was Victorio's uncle, the old man was by his side on most of the raids."

Ross added, "Victorio was finally trapped in a pincher operation in one of the rare cooperative ventures between the Mexican and American armies. Nana actually led his most famous attack after Victorio's death at Tres Castillos."

Philip interrupted, "Clarence was talking about his grandfather chasing the Apaches into Mexico. I wonder if the Buffalo Soldiers were involved in that."

"They were."

Sarah continued, "Nana escaped to lead a few survivors to safety. Then he went on retreat with The Dreamer at Cibecue in southern Arizona. While in a trance, Nana saw the ascent of Victorio and the other great Apache chiefs into heaven.

"Clarence mentioned that too."

Sarah nodded. "That vision had a big impact on Nana and his followers. Then the half lame seventy-year-old medicine man went on a raid that is still considered to be one of the most formidable guerilla actions by a small group of warriors in history. Afterwards, he just disappeared into Mexico to join Juh's Chiricahuas and mourn for his lost companions, their homeland at Ojo Caliente, and the loss of their way of life."

Ross agreed. "You're right about Nana's raid in the annals of military history, the archetypal horseback guerilla raid. That was also the end of the Apache wars for the Warm Springs band. The Chiricahuas continued to fight for another five years until Geronimo surrendered in eighteen eighty-six. The United States had spent millions of dollars, and killed fewer than one hundred Apaches. Meanwhile the Apaches killed about a thousand Mexicans and Americans as well as stealing countless head of cattle and horses."

"You can see why I think that they were the greatest guerilla fighters in history."

Ross nodded. "But what a sad ending. All of the Chiricahua and Mimbres were sent to Florida, then Alabama; most of them died from malaria in the swamplands. The remainder finally joined up with the Indian Nations in Oklahoma. Although he had been an old man during the Apache Wars, Nana lived there until after the turn of the century. He never returned to Apachería and died near Fort Sill, Oklahoma."

Philip stood up. "No wonder Adams was uneasy about returning in the eighteen seventies. He had been caught between an irresistible force and an immovable object, the collision of cultures."

After packing up the remainders of lunch, they rode back along the Chain of Craters. Ross explained how the cones were formed by the accumulation of clinkers, bombs, and lava from the vents. The lava built up until it finally spilled over the side, breaching the wall of the crater to form crescent-shaped hills. The stunted forest of *piñon* and juniper flourished on the north sides of the hills. Stands of *chamisa* and sage grew along the sides of the arroyos, while yellow sunflowers and purple asters crowded the moister areas. Wild flowers bloomed in their glory days following the summer rains. Sarah pointed out the blue Rocky Mountain penstemon, the bright red Indian Paintbrush, and scarlet globemallow. Gray-green stalks of wooly mullein stood sentinel among the dark clinkers.

Sarah wiped her brow and took a drink from her water bottle. "It's funny how memory works. Since talking to you two about Apache history, I've been thinking about what I read in that seminar. One of the books was an oral history told by Nana's grandson. He related how

Nana thought white eyes were obsessed by gold, that they coveted it above things that were more valuable, such as family and community. Nana told him that there were many places in Apachería that contained gold and silver, including a canyon to the west of Ojo Caliente that had nuggets of gold the size of kernels of corn."

Philip and Ross looked at one another. Philip said, "The more I hear, the more likely the story of the Diggings sounds. Clarence's grandmother said that she had heard of Sno-ta-hay from Nana as well. I don't think we're going to find it today, but I'm more certain that Buck did."

When they returned to the truck, Philip pulled Tecates from the cooler. They unsaddled the horses whose backs were damp with sweat. They drank a lot of water. "For this short jaunt, we could just leave them saddled, but they're hot. They were having such a rough time maintaining their balance on the way in. I'd like to make it as easy as possible on them."

They drove back down the muddy road to the Hole in the Wall turnoff. They were back on the plains. Horizons stretched into the distance. When they got to the West Malpais Wilderness boundary, they parked, saddled up, and got back on their horses. They rode over an expanse of rolling country alongside the lava until they crossed the lava flow. A cinder-filled road stretched on until they finally reached the *kipuka*.

"I bet the tourists are really beating a path through that section. How many miles was that to get here?" asked Philip.

Sarah replied, "A little over three, but you're right. I bet it feels really long and boring on foot. Most people don't have the privilege of doing this on horseback. I think it would get visited more often if they had opened it to mountain bikes."

Ross looked around. "Hank was right. It doesn't look like the kind of geography that's going to have dramatic canyons or waterfalls, just lava over prairie. By the way, this prairie covers an ancient lava flow that goes all the way to Fence Lake. This recent lava flow just isn't deep enough for the kind of canyons that Adams described. But it's an interesting phenomenon, and it's good grazing country. I just don't think what we're looking for is going to be here."

"You men are so goal oriented. Can't you guys just enjoy a beautiful ride in a unique environment?"

Philip furrowed his brow. "You do seem to be forgetting that I have a job to do. I think Ross is right; this place doesn't look real likely for the Diggings. Let's take a look at Bob's left foreleg. He seems to be favoring it."

They dismounted and Philip picked up the horse's foot and found a clinker caught under the shoe. He worked it out with his knife.

"There you go, Big Red." They remounted. "Sarah, take our minds off our disappointment. Give us the Park Service lecture on the Hole in the Wall. The name sure had me thinking about the little door."

Sarah turned in the saddle as she rode ahead on *Mija*, "The name got me interested as well, since I grew up near the Utah version of the same, but this Hole in the Wall isn't nearly as exciting. It wasn't a gathering place for outlaws, just shepherds. As Hank was saying, they were mostly Basque. That's a unique subculture. They've kept the language; Spanish is probably Hank's second language. They still use the horse-drawn 'gypsy' caravans for sleeping quarters and chuck wagons."

Philip caught up with her. "The gypsy life sounds romantic."

Sarah smiled at him. "I like to hear you talk about romance, but that's not how it works for the Basques. The women and children live in the small towns, while the men run sheep in some of the wildest country imaginable. The Basques left here years ago, but there are communities of them in the Great Basin and the northern plains. There's not a lot of money in it, but the Basques have always been fiercely independent. Remember, they're still fighting for a separate state from Spain. Neither the Spanish nor the French governments have been able to control them, because the Separatists just disappear into the Pyrenees."

"You would have thought Buck might have had something in common with them."

Ross shouted from behind them. "He probably did, at least as much as he could feel such things. You certainly didn't find him hanging out with the Mormon ranchers. These people were all drawn here by the bleakness of the lava." His eyes took on the haunted look again and he gestured at the kipuka around him. "An emptiness that even God couldn't fill." He pulled out a flask and raised it in a salute. "'Strangers in a strange land.'" He drank deeply; then he reined his horse around.

They returned to the truck and unsaddled the horses, put on halters, and gave them water. They rinsed the salt off their backs and brushed them. The horses seemed eager to get back in the trailer. They drove back to County Road 42. Philip had to concentrate on driving, but he noticed that his companions were quieter than usual. When he got to the end of 42, he turned the hubs back and shifted the truck back into two-wheel drive. As he turned northeast onto the pavement, he asked, "So do you two think it's worth looking at the Little Hole in the Wall area?"

Sarah answered, "Yes, it's the last area that could fit Byerts' description, and it's practically in Buck's backyard. Besides, you could check out the Braided Cave, it's my favorite lava tube."

Philip said, "You're the only person I know with a favorite lava tube."

"There are lots of us, but I'm only an amateur. I've just visited the main structures. There are back-country tubes that have unique features that I haven't even seen yet."

Ross intervened, "Sarah's right. When I was in Boy Scouts, we visited a couple of the others. I agree with you, the Braided Cave is wonderful. I haven't seen it in almost thirty years. Maybe Adams' zigzag canyon was a collapse structure."

Philip agreed. "At least there could be canyons on the west side. How tall was that lava wall that we saw on the way to the Big Tubes?"

Sarah replied, "About a hundred feet. It's certainly more rugged country than this, all right. I can't join you tomorrow, I'm booked all day."

Ross leaned forward. "I could go in the morning. They're used to me calling in sick on Monday mornings. Besides, this is contract work, I just bill for the hours worked. I've got a report I've got to finish tomorrow afternoon, but I'd like to go if you can get me back by around one o'clock."

Philip grinned. "We'll need to get an early start. Let's do it."

13

As they approached La Ventana Arch, Philip watched a dot in the distance materialize into a Harley-Davidson and rider. When he could identify the rider, he exclaimed, "Gruber!"

As the motorcycle roared past, Sarah said, "You were right, Ross. He does look good in a uniform. I especially like how the leather helmet and goggles add to the Brown-Shirt look."

Philip looked in the mirror. "This isn't funny. He's turning around, and I sure can't lose him with this rig."

⁄⁄ ⁄⁄ ⁄⁄

Derek Gruber couldn't believe it. Habib, the ranger collaborator, and the Arab sympathizer were together right in his neighborhood, coming right at him. They obviously didn't get his warning the other night. As he suspected, Habib's response was the result of his military training. One of his Internet buddies had found Habib on a veteran database; it showed him serving with the Marines in Jordan and Lebanon. His friend was a jarhead too. He knew some of the covert-operations desert rats who had served several tours in the Middle East. His buddy would ask them about Habib and get back to him. Derek followed the conspirators north on 117. With that stock trailer at this hour, they were probably going back to the Habib family's ranch. Where had they been with the horses?

Pulling off at La Ventana Arch parking lot, Derek let the hog idle. He was off work for the next three days, so he decided that the time would be dedicated to the Arab conspirators. They were traveling together openly now, but it looked like they were heading home. He would go back home as well and equip himself for serious surveillance and possible intervention. They were obviously searching for something in the backcountry, but he just couldn't get a fix on the purpose of their pursuits. Maybe somebody had stashed something and didn't live long enough to say where it was. Anyway, tomorrow he would follow these traitors and find out what they were up to. The vigilance of the American militia would be made clear to them. No Islamic militants were going try anything in his territory without meeting his wrath. The terrorists in America were just biding their time, waiting for an opportunity. With the Bush Administration distracted by the deteriorating conditions in Iraq and their fumbling attempts to find Bin Laden in the tribal lands on the Afghani-Pakistani border, there were plenty of opportunities for covert operations in this country. *Al Qaida* operatives had gone to Iraq to engage the U.S. in guerilla warfare there, but others had maintained their focus on the Great Satan. In Washington, they were still bickering about the legal status of the detainee camps and Bush's contempt for the Constitution. Meanwhile our borders were like sieves, and terrorists had massacred more innocents in Madrid and London. The fate of this country was in the hands of the citizen soldiers.

ℓℓ ℓℓ ℓℓ

After Gruber stopped tailing them, the mood in the truck lightened considerably. They were still unable to find a connection between Gruber and their investigations. So Sarah suggested that they just focus on the Diggings. She insisted that she and Ross should talk with Fred Russell.

"We could put our heads together for a strategy session, besides I want to meet him anyway."

Ross agreed. "The last time I talked to him about the Diggings was over twenty-five years ago. He's got more first hand knowledge than anyone I that know. Let's go see him."

Philip looked at his watch. "I think there will be enough daylight to be able to get to his place if we hurry. I don't want to try to find my way to Fred's in the dark. We can use the GPS to get back out, so we can stay as late as we want to."

"I'll bet there's some place in Thoreau where we could get take-out Navajo tacos," Ross added.

"Good idea. We'll have to be efficient putting up the horses and tack. When we finish, Sarah, you'll need to take Ross home right away. If we each jump in the shower and get dressed in fifteen minutes, we can do it. I'll pick you up in the 4Runner."

There was indeed a restaurant in Thoreau that made Navajo tacos. The three adventurers were glad that they had also bought chips and salsa to snack on. The smell of the meat, beans, *chile*, and cheese from the Navajo tacos leaked out of the foam clamshells. The aroma was driving them mad with hunger.

The sandstone of the mesas and canyons north of Thoreau glowed carnelian red as the setting sun intensified their hue. After they turned off the pavement onto the road to Fred's place, Philip handed the GPS device to Ross in the back seat.

"Could you give me a hand? Since Sarah has made it clear that she thinks that topos and GPS are guy things, would you set some waypoints for us? You'll probably have to roll down your window to 'see' the satellite."

"We use these in geological exploration all the time. I'd be glad to."

Sarah scanned the canyon that they had entered. "The vegetation looks pretty sparse."

The sunlight disappeared as the canyon fell into dusk. Ross answered, "Except where water flows. Springs, arroyos, collection pools, and places where water channels off slickrock and hits soil all have micro communities. Not only do riparian plants live there, but animals also come to water. It's not just water in liquid form that sustains them. A lot of desert animals can go long periods without actually drinking water, because they absorb the water that's stored in grasses, leaves, fruit, or their prey."

A broad valley opened up where the roads divided. Philip took one that angled over to a wide canyon and followed it until it branched again. Dusk was descending into darkness as they reached Fred's trailer. Philip flashed the lights and honked.

Fred opened the door and shouted, "I ain't had this much company in years.

I knew I hadn't seen the last of you, Philip Habib. Who are your friends?"

Ross held the Navajo tacos steady with his chin, and held out his hand. "Fred, do you remember me? I'm Ross McIntyre. We talked about the Diggings almost thirty years ago."

"Sure do. And who is this lovely lady with the twelve-pack of Coors?"

Philip came around the SUV. "Fred, this is Sarah Johnson. She's an intern at the Malpais Monument. We come bearing supper. Even if you've already eaten, you've got to have one of these Navajo tacos."

"Always a pleasure to eat something I didn't have to cook myself. Come on in, but let me clear off the table first."

They squeezed into the small dining space, and the food tasted as good as it smelled. The fry bread was just the right crispness, and the lettuce and tomatoes were fresh. The beans, beef, and cheese added a hearty flavor, and the salsa was homemade. They chatted and laughed until they finished eating.

Philip asked Fred, "What's this bear trouble Hank was talking about?"

"That turned into Game and Fish trouble. A month ago, this bear decided that I was eating better than he was. So he was going to do something about that. He started going through the garbage and then sniffed at the windows. I guess I'm like the rest of the old timers. The way we used to solve problems seems good enough today. So, I went into town, got a slab of salt pork, shotgun shells and bullets. I put out the salt pork, and pointed the truck at the picnic table it was on. I can't see that good any more, and my aim is shaky, so I opened the driver's door, rolled down the window, and figured to use it to prop the rifle. I got in the cab around dusk and had the shotgun for back up. About an hour later, when it was almost full dark, the bear came into camp. I waited for him to get the salt pork. Then I pulled on the brights. He was the most amazing color I'd ever seen; so light he was silver. He reared up and roared, and I plugged him four times."

Sarah grinned as she grabbed another Coors. "It sounds like you've still got an eye for hunting."

"Damned cataracts are getting worse every day. Anyway, I called Game and Fish then, and they weren't happy. I got off with a warning, but now I know to let those boys handle it their way. Imagine trapping a bear and moving him to another range. Last week I saw a silver bearskin in one of the Gallup Indian trading posts with a hefty price tag on it. I wonder who sold it to them and how much they got for it."

"'To the victor, go the spoils.' Good story, Fred."

Ross said, "That's a great bear story. Philip said that you two talked about the great old prospectors the other day. Didn't Nat Straw have a story about riding a bear?"

Fred laughed. "Now there's one I heard around a campfire a long time ago. Nat Straw wasn't just a prospector, you know. He was a rancher and a hunter too. He would guide hunters who were looking for a grizzly or a cougar. After Teddy Roosevelt came out to the Gila, it got to be pretty popular. I would have never guessed then that they could have hunted the griz into extinction in this part of its range."

Philip asked, "When was that?"

"Late twenties, early thirties, don't recollect exactly when. Can't say I miss them, black bears are bad enough. Anyway, Nat Straw guided a party of hunters to a female grizzly. But it wasn't until after they killed her, that the cub came out of the woods. He was a cutie, cinnamon-colored. He was old enough to wean, but not old enough to really take care of himself."

"Poor baby," Sarah sighed.

"Nat felt sorry for him too, and took him in. After a while the cub looked on Nat as his daddy, and they were best of friends. When the cub got bigger, he could run up mountainsides faster than Nat. So Nat got the idea that he could train the bear to halter. He just rode him bareback. They got along great together. Sometimes he would take the bear on a ride just for the pure pleasure of it, but he also used the bear's instincts to hunt grizzlies."

Fred spat into a tin can. "One day they approached a bear wallow, and there was a big cinnamon griz in it. Nat's bear reared up, and Nat took off the halter. The other bear reared up and they tore into one another. They swatted, bit, and wrestled. They were about the same size and color. While they were fighting, it was just a cinnamon blur with fur flying. Finally, they stood apart from one another. Nat, fearing for his bear's life, jumped on his back and rode out of there. The other bear was close on their heels and roaring up a storm. Nat couldn't control the bear, so he reached for his ears to guide him. He felt a huge tear in the bear's ear that had scarred over. He was riding the wrong bear."

They all laughed. Sarah asked Fred, "Did all the old prospectors have stories like that?"

Fred replied, "Nat was a lot more sociable than most. Yeah, us prospectors see strange things. We have the time to work up the story pretty good by the time we hit town. Most of the time, stories are all we've got. No, most of the old prospectors were more of a solitary sort."

"More like Mike Cooney?"

"Mike Cooney was pretty solitary in his later years, but remember that he was a member of the state legislature when he was younger. You've got to be friendly to get elected."

Sarah persisted. "Isn't he kind of a hero to prospectors? After all, he died with his boots on, going after the gold."

Ross smiled. "If he can only get three miracles credited to him, he'll be the patron saint of prospectors."

Sarah kept up her inquiry. "What are some of the places that you know are possible sites for the Diggings, Fred?"

Fred put in pinch of Copenhagen in his mouth. "Most of the time, Adams started out from Reserve. So the Mogollons, Allegros Mountain, Mangas Mountain, the Sugar Loaf Mountains, the Datils, the Gallinas, the San Mateos, and the Black Range have all been scoured for the Diggings. I'm not the only one who has gone over the Zunis and the western edge of the *malpais* looking for them. The other day Philip and I talked about Shaw and Brewer heading east from Springerville looking for them."

Ross asked, "What about the searches that started out from Socorro. I think Adams started from there a time or two. But the most interesting one I remember was the Sturgeon-Dowling expedition."

"Yeah, Doc Sturgeon treated Adams and Davidson at Fort Whipple after they got picked up by the cavalry."

Sarah jumped up and began to shimmy, singing in a pouty voice, "Like a Sturgeon, just like the very first time."

Philip and Ross howled with laughter. Fred looked very confused.

"I think the lyrics sounded like Weird Al Yankovic," Ross said.

Philip nodded. "But the delivery was pure Madonna. Come on, this is important. I remember skimming through this in Dobie, but the stories started running together."

Ross turned to Philip. "This is what I mean about the human element of the story. Dobie writes about Sturgeon's twenty-year obsession with the Diggings while trying to live a normal life in Ohio. He finally gathered some partners, and they outfitted an expedition with the best camping gear money could buy. However, these greenhorns didn't even survive the stage coach trip to Socorro from Las Vegas, where the railroad stopped back then. So Sturgeon, within miles of his goal, felt a misplaced sense of obligation to the men. He agreed to lead the retreat and return with them."

Ross took a long drink of beer. "He found John Dowling, a mining engineer, who was knowledgeable about central New Mexico. He hired him and outfitted him for the trip to the canyon. Sturgeon had heard a lot about the canyon from Adams and Davidson and so he was able to give quite a description and, most importantly, a map to Dowling. Sturgeon insisted that one of his partners had to accompany Dowling. Dowling brought along a couple of men who had worked for him in past. There was dissension from the beginning. The well-heeled tenderfoot refused to help around camp or care for the horses."

Fred interrupted, "You can't act like that on a prospecting trip."

"That's right. Dowling's men weren't guides who were used to catering to dependent, useless hunters. The Code of the West dictates that everyone pulls his own weight, and everybody helps in camp. The boys refused to accept the selfish, superior attitude of the Easterner. Dowling had to physically restrain his employees from shooting the parasite right there in camp."

Philip was having a hard time concentrating on Ross' story. Sarah had placed her hand on his thigh, and leaned into him. Patchouli wafted into his nostrils. He placed his arm around her and forced himself to focus on Ross.

"Eventually, they came to two haystack mountains, but Dowling didn't tell the others that they were near their goal. In the morning they rode into a canyon that wound into the mountains. Dowling sent his boys up one fork and went up the other with the dude. Dowling saw a grove of stumps and, further up the canyon, the burned-out cabin. The dude was oblivious. At camp that night, tempers flared again. Dowling decided that they had to go back to Socorro the next morning in order to save the dude's life. He would return later to prospect and survey, after he contacted Sturgeon."

Fred barged in. "This is the part that makes me crazy. When you hire on with someone, you ride for the brand. Dowling had an obligation to Sturgeon that he didn't honor. Talk about opportunity slipping through your fingers."

Ross continued. "Thirty years later Dowling decided to search again. He was half blind, so he gave one of his employees the description and the map. The man was gone about ten days. He came back to say he couldn't find anything. Years later, Dowling found out that that the man had gone to friend's ranch and stayed drunk the whole time. In his telling of the story, Dobie emphasizes that breaking faith is part of the human condition. 'You will betray me three times before the cock crows.'"

Ross grabbed his flask and went outside.

Fred shook his head. "Is he always so bleak?"

Sarah came to Ross's defense. "Only some of the time. Other times, he's a perceptive, intelligent man."

A coyote howled from the upper canyon; the plaintive cry echoed off the cliffs. She looked towards the door. "Fred, where do you think the Diggings might be? You've probably spent more time looking for them than any other living prospector."

"I can tell you where they aren't, but I think everyone has to find that out for himself. I was telling Philip that some of the great prospectors spent their whole lives looking for the Adams Diggings. It's an itch that has to be scratched. I thought I'd given up on it until you folks came around. You either do that or die trying."

"Do you think Buck could have found them?"

Fred spat into the can. "I guess the thing that bothers me so much is that he could have. I really hate being beaten by that conniving, self-centered scalawag. From our conversations when we met on the trail, I could tell that he knew something about the legend. He sure spent a lot of time in some of the loneliest country that I've ever seen. He was not only smart enough to find them, but he was also just the kind of guy who would be able to keep it to himself."

They navigated their way back by moonlight and GPS. After they dropped off Ross, Philip and Sarah returned to her apartment. They wasted little time on preliminaries and went into Sarah's bedroom. As Philip was stripping off his clothes, he saw that there was a bottle of white wine and glasses on the dressing table. Sarah lit candles and turned out the light. She handed him the wine bottle and led him to the bed.

She smiled as she lay down. "*Liebfraumilch* is usually served cold, but for our purpose, it's better at room temperature. *Liebfraumilch* means 'dear wife's milk' in German. Since I detected some unmet oral needs yesterday, I suggest that you pour this sweet nectar on my nipples and fulfill yourself."

Philip followed her wishes, but the exquisite experience didn't satisfy him. His tongue was only tantalized. He gave her the bottle and she drank deeply. Then he slowly poured wine into Sarah's navel and lapped it up. Then he trickled some across her delta of Venus and licked his way to satisfaction. Sarah cradled his head in her hands and rocked her hips gently. Her rocking intensified until she arched her back and cried out.

As she lay back against the pillow, she gave him a languid smile and said softly, "What a lover."

Philip returned the smile. "I had a fantasy too."

He pulled her over to the dressing table and turned her to face the mirror. He placed her hands on the dressing table and kissed her. He pressed against her back and thrust himself into her silky wetness. Their eyes met in the mirror as she straightened and began rubbing her breasts. He held her hips to guide their rhythm. The reflection of Sarah's beauty heightened his pleasure, and he came quickly.

She turned and pushed him back onto the bed. "Maybe now it's time to drink this wine from glasses. I do have another bottle chilling in the refrigerator."

14

Philip had some difficulty getting started in the morning. He was more hung over from the intoxication of love making with Sarah the night before than he was from the wine they had drunk. The Turkish coffee gave him a jumpstart.

He picked up Ross in the 4Runner. As they headed toward Highway 53, Ross told him about his phone call to a friend who was a professor of geology.

"I knew that I had read more about Byerts at the School of Mines. So I called an old college friend of mine who teaches there; now it's called New Mexico Tech. He told me that I was right. There's an old newspaper clipping about Byerts in the library that gave more explicit directions to the Diggings. A few years ago, he followed the directions from the article. They led to an area in the Ramah Navajo Reservation. He said that it was more likely than where we're heading today, since there were canyons there. However, he acknowledged that it was all sandstone country; he couldn't imagine finding gold there. He invited me to Socorro for the Festival of the Cranes in November and asked me to let him know how our search turned out."

Philip turned into the drive through in fast food city. "Ross, you've got some good contacts. I appreciate your research, but it sounds like there are just a lot of dead ends out there."

They grabbed bags of breakfasts and rolled south on NM 53.

They unwrapped their greasy fare as they passed through San Rafael. Ross washed a sizeable portion of cholesterol-filled sausage down with cardboard-flavored coffee and turned towards Philip.

"You know, I poked around a little on County Road Forty-two in my youth. It's interesting country; I'm looking forward to this. Byerts wasn't the only searcher who felt strongly about this area. Charles Allen wrote an account of the Diggings that traced the route of the original miners to east of what's now Springerville, Arizona. If they had kept the same northeasterly heading, they would have ended up somewhere around here."

A county sheriff's cruiser passed them on the wide straight stretch of 53 just south of San Rafael. Philip and Ross waved to the deputy who touched the brim of his hat in response.

Ross said, "I sure hope the deputies find Gruber and have a chat with him. Now back to the story, both Allen and Byerts had prospected with Captain Shaw, Adams' primary apostle. They wrote Adams' story as it had been told to them by Shaw, but Allen had another source. He heard a different version from a man who had known Jack Davidson, Adams' companion in the escape from the Apaches."

"This is the guy that Sturgeon had treated, right?"

"The same one. This old soldier talked to Davidson when they were at Fort Whipple. The two versions are close, and they both point east by northeast of Springerville. Remember, Shaw made several searches east of Springerville."

"Let me get this straight. Neither you nor your friend at the School of Mines and Technology thinks that this area is likely geologically, but we're going to look because everybody else did."

Ross took another sip of coffee. "When have you let a fool's errand discourage you before? You know what's always bothered me about this whole area for the site of the Diggings?"

"If it's going to make today's treasure hunt seem less likely, I don't know if I want to hear it."

"When Adams himself was searching, why did he start the search so far away from here? His primary base of operations was out of Reserve, and he started from Socorro a couple of times. Both are a long ways south of here. However, as Sarah said, this area is practically in Buck's back yard, so I guess we should check it out. Speaking of Buck's backyard, aren't we close?

"Just a few minutes away. Well, regardless of the outcome, it's a gorgeous morning. I enjoyed hiking in the lava with Sarah a couple of days ago."

"Sarah gave me a copy of that Internet history, so I read it last night. There have been some new researchers, and they've come up with some new ideas. Didn't you pick up Dick French's book? From the way it sounded in this article, I'd sure like to read it."

Philip answered. "I've got it in my bag; you can borrow it tonight. He's got a lot of information from a variety of original sources, as well as first-hand prospecting experience. I just skimmed it and looked at the maps and photos. And he would agree with you; it looked like he was pointing south and east of here. I also bought Feldman and McPherson's book, which looks like it will be fun to read. I gave it to Sarah last night. They place it in Arizona, which doesn't quite match up with the number of days the miners were supposed to have been on the road. I think that Arizona would be out of Buck's territory. ¿Quién sabe?"

Ross thought for a moment. "Buck is the wild card here all right. We can logically search west-central New Mexico according to the legend. But the topos, GPS, or even a fly-over won't give us the kind of information that Buck would have had. To hear Hank tell it, Buck was always vigilant. He absorbed details from every bit of ground he covered, and he covered a lot of ground. It would help if we could get a better feel of what his territory really was. We know that he knew the malpais like the back of his hand, but how far south did he go?"

"Hank said that Buck used to be part of the cattle drives down that corridor from the western part of the state across the Plains of San

Agustín to Magdalena, so he probably knew that part of the country well. If he was like most drovers, he washed down the dust of the cattle drive at the railhead. I bet he hung out in the saloons in Magdalena."

Philip pointed to a gate that was partially shaded by ponderosas in the park-like grasslands. "And here we are; Buck's ranch is down that road."

"Magdalena was pretty wild in those days, and I bet Buck fit right in. There's quite a contrast in character. Here he's the isolated rancher, and whenever he's in town he's a party animal. Magdalena was not only full of cowboys and shepherds; there were miners from Kelly as well. In fact, there's a story about Adams almost getting his throat slit in Magdalena. Remember, I was telling you about how I liked to read Howard Bryan's column in the *Albuquerque Tribune*. Many years ago, he interviewed Bob Lewis, who used to be Magdalena's Town Marshall and was quite a character in his own right. Lewis told him that he had once saved Adams from getting knifed after he was caught telling a lie in a bar in Magdalena. Lewis put Adams safely on the train to Socorro. In gratitude, Adams told him to look for the bodies of the supply party that were stashed in a deep crack in the sandstone. Adams said that the Diggings were within a few miles of the massacre, but that he would need Adams' help to find it from there."

Philip shifted the SUV into a lower gear as the road climbed. "Did Lewis ever find them?"

"Years later, after Adams died. At least he found some skeletons stuffed in a crack in the rocks, and the clothing remnants were from about the right era. That was in the Datils. But after an extensive search in a ten mile radius, he didn't find any gold."

"It sure sounds like that area is worth looking into."

"I'd like to go with you again tomorrow, *con su permiso*. That is, if we don't find the richest gold mine in New Mexico this morning."

"Well, we better start paying attention to that. Here's Forty-two."

Ross craned his neck around to get a better view of Cerro Bandera.

"I'd forgotten how big it is. See how the south side of the crater wall has been breached. Look at the difference in both the quantity and quality of the lava compared to the southern cones. This aa-aa field is incredible, flooring from hell."

"This road could become driving from hell in the mud. It's bad enough with these truck-eating puddles. I'm going to go via the Big Tubes since at least part of that road has been graveled. I want to look at that lava wall again."

After a few miles, Philip said, "I've had a weird feeling ever since we went by Buck's place. I feel like we're being followed, but I haven't seen anyone."

"Maybe we picked up Buck's ghost. It's probably what the Navajos call a *chindi*, the evil that persists after death."

Philip drove on in silence, but he kept an eye on the rear-view mirror. They turned off 42 at Cerro Rendija, and then pulled off the road at the highest point of the lava wall. The lava cliff was steep, rough, and intimidating.

Philip walked towards the wall. "We're approaching this from the south the way Byerts said we should. Now, I bet this could have a zigzag canyon in it."

Ross followed, shaking his head. "With trees and a waterfall and an approach that horses can walk through? Maybe, but unlikely. The important issue is what's under it. Look at what you're standing on." He kicked a hole through the dirt, stirring up dust. "This is just older lava. I bet it's from Cerro Rendija over there. There are layers upon layers of lava from different time periods. This wall is a relatively fresh one. But what's under the lava? Most of the places we've seen on the east and south sides have had that light-colored sandstone poking through. Sedimentary rock, that's not consistent with gold. However, this far northwest, there might be igneous rock under it, the same stuff that's found in the Zunis.

He was interrupted by the trill of a meadowlark. They looked across the grass and wildflowers trying to spot it. A large raven was gliding on the thermal updrafts until it disappeared high over the lava.

Ross continued. "Didn't you say that Fred had a claim with gold and silver ore on it near Mt. Sedgwick?"

"Yes, that's maybe fourteen or fifteen miles from us now."

"We're at least in the realm of geological possibility around here. It would have to be under these layers of lava or exist as a protrusion above it. I really think that Adams would have remembered trying to take horses through a lava field."

Philip asked, "Who knows what he remembered. How far away are we from San Rafael? I don't think it would have been a four-day ride to Old Fort Wingate from here, at the very most two."

They got back in the SUV and drove through the Big Tubes parking lot past a small sign to the Braided Cave. The road deteriorated precipitously. It was a two-track with lava obstacles. They bounced along unremittingly until the road divided. They took the east fork into the Little Hole in the Wall.

Philip grimaced as he heard the scrape of the 4Runner's skid plate striking a lava ledge. "I'll bet this area doesn't get a lot of tourist traffic."

Ross braced himself on the dash. "Probably not, but it's a checkerboard area. There's some private ranch land back here that does get regular traffic. Can you imagine owning the Lost Adams Diggings and not knowing it?"

Philip glanced at the *Malpais* map. "I think that would only be possible on a really big spread. Aren't these just alternating sections?"

"You're right. From what I see, I don't think we're likely to find it here, public or private."

They drove to a trailhead shown on the topographic maps. As they got out of the SUV, Philip thought he heard the sound of a truck lumbering in low gears off in the distance.

He asked Ross, "Did you hear that?"

"What?"

"It sounded like a truck in low range. I've still got that feeling. Let's keep a look out."

They went a short ways down the trail where ponderosa pines dominated the sparse vegetation. In the low spots, aspen were beginning to turn yellow and three-leaf sumac bushes were transforming into bright scarlet.

Ross said, "That looks like the burning bush; maybe the voice of God will give us some answers. Have you got one of your maps handy?"

Philip pulled out the close up of the Ice Cave quadrangle and handed it to him.

Ross studied it. "If there are trails, there must have been some reason to cross the lava. In fact, it looks like this trail goes to the Hole in the Wall. This must be how Buck got to the *kipuka*. Look, there's a feature named Mesita Blanca. I'll bet that's an outcropping of the white sandstone, so there may be sandstone underlying the lava here too. This area doesn't look anything like the country described in the legend, only lava upon lava, and lots of it."

Philip concurred. "Another dead end. Let's go to the Braided Cave. If we're going to go through these lava fields, let's have a destination that isn't just more of the same. You and Sarah piqued my curiosity about that cave. You made them sound like something out of Mark Twain."

They got back into the 4Runner and bounced back up to the fork and turned south. The road became almost invisible, only a hint of a two-track guided them. Finally, a wide space marked where the road gave out. They parked and walked over to the mailbox at the trailhead. Philip looked at the log.

Ross asked, "When were the last visitors here?"

"It looks like three days ago. There are maybe three or four parties a week on average. I'll sign us in. Let's grab our packs and hit the trail. Have you got gloves, flashlights, and water?"

"Remember, the last time I was here was with the Boy Scouts. I am prepared."

Philip felt a little less confident about Ross' memory after thirty years than he had about Sarah's. He got out the GPS and set a waypoint at the trailhead and took a bearing down the trail. They appeared to be heading southeast.

Ross observed, "You know, that's a lot better than a compass around here. The iron content of the basalt can be so high that it will throw off a magnetic reading."

Philip felt the same way that he had on the other trails in the lava. The sharp black rock lent an ominous oppressive mind set. Although there were differences in the terrain, there was also a sameness that made it difficult to remember landmarks. They followed the cairns, and Philip entered waypoints when they changed direction. The cairns seemed to be at the very limit of visibility. It sometimes took them a minute of searching to spot the next one. The rough lava held no imprint of a human foot; to call it a trail was a stretch. Philip and Ross sometimes each found their own way to the next cairn because there was no obvious path. Philip found himself drawing upon the yogic training in mindfulness that he had received from the Sikhs. Each step had to be conscious to avoid turning an ankle. The overall direction of the trail had to be remembered in order to find the next marker. They didn't talk. At last the ponderosa cleared, and a collapse structure appeared before them. The basalt cliffs descended to the rubble from the fallen roof of what had been a lava tube.

Ross was excited. "I remember that we didn't enter the first one. See, there are a series of pits and bridges."

They walked to the fourth opening, but had to backtrack to the third because there was no way down. Scrambling down the tumbled blocks of basalt, they arrived at the floor. The bridge loomed over them as they worked their way through the rock piles to the entrance of the tube.

Ross looked at the entrance. "I think we went in the right channel and stayed right on the way in. It branches a lot."

The openings were smaller than the Big Tubes, but they still were substantial. There was a lot of breakdown at the entrance, so they continued to scramble. By the time they needed their flashlights, the floor was relatively easy going. The cavern branched occasionally with smaller passages to the left. They played their flashlights down the tubes, but couldn't see the ends. As they continued on the main right branch, the passageway became smaller. Philip noticed that Ross was slowing down and his movements were erratic.

"What's up, old man?"

Ross' voice was breathy, and his speech was halting. "I've got a bad feeling. I haven't been in here since Vietnam. Even though this is a lot bigger, it reminds me of the Viet Cong tunnels. After Charley had been cleared out, they would send us engineers in to study the workings of the tunnels. Sometimes there were still VC in them in secret passages. I didn't like that, and I don't like this now."

Philip noticed that Ross was sweating. He couldn't tell if his color was pale or if it was the effect of the flashlights. "Let's take a break. How about some water?"

Philip took off his pack and set it on a basalt outcrop. In the soft glow of the lantern, he watched Ross carefully as they passed a water bottle back and forth. Sweat was forming faster than Ross could mop it up, and he shivered occasionally. Philip decided that they needed to leave quickly. He stood up and threw his head back to take a last pull from the water bottle.

"Watch out!" Ross shouted.

Philip ducked and pivoted, but he didn't see anything behind him.

Ross' laugh was high-pitched as he apologized. "I'm sorry. I didn't mean to scare you, but you were about to step back into that area that's marked off by yellow tape."

Philip saw the line of dirty tape on the floor of the tube and remembered the warnings not to disturb the bighorn sheep remains in the cave. Philip shook his head. "Maybe we've had enough caving already. We're both on edge, and we've got to get you back to work. Why don't we turn around?"

"Thank you. I'd like to get out of here as soon as possible."

Following Ross out, Philip noticed that his friend's light wasn't steady. He realized that his friend was having Post Traumatic Stress Disorder symptoms, and he felt badly that he had brought him to this dark cavern. He knew that Ross had asked to come, but he still felt responsible. Ross had hoped to recapture his boyhood, but fear had found him instead. As they approached the light at the entrance, Philip felt his own mood brighten. They clambered over the breakdown and made their way under the bridge. They had to use their hands and feet to climb out of the collapse pit.

Just as Ross reached the top, the world exploded. Automatic-weapon fire raked the ponderosas above them, sending a cloud of needles and branches raining down on them as they clawed their way to cover. Philip pulled his Sig-Sauer 9 mm. out of his pack. He saw Ross grab an Army Colt 45.

Philip swore. "It must be Gruber. What the hell does he want?"

Ross looked over a basalt boulder. "I don't know, but we're completely exposed here. If he goes to the north side of the pit, he can pick us off at his leisure."

Philip moved his head to try to spot movement. "So do you want to head back into the cave?"

"Hell no. I was scared in there before someone started shooting at us. Besides, we'd be trapped. Nobody is likely to come here for a couple of days, and we'd be out of light and water. No, we need to increase our options, not limit them."

"I defer to your combat experience, Lieutenant. What do you want to do?"

"If you could draw his attention, I could make my way across the bridge and over to the other side. Then we can each work our way forward and cover both sides of the pit."

Philip found a rock that provided protection near the rim. He tied a handkerchief to a stick and waved it, shouting, "Gruber! This is Philip Habib."

Ross made his way to the top several yards behind Philip.

"Whatever it is that you want, I'm sure we can work something out."

Ross rolled onto the surface and hid behind a ponderosa.

"I don't know what we've done to upset you. But if we talk about it, maybe we could make it right."

Out of the corner of his eye, Philip saw Ross run in a crouching zigzag across the bridge behind him to a ponderosa on the other side.

Philip crawled out of the pit and found cover behind a lava pressure ridge. The only sound was the wind whistling through the pine needles. He searched the area for movement. Seeing none, he motioned to Ross. They crept forward on each side of the collapse structure, resting behind trees and lava outcrops. On the far side of the next pit, Philip found some 9 mm. shell casings. He used a twig to pick up a couple of shells and dropped them into an outside pocket in his pack. They continued their sweep, cautiously keeping near cover when possible.

*⁄⁰ *⁄⁰ *⁄⁰

Derek Gruber laughed to himself as he headed up the trail. The traitors couldn't ignore the warning this time. He really got a kick out of their white flag. Habib sounded just like the anger-management counselors in the service. On one of his covert operations, he was reprimanded for the use of excessive force and ordered to go to an anger management class. He just didn't understand it. First, they trained you to give no quarter in hand-to-hand combat. Then they expected you to solve your problems like pansies. "You have to talk out your anger." They didn't understand that anger was a weapon in combat; it strengthened your determination

Just wait till the terrorist conspirators found the surprise in store for them. He'd see how well these renegades could negotiate actual combat conditions. Jogging through the woods, Derek wondered what Habib and McIntyre were doing in the Braided Cave. And why did they go to the Little Hole in the Wall? As he moved through the trees, he had seen McIntyre moving cautiously across the basalt bridge, as well as their two-pronged pursuit. They both had pulled semi-automatic pistols and carried them like they knew what they were doing. What were these combat-trained Arabic speakers looking for in the *malpais*? He had learned that McIntyre had done a tour as an army lieutenant in Vietnam. They had both volunteered to serve their country. What had caused them to go over to the other side?

ll ll ll

When Philip and Ross got to the trail head, they breathed a sigh of relief.

Ross stared back towards the cave. "Jesus! What do you think that ambush was about?"

"No idea, but it pisses me off. I've been asking myself the same thing since the other night. Sarah has never met Gruber before, so it must have something to do with our investigation. Since he didn't really engage us, just scared the crap out of us, this must have been another warning. But what could the warning be about? Stay away from what?"

"Maybe the Adams Diggings, maybe Buck."

Philip was perplexed. "Why?"

"I don't know. You've made no secret of your inquiries about Buck and the Adams Diggings, so he might have some reason to react to that. But I think the anti-Arab hate crime angle might be worth looking into."

"There was the Arabic road rage, and he's involved with the Aryan Brotherhood. Those nine millimeter casings could've come from an Israeli military Uzi for whatever that's worth. I agree that racism sounds more likely than the Diggings. Why is he following us out here? He's already got us so spooked that we both brought pistols."

"I'm glad we did."

"We better be careful on the way out. This trail is the perfect place for another ambush."

Ross scanned carefully around them. "What trail? I don't see a cairn."

Philip felt panic rising. Ross was right. There wasn't a cairn in sight. Gruber must have knocked them down. Philip had to consciously deepen his breathing. He knew that using the GPS would get them back eventually, but he felt very vulnerable. Who was this guy, and why was he harassing them anyway? He got out the GPS device and showed it to Ross.

"We'll get out of here, but it will take a little longer. You're going to be late for work."

"To hell with work. This is the most excitement I've had in years. You didn't make any enemies when you were a spook in the Middle East, did you? I keep thinking there's got to be a reason for this."

Philip tried to recall any possibilities. "I don't think anyone penetrated my cover. I did have a confrontation with a dean at the American University of Beirut, but he must have really pissed off someone else. One of the students shot and killed him a couple of years later."

Ross smirked. "Ah yes, the tranquility of the academic community. Keep your eyes open for booby traps. There could be trip wires for Claymores or some of the newer land mines. These days, we're the only country that still makes them. The rest of the civilized world thinks they're barbaric."

They made their way back slowly, following the waypoints on the GPS device. It was hard walking. The device didn't have pinpoint accuracy, so they found themselves in rougher country than they had been on with the trail. About half way back, they heard a shot.

Ross looked over at Philip. "Small arms fire. Probably at the parking lot."

The sound of a truck revving up and taking off reverberated over the empty landscape. Philip was having a lot more difficulty maintaining his mindfulness in the rough rock than he had on the way in. He kept trying to fit Ross's ideas with Gruber. He didn't see the connection with Buck. Buck had died years before Gruber moved here. The Adams Diggings? It's possible, Philip thought, a lot of other people had been hooked over the years. Was Gruber protecting what he found? What about the Middle Eastern connection? Ross's biker connections confirmed that Gruber was a Gulf War veteran and that he loved to talk about his Special Forces experience. What did that have to do with them? Philip's stint in the Arab world had been many years before Desert Storm. As he had told the feds, he hadn't heard from his Palestinian radical contacts in decades. Most of them had settled down. Now his best friends in the Persian Gulf had a Land Rover dealership in Bahrain. If there was a connection to Beirut, he couldn't see it.

Suddenly the cairns appeared again and they made their way back to the trailhead. He could see that the 4Runner was listing to port. The back tire had been shot out.

Ross was pensive. "Shooting out only one tire makes it another warning. Of course, he wanted to keep us from following him. But we'd be walking if he'd shot out more. He wants to keep us in the game. I sure hope your spare is good."

"It is, if he didn't tamper with it. These tracks sure look like they could be from big off-road tires from a Power Wagon. Let's take some pictures and change this tire."

After Philip dropped Ross off at his house, he drove over to the sheriff's office. He tracked down Don Abeyta in his cubicle and told him about the morning's events.

Don shook his head. "You never saw him, and Ross didn't catch a glimpse of him either? I can understand why you think that Gruber's pattern of behavior makes him the likely culprit."

"And we have some physical evidence that might be useful. I picked up these shell casings; they might have prints. I left the others in place in case you want to check out the scene." He showed Don the screen on his digital camera. "Look at these tracks; they could link him to the scene."

"Let's download that to my computer and print it. Let me track down a USB cable."

There were a couple of deputies working the phones. Another looked like he had a deteriorating relationship with his computer.

Don returned with the cable. "We can't run ballistics on your tire shootings. But since he shot at you too, we'll check the shells for prints. I'll call the security company that he works for and see if he's been at work today. I'll also get his physical address from them. We know that he lives near Pie Town. Then, I'll call our friends at the sheriff's department in Catron County and ask them to talk to him. Our deputies will be on the lookout for Gruber to stop him for questioning."

Don's phone rang. He told the caller that he would meet with them in a few minutes. "The joint is jumping. I'll call the monument too, to tell them about the missing cairns. You might be able to get them interested in the destruction of federal property. But I've got to warn you, this happens now and then. Apparently, there's a group of eco-terrorists who take down the cairns. They think they can cut down tourist visits and better preserve the land that way."

Philip raised his voice. "Are they the kind of terrorists that use automatic weapons? Don, this wasn't a random event."

"OK, Philip. You've got it on record, and we've got a plan. It's hard for us to get really aggressive on this when the worst offense that you've actually witnessed him doing is kicking your truck. You could file a restraining order."

"I'll do that if it continues."

"I'm sorry that I can't do anything more. Have you heard that Mary is having everyone over for dinner tonight? It's Melissa's birthday, you know, and the family expects your presence. Not that I'd think you'd miss a chance at my mother-in-law's cooking."

"You're right. I can't let this guy dominate my life. I'll be there. *Hasta la vista*. Thanks, Don."

␣␣␣

Derek Gruber grinned as he passed through security at the Grant's women's prison. He had locked anything that they would consider contraband in the toolbox of the Dodge. He was excited about the prospect of seeing Gloria. He couldn't wait to tell her what he had found out about Habib. She had sounded interested in the operation during their phone conversations, but she was skeptical about whether the conspirators really had terrorist connections. After the cell phone message he had just picked up, there was no doubt.

He sat at the table in the visitor's room and waited for her. There seemed to be more visitors who were parents and children than there were husbands or boyfriends. He stood when Gloria approached. He loved to watch her walk. She held her head high, and moved with feline grace. Her well defined muscles demonstrated the amount of time she spent working out. Her short red hair emphasized the beauty of her face, and her smile reached her green eyes. He liked the way that she looked at him, lingering on his muscular body. He loved feeling her body against him during the brief embrace that the guards allowed.

He couldn't believe his good fortune in finding her. Her brother was a Harley mechanic that he had met through the Aryan Brotherhood. Gloria's incarceration as an accessory to drug manufacturing had opened her eyes to the power of the government, especially to Fourth Amendment violations. When her boyfriend had ratted on her, the narcs had no other evidence of Gloria's involvement. That didn't stop them from getting a search warrant and finding a boatload of meth. Even though she had a hard time trusting men now, Derek's views on illegal search and seizure had been the beginning of a relationship based on a common mistrust of the government. Although she didn't completely embrace her brother's political views, prison life had taught her that there were only a few people who would watch your back.

They sat down at the table. She leaned forward and smiled as she watched Derek's hungry eyes go to her cleavage. "How's my counter-espionage expert?"

"I had an exciting day, and I've got news on the terrorist front."

Her eyes sparkled. "Have you found Osama Bin Laden?"

Derek leaned closer so that they could speak softly. "Not quite yet, but I've got proof that Habib is a traitor. I got a message that Habib was a spook in Beirut. My guy said that the rumor was that he had gone over to the other side. They say that his involvement in Al Fatah, the militant branch of the Palestine Liberation Organization, went way beyond intelligence gathering. He's going to email me the details."

Gloria beamed at him. "You sure can sniff out a rat, Derek. What are you going to do about it?"

"I've already started. I gave them a strong warning today. I followed them to the *malpais* and watched them go into the Braided Cave. When they climbed out, they had a surprise. I shot down the ponderosa branches over their heads and watched them scurry for cover. Habib started waving a white flag and giving me this 'let's resolve our conflict' bullshit."

"What did you do next?"

"This is the best part. I didn't let them see me and left on the trail to the parking lot. I knocked down all the trail markers, so they had to find their own way back across the lava."

More visitors entered the room and the noise level grew. Gloria nodded approval. "Clever. That lava freaks me out. So, big bully, do you think that they'll find their way out?"

"Probably, they're both military trained. But I also slowed them down by shooting out a tire."

"Quite a day, my master of threats. Do you think they knew that it was you? Did you tell them you were on to them?"

Derek started rubbing his forehead. "Habib called my name when he was trying to get me to talk to him. He must have taken down my license-plate number when I confronted him the other night. You're right. I got so caught up in the clandestine operations that I missed the opportunity to tell him that I knew they were traitors. I blew it. Obviously, I need a woman to help me communicate."

Derek looked around the medium-security visiting room. The children had a hard time dealing with their separation from their mothers. Some were clingy, some were withdrawn, and others acted out their anger. Gloria's brother's friends teased Derek about his romance with Gloria. They made these cracks about what good is a woman when you're not getting any. The idiots didn't understand that she was the sounding board that he needed. He recognized that he could be shortsighted in his obsessions, and she gently guided him to more strategic approaches. No woman had ever listened to his plans the way that she did. Those bozos were just jealous because she was so buff. What a body! Although she was strong, she had curves in all the right places. He had no problem waiting for her.

The other security guards and corrections officers that he played pool with teased him too. They joked about jailhouse romances, how it was usually a woman's game. The lonely hearts were attracted by the brutish violence, but were kept safe from having to deal with it up close and personal by the cell bars. The correction officers also teased him about Gloria's tough reputation in the joint. They said that he must be looking for a dominatrix. The image of her in leather with a riding crop did excite him, but there was no way that he would ever allow himself to be completely dominated by anyone.

She told him stories about the petty conflicts of daily life in the prison. Then they talked about the future when she would be free, and they would be together. Derek whispered to her, telling her how beautiful she was, and what he wanted to do to her tempting body. Gloria delightedly told him in a soft voice how she was going to make passionate love to him. They looked into one another's eyes with powerful desire and relished the sense of arousal in their bodies.

Before he left, Derek told her about his plans to follow the traitors tomorrow. He promised her that they would have crystal-clear knowledge of why he was going to prevent the success of their sinister schemes. Their quick embrace and kisses on the cheeks only intensified their unfulfilled lust.

15

After Philip replaced his tire, he picked up a birthday card for Melissa that would appeal to a youngster's sense of humor. Then he drove back to George's law office.

George greeted him. "The knight errant returns. Does this job make you feel like you're tilting at windmills?"

"The windmills have started tilting back." Philip sat down in the client chair across from George's desk and told him about the incident at Braided Cave.

George scowled and tapped his pencil hard against a legal pad. "Don's right. You don't have much for him to work with, but this investigation is out of control. I certainly had no idea that this job would put you in harm's way. Marlene called this morning and set up an appointment for four o'clock. I think we should summarize what you've got and then call the whole thing off. You've developed some interesting ideas, but it's not like you're following any hot leads."

Philip launched himself out of the chair and started pacing. "Gruber might be the hot lead. If this search has him so stirred up, he must have something to hide. At this point, Ross and I think that the most likely remaining place for the Diggings might be somewhere near the Datils. Gruber lives outside of Pie Town, not far from the Datils. There could be a connection."

George threw up his hands. "So you want to go to this guy's

backyard after he's shot at you twice. You're nuts! And you're going to endanger that lost friend of yours as well. *Dios mio*, you really are acting like Don Quixote and Sancho Panza. You're both crazy."

"It's not finished. I'm not going to let this survivalist creep control my life. I said I would investigate this, and there's one more place I've got to look. I'm hoping that the county mounties will talk to Gruber and find out what's going on. That will also put him on alert that the law is watching him. I'm not planning to confront him myself. As for Ross, he's the one who's pushing to go down to the Datils. He's excited by all this. Besides, he's not drinking as much since he joined in."

"He doesn't have to. He's found a new way to kill himself. Is your will up to date? We drew that up a while back, but it's not like you've added any dependents. I think both of you are totally self-destructive. Maybe it's the gold that's done this to you. Remember what happened to Bogart in *The Treasure of the Sierra Madre*. It brings out the worst in people."

Philip decided to retreat. "I'm going to get my laptop out of the 4Runner. I'll write up this morning's report and we'll present it to Marlene. Let's see what she wants to do."

George stared at him in disbelief. "You really have gone round the bend. You've insulted her so much by rejecting her that she wishes that you were dead. And now you're going to let her make the decision whether or not to proceed against a madman with an assault rifle. This is going to be like a *bon voyage* party for the Titanic."

At four o'clock, Marlene entered the office togged out in Santa Fe chic. She wore the gambler's hat again and black riding boots. Her burgundy silk blouse and long skirt were accented by a shimmering silver concho belt. A black embroidered bolero jacket topped off the outfit. She asked haughtily, "So do you two have anything to show for your efforts."

George took up the challenge. "In the last five days, we've made considerable progress. You were right that Buck could not have supported himself in his inimitable style from the proceeds from the ranch and acting as a guide. It's become clear that your grandfather made periodic trips to Mexico and returned with money. The apparent origin of that money was gold. Philip has uncovered two possible sources, but the A and P robbery seems unlikely for ongoing revenue. Mr. McIntyre, our consulting geologist, has suggested that Buck's pattern of behavior is consistent with placer mining. There is a persistent legend of such a lost gold mine in this area. Philip has investigated this through scholastic research and field exploration. He and Mr. McIntyre have eliminated some of the possible sites through examination of the topography and geological analysis. During their search of a geologically promising area this morning, they encountered armed resistance. Philip believes that the perpetrator is connected somehow to either Buck or the gold."

Marlene batted her eyes. "How exciting. Let me guess, he got away."

Philip had been watching this exchange suspiciously, but he couldn't restrain himself. "Yes, he shot out my tire and escaped. We don't know why he was shooting at us, but it may be related to the investigation. There is one more area that Mr. McIntyre and I would like to explore."

Marlene gave him a cold stare. "So you want to continue to spend my money chasing legends."

George interrupted. "That's an important point. Mr. Habib has not received any money from you. He presented you with a bill yesterday and has incurred two more days' expenses since then. Do you have any problems with what Philip has submitted thus far? If not, I would ask you to pay this invoice now."

Marlene retorted, "I don't feel that I'm getting my money's worth."

George asked Philip, "Has Mr. McIntyre asked you for a consulting fee?"

"No, he's been doing this as a personal favor."

George turned back to Marlene. "Do you have any idea what it costs to hire an experienced geologist with local knowledge to do this kind of field research? Philip's contacts have opened doors that would have cost you many times more if you had to pay for their services. Philip, do you have your reports and expenses for the last two days? Good, we'll be happy to wait for you to write his check for the full amount before we proceed."

Marlene slammed her purse down on the desk, and angrily retrieved her checkbook and pen. She threw the check at Philip. "I'll give you one more day to find something. And it better be more than just chasing ghosts."

She got up and stormed out of the office. Philip and George breathed more easily.

George looked at Philip. "Well, you got what you wanted. I just hope that psycho doesn't put holes through the two of you tomorrow."

Philip put his arm around George's shoulder. "Thanks for your concern, *ibn 'amma. Shukraniktir* for the way you handled Marlene. That was a very impressive summary. I especially liked the way that you convinced her that she was getting a real deal here. I didn't think I was ever going to get paid after yesterday."

"Years of experience, *ibn khaal*. I still don't think you should go tomorrow. Don't forget, Mom has invited you over for the condemned man's last meal tonight. Can you bring *Sitti* with you tonight? She doesn't drive after dark. Don't worry about your date; I'll take *Sitti* home. We'll look for you around six thirty."

/h /h /h

His breath was coming hard, but he'd run a good distance. Derek could feel the muscles of his legs burn as he slowly jogged up the last rise on his way home. Shadows were lengthening in the canyons and the bluffs picked up the red of the setting sun. As he crested the hill, he immediately saw that something was wrong. Someone was at his trailer. He crouched behind a sandstone boulder and got the binoculars out of his pack. The hair on the back of his neck rose as his stomach fell. There was a Catron County Sheriff's cruiser and a uniformed deputy. The cop knocked on the door of the trailer, and walked around the house trying to see through the reflective covering on the windows. He went over to the Power Wagon and shielded his eyes from the glare on the windows and looked inside. Gruber knew there was nothing to see; he always kept anything incriminating out of sight. Next the deputy took out a camera and took a picture of his tire tread. He went over to the oversized shed where Derek kept his Harley. The wire-embedded windows were frosted so nothing on the inside could be made out. He tried the lock, but Gruber knew that the padlock was as strong as they come. The deputy ambled back to the front door. He took something out of his wallet, wrote on it, and stuck it in the doorframe. Finally, he looked around the barren yard and climbed back in his unit. The cruiser turned up the road and headed back to the highway.

Derek waited until the car was completely out of sight before putting the binoculars back in the pack. He walked cautiously down the slope to the house. He found the deputy's card and turned it over. "Please call" was written on the back. He laughed. If they wanted him, they were going to have to find him.

So the conspirators had gone to the police. He wondered what kind of a spin they had put on their story. Probably poor innocent tourists assaulted by a backwoods gun nut. He knew that he couldn't trust the local yokels. They couldn't find a conspiracy if it walked into their front room. He remembered how the Saudi and Kuwaiti rag heads had manipulated the American leaders with exquisite parties and lavish gifts. These people knew how to use their money to get what they wanted. Besides, he had heard rumors that Habib had a cousin who was a sergeant in the sheriff's office. Family counted for a lot around here; he wouldn't get a fair shake from any of these cops.

He wondered how much Osama Bin Laden would be willing to pay for enough uranium to build a bomb. He could have bought the centrifuges that were necessary for bomb making from that rogue Pakistani nuclear scientist. The real question is how much nuclear material would *Al Qaida* need to make a dirty bomb? That would be far easier to assemble. That's what they would use next time so that more people would be affected by the spread of the radiation, and the survivors' medical problems would go on for years. Last time they had attacked the symbols of America's economic and military power. Now, the use of radiation would underscore the fact that the United States is the only country that has deployed nuclear weapons against civilians. He renewed his vow to keep that from happening.

He put his pack in the front closet, grabbed a Coke, and went into his gunroom. He had converted the smaller bedroom into space for his arsenal. He had lined the closet with steel, put in a false floor, and hung a safe door on it. His dad had given him a small inheritance when he died, so Derek had decided to use it for weaponry and surveillance equipment. He dialed the combination, opened the heavy door, and looked upon his beauties.

He pulled out the Kimber Gold Combat .45 ACP and racked the slide. He loved the feel of this gun and the sound of the action. There were dozens of manufacturers who made semi-automatic forty-fives that were based on the Colt 1911 frame. There were also legions of gunsmiths who would customize something for you. The Kimber production process was a precision high-tech manufacturing operation, uniquely twenty-first century. The design team had used a CAD/CAM system that interfaced with computerized numerically controlled machines to produce pistols with tolerances of less than one ten-thousandth of an inch. Why would anyone buy something made in a pre-WWII European factory with ancient machines when this was the alternative? American technology again proved that we were the ultimate weapon-makers on the planet. He had lightened the trigger pull, but otherwise he was quite pleased with the production model. The blue steel gave it the look of a tactical weapon, but the rosewood grips made it a thing of beauty.

Tomorrow he would bring the sniper rifle. He looked forward to the opportunity to try out his new Heckler and Koch SL8-1 under combat conditions. He liked the commando of the future look of the carbon-reinforced polymer frame. It sure wasn't styled like your daddy's deer rifle. He had added a custom scope and a laser dot sighting system. The H & K certainly lived up to the company's reputation. Its accuracy was helping him shoot tighter clusters at greater distances. He hefted it. The SL8-1 was certainly lighter than military issue rifles that he had used. Stepping into the hallway, he looked down the scope into the living room, and imagined the deputy breaking down the front door. He could understand the Washington D.C. area snipers' desire to shoot human targets. He had never lost the taste for it either, but why waste your life on a random shooting spree? Military marksmanship training had the goal of protecting the nation's security, and the skills acquired there should really be used for that purpose.

Gruber chuckled when he remembered shooting the branches above the infiltrators' heads. That little Uzi was lots of fun. He kept the assault rifle under the false floor of the closet with his other illegal weapons. He usually tried not to leave his brass behind like he had at the *Malpais*, but he couldn't help tantalizing Habib by leaving the shell casings as a clue. He had wiped them clean. They couldn't be traced back to the Uzi unless he was captured or killed, and then it wouldn't matter.

He put the rifle and pistol back in the gun safe and sat down at his hand loading station. His dad had taught him to reload cartridges so that they could save money while target practicing. He smiled at the Blue Press calendar with the voluptuous blonde leaning against the reloading equipment. Because he had grown up with it, hand loading was comforting to him. Measurements with scales and calipers required precision and concentration. His Dillon RL 550B press operated with ease, and he found the repetitive movement soothing. His father had been a good machinist, but he didn't really understand the physics of shooting. He just tried to duplicate factory loads. Derek was a bit of a wildcatter. He increased the grains of gunpowder himself to boost the power of his loads to +P levels. He had learned long ago the round-nosed .45 caliber bullets didn't have the destructive impact needed to stop an assailant in his tracks.

To hone his skills, he had hunted deer with a handgun for years. He felt that it gave him an edge to practice getting close enough to a wary target to be able to bring it down with a pistol. At first, he had used a sniper's Gillie suit for camouflage, but that made it so easy that it took some of the fun out of it. Last year he had used a new combination in the Combat Kimber. This load stopped a four-point buck with the first shot at fifteen yards. In his research, he had learned that most lead hollow-point bullets weren't all that they were cracked up to be. The new half-jacketed hollow points with redesigned heads expanded to leave a huge wound channel, so you didn't have to chase all over creation following blood droplets from a wounded deer. He had test fired his loads into sides of beef and found the optimal powder weight and bullet seating in the cartridge. Some of the other wildcat reloaders that he knew didn't realize that if you kept increasing the powder, you would get too much recoil and slow down the cartridge replacement rate. This combination tested fast on the tachometer and still worked well on the combat range.

He was going to follow his terrorist suspects again tomorrow. From what he knew about Habib already, it might turn into an opportunity to use his skills and his weapons.

l l l

Philip escorted his grandmother into his aunt's house amid a tumultuous greeting. Children surrounded them. His cousin, Priscilla, was tying the shoe of her littlest one. She gestured for their grandmother to sit by her, but *Sitti* refused.

"Philip, you go sit with Priscilla. I helped Mary cook this, so I'm going to help her serve it. I'm still the little red hen, fixing food for the brood."

Philip gave Priscilla a hug and struggled to recall how old Melissa was. He was saved by the arrival of the birthday girl with her missing front tooth.

Philip asked her, "Is the other one loose yet? You know that it's a rule that no second graders can have front teeth. In fact, sometimes the second-grade teachers don't have front teeth either."

Melissa laughed and ran away. Priscilla asked, "Do you want to get seated at the kids' table again, Philip?"

Philip looked around the room. "As much as I'd enjoy that, I don't think there going to be enough room at the kids' table. I guess I'll have to join the grownups."

Priscilla shook her head. "Sometimes I wonder if you're ever going to join the grownups. Don told me you stopped by today." Concern clouded her face. "Philip, you've got to be careful."

"Now, now, Priscilla. You're taking over your mother's job without asking her permission. I wouldn't want to deprive her of her time-honored role of nagging me to grow up." Standing up, he looked around the room. "I better go find her right now."

He waved as Don's sister and her family arrived. When Philip entered the kitchen, he saw a flurry of activity. *Sitti*, Mary, and George's wife, Tammy, were bringing the meal to fruition. He gave Tammy a kiss on the cheek as he walked by and gave Aunt Mary a big hug. She stood in front of simmering pots of beans and red chile. Philip sniffed the air. "What's on the menu tonight?"

Mary's face was flushed from the heat of the kitchen and her level of activity. She said, "When we get everybody together, we've got to have both Lebanese and Mexican. Everybody likes the cabbage rolls and *papas fritas*. We made tamales and put chicken in the ones over there for everybody whose cholesterol is over two hundred. I also made some sweet ones for dessert because I know you like them."

Philip loved homemade tamales, and Mary's unique sweet ones brought back pleasant memories of childhood. She made a filling of pine nuts, apples, and raisins in a sweet butter sauce with cinnamon and nutmeg, and then she drizzled the *masa* with honey. "I can hardly wait. What's on the grill?"

226

"Shish kafta and we've got mint and garlic yogurt sauce for it. Go say hi to your Uncle Joe."

Philip continued through the kitchen and out to the back yard. His uncle Joe was tending the skewers of ground lamb, onion, garlic, and cinnamon while Don and George were drinking beer and telling stories. He shook hands and grabbed a beer.

Joe asked, "Did I see your rig at the dealership today?"

Joe ran the used-car department at a car dealership that was owned by relatives.

"Yeah, I had to buy a tire. I'm sorry I didn't have time to stop by, but I knew I'd see you tonight."

"So you had a tire shot out."

"And got dusted by pine cones from assault-rifle fire over our heads. It was quite a day."

Don said, "I've only got a little more for you, Philip, since we talked this afternoon. Those shells were clean, no prints, not even partials. Gruber wasn't at work today and isn't due back for a couple of days. One of the Catron County Sheriff deputies went out to his trailer, but no one was home. His trailer windows have dark reflective material on them, so he couldn't see much. It looks like the tires match, but that doesn't prove anything. They'll keep trying."

Joe asked, "Isn't that the guy with the Power Wagon and the pan-head Harley? Both of them are classics and they're in good shape. A collector would pay big for those."

George laughed, "Dad, is that the way you look at people? Boy, could I make some money off that car."

Joe disappeared in smoke momentarily. "Tell me you haven't noticed those vehicles around."

"Okay, but I was only aware of the Dodge."

Don added, "One of our snitches says that Gruber doesn't hang out with the bikers all that often. I hear that he's too political for most of them to be really comfortable with him. It sounds like he's the type with the 'You'll get my gun when you pry my cold dead fingers from around it' bumper sticker."

Joe shook his head as he used tongs to turn the skewers. "And he lives in Catron County? Some of those militia types down there are pretty far gone. Every so often, a couple of them will drop by the American Legion in Grants. They wear camo and sound like they haven't given up soldiering. They're a piece of work. For a bunch of guys who served their country, they sure are antigovernment. They don't use bull's eyes to practice marksmanship. They shoot at human figure targets with FBI and ATF badges. Now they've got an outside enemy, so they're firing at Osama Bin Laden targets too."

George turned to Philip after he popped open another beer. "Don't you hear what kind of a flake this guy is? Don thinks he was probably in on the post nine-eleven anti-Arab backlash too. Do you know that there have been over a thousand unprovoked violent incidents against Arabs in America since nine-eleven? So you want to be part of the body count now? Whatever his beef is with you, let the police handle it. Stay away from him."

Don agreed. "Listen to your cousin. You already know how bad it can get. The last time that you were a target for prejudice, we could take care of it through the courts. With these guys, there's no appeal."

Philip tried to lighten the mood. "That reminds me. Did you hear the one about old Mustafa? He was a retired Lebanese waiter back east, who wrote an email to his son, Walid, who was studying engineering at Stanford. Mustafa complained that he was too old and tired to be able to dig up the garden anymore to plant vegetables. He begged for Walid's help. Walid replied that he wouldn't be able to get away from school, but he wrote in his return email, "Whatever you do, don't dig up the garden. That's where I've hidden 'the mother of all evil.'"

"That afternoon, dark SUVs full of FBI and Alcohol, Tobacco, and Firearms agents surrounded the house, and the feds presented Mustafa with a search warrant. They went through the house, but concentrated their efforts on the garden. They dug up all the dirt and carefully sifted the soil. After a few hours, they left, greatly disappointed because they found no contraband. The next day Mustafa receives another email. "*Abu*, I hope that the garden has been dug up by now. That's all I could do from here. Walid."

A chorus of groans was silenced by Mary shouting from the kitchen. "Bring that meat in and then dish up a plate for yourselves."

After the men took their plates to the dining room, Mary told the teenagers to turn off the MTV in the den. "You kids set up some TV trays in there, and no music until the adults have finished eating."

The women served the younger children in the kitchen and finally joined the men in the dining room. Philip had forgotten the logistics necessary to feed the Habib clan. In spite of all of the clamor and hubbub, he enjoyed being part of something larger than himself, a family. After the sweet tamales, he wished Melissa a happy birthday and said goodbye.

Modern swing music spilled out as Sarah opened the door of her apartment. She was wearing a floor length black cowboy duster. She kissed Philip hard. As he licked her ear, Philip thought that he spotted high-heeled pumps peeking out from under the long coat. Sarah stepped back and removed the duster strip tease style. She revealed that the pumps were accompanied by black stockings held up by sleek black garters. High cut black lace panties and a matching bra completed the ensemble. As the band segued into a Latin rhythm, her body moved to the music. She slipped out of her bra seductively and shimmied as her panties dropped down around her ankles. Stepping out with her left foot, she kicked the black lace right into Philip's face. He inhaled deeply. Then he threw them down, scooped her up, and carried her to the bed. He ran his hands over her body. Then he reached between her legs and fondled her until Sarah's breath was coming in short gasps. He ripped off his own clothing. As he lowered himself onto her, he watched Sarah's eyes widen as he penetrated her. Their lust drove their coupling. Sarah wrapped her black-stockinged legs around him and pressed the heels of her pumps into him. Philip raised up to let his hips rock rapidly, thrusting himself against her until they both wailed. He fell onto her as his pelvis gave its last spasmodic jerks. In a few moments he rolled onto his side and moaned softly.

Sarah appraised him. "Well I guess I don't I have to ask if that was good for you. Do you really like lingerie that much? You were an animal."

Philip realized that some of his anger had found release in their encounter. "The lingerie was exciting, but your striptease . . . You were pretty lewd yourself, my little vixen. You know, you never told me what kind of work you did in Las Vegas."

Sarah giggled. "I don't have enough tit to do that in Las Vegas. I was a blackjack dealer."

Philip snuggled against her and lay quietly as their breathing slowed and they relaxed in the afterglow. He was amazed by what a provocative woman Sarah had turned out to be. He could get addicted to this.

"Well, what did you think of the Braided Cave?" asked Sarah.

"It was bewitching. The way that the passages twisted off made me feel like I was Theseus in the Labyrinth, on my way to find the Minotaur. Unfortunately, it reminded Ross of Vietnam. The power of his subconscious manifested a firefight."

Sarah sat upright. "What are you talking about? You're not making any sense."

Philip tried to calm her. "I'm sorry. I was uncomfortable telling you about this, so I was sarcastic. When Ross and I were climbing out of the cave, someone shot over our heads with an automatic weapon and pinned us down. Then whoever it was knocked down the cairns, so we had to find our way back with the GPS. Finally, they shot out a tire on my SUV. We think it was Gruber, but we didn't see him."

Sarah got up and put on her robe. Worry furrowed her forehead. "This gives me the shivers, just thinking about it. What did you do?"

"I reported it to Don at the sheriff's office. They're going to contact

Gruber, but they weren't very hopeful that they could stick him with any charges."

"Isn't there an anti-stalking law now? Can't they charge him with that?"

"They'll warn him, but they probably won't pick him up."

Sarah sat down hard in her rocking chair and started rocking agitatedly. Her voice sounded constricted. "What's he got to do? Kill somebody?"

"I gave them some of the assault-rifle shells, but there weren't any fingerprints on them. Ballistics won't help until they've got some matching casings that can be traced to Gruber, or they have the gun that fired them. I took a digital photo of his tire tracks. The Catron County deputy said that it matches his tires, but lots of people drive on that tread. We don't have any real proof."

Sarah's voice was high and constricted. "Why is he doing this? Now I feel like I've entered a labyrinth. How do we get out of this?"

Philip pulled on his boxers. "Ross suggested that this either had something to do with the Middle East or with our investigation. If it's the investigation, we might be getting close to something that Gruber wants to stay hidden. It might be a lead."

Sarah's volume increased several notches. "A lead! That wasn't a clue; it was a threat. So I suppose you're going to walk up to Gruber's door, ask him why he shot at you, and give him the opportunity to do it again."

Philip crossed over to her chair and tried to calm her. "We're not going to talk to him; the deputies are going to do that."

"But you're going to keep looking for the Diggings, aren't you?"

"I haven't finished the job I was hired to do. There's one more area that Ross and I think is promising. We're going to go there tomorrow, and then I'm done."

Sarah stormed out to the kitchen. Philip put on his jeans and followed. She was pouring herself a shot of Jack Daniels. Without looking at him, she threw it back. "So a man's got to do what a man's got to do, huh?"

Philip poured himself a shot. "I'm sorry that this is upsetting you. But you're right. It's what I do, and why I came here. I'm not going to let this punk keep me from finishing my job."

Sarah pretended to hold a gun on him and growled, "'Make my day, punk.'"

"It's not like that."

"It's always like that when men get in a pissing contest."

Philip poured them each another shot. The silence was deafening and the lighting was harsh. After a couple of minutes, Sarah sullenly asked. "So, now where do you and Ross think the Diggings are?"

"Maybe near the Datils."

"Great, just where we last saw Gruber." Sarah chewed on her lower lip. "I hate to encourage this madness, but I glanced through that *Zigzag Canyon* book you loaned me last night. They don't even think the Diggings are in New Mexico; they place it near Clifton, Arizona. The book is ninety percent fiction and ten percent fact, but it's entertaining fiction and provocative facts. The facts include some original research, and I really liked the way they portrayed the Apache perspective. So anyway, Feldman and McPherson say that 'the legend' is wrong. They use Lieutenant Emory's eighteen forty-eight diary of his exploration on the Gila to propose that the original gold find occurred several years earlier. They say that Adams' eighteen sixty-four escape with Davidson was the result of a search for the lost mine that had been found decades earlier. They also suggest that the gold under the hearth was found by one of the better-known treasure hunters from the early part of the twentieth century. When they were digging at the site, they found a section of railroad track like the treasure hunter used to carry as an anvil.

"So Feldman and McPherson didn't really find it. They just think they know where it might have been."

She sat at the chrome dinette. "Right. And they didn't run into armed resistance either. You two are just as foolish as Adams' party, looking for gold in enemy territory. You know, maybe it wasn't Gruber."

"What do you mean?"

Sarah appeared to go into a trance. "The Apache chiefs have finally been awakened by the Dreamer's dance at Cibecue. They are protecting the squaw metal from the greed of the white eyes. Ussen, the one god, has given them the power to prevent the rape of the land, the last insult to Apachería. Nana has returned to guard the sacred canyon."

16

As he sipped his morning coffee in his grandmother's comfortable country kitchen, Philip reflected on the night before. His poor track record with women had pushed him to try to become a sensitive New-Age guy. He had a couple of parts right: he was able to listen and to express his own emotions most of the time. Try as he might, he was unable to shed some of the vestiges of his macho upbringing. He had expected an argument with Sarah last night. He had thought it would be about whether or not she would accompany them to the Datils. Not only wasn't she interested, but she also thought that he and Ross must be suffering from testosterone poisoning. She made him promise that they would check in with her every couple of hours. She was explicit. If they didn't have a strong enough signal on the cell phone, they were supposed to drive or climb until they got one. He also promised to call Don at the Sheriff's office and tell him their plans. There was still tension between them when he left.

Ross' old Ford pickup rattled up the driveway. As he climbed out of the truck, Philip was surprised to see him in a desert camouflage outfit. Ross called out, "*Sabah al khayr.*"

"*Sabah al nur.* Good morning, General Schwartzkopf, it's good to see you again."

Ross laughed. "A few years after Desert Storm, all the *suqs* along the Gulf were full of this stuff. I couldn't resist. Anyway you should talk, wearing olive-drab cargo pants and T-shirt, and khaki commando sweater. After the surprise attack yesterday, I guess we both needed to feel battle-ready today."

He pulled out his camouflage patrol pack, reached into the truck for a scoped army M-16 rifle, and put them in the back of the 4Runner.

Philip looked at the rifle and asked, "Do you really think we're going to need that kind of firepower?"

"I hope not. After yesterday, I'd like to have a chance at defending ourselves if we have to. Pistols aren't much use against assault rifles. You don't happen to have a grenade launcher by any chance?"

Sarah was right about the way that men deal with conflict. He and Ross were approaching this expedition as though they had a score to settle. On some level, they stung from the humiliation they had experienced yesterday. Their fear had made them uncomfortable, so they had transformed it into anger. Now their reaction was primitive and vengeful, but he recognized that Ross was right. A long gun might save his life.

Philip asked his grandmother, "Do you still have *Jiddi's* deer rifles?"

Sitti's anxiety showed in the deepening of the lines of her face and the tension in her body. "*Ma"loum.* I keep them for bears. Remember what happened to that old lady in Mora a couple of years ago. I wish you two would forget this foolish idea. Guns bring trouble."

"*Sitti,* I'm doing the job I was hired to do. The guns are to protect us."

"Staying home would protect you, but you've always been too stubborn to listen to your grandmother's advice. I hope that it doesn't get you killed this time. I'll go get the key."

Philip followed his grandmother into his grandfather's study where she unlocked the door to the glass-fronted gun case. *Sitti* said, "George is the one with the fancy elk-hunting rifles, but these were good enough for your grandfather."

Philip chose the scoped Remington Model 700. "I haven't used this since I was a teenager hunting deer. I remember that *Jiddi* got a buck with it every fall until his eye sight started to fail. Have you got any bullets for it?"

Sitti pulled out the drawer below the rifle racks and handed Philip a box of cartridges. "Here you go. Hank and I go plinking every so often to keep our eyes tuned up. I've always liked this rifle. Your grandfather said that it was the scope that made it so accurate, but he was just being modest. I think about him every year during deer season. He was so proud of being a good hunter."

As Philip looked through the scope, he smelled gun oil. He wiped the rifle down, checked the bolt action, put it in a canvas transport case, and placed it and the cartridges in the SUV. Ross put the extra water and the gold pan in the back. Philip also placed the canvas attaché bag that contained the maps he had generated last night as well as the cooler that his grandmother had prepared on the back seat. He reassured her that they wouldn't take any chances, and they would call for help immediately if they ran into Gruber.

He bade Sitti goodbye, "*Bhatrik.*"

"*Ma" salaami.*"

The standard Arabic response seemed especially poignant today. His grandmother's worried look made it clear that she explicitly and sincerely wished that peace would be with them.

/ı /ı /ı

Through his binoculars, Derek watched the Arab and his camouflaged lackey load the rifles in the SUV. The traitors were arming themselves for battle. He wondered where they were headed today. He had placed a GPS transmitter on the 4Runner before dawn. It would allow him to track them in real time on his laptop wherever he had cell phone reception. He could hang back and still monitor their movements.

He had been able to stay close to them through most of the *malpais*. If they stayed on the plains, the long line of sight would mean that he would need to give them a good head start. From what he learned yesterday, Habib really fit the profile of a terrorist. Not only was he an Arab, but he had been part of a militant Palestinian organization years ago. McIntyre had also spent a lot of years in Saudi Arabia and the Gulf States, as well as being an emotionally unstable drunk. Wherever they were going, he would follow and stop them from carrying out their treasonous schemes.

/s /s /s

As they drove out, Philip asked Ross about his previous exploration of the Datils.

"Bob Lewis said that he found the skeletons about thirty-five miles northwest of Magdalena. He thought that the *Tres Montosas* west of Magdalena were the haystack mountains. So I approached the Datils from the southeast, the way I thought Lewis had gone, and went up Main Canyon. I had my old duckbill orange nineteen fifty-two Willys Overlander, and I drove all around that area one weekend. There are lots of little peaks that could be haystacks or *piloncillos*, but I couldn't find any skeletons or zigzag canyons. Some of the rock looked like it could have been gold bearing, and the weathering was about right for placer finds. There were deposits of black sand in some of the streambeds, but I didn't find any gold."

"But the geology was possible."

Ross agreed. "Anything is possible; but no, it wasn't sedimentary. The Datil Mountains are composed of igneous rock. Although, even sedimentary rock can have igneous intrusions. Look, there are a lot of volcanic plugs around Mount Taylor, just like those off to the east there, past Cubero."

"You mean those black rock towers."

"Yeah. The softer material has eroded, leaving the harder volcanic rock that intruded into the sandstone. You usually find gold in what are called mineralized areas, which means igneous or metamorphic rock. Mineralized areas might also have silver, copper, zinc, or lead like they mined in Kelly just southwest of Magdalena."

Philip looked at the rear-view mirror. There weren't any vehicles behind them, but he had the feeling they were being followed again. He chalked it up to his anxiety and asked Ross to grab the canvas bag. "Could you look for an article that comes from the WPA Writers Project during the Depression? It's another Bob Lewis story that I found on the Internet last night. It places the skeletons by North Lake, a *playa* at the juncture of the Datils and the Gallinas Mountains. The track for the Very Large Array, the radio-telescope system on rails, ends near there."

"I didn't look that far east last time, and the VLA didn't exist back then."

"Nobody could have imagined it back then. Back to the WPA story, it said that Lewis called Adams a liar and a drunk. He thought that Adams' assailant in that knife fight in Magdalena was probably right. The cavalry captain said that Adams had stolen the nuggets from the party of California miners he had hooked up with and killed. The captain insisted that there wasn't any mine. Lewis also reported that an old man he knew, José María Jaramillo, found twenty thousand dollars worth of loot five miles north of North Lake, near where he had found the skeletons. Jaramillo wouldn't tell Lewis if it was gold, but Lewis thought that he must have found whatever Adams had hidden."

Ross smiled. "Should we turn around?"

Philip returned his grin. "And give up this expedition just when it's getting good? No, there are so many conflicting stories that I don't put too much stock in any one of them. Besides, we need to stay focused on what Buck might have found, because it sure looks like he found something."

"The question is still what and where. Lewis's story sure puts Adams in a different light doesn't it? I hadn't pictured him as a mass murderer. Death is a central part of this story, no matter how it's told."

Philip saw Ross's eyes start to glaze over again, so he tried to keep him engaged. "When I was web surfing, I found that the ranch by North Lake has a web site. They've closed off part of the ranch to cattle, and they're hosting hunting expeditions for elk and deer. I emailed them yesterday. They replied that there had been a lot of prospecting on the ranch over the years. Could you look for that thermos? I think that there are a couple of cups, too."

Ross poured them each a cup of steaming coffee.

"Thanks. Bob Lewis was the town marshal in Magdalena. He wasn't shy about telling a story, so every cowboy who came to the railhead probably knew something about the Diggings. When the mines at Kelly played out, there were a lot of unemployed miners in the area. I bet some of them took up prospecting. Anyway, it sounds like the area past North Lake has been pretty well explored over the years, starting with Bob Lewis himself."

As they drove past La Ventana Arch, buff-colored sandstone framed blue sky. The sun shone brightly and promised a hot day for hiking.

Ross said, "Let me tell you a yarn about the other end of the Datils. Since we're in the middle of a buddy expedition, I'm reminded of Uncle Jimmy McKenna's retelling of Jason Baxter's lost-canyon story. Baxter was a prospector who made and spent several fortunes from prospecting and mining in Colorado. He cut a pretty wide swath in Western New Mexico, and he was quite a storyteller too. When they were soaking in the Gila Hot Springs in the eighteen eighties, he told Uncle Jimmy about his attempt to find the Snively Diggings. Snively had told Baxter about his gold find when they met up in Piños Altos in the mid eighteen sixties. He brought out at least ten thousand dollars worth of gold and considered himself lucky to have escaped the Apaches. Snively told Baxter that the gold was a hundred and twenty-five miles north of Fort West."

"This is same time frame as Adams' story, as well as the same area.

Could Snively have been the German who left with his own gold?"

Ross looked pensive. "It's also about the same amount of gold. It's quite a coincidence, isn't it? By the late eighteen seventies, Baxter thought that it was safe to look for Snively's diggings. Since the placers at Piños Altos were about played out, he was able to convince his friend John Adair to accompany him. Baxter supplied the grubstake. He bought horses, pack mules, grub, and one of the first repeating Winchester rifles in western New Mexico. Adair brought a lifetime of experience mining placer gold and his fifty caliber Sharps buffalo gun. What's in the coffee? It reminds me of Arabia."

"*Sitti* put a couple of cardamom seeds in the thermos."

"So they headed north out of Silver City, crossed the mountains and the Plains of San Agustín. They made their way north into the foothills of the Datils, but were unable to find water that night. They made a dry camp and picketed the horses and mules. One of the mules had belonged to Mexican shepherds who had worked this area. In the middle of the night, the Mexican mule broke free from its picket. They found it the next morning several miles away where it had caught its lead rope on a mesquite bush. It was headed northeast toward a group of mountains that looked like pyramids in the desert. They loaded him and turned him loose. As they approached the island mountains, the country got rough. They climbed a hogback ridge and then the mule led them into a box canyon. He went straight to the end and disappeared behind a huge boulder. They followed him through a passageway that led into a park."

Philip interrupted. "This is starting to sound familiar. Where did you find this story?"

"I went to the library yesterday evening and looked up Jimmy McKenna's *Black Range Tales*. I had read it before, but it's better than I remembered. The best part is that it's completely independent from the Adams' legend. Baxter and Adair went through another canyon to a larger park where a gulch cut through the middle. The mule started pawing in the sand and soon water appeared. They continued further up the canyon to where there was a flowing steam in a meadow. They made camp and started panning. Soon they had color in their pans. They followed the stream up to where there was a band of rosy quartz in the canyon wall. By then it was too dark to pan, so they bedded down under an overhang. They built a low rock wall in front of them."

"Since the stories seem to parallel one another, I can guess what happens next."

"You're right. In the middle of the night, they were awakened by the Mexican mule nuzzling them and heard strange birdcalls. Suspecting Indians, they built the wall higher. At first light, the Mexican mule ran past dragging a lariat. That was followed by a hail of arrows. An Apache threw a lance at them, and Adair shot his Sharps at the warrior. Immediately, the Apaches rushed them, but Baxter picked off several with his Winchester. The Indians had never been up against a repeating rifle before and retreated in confusion. The Apaches kept Baxter and Adair pinned down all day, until a lance from above pierced Adair's foot. Clouds had been building up all day, and at nightfall, the storm broke. It was a real frog-strangler; so Baxter and Adair took advantage of the poor visibility to head up the canyon, splashing through the floodwaters. They found the Mexican mule. Adair turned the lariat into a halter and rode him. Flashes of lightning revealed a burned out old log cabin and two piles of bones. They didn't know Adams' story about the hearthstone and hurried past the ruins to distance themselves from the Indians. They followed the west fork out to a game trail that led them out of the canyon. They made their way west, and eventually followed the Tularosa River to Clifton, Arizona. They got Adair's foot doctored, and they returned to Piños Altos."

Philip was all ears. "Did they ever go back?"

"Several years later, after Adair died, Baxter took Uncle Jimmy McKenna and another friend back to the pyramid mountains. Baxter was shocked by the changes in the geography. He thought that there must have been an earthquake or maybe flash floods that totally changed the landscape of those canyons. He knew that he was in the same area, but it was unrecognizable."

Philip asked, "Did the Apaches make him forget too?"

Ross shook his head. "No, Baxter was clear that he was in the same place, but that the place had been rearranged. The area north of Socorro is the most seismically active area in New Mexico because of the tectonic activity along the Rio Grande. I looked up fault lines in the Datils, and it might have been possible. After all, nobody was living near enough to report any tremors. It's more likely that flash floods were responsible for the changes, or there could've been an earthquake followed by flash floods."

Philip pulled off at the Lava Falls parking area and looked at the atlas. "Island mountains northeast of the Datils? The way Lewis described it, the area north of North Lake must have been in the Gallinas instead of the Datils. But that's a mountain range, not an isolated pyramid."

Ross looked out of the window pensively. "You know, not only has the gold remained hidden, but almost everybody who has looked for it has also had some tragedy befall them. I know that the Apaches were desperate to protect their homeland during Adams' and Baxter's time, but it's more than that."

He turned back to Philip and the haunted look was on his face again. "Do you believe in curses? It seems like there are some things in life that are doomed to failure. I feel that way a lot. If this really is a sacred canyon, maybe there's some kind of spirit guardian placed there by the Apache medicine men."

Philip felt very uneasy. "Sarah said the same kind of thing last night. She said that it wasn't Gruber at the Braided Cave; it was Nana or Gruber channeling Nana. I don't know. I've seen too much misery to doubt that there is evil abroad in the world, but a haunting? I think that spiritualism is only invoked when we can't explain things otherwise. These days I just like to leave them unexplained."

He continued south on State road 117 until he turned left onto County Road 41. They were silent as they passed the King Ranch headquarters and continued across the North Plains. The plains were flat, desolate, and dusty. There was a line of mesas off to the east, but it was mostly blue grama and buffalo grass, *yucca*, and *cholla*, with an occasional small herd of cattle. Philip put the Egyptian diva, Oum Kal Thoum, on the CD player. He preferred haunting to be confined to melodies.

Ross pointed out some small peaks on the western horizon. "I think that's Veteado Mountain. The famed community of Adams Diggings is a little south of a line between here and there. Supposedly, a treasure seeker named that wide spot in the road. It had a post office for a while, but it isn't near any zigzag canyons that I could find. When Richard French was tracing Adams's route, he saw the twin peaks of Veteado from Mt. Baldy in Arizona. He thought that it could have been the landmark that Gotchear pointed out to Adams on the way through the White Mountains. But he didn't think that they were the haystack mountains at the end of the journey." He started rummaging around in the back seat and pulled out the book.

"Did he have any candidates for the end pair?"

"Actually, they were suggested by Gary Tietjen. I knew that Gary had written extensively about early Mormon history in New Mexico. French found a reference to the Adams Diggings in which Tietjen promoted Bell Butte and D Cross Mountain as the twin haystacks. They're east-south-east of here."

"Are they possible?"

"Yeah, take a glance at this picture in French's book. They do look like haystacks. I think we should check them out. I noticed that you had already printed those quadrangles."

"I printed everything around the Datils."

"Well, look at these canyons. How many zigzag ones would you like?"

Philip slowed and glanced at the map. "There's a lot of topography all right. It's certainly a contrast to what we're driving through now. Did French explore them?"

"Yeah, he thought that the wagon road that Adams's party crossed was probably a supply route between Fort Craig and Fort Wingate. He suggested that it ran parallel to the road we're on now. So he and his wife looked just east of here, in the Rio Salado drainage."

"I take it that they didn't find the gold."

Ross grinned. "At least not by nineteen ninety-four, when he published the book."

"Why are we continuing south then?"

"Because he didn't find it. He gives a pretty compelling argument for the location based on his research. It's pretty much a straight line from Springerville to this area if you maintain a northeasterly heading, and it's somewhere around one hundred twenty-five miles from where Fort West used to be. I just don't buy the geology. The canyons of the Rio Salado cut through sedimentary rock. French said that they found traces of gold, but nothing exploitable. On the other hand, just south of there, Alamocita Creek drains the north slope of the Datils as well as the south slopes of Bell Butte and D Cross Mountain. There's a better chance for a mineralized area there. And Bell Butte and D Cross are isolated peaks northeast of the Datils, so they might also fit Baxter's description."

Philip pulled over to the side of the road and picked up the atlas again. "And they're just a little more than ten miles from North Lake. I'd also guess that they're less than forty miles from Buck's ranch as the crow flies."

He leafed through the quadrangles until he found what he wanted. "Let's go in on Forest Road Six on the northwest shoulder of the Datils, down to Ox Springs Canyon, and then go east at Webster's cabin. The next two canyons look like they line up with the haystack mountains."

Ross was hesitant. "I don't know; it's possible, but there's another way in. Look at the atlas. French also said that there was an old Indian and Spanish trail from Tres Lagunas down Alamocita Creek to the Rio Salado. It continues the straight line from Springerville, so it might have been Adams' route. Anyway, it looks like some of the stories could converge here."

Philip was puzzled. "Let's check with the people in Datil. The atlas shows a road down Alamocita Creek, but the topos don't."

When they reached the small gathering of houses that was Tres Lagunas, Philip stopped to match up the map with the territory. He studied both the atlas and the quadrangles.

"There's a maze of roads heading east from here. There would be a lot of trial and error to get to Alamocita Canyon, besides Forest Road Six-A would take us to the mouth of the canyon."

"I wonder where Gruber lives." Ross scanned the horizon. "We'll probably pass his place somewhere along here. There's the Catron County line. We're in his territory now."

The uneasiness Philip had felt earlier returned. In his excitement about the Baxter story, he had momentarily forgotten their adversary. Was the gold driving Gruber, or was there something more sinister in his obsession with them?

They went into Datil to gas up. The gas station, grocery store, and restaurant combination seemed to be the meet and greet center for many miles around. Although the price of the gas was high, Philip felt better heading into the mountains with a full tank. Philip pulled out his maps and asked the woman behind the counter about the discrepancies.

She smiled. "The reason why one map shows a road down Alamocita Creek and the other doesn't says more about how adventurous the surveyors were. There isn't really a road, but the fellows who ranch over there drive down the creek bed when it's dry."

"Could we make it down the creek bed now?"

"Since we're in the tail end of the rainy season, I wouldn't advise it. The water cuts back and forth across the streambed. When the streams cross, there's usually quicksand. They've lost a few cows that way."

Philip traced a route on the map. "It looks like we could get there this way too."

"You're right; you could also get near the two peaks by taking Forest Road Six down Ox Springs Canyon and then heading east. You boys take care; it's awful lonesome out there. There's an old boy who's eating in the café that lives near there. Do you want meet him?"

"We'd love to, but first, did you know Buck Cavanaugh?"

Suddenly she looked suspicious. "Why do you want to know?"

Philip smiled reassuringly. "I'm working for his granddaughter. She wants to know more about him, and she remembers that he used to come down here."

The woman called into the café. "This here gent wants to hear Buck Cavanaugh stories."

She looked back at them and said, "Buck's a local legend. He'd come down from his place in the *malpais*, and go hunting or whatever he did for a week or so. Then he'd come back here, buy supplies, and tell us that we cooked the best food on earth. After he'd had a cup of coffee, he'd invite the boys out to his truck to have a snort. A lot of lies were told while that bottle was being passed around. When the bottle was empty, Buck would drive up to Datil Wells and sleep it off in the back of his truck. We miss having him around here; he was a hoot. Let me introduce you to Pete."

Pete's face was lined from years of being out in the weather. He pushed back his sweat-stained hat and invited Philip and Ross to sit with him. The proprietress brought them coffee and refilled Pete's, and they ordered the breakfast special. They told Pete about their interest in the area.

Pete sipped his coffee. "I've heard some of those stories, but in all the time we've run cattle back there, we haven't seen anything that looked like gold. I do remember Buck driving his four by four in the backcountry around my place, but I thought that he was checking out places to take his greenhorns during the elk hunt. He loved to tell stories about how useless his hunters were in the wild. Some of them were pretty funny, like one of them hearing a bull elk bugle and getting out of the sack for reveille. Anyway, if you see any loose cattle past the windmill in Remuda Canyon, they're from our neighbor's herd. Let me know if you see any signs of them."

While they ate their breakfasts, a couple of the other diners related stories about Buck's ability to pick off an elk at great distances. A bow-legged old cowboy ambled up and told them about riding with Buck on trail drives before they closed the stockyards in Magdalena. Everyone waved as Ross and Philip left the café.

Ross said, "Friendly folk. It sure sounds like Buck used to spend some time here. Do you think he was just looking for elk?"

As they drove back to Forest Road Six, the highway followed a beautiful canyon that cut through the foothills of the Datils. Ross pointed out the turn off to the campground at Datil Wells.

"Do you know the history of that well? Datil Wells was part of the cattle driveway from Western New Mexico to Magdalena. There was a swath ten miles wide that paralleled this highway. This was the last place for the cows to drink up before crossing the Plains of San Agustín."

Philip looked over at the washboard road to the wells. "It sounds like Buck was here a time or two on horseback with a herd."

As the highway wound upward Ross gestured to a freestanding pillar at the end of a ridge of volcanic rock. "That's the kind of erosion that could make a 'Little Door.' You see it in sandstone too, a plateau crumbling at the edges."

They turned onto Forest Road 6 and drove north until they encountered a group of trailers and portable buildings. There were a few horses and some kids tending to them as well as the usual barnyard menagerie.

"Either it's a boys' ranch, a religious retreat, or an *Al Qaida* training camp," observed Ross. "Keep your eyes peeled for weapons."

Philip shook his head. "I think the boys' ranch hypothesis has a slightly higher probability. Besides, there were very few swarthy kids and no adults with beards and turbans."

The road to Davenport Lookout appeared on the right, and bulldozers were cutting new roads for a subdivision on the left. They continued north through ponderosa forest until they heard logging equipment. They watched a skidder moving logs as they drove past, and talked about the similarities between these mountains and the Zunis.

Philip pulled off the road before it crossed a cattle guard heading downhill. There was a long view of the canyon country they would be exploring and no sign of any dwellings below. "This looks like the best place for cell phone contact. I'm going to try Sarah."

The receptionist at the monument tracked her down. Philip told her where they were, and where they were planning to go. He expressed concern that they were heading into canyon country, and wireless reception might be tricky. He assured her that they would be back in five or six hours, and that he would call her as soon as he had a signal. He walked away from Ross so their argument wasn't as audible. She was upset that he wasn't going to keep his promise to call more frequently. She said that she would call Don if she didn't hear from him in a few hours. He tried to express the enthusiasm that he and Ross felt about the haystack mountains, but she would not be placated. He apologized again and hung up feeling frustrated.

When he walked back to the truck, Ross put his hand on Philip's shoulder. "You can't win. Even if you called every two hours, she doesn't want you to be here. She's right about Gruber being dangerous, but you've got a client who gave you twenty-four hours to finish this, and we've got a good lead. We'll keep our eyes open and watch each other's backs. If we survive, you'll ask for forgiveness. If we don't, it won't matter. Let's roll."

17

After they crossed the cattle guard at the crest of the hill, they found themselves descending on a narrow one-lane road along the edge of a steep canyon. Philip shifted into four wheel drive. Douglas fir and spruce clung to the north side of the mountain, and aspen filled the valley bottom. Philip breathed a sign of relief when the 4Runner arrived at the bottom without encountering uphill traffic. The canyon leveled off to a Ponderosa and *chaparral* parkland with grassy meadows opening up the views. The jagged edges of the red and cream-colored Sawtooth Mountains appeared through gaps in the trees.

Ross pointed out the passenger window to a ridge. "I might have to change my mind about the earthquake hypothesis. Do you see that red slash on the slope to the east? I think that's the result of a landslide."

Philip stopped the truck and craned his neck to see where Ross was pointing. "That was one hell of a landslide."

Ross rummaged through his bag, pulled out a book, and found a map of the Datils. "This geological map puts a fault line right through this area. If you combine a small quake with torrential rains, you could get the landscape rearrangement that Baxter described. The amount of material from a landslide like that could fill a canyon, and the water could carve a new channel. A half a century or so later, who knows what Buck could have been looking at."

"First there is a canyon, then there is no canyon, then there is.

I always thought that kind of statement was a Zen metaphor for the process of enlightenment. You're saying that it actually could have happened over a lifetime rather than through centuries of erosion."

"It isn't likely, but it's possible if the tremors and the rains came at the right times. All the old timers say that this area used to be wetter before it got overgrazed. The elders say that the grass around Bluewater village was as high as a horse's belly."

"Well, I haven't seen any grasses that tall here, but there are enough meadows to match Adams's description of the journey to the canyon. Let's see what develops as we get closer to Bell Butte and D Cross Mountain. Baxter's story said that the Snively Diggings were one hundred and some miles north of Fort West. Where was Fort West, anyway? I've never heard of it."

"It only existed for a couple of years. It was abandoned just before the Adam's party arrived in New Mexico in eighteen sixty-four. It was on the Gila, about twenty miles west of Silver City. Let me look at the atlas. By my reckoning, that puts us roughly one hundred and twenty miles northeast of Fort West, just about as far away as Snively said it was. This is getting better all the time. When will we get a view of those mountains?"

"I think we should be able to see them soon. When there's a meadow that gives us a view to the northeast, I'll pull off. Listen. It sounds like there are some wood cutters over on the left."

Ross spotted them amongst the trees. "They're Indian. I'll bet they're Navajos from the Alamo band. Pull over."

They climbed out of the 4Runner and walked over to the men. They stopped cutting and loading the pickup and trailer as Philip and Ross approached.

Ross greeted them. "*Ya'aht'eh*. That's a nice load of wood. I'll bet the alligator juniper makes a good fire."

The oldest man answered, "It lasts all night if you get it going right. Are you two scouting for good places to hunt elk?"

Philip shook his head. "No, we're hunting for gold."

The men looked at one another and smiled. It was probably best to humor these crazy *belaganas*.

Ross jumped in. "There's an old story from the eighteen-sixties about a group of white men who found a canyon with gold nuggets. They said it was in a zigzag canyon near two mountains that looked like haystacks in the setting sun. We thought that D Cross and Bell Butte could be those mountains. Nana's warriors killed most of the miners, but one who got away said that Nana had called the canyon *Sno-ta-hay*. Have you ever heard the name?"

The older man looked pensive. "My uncle may have mentioned this place. Some of our people were Apaches who joined up with the Navajos. He likes to tell the old stories. I'd have to ask him."

Ross persisted, "How about a zigzag canyon? They said you entered it through a passageway through a rock wall."

The men conferred, softly speaking Navajo. One of the younger men spoke, "We've been hunting in this area all our lives. We've never seen this hidden canyon and we sure haven't found any gold." He pointed with his lips to the northeast. "Those mountains do look a little like haystacks."

Philip gave a card to the older man. "If your uncle remembers anything about *Sno-ta-hay*, call me collect. Thanks for your time."

On their way back to the SUV, they heard gales of laughter behind them. A chain saw started up and all other sounds were silenced by the growl of the saw.

They continued north, winding through the *piñon*-juniper forest. After they passed a shallow water-diversion tank, a large meadow opened up on the right. Philip pulled off the road and parked. They couldn't believe what was in front of them. Philip grabbed the camera as Ross tumbled out of the passenger side.

Ross shouted, "Haystack mountains, island mountains, or pyramids in the desert?"

Philip replied, "Could be. But they don't look like the pyramids at Giza as much as the Step Pyramid and the Bent Pyramid at Saqara."

Philip remembered the leisurely horseback ride south through the villages along the Nile to Saqara. He had the same feeling of excitement about buried treasures now as he had when they crossed the sand to the pyramids. As they walked further into the meadow, an additional peak appeared to the west of the others, past the trees.

Philip asked, "Didn't someone say that Adams had told them that there were three mountains?"

"A couple of people claimed that Adams said three. Depending on your angle, you could say there were two or three. What I like about this locale is that not only are there haystack mountains, but it's also an area where there are no major roads. You can't see those peaks or these canyons from any highway. The woman at the store had it right; it sure looks lonesome out here."

Philip took a picture and turned back to the 4Runner, "Let's see how close we can get."

After they rounded the corner, a side road led off to the west to one of the Sawtooth Mountains. A sign at the intersection caused them to stop and stare. It read: DANGER! U.S. Army Missile Impact Area. Closed from 3:00 a.m. to 6:00 a.m.

Philip let out a low whistle. "What the hell is that about?"

Ross chortled. "Star Wars."

"What do you mean, Star Wars? Is the Army working with the Empire or the Rebel Alliance? Is this is the test range for the Death Star?"

Ross explained, "That's close. Before we realized that terrorists could turn our own technology against us, G.W. Bush revived the Strategic Defense Missile Initiative. It's a defense project that was proposed during either his father's reign or Reagan's. The idea was that an enemy with nuclear capabilities might launch a missile against us. Therefore, we needed to develop a system that would track and intercept incoming nuclear missiles. Originally the system was supposed to operate from space, thus the Star Wars moniker, but the international community demanded that we follow the treaty prohibiting weapons in space. A couple of tests have involved attack missiles that I think were launched from Fort Wingate, or maybe somewhere in Utah. Anyway, the interceptors were launched from the White Sands Missile Range. I had forgotten that the Datils were supposed to be the point of impact. Both shots missed."

"Unbelievable. Did any of the interceptors connect?"

"Eventually, but their track record is still pretty bad. After he identified the Axis of Evil, President Bush pushed hard for a multi-billion dollar appropriation to build the system, but it seems to have fallen off the media radar screen. I hope we're not going to be here between three and six a.m."

/// /// ///

Derek Gruber had been following the 4Runner at a safe distance, but when he came to the missile impact sign he stopped dead in his tracks. He felt like a fool. The Arab wasn't just looking for uranium and places to cache weapons; he was investigating the Strategic Defense Missile Initiative. There might be something out here that would give them information about the weaknesses in the missile interceptor system. That intelligence could give any rogue state a way to overcome our defenses in order to use their weapons of mass destruction against us. His hatred for Habib came to a boil. What a traitor, pretending to be a Marine! Which side was he really working when he "infiltrated" the Palestinian militants? His friends in the intelligence community had warned him that Habib had gone native, but Habib may have come by it naturally. He was only two generations removed from Lebanon, and blood was thicker than water, after all. No wonder that he had blended in so easily with the radicals at the American University of Beirut. His cover wasn't good acting; it was a reality show. The *Al Fatah fedayeen* had turned him. Gruber wondered who was running Habib now. Was it *Hezbollah, Hamas, Al Qaida,* or something that we didn't even have a name for yet?

What had happened to the Mormon Eagle Scout? His Internet research had revealed that McIntyre had been decorated during his tour of duty in Vietnam. McIntyre had been a patriot once, but that was before he went mad. The grief-stricken drunk had spent many years in the oil-producing areas around the Persian Gulf. It was obvious now that the wealthy oil sheikhs from Saudi Arabia and the Gulf States had bankrolled Osama Bin Laden. How had they recruited McIntyre? Was it just money, or had they exploited his alcoholism somehow?

Gruber vowed that these turncoats wouldn't retrieve their remote sensing device, much less send it to their Arab masters. He would stop them or die trying. He put the Power Wagon in gear and followed the traitors.

ll ll ll

Philip and Ross continued north down rutted roads across meadows, piñon and juniper forests, and over rocky ledges. A fence appeared on the right as a valley opened up into a meadow with cottonwoods. They drove by a corral and saw the cabin ahead.

Ross pointed to the spot on the map where a road branched to the right. "This must be Webster's cabin. There's the sign; we take Forest Road Five-O-Seven to the right, but take a look at our road. This little lane is sure narrow and lopsided."

As they approached an arroyo where the sand in the bottom looked dark brown and wet, Philip stopped. The road ran across the bottom of the arroyo for about thirty feet and then steeply climbed a sandstone shelf.

"Ross, would you do the honor of walking across?"

Ross strolled across the arroyo. "I didn't sink at all; I'll meet you up ahead. Be careful when you climb up that bank."

They drove over a hill to the next arroyo. The road followed the sandy bank of the arroyo then crossed it. Ross walked it ahead of the SUV.

"There are a couple of places where I wouldn't linger, but I think you can make it. Let's take a break over by the windmill and tank."

Philip pulled off the road into the shade of a low sandstone cliff. He got out and stretched. "We've really got to watch the weather. We're not going to get across those when they're running. We've got to be on the other side of these when the floodwaters come down from the mountains."

Ross pulled a couple of beers from the cooler. "The sun is over the yardarm somewhere in this time zone. Have one."

"*Shukran*. After all this bouncing, I wouldn't mind taking a minute to relax." He looked up to the cliff above them. "That would be a good place for a deer or elk stand."

Ross grinned. "I'll bet there are a few people in line ahead of you. You wouldn't believe how crowded this country gets during hunting season."

They got back in the vehicle and drove steeply out of the canyon onto a plateau covered by meadow interspersed with *piñon* and juniper. The road became a sandy streambed between banks of native grasses as they ascended the hill. Coyote tracks were visible in the muddy spots. When they crested the hill, they were driving on sandstone ledges dropping down into a broad valley. The road grew harder to follow; the SUV leaned precipitously over washed-out sections. Philip dropped into low range and stayed in first gear. Just as he was beginning to doubt whether they could continue, the road leveled out and dropped into the valley. A windmill was silhouetted on a ridge in front of the sandstone cliffs.

Philip observed, "There's another windmill and tank as well as a fairly sturdy corral. This must be the place that Pete mentioned. We're in Remuda Canyon."

They followed the road across the meadow and stopped in the shade of cottonwoods next to the arroyo. Ross walked down the road and onto the wet sand.

He called back to Philip, "There's some alluvial gravel in the bank, but I like what I see in the sand even better. Turn off the truck and come on down here."

Ross bent down as Philip advanced down the slope. "This is the black sand that Fred was talking about. There isn't much of it here. See how it's in the deeper channels, and it congregates where the water slows down, like in those riffles and on the inside of the bend. That's because it's heavier then the other minerals and therefore it's deposited much the same way that gold is. It seems to peter out downstream, so let's go up a ways."

The black sand became sparse after they rounded the bend in the low canyon. Philip shielded his eyes from the sun, as he looked upstream. "It seems to open up after it passes this hill. I don't think we're going to find any zigzag canyons up there."

"You're right, but I think we're on the right track. There isn't enough black sand here to fool around with, but somewhere near here, there's a deposit of minerals. It's not just sandstone."

Philip got out the map pouch. He found the Cal Ship Mesa quadrangle and used a hand magnifier to examine the area where they found themselves.

"It shows the next section of road as a jeep trail. But from what I can see across the arroyo, it looks about the same as we've been driving on. Let's check it out."

They slowly crossed the arroyo and climbed up the sandstone benches to a rough road that climbed the hillside. Around the bend, they encountered the steepest, most rutted pretense of a road that they had seen so far. Philip kept it in low range and crawled carefully up the hill as they bounced over rocks and ruts.

At the top Ross yelled, "Whoa, Nelly Belle! Now that's a jeep trail."

The road gently climbed the mesa until it turned a corner and went up a side canyon. They faced a hillside that looked a lot more like an eroded mountain streambed with waterfalls than a road. The ruts were deeper than the 4Runner's axles and there were big boulders everywhere.

"Whooee! Now that's a trail I wouldn't even take a jeep on."

Philip pulled off the road. "I had an old Toyota FJ Forty that could've made it. The body metal was thicker than most cars' bumpers, and it had a power-takeoff winch that could lift the FJ Forty's weight."

Ross smiled. "I always love those ads in the paper that offer a jeep with wench. I thought that it was only motorcycles where the wench came with the vehicle. Anyway, I'm glad you stopped. I'm ready to stretch my legs some. How far does it look to the next canyon?"

Philip checked the map. "Maybe a mile and a half, not far."

He pulled off the road and parked the SUV. They climbed out and opened the tailgate.

/⁄ /⁄ /⁄

Derek Gruber stopped his truck and found an overlook where he could watch the Toyota's progress across the meadow to the next arroyo. He heard the SUV climb the stone staircase and watched it disappear up a side canyon, but then he couldn't hear the engine anymore. He got back in the Power Wagon and descended quietly into the valley. He could only hear birds and cicadas, so he turned down onto the valley floor and parked amongst the overgrown cottonwoods. The conspirators must have left their vehicle. He parked the Dodge, strapped on the Kimber, and picked up his field pack and the H & K rifle. He set them against a gnarled old tree. Then he threw a camouflage net over the truck. Hoisting his pack, Derek looked forward to the hunt.

/⁄ /⁄ /⁄

Philip reached into the back of the 4Runner, handed Ross his pack, and started rummaging through his own. "Let's think about what we need in these packs. What's so heavy in yours, Ross?"

"Water. 'A pint's a pound the world around.' I brought a couple of gallons and my gold pan like you asked me to. There's an army surplus tri-fold shovel in there too."

Philip bowed. "Thank you for bringing the prospector's tools."

Ross added, "I've got a couple of vials and some tweezers too, for when we find the gold."

"Let's each carry a gallon of water. So, what part of your arsenal are you taking?"

"Just the carbine and my Colt. I carried a rifle with a pack for years in Nam. Will you put your grandmother's lunch in yours? Let's boogie."

Philip packed the lunch, zipped the topo map and GPS in an outside pocket of his pack, and shouldered it. He loaded cartridges into the rifle and zipped it back into the rifle case, put spare cartridges in the case's pocket, adjusted the sling, and put it over his left shoulder. Then he checked his access to his holster on his right hip. They walked up the so-called jeep trail that really had room for only one set of tires.

Ross reached down for a rock. He held it up for Philip to see how it sparkled in the sunshine.

"Now this is a pretty unusual alluvial deposit. This beauty is petrified wood. The original cell structure was replaced by silica crystals, thus the sparkles. Those dark smooth ones over there are granite, and this heavy round rust-colored rock is iron ore. Now look at this, rose quartz." He held it up to the light. "The gravel plays out as we top the climb. Let me catch my breath. Look at how the gravel disappears when we cross this sandstone. Soon we're back to sandy dirt with an occasional pebble. We're only going to see the gravel in the canyons."

Philip also stopped, and a big fly buzzed around them. "So let me make sure I understand. Do you think that the black sand is associated with the layer of alluvial gravel?"

They continued walking and the hill leveled off into a meadow with a few trees.

"It's certainly possible. There aren't any other mineral-bearing rocks around here. We'd have to go quite a ways further up into the foothills to hit the igneous rock that the mountains are made of. Besides, this gravel doesn't match the volcanic rocks I saw on the way in. We just need to keep our eyes open when we get to the next canyon."

Ross was walking faster now and Philip had to lengthen his stride to keep up. "Didn't Adams say that the Diggings weren't in a mineralized area?"

"Yeah, and no prospector would find it if they were looking for the usual places for gold. That always confused me. I always assumed that the Diggings were just downstream from a mineral-bearing rock, but I never thought about a gravel bed that wasn't in a mineralized area."

"Ross, you're setting a pace that's a little bit faster than when we were in the *malpais.*"

Ross turned with a grin on his face. "I'll admit that I haven't felt like this in some time. You're right; I'm excited. Nothing else that we've looked at has had any real promise. When I looked for the Diggings before, I never felt like I came close. I always prospected on my own back then, so it's a real pleasure to have someone share my enthusiasm. Thanks for inviting me to leave my misery at home."

"My pleasure, Ross. It's good to see you smiling again. Look at this country. It sure gets green out here after the summer rains; this meadow is filled with wildflowers. Take a look at that view past the stock pond over there. What do those hills in the middle distance look like to you?"

"They're everywhere, pyramids in the desert. Those really look a lot more like the view at Giza than the other ones." He looked toward the water. "From the look of those tracks in the mud, cattle have been down to the pond recently. We'll have to tell Pete."

They walked across the meadow to another fence line. They began their descent into Red Canyon.

Philip looked down the hill. "The trail is starting to hit sandstone again. That next stretch is nothing but rock. You have to look carefully to see where the trail picks up again in order to know where to cross this sandstone ledge. Remember, Fred said that Adams and Davidson escaped across a rocky area so they wouldn't leave prints."

"Look off to the northeast here, Philip. There's a sandstone outcropping that would be a waterfall during the wet times. It drops into that box canyon."

Philip walked to the edge. "I would say close but no cigar. Then this would have to be the sacred place above the falls. There's just a low hill, and there isn't any gravel or black sand."

As the road descended, the gravel began to appear on the trail again. There was an overlook with a view to the south where they saw sandstone canyons converge. There were hoodoos and nooks and crannies in the rock. Reflections from scattered pools sparkled in the streambed. A green carpet of *piñon* and juniper spread before them. Patches of grass were sprinkled across the low hills and into the ponderosa-covered highlands. The volcanic peaks rose to rocky heights. Puffy cumulus clouds dotted the deep blue sky.

Ross spoke softly. "This could be a sacred place. Not only because of the beauty and the contrasts, but also because the Athabascan people respect the gathering of waters. The Animas, La Plata, and San Juan rivers join up in Farmington. The Navajo word for the area is *Totah*, the Meeting of the Waters."

They stared at the beauty of the panorama before them. The shrill scream of a hawk split the silence. They watched it soar in ever widening spirals as it sought its prey.

Ross broke the spell. "Let's look at the sand in that gulch."

As they approached the arroyo bottom, Ross ran ahead. "Look at the opposite bank. It's fused alluvium, an aggregate of gravel and sandstone. It's an ancient stream bed!"

He jumped into the bed of the *arroyo* calling, "Would you look at the black sand here. Philip, an ancient streambed is a prospector's wet dream. It's where a stream deposited gravel and then changed course. Since there's no water associated with them any more, you only find them like this, when a stream cuts through and exposes it. A couple of ancient streambeds that were found during the Cariboo gold rush in British Columbia produced millions in gold. Look, there's more fused gravel upstream in the canyon to the west."

Ross ran up the canyon. Philip called after him, "I haven't run with a pack since basic training. I'll catch up with you."

Ross ran an erratic course through the canyon bottom. He would look down at the sand and then pinball from one side of the gravel outcrop to the other. He disappeared around the corner.

When Philip rounded the corner, Ross was coming back. He shouted, "The black sand and the gravel bed both run out up there. The canyon opens up to grasslands. Let's look below the trail. Take a gander at how the sand and gravel alternate on the wall of the canyon here. This area was deposited during some big changes geologically. The river may have been changing course because it was nearing an inland sea. The Plains of San Agustín used to be a lakebed. Anyway, this gravel is different from the rock of the peaks, because there were different peaks then. This gravel deposit was made by a stream that flowed here millions of years ago."

Philip pointed up the other canyon that converged from the south. "What do you think?"

Ross walked over so that he had a view up the canyon. "I'd say that it looks like it has less gravel than the other branch. Let's go downstream. You can see that the congregate rock is softer than the sandstone below it. The sandstone bedrock peeks out of the sand here and there in the streambed. Again, this is good news for prospectors. The weight of gold brings it down through the sand and gravel to bedrock. If you don't have to move too much fill, you can get to the best gold-producing areas at bedrock faster. Look at the sandstone that's protruding over there by that little muddy pool. See how it has these horizontal cracks in the top. Crevices like this can be catch bins for gold."

Philip felt himself caught up in his friend's enthusiasm not only because it was so genuine, but also because it was so rare. Ross took off his pack and faced an alcove in the fused gravel canyon wall.

"This little side stream cuts straight through the gravel. Sometimes gold stays near where it falls. We should take a closer look here."

Philip traced the black sand around the bend. As he followed it, his heart leapt. Ahead of him lay a sandstone ledge where the canyon dropped straight down fifteen feet. It would be a significant waterfall when water flowed. The canyon walls made sharp bends with sensuously curving lower levels and jagged heights with pinnacles that reached to the sky.

"Ross, come here. I think we've found our zigzag canyon."

18

Ross stared in wide-eyed astonishment at the sandstone canyon dropping away from the waterfall. He pointed downstream to a narrowing of the canyon walls.

"Doesn't it look like a man could touch both sides at once, *khayee?*"

"It does, and maybe on the top too, from the way that overhang juts out. It reminds me that the last time we looked at something like this together was the *Siq* at Petra in Jordan. Remember when we went off to that Bedouin dance up in the *wadi*, and our friends sent the Jordanian army out to look for us."

"Yes, only this canyon is khaki-colored instead of rose red. I hope they won't have to send the army out this time."

"It also looks like you couldn't get out of this end on a horse, making it a canyon with one entrance like Adams described. In fact, it looks like you couldn't get out of this end without some mountaineering skills. There's a little trail on the west side. Maybe there are some cracks where we might get down. Let me set a waypoint on the GPS so the Apaches can't make us forget."

Ross halted a short way down the faint game trail. "It sure does zigzag. There's a side canyon where you might get down to the bottom with gloves and some bouldering, but there's got to be a better way."

Philip pointed across the canyon to an area on the east side where a watercourse cut through the sandstone overhang.

"That looks like a possibility; let's go over and give it a try. Take a look downstream. It looks like your waterfall side-canyon from up the road enters this one at the bend, Ross."

As they crossed the streambed above the waterfall, Ross said, "I'm glad I brought the gold pan. Waterfalls are good sites for placer findings. They create deep pools and eddies where gold collects."

They followed another game trail along the hill on the eastern side of the canyon until the side stream cut through the sandstone. They had to pick their way down though the rock. At one point, an overhang made the access tight. Ross followed Philip, but his pack caught the overhang, forcing him further out from the sandstone wall. The rock under his feet moved, so he heaved himself back against the rock wall up the trail.

Philip called, "That was too close for comfort. Ross, give me your rifle. I'm going to put the guns and my pack on that ledge near the bottom."

When he returned, Ross handed his pack to Philip. "Be careful with that."

He proceeded cautiously, keeping close to the wall. They reached the bottom without mishap and walked back along the canyon floor to the waterfall. The top of the sandstone cliff hung over the bottom of the canyon, creating cave-like alcoves. The sky was only visible as a narrow slice above their heads. Curvaceous shelves of rock accentuated the serpentine bends of the canyon. Deposits of black sand demonstrated the flow patterns of water across the sandy bottom. They put their packs on a ledge and approached the horseshoe-shaped cavity behind the edge of the falls. Water dripped slowly from a crack in the waterfall's stone edge into the center of the sandy streambed.

Philip spoke in hushed tones. "I think that this should be the sacred area. It feels like the nave of a church in here."

He advanced towards the dripping water. Suddenly, his eyes widened and his mouth fell open as he dropped six inches. His boots disappeared into the quicksand, and he began to struggle to extricate himself. Ross carefully stepped closer and reached over to him. Philip grabbed his hand and thanked Ross as he pulled himself out. As they warily retreated, the sand underneath them trembled while they sank in a couple of inches with every step.

When they reached less shaky ground near the sandstone ledge, Ross laughed. "That looked like an old Tarzan movie for a second there. Obviously, the sand holds water pretty well here."

Philip stomped his boots on the sandstone and tried to catch his breath. "I have to admit that I was shocked. I've been in quicksand before, but never anything that was that quick. The last few minutes are reminding us that Gruber isn't the only threat here."

"You're right. We need to be very aware of the weather. If a flash flood caught us in this box canyon, there would be no escape." He surveyed the canyon bottom. "The center of the pool could get scoured clean by the force of the falling water anyway. These edges and that eddy on the other side of this ledge would be better for collecting gold. There's a lot of black sand in that eddy."

"Why don't we pan here? I'd like to see how it's done."

"This is as likely a spot as any. Let's get the stuff from my pack. I really like these new plastic pans, especially if you have to carry it any distance. They're a lot lighter."

Philip watched as Ross took a shovel full of sand with a concentration of black sand into the pan. He added another half-shovel of sand until the pan was almost three-quarters full and then poured enough water over the sand to cover it. Shaking the pan from front to back and side to side, he reached in and fished out the larger pebbles and inspected them. Then he began rhythmically rolling the slushy mixture around the pan, making Elvis-like gyrations.

Ross shouted, "Rock and roll!"

Water and sand spilled over the front edge with every rotation. The remaining slush grew thick.

"Philip, can you grab the water jug and add water when I tell you to? It's harder to pan when you don't have a stream to use. This has a lot more sand, less dirt, and fewer pebbles than you usually find in high-country mineralized areas. We have to keep it wet so the heavy material will sink to the bottom."

Ross rocked the pan and Philip added water until they were down to a thin layer in the bottom of the pan. Ross reached into his fatigues for a pair of tweezers. He picked at grains of quartz and tiny yellow stones. He sloshed the concentrate across the riffles on the pan.

"I like the new riffles on these pans too. It creates a mini-sluice in your pan. The heavier material gets caught up in these ridges, but there's no gold here."

"With all of the signs that we've found that led us here, I thought we'd get at least a fleck or two of gold. Let's find a place with black sand where we can go down to bedrock. Maybe that area over there." Philip pointed to an eddy between sandstone ridges. "Can I borrow your shovel, Ross?"

Philip dug down about two feet until he hit sandstone. He shoveled the layer of wet sand just above bedrock into the pan. Ross repeated the panning process until they got down to concentrate. He pulled a plastic pill bottle out of his pocket and picked up the tweezers. He fished out a miniscule stone and held it up to Philip.

"Gold from the Lost Adams' Diggings."

Philip squinted at the tiny grain of gold. "It sure isn't the size of an acorn."

Ross placed it in the vial and continued working the concentrate. He pulled out a couple of gold colored flecks that he said were possibilities, and then he dumped the pan.

"I don't think this is going to turn out to be the richest placer mine in the Southwest. What do you want to do?"

"We shouldn't base our judgment on just two pans, but I need a higher rate of reinforcement or I'm going to get bored with panning pretty quickly. I don't think that Buck would have panned an area that yielded one fleck every other pan either. Let's try a couple more places."

Ross suggested, "Let's scoop up this recent layer of black sand and pan it. That will tell us if any gold washed down during the last storm."

Philip skimmed off the black sand from several likely spots and put it in the pan. Their bedrock hole had gradually filled with water.

Ross looked into the hole. "This is typical of New Mexico rivers. Too thick to drink, too thin to plow."

They used the muddy water in order to conserve their own supply. Ross worked the pan and Philip scooped up water. They found a couple of flecks that Ross certified as gold, but they were so miniscule that Philip had to take the tweezers from Ross' shaky hands. He carefully put them into the vial and held it up so they both could see the tiny granules of gold.

Ross said, "Well there's some gold in this canyon, but this is still not a promising rate of return. What's next?"

"Let's explore the canyon further. Maybe we can find the cabin and the gold under the hearthstone. Then we won't have to pan for it."

Ross laughed. "Dream on and lead on. We can come back and pan some more later."

They grabbed their packs and rifles and headed downstream. The narrows downstream didn't actually have walls that were close enough to touch, but the effect of large amounts of water squeezed into a narrow canyon were apparent everywhere. Deadwood was lodged high on the rugged canyon walls. When they passed the narrows, a stand of scrawny willows stood about head high. Grasses and dead leaves from other trees festooned the willow stalks.

Philip examined the debris near the top of one of the willows and bent it over.

"It looks like water at least four feet deep has run through here recently. This canyon gets some serious flash floods. We've really got to keep a weather eye out, or our pummeled bodies will be found in

Alamocita Creek. It's harder to get the big picture of the cloud build-up down here, so we've got to look up the side canyons to see other slices of sky. It already looks like there are a lot more clouds than there were when we were at that overlook. I'm concerned about what's happening up in the mountains. We need to find a place where we can see if the clouds look like rain upstream."

Ross continued walking down the canyon. "I agree; we have to be vigilant. It looks like it opens up a little past the side canyon. We can get a better view there. The combination of these overhangs and flash flooding sure makes this look like it could be Baxter's lost canyon."

They picked their way through a field of large boulders. Water emerged as a tiny stream where the canyon floor dropped, only to disappear again into the sand. Boulders channeled the streambed into a four-foot-high dry waterfall. They clambered down the rocks.

When he reached the sandy bottom, Ross shouted, "My turn."

His boots were half-covered on each step as he ran across the quicksand to stone.

Philip smirked. "And my turn to be amused. You looked like one of those Jesus lizards that walk on water. We've really got to watch our step around here."

Ross stamped his feet to get the sand off. "I don't need any more convincing; you really sink fast in this stuff. I'm going to try to stay near the edges."

The side canyon joined them from the west. Water trickled down a sandstone formation with horizontal cracks forming small ledges. It was the kind of place where people get flagstone. The water flowed down the mini-stair steps and vanished into the sand as it entered the main canyon.

"I am a trained hydrologist. I will not let Red Canyon pull me into her depths. I still want to check out this side canyon, but I am going to cross the streambed above the place where the water enters. If you want to wait here, I'll be back in a few minutes."

Philip watched Ross scramble up the little canyon. Within seconds, he had vanished. Philip took off his pack and rifle. He sat on the ground and used his pack as a backrest. The sun went behind a cloud and the canyon cooled slightly. He closed his eyes and felt the gentle breeze flowing up the canyon. Slowing his breathing, he considered their situation. There were lots of indications that this could be the zigzag canyon. Why couldn't they come up with enough gold to confirm it? He listened to Ross clambering around above him and tried to let himself relax.

/ˌ /ˌ /ˌ

Derek was concerned. They had split up, and McIntyre was heading right for him. He took cover behind a rock on the west canyon rim. He had followed the traitors to the canyon but decided that high ground would be a strategic advantage. McIntyre wasn't climbing out of the canyon towards him. The camouflage-covered coward scrambled past, following the little canyon. He looked like he was examining the canyon wall again, the same way that he had done up higher. What were they looking for? Could the gold panning have been an attempt to find the gold plating from battered high-tech electronics? Were the terrorists trying to recover part of the missile or one of their own tracking devices? By now, he had no doubt that the Strategic Defense Initiative was the reason they were in this part of the Datils. He had difficulty coming up with a reason why they needed a geologist to find whatever they were looking for. He would continue to follow them until he knew why the terrorists were exploring Red Canyon. McIntyre came back down past him, empty-handed.

/ˌ /ˌ /ˌ

Ross called out to Philip, "There's more gravel and black sand up there. But there isn't that much of it."

"Let's keep going downstream. I just want to see if there's a place where they could've built a cabin."

As they made their way downstream, they crossed back and forth across the canyon to stay on terra firma. There were places where the banks were higher, but even those areas showed signs of flooding. The canyon widened, and there were places where erosion made it possible to clamber out. After they rounded a bend, the streambed dropped down several feet. The banks were now high enough above the flood plain to sustain tall junipers. They walked across to a low tree-covered terrace, made their way up the bank, and surveyed the area.

Philip said, "This site is big enough and high enough to support a cabin and has enough room around for outdoor activities too."

Ross marched over to a large flat rectangular rock that had a diagonal crack across it. "Could this be the hearthstone?" He lifted up the larger piece. "And guess what's under it? Ants and lots of them. I'm going to get out the shovel and dig a little. I'm going to piss the little buggers off, so stand back."

Ross danced a little jig while he dug to try to keep the ants off him. After scooping a few shovels, he retreated. He pulled up his pants and brushed off several ants.

"I'm not willing to dig further. These little red devils have quite a bite. There's just sandy loam under that rock. I don't think anyone buried anything there. The treasure could be deeper, but then why would the hearthstone be on the surface? Let's explore a little further to see if we can find the little door."

Philip agreed. "I think we should check it out, but we need to be quick. Look up, there's more cloud cover than blue sky. We can't stay here much longer. Besides, I don't see black sand anymore."

As they continued down, the canyon grew wider and the cliffs began to break down into low hills. They could see the far side of another canyon with higher walls coming together with theirs.

Ross laughed and pointed to a black band at the bottom of the cliff. "Here's Fred's next coal mine. It looks like it's pretty good quality too. We'll have to tell him about it when we report finding the zigzag canyon."

"Let's find the little door first. This canyon is disappearing. Unless the little door is in the tall cliff on the east side where the canyons merge, I don't think we have a match."

The confluence of the streams was disappointing. The streambed looked more like a broad valley. They walked up the other canyon a short distance and climbed up a five-foot ledge. They looked up and down.

Philip said, "Not much in the way of black sand here either, and I sure don't see any signs of a little door."

Ross turned and went back down the ledge. "I'm disappointed too, but remember that Baxter said that the geography had been rearranged by an earthquake. We certainly can't say that there isn't gold somewhere in Red Canyon based on just three pans full of sand. Let's go back up and try a couple more places."

Philip surveyed the sky. "We might have time for one quick pan. We need to go back soon regardless of where we are on the search. The clouds are turning gray, and they're really building up over the peaks."

"They're forming a typical monsoon season anvil-shaped cloud. I like the way they glow in the sunlight at the top, then get darker at the bottom. But, you're right. It doesn't matter if it rains here, it going to rain upcountry for sure. We could have some real gully washers plunge down these slopes. Let's see how it looks when we reach the upper canyon."

/i /i /i

Derek watched the conspirators scurry up the canyon. He had been able to follow them while remaining on higher ground. He held the sniper rifle up to his shoulder, cradled the stock with his cheek, and sighted down the scope. He could pick them off easily, but dead men don't talk. He needed to interrogate them to find out exactly what they were doing. Although the Strategic Defense Initiative seemed like the obvious reason that they were in this canyon, their behavior was confusing. If they were retrieving something, they certainly didn't know where it was. He was perplexed by the geological activity. Was McIntyre recruited because a geologist was necessary for this project?

Derek felt his anger rising. How could a decorated veteran sell out his country? Alcoholism dominated McIntyre's life. He got enough contract work to support himself, but he blew it all at the bar. Derek was sure that money was a motivator for the traitor. Was he so alienated that he didn't care what happened to his native land? Or was he so angry that he wanted to hurt other people to drown out his own pain?

Then there was Habib, using the espionage training that he had received from the U.S. military and turning it against his own government. An Internet buddy had tracked down a retired CIA agent who was active in Lebanon at the same time that Habib was there. The spook reported that there had been doubts about Habib from the beginning. He made contacts too easily, and some of his pinko university friends had strong connections to the *Baathi* party in Iraq. The intelligence reports that Habib generated were sometimes useful, but they were always viewed with some skepticism. The retired agent had told Derek's friend some interesting stories about Habib. It looked like his friends from Saudi Arabia and the Gulf States must have made him an offer that he couldn't refuse. They must have waited until fundamentalist Islam reached critical mass.

Derek had to give Habib some credit. His woodcarving made him appear to be a sensitive artistic type, and the part-time private investigator gig was perfect cover. The investigations kept him active enough to maintain his skills as well as allowing him to do some covert work for his masters without appearing obvious. The P.I. license gave him a reason to access espionage equipment. So far, Habib had only revealed his skills with his hand held GPS, but Derek was sure that he had a few other high tech devices up his sleeve. He walked toward the point where the side canyon came in from the west. He scrambled down and took a position on the other side. Once they were past the side canyon, he could cover all the possible routes out of Red Canyon.

/h /h /h

Philip and Ross could feel the effects of their pace up the canyon. The wet sand made the canyon bottom feel humid. They were sweating profusely by the time they reached Ross' side canyon. They pulled out their water bottles and drank thirstily.

Ross looked up the narrow opening. "I'd like to spend more time up there some day, but from the looks of those clouds I think we should continue on out. I don't think we're going to get dramatically different results from one pan. This canyon is going to have to be systematically examined in order to know what's really here."

"I agree. This canyon matches the Adams's legend better than anywhere else we've been, but I don't think we should linger. Those arroyos that we have to drive across are still a mile and a half away by foot. Let's hit it."

19

Derek waited until the turncoats made their way past the side canyon into the narrows. As they clambered up the low dry waterfall, he stood up and shouted, "Drop your weapons, traitors."

Philip and Ross exchanged looks, and then each dove behind a large boulder on either side of the streambed. Philip drew his pistol. Ross shrugged off his pack and brought up the M16.

Philip called out, "Gruber, what do you want from us?"

"Stop playing innocent, Habib. You know that I've been watching you. I don't understand all of your treasonous actions, but we both know what you're doing here now."

Ross yelled, "We're not claim jumpers. We were just trying to find the placer mine for Philip's client. We're on our way out anyway."

"Nice try, McIntyre, great cover story. I don't know why you were actually using that pan, but gold isn't the real reason you're here, is it?"

Philip turned to Ross and shrugged his shoulders. "I don't know what you're trying to make us say, but the reason that we're here is to search for a lost gold mine."

Derek laughed. "You two have already found your gold mine. I bet your Arab masters pay you very well."

Philip feelings went from confused to angry. "What are you talking about? My client is an Anglo from California who is looking for a gold mine that her grandfather might've found."

Derek aimed at a taller boulder behind Philip and fired. The copper-clad hollow-point bullet mushroomed and scattered rock fragments as the shot resounded in the canyon. Philip felt pain in the back of his neck and realized that he had been nicked by shrapnel.

Derek continued, "I'm serious. I know that your training won't allow you to betray a mission this easily. Maybe somebody else would buy that crap, but I did my homework. I know who you are."

As Philip pulled the Remington out of the case, he whispered to Ross, "Can you see him?"

"No, but it sounds like he's on the west side behind the sandstone rim above us, south of the side canyon about fifteen, maybe twenty yards away. Let me try."

Ross shouted, "Gruber. I'm a geologist. Why do you think I'm here?"

Derek replied, "I don't know why they need a geologist, but you're here because you're a sand-nigger lover."

Philip couldn't contain himself. "What the hell does this have to do with Arabs?"

"Besides the fact that I'm talking to one? Besides the fact that you were part of *Al Fatah* in Beirut? Are they still running you, or did you branch out?"

Philip retorted, "I was working for the United States Marine Corps in Beirut. What does that ancient history have to do with this madness?"

Derek sneered, "You tell me, jarhead. Why are you really in the Missile Impact area?"

Ross yelled, "Philip didn't even know about this area until we got here."

"He didn't have to because he had Benedict Arnold with him. McIntyre, you won the Bronze Star in Nam. How could you turn your back on your country? Is it worth what the *Saudis* pay you?"

"Gruber, you're nuts! We're here looking for the Lost Adams

Diggings. I have never taken money from the *Saudis*. I lived in Saudi Arabia, but I worked for American oil companies."

"So how did the Islamic militants turn you? Did your drinking land you in jail? Did you kill a whore? Maybe it was a boy. My biker friends and I loved how sweetly you sang to Habib in Arabic."

Ross leapt up and squeezed off a burst of bullets. Derek returned fire, hitting the rock that Ross had ducked behind.

Philip tried to calm his distraught friend. "He's trying to get our goat. Don't waste your ammo."

Then he shouted, "Gruber, you're right. Both us of have lived in the Middle East; we both speak Arabic. But think about it. Would Ross live like he does if he had the big bucks? That truck of his sure doesn't look like a Saudi Land Rover."

Derek snickered. "Just more cover. I'd like to see your offshore accounts. McIntyre's a pathetic has been, so he needs to reinvent himself. What's your excuse?"

Philip saw that Ross was wound up like a spring. He whispered, "Ross, don't bite; he's baiting you. Everybody knows that you've had your troubles. I admire you for going forward in spite of everything. Don't let him get to you."

"Well, master spy. Are you bringing your asset back under your control? Does your boy need to have his hand held?"

Philip motioned for Ross to cool it. "I don't know what this has to do with anything, but I was a spy for military intelligence over twenty years ago. I didn't like it, so I quit."

"You quit. That's bullshit! You just quit working for America. So why were you arrested after nine-eleven?"

Philip felt his attempt to use negotiation tactics slipping away as his anger grew.

"They arrested me because of racial profiling, and they released me because there was no evidence."

Derek yelled, "That's just because they didn't look hard enough.

Racial profiling, my ass! I know that you're a *Baathi* spy. What do you know about the Strategic Defense Initiative?"

"I am not a *Baathi* spy."

Derek said mockingly, "Is that so? Then why did you stay at the Iraqi ambassador's house in Damascus? Were you connected to both the Iraqi and the Syrian *Baathi* parties or just to one?"

Philip had to unclench his jaw to answer. "I stayed at the ambassador's residence in Damascus because his son was my friend. Samir invited me to visit Damascus, and his parents were the most gracious, generous hosts I've ever met. I've hated the *Baathis* ever since Samir's father was recalled to Baghdad by Saddam Hussein who was the Iraqi Chief of Security at that time. The ambassador disappeared forever; and my friend lost a father and his country."

Derek replied smugly, "So you admit a connection to Saddam Hussein. You know how easily hate can turn into love."

Ross shouted, "You're totally paranoid. You're twisting everything to match this Arab conspiracy theory of yours."

Derek fired at the overhanging rock ledge above Philip and loosed a rain of sandstone. "I am not paranoid. You're the one who's delusional if you think that there isn't an Arab conspiracy. What was nine-eleven? I could be wrong about the *Baathis*. After all, the *Saudis* are the ones with the deep pockets. How many of the hijackers were *Saudis*?"

Philip was enraged. "Neither of us works for the *Saudis* or any other Arab government."

"Not a blemish on your patriotism. What about that time in Beirut when you were throwing rocks at the American Embassy with your Palestine Liberation Organization comrades. Why did the crowd scream, 'Saudi spy'?"

Philip turned to Ross again in bewilderment. "Where's he getting this stuff?"

Philip tried to explain. "I had to join my PLO friends; that was my cover. And my girlfriend's brother, Fuad, had worked as an intern for

Saudi television the summer before. That's why they were yelling 'Saudi spy."

"That's right, the *Saudi* princess. I bet she had beautiful eyes. Are you denying your connection to the *Saudi* royal family too?"

Philip felt like a volcano ready to explode. "She didn't want anything to do with *Saudi* royalty. She moved to New York after she graduated from the American University of Beirut."

"And you haven't seen her since, of course. Well, I've got to admit that you've got a comeback for everything. Maybe you're not as inept as I thought."

Ross whispered, "He's totally paranoid. I met some guys like him when I was on the psych wards at the VA Hospital in Albuquerque. Most of the guys I knew were Vietnam era, so they focused on the Asian neighborhoods around the hospital. Some of them had to ride the bus with Vietnamese speaking passengers. By the time they got to the VA, they were raving about gooks and hootches. Maybe he's taken his Desert Storm duty a little too far."

"You're probably right, but this guy isn't some disorganized loony tunes. He's had to do some serious research to come up with some of this stuff. He must have talked to some spook who knew me in Beirut. I gave reports to my superiors about these incidents, but I'd half forgotten them."

Gruber yelled, "Don't even think about escaping. There's no way out on the west side of the canyon, and I've got the east side covered. You're not leaving until I find out what you traitors are doing."

Ross responded, "We're not traitors or spies. Why would I carry a gold pan if we're not looking for gold?"

"I haven't figured that out, but I know why you're carrying weapons because you've already tried to shoot me. Besides, most prospectors don't wear desert camouflage and carry an M-Sixteen."

Ross' frustration was mounting. "Our camo and weapons are a response to your ambush yesterday. You started this."

"Did that line work with your parents when you were fighting with your brothers? You both pulled pistols immediately after I shot over your heads yesterday. The only difference today is that you brought long guns."

Philip turned to Ross. "It's no use. Logic won't work; he's delusional. Nothing short of a confession that we're *Al Qaida* operatives trying to destroy America's defenses will satisfy him. He's going to kill us, but he likes this cat and mouse game. He's got us between a rock and a hard place. We've got to find a way out soon. Look at that sky; it looks as dismal as our situation."

Ross looked up. "You're right, but he's got us trapped. You could get out on the west side of the canyon if you had climbing equipment and plenty of time, which we don't. And there are some other possibilities besides the way we came down on the east, but we'd be easy targets. If we tried to go downstream, we'd have to go right in front of him. He picked his ambush well."

"We may end up going downstream with a wall of water. If we can't flee, we're going to have to fight. Ross, you've got more experience in firefights. What should we do?"

Derek's tone was more strident. "Okay, renegades. We've wasted enough time. Tell me what you're doing here now. You're not getting out of here until you come clean."

Ross fired a shot at the sandstone rock in front of Gruber. He said to Philip, "He's got the high ground advantage, but we outnumber him. We're trapped, but he can't get to us without giving up his position. We could wait him out, but the storm isn't going to give us that opportunity."

"I can't believe that we're sitting here in this box canyon with a thunderstorm building. Even without Gruber, I'd be nervous. So how can we use our superior numbers to our advantage?"

"I could be the decoy to make him leave cover, so that you could shoot him. How good are you with that rifle?"

"You don't mean decoy, you mean sacrificial lamb. I'll bet that Gruber is quite a marksman with that futuristic sniper rifle. What's that stock made out of anyway?"

"I think it's a polycarbonate, definitely state of the art."

"I used to be pretty good as a sharpshooter, but it's been a while. These Remington Seven Hundreds were good sniper rifles in their day too. I haven't even had a chance to sight this in."

"No time like the present."

Derek interrupted them. "Come on, camel dung. Fess up."

Philip's marksmanship skills had developed through his spiritual searches. During his freshman year at the University of New Mexico, one of his friends was a practitioner of the Japanese art of *kyudo*, the way of the bow. He brought Philip to an archery range, but he didn't give Philip hands on instruction. Instead, he talked about the interconnectedness of the archer, bow, arrow, and target. He emphasized that attitude, movement, and technique existed in perfect harmony. Philip didn't develop much skill at nonattachment while his arrow was going wild. During his rifle training in the Marines the following year, the message hit home. He could release the pain that had driven him to enlist by achieving oneness between the marksman, rifle, bullet, and target. There was a world of difference between the sanctuary of the shooting range and the turmoil that he was experiencing at the moment. He couldn't allow himself to think about Gruber's paranoid ravings or the impending storm.

There was a jagged break at the top of the rock that he was sheltered behind that he could use for partial cover while shooting. He held the Remington to his shoulder, placed his cheek on the stock, and sighted through the scope. He slowed his breathing and found a fair sized branch in the juniper above Gruber's hiding place. He held his stance, held his breath, and squeezed the trigger. The branch exploded and Gruber let out a string of curses.

"Jesus," cried Ross. "I guess you've got it sighted in."

"Actually it shoots a little to the left. Jiddi let me use this rifle while we were out hunting deer. I've always liked it. It sounds like Gruber doesn't think much of our mothers. Now what?"

"Can you do that again? There's another boulder a few yards down that's big enough to provide cover for me if you can keep him occupied. We've got to separate far enough so that he can't keep both of us in his sights at the same time. I'll keep doing that until I get close to the side canyon."

"I don't like it. You'll be putting yourself in mortal danger. However, I just felt a drop of rain. We've got to do something fast. If we're not out of the narrow part of this canyon by the time the flood hits, Gruber will be the least of our worries."

"I just felt one too. Gruber's Arabic training seems to have given him a fairly good command of profanity. If being part of the militia fits the Identity Church profile, he's a homophobe. So you know what to shout after you put it to him. I'll give you a nod when I'm ready."

Ross nodded and Philip shot another branch over Gruber's head. Philip yelled "Ari fiki."

Ross had been right. Gruber became enraged at the idea of being sexually dominated by a male. He shot back at Philip, narrowly missing him as Philip ducked behind the rock. Ross made it to his boulder. The raindrops were closer together now.

Philip laughed at the sight of Ross successfully scurrying to the boulder. Then reality hit. All they had accomplished was making sure that Gruber couldn't pick them off at the same time. Even if Ross got to the side canyon, wouldn't he be just as exposed there? Philip looked around. He saw that if he went up canyon, he could be up on a ledge under overhanging rock where Gruber couldn't possibly have a shot at him from his current location. He could have hid out there for a while. But the big splatters of raindrops that were hitting now made a wait seem unlikely. Besides, if he didn't continue to participate in the exchange, Gruber would just focus all his energy on Ross.

Philip taunted Gruber. "That sure sounded like an over-reaction. Maybe you Neo-Nazis are just like the Nazis. I know some of the Gestapo liked boys. Don't you militia guys get together for sleepovers?"

Derek hissed through his clenched jaw, "I don't like boys. I have a girlfriend."

Philip relished having some inside information on Gruber. "That's right, the one at the prison that you can never have sex with. Pretty good cover, Gruber."

Derek stood up and roared, "I don't love men; I love my country."

Ross squeezed off a burst and caught Gruber in the left shoulder. He ran for the next rock, but tripped. Gruber bellowed like a bull, but he brought the rifle up and shot Ross in the leg as he stumbled toward cover. Ross screamed in pain and rolled behind the boulder. Philip shot hurriedly and knocked Gruber's hat off as he disappeared behind his cover. His shot might have grazed his head.

Derek called out. "Just flesh wounds, boys, but if you had any thoughts about leaving this canyon alive, forget about it. No murderous traitors will get past me!"

Philip couldn't see Ross. He knew that Ross carried a first aid kit, and he hoped that the vet could do his own field dressings. He needed to give him some time. He replaced the two cartridges that he had shot.

He yelled, "You never intended to let us leave this canyon alive. In order to justify your paranoia, you have to kill us. Face it Gruber, you've gone round the bend. No real counter espionage agent kills off potential informants, and no disciplined military man would be doing this lone ranger bit. Admit it, you're Section Eight."

"You're the one who's crazy. You're saying that I should trust the Federal Government's intelligence agencies. If I turned you in, your information wouldn't get to a decision maker for weeks. I think the code of the West works better here. If a man is rustling your herd, kill him."

Philip replied, "People know our location and that you've shot at us before. You'll never get away with this."

"Stopping you is more important than what happens to me, but I can be packed and gone before they even find your bodies."

Philip was now certain that that they would have to immobilize or kill Gruber if they wanted to live. It was really raining now. He slipped his poncho over his head. He could hear water splashing down the waterfall. A stream was forming in the middle of the canyon. His fear was growing. He remembered the tragic flash flood in Albuquerque a few years before that swept a car down an arroyo and killed its young driver. Six inches of rain had fallen in an hour over the foothills of the Sandias, and every arroyo became a raging torrent. But he was more worried about Ross. He hadn't heard anything from him since he'd been shot.

Suddenly Ross yelled, "Plan B!"

Philip shot at the rock that Gruber hid behind. He was shocked to see Ross hurl a stick of dynamite toward Gruber. As Philip fired again, Ross pointed what looked like a television remote at the top of the cliff. When the dynamite reached the top of its trajectory, a deafening roar filled their ears and debris pummeled them. Gruber's body flew through the air, bounced off a ledge half-way down the cliff, and splattered onto the quicksand below the small waterfall.

They stared at his still form as rocks continued to tumble down the hill. Just as the rain settled the dust, they heard a roar above them. They both turned to watch a three-foot wall of muddy water plummet over the waterfall. Philip scrambled up the cliff side and wedged himself into a crack. Ross hobbled up to an over-hanging tree trunk and pulled himself up. Water plunged through the narrows, rising rapidly, and pulling at their legs. Philip managed to support his body by his elbows, but the torrent threatened to yank him away from safety. The surging flood tugged at the front of his poncho until a jagged juniper branch caught it. The impact almost jerked Philip off his perch. The force of the branch swirling in the water was choking him. He braced his downstream arm against an outcropping and brought up his left leg to wedge his knee in another crack. He was able to reach down for his combat knife and sliced the poncho away from his neck. He breathed a sigh of relief and leaned back into the cliff.

He watched the tumbling floodwaters forcing Ross' legs downstream as he clung to the tree trunk. Abruptly the rain stopped, but the rushing flood continued to tear at them. He shouted at Ross but he couldn't be heard over the roar of the cascading water. Gradually the torrent subsided. Ross was able to swing his good leg over the trunk. Philip found a better purchase for his feet above the water and took some of the strain off his arms. He looked at the point where Gruber's body had fallen. Debris filled water tumbled over the low falls and covered the breadth of the canyon.

Philip was glad to see that Ross had his pack dangling off one shoulder. His own had been swept away, but he'd held on to the Remington. He pointed to his leg and shouted, "Ross, how badly are you hurt?"

Ross gave him the Okay hand sign, but Philip didn't think he had really heard him. He looked at Ross's torn pants and the blood dripping down his calf. The elastic wrap that he had seen earlier must have been torn off by the floodwaters. The receding waters revealed a ledge upstream that Philip leapt onto. He sat down and was suddenly swept with chills. He yelled to Ross again, "Can you walk?"

Ross shouted back, "I'll need a splint and some help."

Philip replied, "When it gets low enough to wade across, I'll join you."

He lay back on the rocky ledge. Gruber was dead and it was his fault. This was the first time he felt directly responsible for someone's death. Years ago, Ross had told him that he had killed several Viet Cong when his company had been ambushed and that he still had nightmares about it. He wondered what level his friend's post-traumatic stress disorder symptoms were hitting now. His own adrenaline rush had passed, and now he felt emotionally drained.

Across the river, a rock emerged near Ross, and he was able to swing himself over close enough to clamber onto it. He stretched out on the rock and lay still. Eventually he sat up and looked at his leg. Philip could see the color drain from Ross's face as he surveyed the exit wound. Was Ross beginning to show symptoms of shock? Philip needed to get over there fast. The water level looked as if it were just over knee-high. Philip looked for a piece of wood to use as a staff. He could see an eight-foot long relatively straight piece of driftwood lodged above the crack that had given him sanctuary. He climbed back up and was surprised to see part of the back of his poncho caught on the rocks. He put the remnant in the cargo pocket of his pants. He reached for the pole. Tugging on it, he was able to jerk it free. Then he went upstream as far as he could on the ledge and eased himself into the water. He scrambled to find footing and used the staff to feel in front of him. The bottom was much rockier than he remembered. Without the staff, he couldn't have made it; a faltering tripod was better than a falling biped. The current pushed him downstream and made him move at a faster pace than he would have liked. He managed to reach the east side a couple of yards above Ross's rock.

"*Kif l-hal, khayee?* Have you been able to stop the bleeding?"

Ross smiled weakly. "Glad you could make it. I've slowed it down some. Can you help me get a bandage on this leg?"

Philip pulled the first aid kit out of Ross' pack and found antibacterial cream and four-inch bandages. As he put the cream on Ross' calf, he felt slightly nauseous. It was an ugly wound. Ross moaned whenever he touched him. Philip asked for the blood-soaked bandana that Ross had used to put pressure on his leg and rinsed it in the stream.

"This water is muddy, but it hasn't been around long enough to gather a lot of bacteria."

He squeezed most of the water out of the bandana and folded the diagonal into a six-inch strip. He asked Ross to hold two of the compresses on the back of his leg while he doubled one over the entry wound. He wrapped the bandana around Ross's leg and tied it tight. Then he found water in Ross's pack and made him drink some. He rummaged through the first aid kit and found some codeine with acetaminophen. Ross washed it down with more water.

"We're going to have to get you up and moving. I don't know if we're going to be able to get out of here in the SUV. At least when we reach the 4Runner, we'll be safe and dry, and I've got food, water, and another first aid kit there. Let's hope that Sarah calls Don and he sends help. Let me find some wood we can use for a splint. I think we can use strips from my poncho to hold it together."

"Before you make that splint, you might want me to check your neck. You're dripping blood, too."

Philip felt the back of his neck. Now that he focused on it, he was aware of the pain. The adrenaline from the fight had masked it before. "You're right, and I can feel a bump. I guess I'm carrying a little lead from that ricochet. Can you put some of that antibiotic and a bandage on it for me?"

After Ross bandaged his neck, Philip found a couple of pieces of wood for the splint. "I'm only going to splint it up to your knee. You won't be able to negotiate this rough ground with a full leg splint. You can use my staff as a crutch, and I'll try to support you when I can."

As he made the splint, he asked, "How are you feeling about Gruber's death?"

"I've got mixed feelings. 'Thou shalt not kill' is one of the Ten Commandments. Taking a life is a terrible thing."

Philip looked Ross eye to eye. "If you hadn't used that dynamite, we would both be dead. Thank you for saving my life."

Ross smiled. "I'm kind of glad I saved mine too. After so many failures, it's good to know that I still have it in me when the chips are down."

20

Philip put on Ross's pack and helped support him while they made their way back to the place where they entered the canyon. Water trickled down their path. Philip helped Ross until they reached the narrow rock ledge with the overhang.

Philip said, "I'm going to go first to make sure that this rock hasn't shifted any more. Give me your staff and I'll put it on the other side. You're going to need to use your hands here."

"This place makes me nervous; I almost fell here before I got shot."

The rock was no more or less unstable than it had been on the way down. Philip set down the pack and staff and went back to Ross.

"Grab the cliff side and put your injured leg right in front of the rock. Step on the inside edge of the rock with your good leg and hug the cliff. I'll grab your left arm and help pull you up when you step past it."

Ross grinned when he reached the other side. "I'm glad we're beyond that. Let's get out of this canyon."

They reached the top and followed the game-trail back to the waterfall. The water was only about ankle deep. They sloshed through it until they were able to climb up a low bank. The mud made for slow going. Ross put his left arm over Philip's shoulder and used the staff to help keep his balance. They crossed the water below the confluence of the two streams and rested on the jeep trail on the west side.

Ross reached into his pack and pulled out his flask. "That was tough going, and this hill isn't going to be much better. My blood alcohol level is dangerously low, want some?"

Philip shook his head. "No, I'll wait until we get back to the 4Runner. I've got some beer in the cooler."

Ross looked up the road. It was even more rutted than it had been on the way in. "We're going to have to take this easy. I'm going to need some rest breaks."

They worked their way slowly up the hill. During their first break, Ross picked up some of the alluvial gravel. He held up a piece of rose quartz and examined it carefully. "I doubt that Red Canyon is really the site of the Lost Adams Diggings. Now the name means blood to me. The ancient streambed has some promise for gold, and Buck could have found it. Maybe there's somewhere else on this mountain where there are better conditions for a placer find."

"Always the geologist. Well, I have had it with the Lost Adams Diggings. You and Sarah were right. They are cursed, and today proved it. I don't really think that Gruber was called by Nana, but I'm not interested in finding out if the Mountain Gods continue to protect *Sno-ta-hay*."

"There it is staring you in the face, Philip. What happened to us had to be a manifestation of the legend. We were ambushed in a box canyon the same way that Adams' party was. My leg wound during a firefight was just like John Adair's when he and Jason Baxter fought off the Apaches in a box canyon somewhere near here. They were saved by a torrential rainstorm that was similar to ours. We've got to be close to *Sno-ta-hay*, and there's obviously some kind of force that repels seekers. Maybe it is from the *Ga'an*, the Mountain Gods of the Warm Springs Apache."

Philip got back on his feet. "I think you are distorting cause and effect. The legend called us to this place, true. We were looking for a zigzag box canyon, but it was Gruber's paranoid delusions that created the ambush, not the Mountain Gods."

He helped Ross struggle to stand up. Ross had to get the last word. "Philip, ever since I've known you, you've been a spiritual seeker who eventually rejects whatever teachings you've embraced. A flood was enough of a sign for the ancient Hebrews. What will it take for you?"

Philip shook his head, and they walked together up the slope. Ross had to take breaks more frequently. They sat on rocks overlooking the sandstone waterfall that had led to Ross' exploration of the canyon below.

Philip tried to encourage Ross. "We're almost to the top of White Mesa, *amigo*. The next part is all level. I wonder how the cattle fared."

"They have enough sense to go to higher ground when the creeks rise." Ross's eyes had that haunted look again. "That flood was really scary. I had a hard time keeping my grip on that tree trunk, but I realized that I actually wanted to live."

"I'm glad to hear that. I was worried about you too; that current had you stretched out downstream. I was really scared when that branch caught on my poncho and almost pulled me off the cliff."

"I wonder how far down Gruber's body went?"

Philip thought about it. "It could have gone all the way to the Alamo Band Reservation. Hell, it could have washed into the Rio Grande above San Acacia, but they'll probably find him near here. It looked like there were a number of wide places below where the next canyon came in. The water couldn't have more than a couple of feet deep there. Most likely, the body would have been caught up in bushes or trees before it made it to Alamocita Creek."

Ross looked mournful. "I can't help wondering if he was dead when he landed at the bottom of the canyon. I mean even if he were still alive, I caused his death in the grip of the floodwaters. Do you think it's bizarre to be obsessed with the details?"

"No, I think that we've just come to the point where we can breathe a little easier, and that's when you think of the details. I was speculating about the same thing. Even if the dynamite killed him, it was purely self-defense. I don't think that anyone could look at your leg and doubt that an extreme response was necessary. I sure was surprised to see you throw that stick. I want to thank you again, *Yslamu dayk.*"

"*Afwan.* I just put that dynamite in there in case we needed to move a little rock around to find the Diggings, but it was the kind of ambush that called for a grenade. The dynamite turned out to be a pretty good alternative. As delusional as Gruber was, he sure had good tactical skills. I still say that part of it was the warriors' shared consciousness phenomenon."

"I'll agree with you about Gruber knowing the way of the warrior. He did well investigating, tracking, and intimidating us. But I've never seen anyone string unrelated stories into an impenetrable delusional system before. What turned his passion to protect America into a crazy vendetta?"

"Who knows? Let's get back on our three feet and get down to your SUV."

The mud on the top of White Mesa made their progress sluggish. When they finally reached sandy soil, they took a break in the meadow where they could look at the stock pond. The sun had moved lower than the dissipating cloud cover and reflected off the pond. The pyramidal buttes were backlit, and the Datils lost their dark foreboding look. The trees looked a darker green, and the dripping water sparkled as it fell from their branches. The thing that lifted their spirits the most was a distant noise.

Ross threw his head back and shouted, "*L'hamdillah!* Praise the Lord. The air cavalry are coming to the rescue. This kind of a wound in Nam would have earned you a chopper ride that led back to the real world, but I'd settle for an emergency room right now. I love that whoop, whoop sound."

"They're going away!"

"Don't sweat it, *khayee.* They'll look in the canyon where your car is first. Then they'll start a search pattern. Hand me the pack."

Ross pulled out a small shiny plastic package and handed it to Philip. "Boy Scout training proves itself again. Open the plastic and get out that reflectorized space blanket. Be careful when you unroll it, it tears easily. Go back towards the center of the meadow and wave it when you hear them come back."

The sound of the helicopter returned and went up canyon for a short distance, and then the chopper rose above the mesa. Philip waved the reflector, and the State Police helicopter headed towards them. It landed in the meadow, and Don Abeyta threw open the passenger door. He crouched and ran to Philip.

Philip threw his arms around him. "Boy, am I glad to see you. Ross has a pretty severe leg wound. He needs to get to a hospital as soon as possible."

Don exclaimed, "What happened here? You both look like hell. You're wet, muddy, and bloody. Let's have a look at Ross."

They strode over to Ross who was struggling to his feet. He shook Don's hand and thanked him profusely for coming for them.

"Gruber's truck is under the cottonwoods not far from yours. Where is he?"

Philip answered, "We don't really know, but we think he's dead."

Don's eyebrows rose. "How?"

Ross responded with his head lowered. "There's some debate about that, but he washed down Red Canyon in a flash flood. No one could have survived that."

"I'm not interested in debating right now. Ross, we need to change that dressing and get you to the hospital quick. Did Gruber shoot you?

Ross looked at this leg. "Yeah, and did a pretty good job of it too. He nicked Philip as well."

Philip protested, "It's nothing. Gruber attacked us in a box canyon. He was delusional about us being *Al Qaida* infiltrators. He had us pinned down and kept taking pot shots at us."

"I assume that you two returned fire."

Ross replied, "We clipped him a couple of times, but that's not what killed him. I threw a stick of dynamite to dislodge him from his sniper nest. He flew off a thirty-foot cliff, bounced off a ledge, and landed at the bottom."

Don urged them back to the chopper. "A homemade grenade, that's about the only way to clear out snipers. So was he dead?"

Philip took up the story. "We didn't get a chance to check. A wall of water flooded the canyon, and we had to find a safe perch in that narrow box canyon. By the time we were safe, Derek's body was long gone. How did you know to look for us?"

"McIntyre, what are you digging for in that pack?"

Ross grinned, pulled out his flask, and finished it off in one movement. He smiled. "I'll bet I'm not going to get another drink in quite a while. Lead on, Sergeant."

The state police pilot had the first-aid kit open. Don introduced them to Tony Messina who greeted them. "Welcome aboard."

They got Ross settled in the back seat and removed the splint and dressing. Don and Tony examined the wound, exchanged a look, and quickly changed the dressing. Philip climbed in, and Don shut the door.

"Seat belts, everyone. When we get in the air, we'll radio the trauma center at the University of New Mexico Hospital. Since we're heading that way anyway, Tony, how about if we follow Red Canyon to see if we can spot Gruber's body?"

"Sounds like a plan, Sarge. I'll keep us low and slow. Let's keep our eyes peeled."

The helicopter lifted and flew east to Red Canyon. Tony kept it high enough to give them plenty of clearance. Philip saw the large side canyon joining in from the northeast. Tony knew about Gruber and his threats from Don. Philip filled him in on what happened in the canyon. He directed Tony to the box canyon so that he and Don could see the site of the shootings.

Don exclaimed, "Damn, he really had you cornered. You were lucky to get out of that alive."

Tony added, "We'll send some crime scene techs, but they aren't likely to find much after that storm." He flew down the canyon past where next canyon entered.

Philip said, "This part of the canyon is a likely spot. Can you keep it slow, Tony?"

"You bet. I'll go from side to side a little to cover the whole canyon. How are you doing back there, Ross?"

"Not too bad, but I feel a little chilled."

"Philip, there's a blanket in that compartment beside you. Can you get it?"

Ross wrapped himself in the blanket and eventually stopped shivering as they continued downstream, but he was very pale and his breathing was faster than normal.

Don pointed at a small tree. "There's something in that juniper. Can you set it down Tony?"

After they landed, Don and Philip ran to the muddy base of a one seed juniper. Gruber's body was twisted amongst the branches. His clothing hung in tatters. His limbs were twisted in grotesque positions. Abrasions and contusions covered his body.

Don touched Gruber's carotid artery. "He's been cold for a while. Let me talk to Tony."

Don returned with a camera. "This is a little unorthodox, but Tony agrees. If we leave him here overnight, the crows and coyotes will get him. Can you go back to the chopper and get that metal rescue basket while I take pictures. We've really got to hurry; I think Ross is getting shocky."

After Don took crime-scene photos, Philip helped him disentangle Gruber from the tree and put him into a body bag. It was strange to see how diminished his form was without its driving anger. They strapped him into the rescue basket and carried him back to the chopper. Tony attached the basket to one of the skids and they got back into their seats. The helicopter rose above the canyons and soared eastward.

Tony turned to Ross, "Hang in there, buddy. I'll be setting this down at UNMH in no time. Drink some more water, you'll feel better."

"It's going to take a while before I feel better. Never mind my leg, that dead body below us is my responsibility."

Don saw that Ross was on the edge of tears, "You're right, Ross, it is your responsibility; but it wasn't your fault. We don't know that the dynamite killed him. If it did, it's still a clear-cut case of self-defense. He tried to kill you."

Tony said, "Don't worry, Ross. The furthest that this could go would be an inquest."

Philip touched his neck. "Our wounds are convincing evidence. Gruber was a pretty good shot."

Don shook his head. "He sure went round the bend. He had to have been somewhat stable to get into Special Forces."

"I don't know. He must have had a lifelong diet of racism. The names he called me and other Arabs rolled off his tongue too easily."

Ross's voice was low. "In the VA psych ward, some of the worst paranoids were the covert operations guys. They were usually ultrapatriotic; that's part of what motivated them to do high-risk operations in the first place. Then, they were surrounded by people of a different race who tried to kill them. Maybe they were intolerant to start with, but the fear turns out to be real. Not only are they trying to shoot you, but the guy next to you in a crowd could be a suicide bomber. Add an atrocity or two, like the ones they've turned up at Abu Ghraib prison, and you've got the recipe for psychotic PTSD."

Tony said, "It's hard to see someone who was one of the good guys go so bad."

Philip asked, "Don, you never answered my question earlier. Did Sarah call you?"

"She sure did. She let me know that she was worried about you, because you and Ross were the biggest fools she'd ever met. I could agree with her about you, but I had to tell her I didn't know Ross that well. I promised her that I would check it out. When I called the Catron County Sheriff's Department, they had just received a call from the storekeeper in Datil. She said that these greenhorns had gone into the Datils looking for a gold mine and were probably trapped by the torrential thunderstorm. The Catron County boys called someone who lived up Davenport Canyon. Those folks said that they hadn't seen you come out, and that you had been followed by a camouflage-painted Power Wagon. Being trained investigators, we put two and two together and decided you were in trouble. There was no way a vehicle could get back here through the water, mud, and quicksand. So Catron County gave the State Police jurisdiction, and we were able to get Tony to fly in. Since I knew the case and we're brother Vietnam vets, he took me along."

Philip replied, "Believe me; we wouldn't have stuck around for the flash flood if Gruber didn't have us pinned down. Sarah is right. We were fools to think we could deal with a delusional paranoid. Thanks for coming through for us. You probably had to do some arm-twisting to make it happen."

"Thank Tony too. He had to push for it just as much as I did. I'm just glad that you two survived, and that we got here in time. Try to get some rest; it's going to get busy when we land."

Philip half-listened to Ross, Don, and Tony discuss MEDEVAC helicopter rides "in country" until Ross faded and settled down to rest. Philip overheard a lot of radio traffic about the logistics of their arrival at the hospital and arranging police interviews, but he was too tired to care and drifted off to a fitful sleep.

21

Philip woke up as they prepared for landing. The helipad was brightly lit, and there was a slew of medical and law-enforcement personnel.

Don turned and said, "We've got quite a crew. There's the University Hospital group to take you and Ross to the emergency room. The Office of the Medical Investigator's staff will take Gruber's body to their autopsy suite. Because this was an unattended suspicious death, they're expediting this one. We're lucky that they didn't have too much of a backlog tonight. Remember that the Catron County Sheriff's office has asked in the State Police to be primary investigators, so one of their officers will witness the autopsy. I'll introduce you to Captain Lewis who's their Albuquerque-based homicide detective. I'll meet with him while Philip is getting stitched up, and then he'll want to talk to Philip. Ross, they'll want to stabilize you before any questioning. Prepare yourselves for being swept away to the ER."

They landed and the UNMH ER crew raced to the helicopter. Ross was placed on a gurney, and Philip was forced into a wheelchair. He was glad that he was on wheels once they started for the ER because these folks were fast. Don was talking to an African American "suit" who briefly stopped the caravan.

"I'm Captain Lewis. I'm glad that Tony was able to perform your med-evac. Good luck and I'll talk with you later."

He waved and they were off again. They flew down the corridors. Philip noted that they had an IV in hand for waiting for Ross. Once Philip was in a cubicle, they helped transfer him to an exam table. A nursing assistant took his vital signs, and an insurance clerk took his vital insurance data. A tired-looking young woman entered his cubicle and introduced herself as his doctor. She took a brief medical history while examining his wound.

"Well it's nice that you got hit on the side of your neck. Bullet fragments in the spinal cord do make things more complicated. I can see the metal fragment, so we can take care of this right here. You're going to be sore, but you'll be fine. I'm going to show you my best precision needlework when I stitch you up. A small scar won't rub your collar as much."

She wore glasses with a magnifying lens and worked under bright light. It seemed to take a long time, but Philip was content to sit and relax. His clothes were beginning to dry out.

When he went out into the emergency room waiting room, he was surprised. Sarah rushed into his arms asking, "Are you all right? How bad is Ross?"

Philip responded, "I'm fine, but I haven't heard any updates about Ross since I got here. He has a pretty significant leg wound. How did you get here?"

Sarah smiled and gestured behind her. "The Habib family telegraph and taxi service."

George strode up, and Philip gave him a hug too.

George said, "God, I'm glad to see you alive. This is the only time I'm going to remind you that you put your neck on the line against my advice. How is it by the way?"

Philip touched his bandage. "I caught a little lead, thankfully very little. It's fine now. My doctor is a quilt-maker, and can she sew. How did you know where we'd be, and how did you get here so fast?"

"Connections, and we just arrived. Sarah called me after she talked to Don. I made Don promise me that he would call me when he found you. So I got a phone call from dispatch. I called Sarah back as soon as I got the scoop. We picked up another visitor on our way out of town. I made Marlene come to see first hand the effect of her encouraging you two to continue this madness. Oops, I promised that I wouldn't editorialize again."

Sarah grabbed Philip back from George. "I made no such promise. You fool! You made me worry so much that I ought to slug you."

Instead Sarah gave him a deep kiss that made Philip forget everything else for a few seconds. When he came back to reality, Philip apologized. "I'm sorry that I made both of you worry. You told me exactly what was going to happen, and I ignored you both. My apologies."

Sarah looked him in the eye. "You're going to have to prove to me that you can regain the inquisitive and compassionate personality that I was beginning to find irresistible. Listening would be a good start, especially when people tell you that you're crazy."

George added, "I understand that there are treatments now that help curb impulsivity. Maybe there's a Twelve Step group too, Machos Anonymous."

"Okay, okay. I hereby promise that I will listen to feedback. And whenever I think, 'A man's gotta do what a man's gotta do,' I'll call my sponsor."

Sarah smiled. "That's better. Now, you've got to tell us what happened. All we know is that Gruber trapped you in a canyon and shot at you, that he washed away in a flash flood, and that you found his body. We know that you both were shot and that Ross's leg wound is serious. What happened out there?"

George interrupted, "Hold on a second. This is why I brought Marlene, so she could hear this story. And there's Don and the State Police detective. Philip, as your lawyer, I want you to tell us all a brief version of the story. Then you, Don, the detective, and I will meet to go over details."

"Since you are my attorney, of course I will follow your advice."

George rolled his eyes.

"I'd like to get this interview with Captain Lewis over with as soon as possible."

George proposed the format to Don and Captain Lewis. He brought Marlene over to an alcove where they all sat down.

Captain Lewis spoke. "This is not the usual way that we interview suspects, but I guess everyone here has the right to hear the basics. Philip, do you realize that this is a public place and we won't be able to maintain confidentiality?"

"I have nothing to hide."

George interjected, "I would like to be able to advise my client whether to respond to your inquiries, so Philip will tell the story, but I ask each of you to hold your questions until he is finished. Then the officers and Philip and I will go to a secure place for further questioning. Does everyone understand?"

Captain Lewis responded, "That's fine as long as I can record Philip's story as part of his statement."

George agreed. "That's fine by us."

Captain Lewis spoke into a small digital recorder giving the date, time and place. "Now Philip, please tell us what happened."

Philip started with their discovery of the ancient streambed and panning for gold. He tried to be as concise as possible as he described the ambush in the narrow box canyon, the firefight, the flash flood, and their journey out of the canyon.

When he finished, Marlene exclaimed, "So you did find some gold. Do you think that you found Buck's diggings?"

George interrupted Philip's response. "As empathic as ever, Marlene. Philip and Ross were working on your behalf when they were shot. You can hold your questions until Captain Lewis and Sergeant Abeyta have completed theirs. Sarah, can you and Marlene find out how Ross is doing while we look for a private place?"

Captain Lewis secured an office and directed the inquiry. "Let's start at the beginning. Don tells me that Gruber had a road rage incident with you. Then, a couple of days later, you thought that he fired an automatic weapon at you and Ross. Why was he after you?"

Philip was pensive. "You'd probably have to have a psychiatric post-mortem to answer that. All I know is that he thought that we were *Al Qaida* or *Baathi* operatives. I had been poking around the *malpais* and the Zunis trying to find out how Buck Cavanaugh got his extra money at Marlene's request. Somehow Gruber misinterpreted my actions as espionage. We thought the loot came from a lost gold mine so Ross got in the act. When he was able to trace us both back to the Middle East, Gruber became obsessed with stopping us."

"You said that Gruber was investigating your experiences in Beirut. What does that have to do with his obsessions?"

George held up his hand. "Philip has already been cleared of any suspicions of traitorous activities. He was fulfilling his patriotic duty in Beirut for the United States Marine Corps. Based on misinterpretations of these decades-old stories, he was falsely arrested on the day after nine-eleven. Captain Lewis, I want to be clear that we are responding to Gruber's delusional associations. If you try to railroad Philip into any terrorist witch-hunt, I will advise him to refuse to respond to any further questions."

Captain Lewis furrowed his brow. "Settle down, counselor. Obviously, something happened during Philip's arrest that made you so defensive. I'm just trying to clear up this investigation."

Philip asserted himself. "George, I can handle this. Captain Lewis, I did intelligence work for the Marines while I was attending the American University of Beirut in the seventies. Gruber must have had Internet access to some network of former intelligence agents. The person that he talked to must have misrepresented some of my friends as operatives of the Iraqi and Saudi governments. They never were government agents, but most of them were members of the Palestine

Liberation Organization. I haven't heard from any of them in years. Those reports from my time in Beirut convinced Gruber that I must be a turncoat spy. It was news to us. He never said anything about his persecutory delusions before he ambushed us today."

"So you had no idea why he had been harassing you before today."

Philip shrugged. "Not really. When he kicked my car door, he swore at me in Arabic. So I thought it was his general Neo-Nazi racism. I didn't know that he was tracking me in particular."

Captain Lewis nodded. "The officer at the autopsy called me. They're still working on Gruber's body. The pathologist's initial finding was that Gruber had water in his lungs. Drowning will be the official cause of death. The coroner will probably call it death by misadventure, but it's possible that there will be an inquest. However, I need to know more about this dynamite blast."

"I was shocked at the time. I didn't even know that Ross had the dynamite. When he detonated it, Gruber flew towards us, bounced off the cliff, and landed with a splat in some quicksand. Before we could recover enough to go to him, the flash flood poured over the waterfall. We had to find higher ground immediately to keep from being carried away in the flood. When I got a chance to look where Gruber's body had been, it was long gone. The whole area was under several feet of water."

Captain Lewis offered some consolation. "The whole thing sounds horrific. You two are lucky to be alive. I'll need to interview Mr. McIntyre next. I may have more questions later, but you can go for now. Thank you for your cooperation. Here's my card, and I've got George's card to reach you. I probably won't be able to reach you directly. Have you tried your cell phone since you submerged it?"

Philip laughed. "Yeah, I tried to call my parents. I guess they don't design them to be waterproof. George will know how to reach me."

As they returned to the waiting room, George looked around. "I guess it's a little early for the Saturday Night Gun and Knife Club to be in full swing, but it's building. It's good to come in the back door bleeding; they work on you faster."

Sarah walked over and put her arm around Philip's waist. "How did it go?"

Philip smiled. "Fine. I'm glad that's over. Lewis said he was going to talk to Ross next. How is he?"

"I'm happy to report that he's doing better. He lost a fair amount of blood, so they started a transfusion. They didn't feel that he was stable enough to operate on his leg immediately. But they've got him scheduled for first thing in the morning. They just sent him up to his room. I talked to him briefly and introduced Marlene. I thought that it was strange, but she went up to his room with him. She actually looked concerned."

George sneered. "It's possible that she might feel some remorse for what happened, but I suspect that she's really trying to find out more about the gold. Philip, I told Sarah about your encounter with Marlene at brunch yesterday. I was pretty sure that you had omitted the details. I thought an explanation might help Sarah understand why her reception was so cool that I didn't have to turn on the air conditioning in my car. Let's go grab a snack at the cafeteria and give Captain Lewis some time with Ross."

After they ate mediocre Mexican food at the hospital cafeteria, they made their way up to Ross' room. Marlene was hovering over Ross.

Philip went to Ross' side and grabbed his hand. "How are you doing, my friend?"

Ross gestured to his leg that was suspended from an overhead rack. "I can't kick. Seriously, I felt better once they got an IV going, and I feel a whole lot better now that I'm only running a quart low on blood. I was also relieved that Gruber was alive when the water hit him. It sounds like they won't be bringing any charges against us."

George agreed. "They may ask you to testify at an inquest, that's all."

Sarah gave Ross a peck on the cheek. "I was so worried about you."

Marlene quickly interjected, "He's scheduled for surgery first thing tomorrow, and he has an excellent surgeon."

Ross chuckled. "Yeah, the doc told me the reason why I felt like my leg was broken when it didn't feel broken to touch. Gruber's bullet fractured my fibula, the smaller bone, but left my tibia intact. They're going to put a pin in the break. He said it would be an easy surgery, they would just use the exit wound to get to the break. You know, I think that it only sounds like an easy surgery if you're not the one with an exit wound. That sucker hurts! But they've got me on good pain meds, and they put me on Librium so that I wouldn't go into DTs in the middle of surgery." He started making dance moves with his arms and sang, "'I feel good, like you know that I should.'"

George was amused. "Before you go into your godfather of soul routine, I want to thank you for everything you've done for us and to express my regret about your injury."

Philip said, "Me too. You saved my life, buddy."

Ross replied, "You saved mine too. If you hadn't tended my wound and dragged me out of that canyon, I would have bought the farm in there. And thank you two for pushing Don to find us."

Philip laughed. "Jolly good all the way around, eh?"

George said, "A celebration is in order. First, Marlene, we need to clarify that you owe Philip another day's wages as well as expenses to both Philip and Ross for their losses. Since Ross wasn't an actual employee of yours, and his insurance will cover his treatment, you will only have to pay for his deductible for his hospitalization."

Marlene responded archly. "George, must you always be so mercenary. I have a check right here for Philip's charges for the day, and of course I will be responsible for the expenses. Philip, as we agreed yesterday, I gave you one more day to investigate, so your services are no longer required."

She sat on the edge of Ross's bed, held his hand, and smiled at him. "Ross and I have discussed your findings, and it is apparent that I need the services of a contract geologist to continue the search for Buck's placer mine or the Lost Adams Diggings or whatever is out there. Ross' experiences on your quest have also convinced me that some kind of force protects the canyon. I will seek advice from the psychic who has helped my friend in Santa Fe. We may have to perform a ceremony to calm the guardian spirits."

Ross smiled back at Marlene. "I won't be worth much for a few days, but I know an outfitter who can take us back there on horseback. He'll set us up with tents, and he cooks great meals. We can bring a case of fine wine and review our progress each evening over a campfire. I know that the ancient streambed will give up more gold than the few flecks we found today."

George, Sarah, and Philip just stared at them. Ross winked and made an okay sign with his other hand.

Philip chuckled. "Ross, I wish you success in completing your life-long quest for the Lost Adams Diggings. Marlene, I'm glad that we were able to get the search for Buck's gold under way. Now you've got the best man to carry that search further. *Mabrouk*, I wish the best of luck to you both. Ross, we'll let you get some sleep. That morning call for surgery will come soon."

He winked at Ross as he turned to leave. Sarah and George said their good byes, and they left Ross and Marlene. They got down the hall a bit before they allowed themselves to laugh.

Sarah shook her head. "Wow! That Marlene sure works fast. She hadn't met Ross before tonight, and they're already planning an outdoor rendezvous."

Philip grinned. "I suspect their rendezvous will occur before the pack trip at this rate. Anyway, it's great that Ross has someone at his side during this ordeal. Maybe she can get her friend's psychic to channel some healing power to him. Do you think it was just the drugs, or was Ross really happy?"

George spoke, "This adventure has renewed a part of his life that he'd forgotten, the returning hero. He saved your life, Philip. However, I think that you not only saved his life, but you also gave him back his dignity."

Sarah said, "You're right, George. He was more at peace tonight than I've ever seen him. He seemed to be riding high after talking with Don and Captain Lewis too. He felt good about his courage under fire."

Philip looked at her affectionately. "And I think that it's wonderful that you're so concerned over him. He hasn't had anybody care about him for a long time. I feel the same way. He's starting to see himself as a good guy again, but he's fragile. The idea of him fulfilling Marlene's fantasy of the gold hunter grows on me. You know Ross cleans up good."

George said, "I think she'll cast him as Stewart Granger in *King Solomon's Mines*."

Sarah joined in. "I can just see him with his hair styled and his beard trimmed. Marlene couldn't stand to be seen with him in his current wardrobe. So, I'm betting on a Banana Republic shopping spree. He's going to be decked out in nouveau safari."

She batted her eyelids and pressed her body against Philip. "Darling, I must thank you for all that you've done. Please accept this as a token of my esteem."

George's eyes twinkled. "I think Ross knows what he's getting into, and it looked like he was enjoying the prospects."

As they waited for the elevator, Philip said, "Seriously, I do hope that Ross and Marlene can find Buck's Diggings or at least that the ancient streambed yields some gold. I really don't think that the Adams' Diggings exist anymore, at least not the way that Adams described them. As we were driving into the Datils, Ross told me story about how Jason Baxter found something that sure sounded like the Adams's Diggings in the eighteen seventies. The Apaches drove him away from the gold canyon too, and he didn't return for many years. When he went back, he was sure that he was in the same location, but the countryside had been completely rearranged by earthquakes or floods. Perhaps Baxter was right. After all, there have been dozens, if not hundreds, of knowledgeable prospectors who have sought the Diggings for well over a hundred years. Maybe nobody can find them, because they no longer exist."

As they entered the elevator, George looked at Philip. "That sounds a little like sour grapes, but you may be right. Too many people have looked for too many years for that zigzag canyon to have it gone unnoticed."

Sarah shook her head. "You men are always chasing after rainbows. Philip and Ross survived, a psychotic killer was eliminated, and I've had one of the most exciting weeks of my life."

As the elevator reached the lobby, they stepped out. Philip said, "I hope that the next few weeks are exciting as well, but maybe a step down from life-threatening."

Sarah kissed him and said, "I think that can be arranged."

ll ll ll

This novel has been printed on acid free paper.
The typeface is Adobe Jenson Pro.

/h /h /h

www.ingramcontent.com/pod-product-compliance
Lightning Source LLC
Chambersburg PA
CBHW011404010726
47495CB00009B/2770